Praise for

GUNMETAL BLACK

GUNMETAL BLACK

DANIEL SERRANO

GRAND CENTRAL
PUBLISHING

NEW YORK   BOSTON

Copyright © 2008 by Daniel Serrano
All rights reserved. Except as permitted under the U.S. Copyright Act of 1976, no part of this publication may be reproduced, distributed, or transmitted in any form or by any means, or stored in a database or retrieval system, without the prior written permission of the publisher.

Grand Central Publishing
Hachette Book Group
237 Park Avenue
New York, NY 10017
Visit our website at www.HachetteBookGroup.com

Grand Central Publishing is a division of Hachette Book Group, Inc. The Grand Central Publishing name and logo is a trademark of Hachette Book Group, Inc.

The publisher is not responsible for websites (or their content) that are not owned by the publisher.

Printed in the United States of America

Originally printed in trade paperback by Hachette Book Group

First mass market edition: August 2011

10 9 8 7 6 5 4 3 2 1

For my mother, Olga Iris,
la flor más bella de Puerto Rico.

AUTHOR'S NOTE

This novel traveled a long way to find you, reader. I worked on it on and off for many years, while going to school and working full time. It began as my college thesis and evolved. On September 11, 2001, I lost three years' worth of work because I kept it at a cubicle inside the World Trade Center. Later that week, I began the story again, from page one.

Originally, I envisioned *Gunmetal Black* to serve as a cautionary tale. I grew up in tough neighborhoods in New York and Chicago and I wanted to speak to urban problems. As I matured, so did the novel. It remains action-packed and gritty; a thriller. It has sexy moments, and a touch of romance. The characters are dangerous and flawed, but I strove to make them complex and human as they face great crises.

While this is commercial crime fiction, it is heavily influenced by the classics. When I began to write at Shimer College, I was steeped in Greek tragedies, Dostoyevsky, Shakespeare, and others. On my own I read

Hemingway, pulp fiction, and detective novels; I studied movies to make the plot fast-moving and cinematic; and I listened to everything from classic rock to hip-hop, and especially to salsa. The main characters are Latino, but *Gunmetal Black* is ultimately an American novel.

I hope you find the story entertaining, easy to follow, and hard to put down. If you do, by all means, recommend it to all of your friends. Enjoy it. Thank you for reading. And be on the lookout for my next novel.

Daniel Serrano, Esq.
New York City, 2007

The wicked roar and growl like lions.
But God silences them and breaks their teeth.

—JOB 4:10

GUNMETAL
BLACK

PRÓLOGO

Murder began when I was ten years old.

It was a long summer's day, in the late seventies, and the sun kicked hard enough to melt your wings. We lived in West Town, a Puerto Rican neighborhood near Humboldt Park, in Chicago. Fifteen minutes and a million miles from downtown.

My father ran bolitas, the numbers, and muscled for a local loan shark.

"I never take nothin' from nobody," he said. "Except what they owe."

My father was tall for an Island-born Rican, nearly six feet, and brown. He was thick from rocking push-ups and pull-ups in the park. His street name was Caballo. Rumor had it he earned it by kicking a deadbeat in the style of a crazy horse.

One time I saw him attack two men in front of a movie theater. He kicked them with his eyes wide and his nostrils flared, and he smiled the entire time. I held his beer. Afterward, we strutted into the theater as if nothing happened.

The houselights dimmed, the curtain rose. My father lit a cigarette and blew a stream into the red light that flickered above our heads. Smoke floated like the wake of some scarlet ghost.

My father looked down at me and smiled. "My partner told me this is gonna be a good flick. It got a lotta action in it."

"Yeah, Pop?"

"Uh-huh." He winked. "He tole me there's a little romance too."

My father smiled down at me, but he must have seen some residue of that sudden violence on the sidewalk. He passed his hand through my hair. "So now you know," he said. "Don't ever be a punk."

One day my mother was at church. My father lingered in the apartment, mopped sweat off the back of his neck with a white handkerchief, and sipped straight rum. He owned congas, two hand drums carved from wood. They were elderly, scarred by chips, scratches, and varicose cracks. Mostly, they slept in the corner. The leather skins stretched across their tops were filthy from a generation of sweat, dirt, oil, even flecks of blood that my father kneaded into them. Some days, if he drank enough, we'd pretend we were in a salsa band. I sang and he beat the drums.

But not that night. Instead, the time came, my father dressed, he headed for the door. I asked where he was going.

"To the moon," he said. "No kids allowed."

"Can you buy me an ice cream, Pop? When you come back?"

The cigarette dangled from the corner of his mouth.

He squinted. "Te estás poniendo grande." He reached in his pocket and flipped me a quarter. "Go down when you hear the truck, OK? But come right back up. And don't let Mami know you was out there."

I nodded. He patted my head and left. I ran to the window and watched my father slide from view, grooving on his private rhythm. I pocketed the quarter and ran down after him.

In the west the sun appeared as a giant bleeding ulcer on the horizon. I shadowed my father. Large metal cars roamed Chicago like modern buffalo, and one custom horn blasted "La Cucaracha." The shells of burnt houses reeked of smoke and stale water and stared sullenly through boarded windows. Children frolicked in the geyser of a corner hydrant. On sidewalks and stoops the adults moved slowly, like chickens on a spit.

My father entered a bar with a sputtering neon sign: LA SIRENA. He exited, rubbed a tall can of beer across his forehead, then cut down a side street to drink and smoke pot.

Finally, he met his appointment: a tall black man in a wide-brimmed hat. Shadows concealed most of the stranger's face, but not his teeth, which were made of gold.

The gold-toothed man slapped my father on the shoulder and grinned. "My brother!" he said. "I thought you got lost."

My father shook his head. The gold-toothed man invited my father into a nearby gangway, and they went.

I crouched in a gutter across the street, between two parked cars. I spotted my face in a curved chrome bumper, and a convex gargoyle version of me stared back. I stuck out my tongue at my distorted self and almost laughed. Somewhere nearby the melody of an ice-cream truck faded and the quarter tingled in my pocket. I held my place and watched the men negotiate as silhouettes framed by the mystery of their business and the final embers of a fiery dusk.

Then came the horror.

Another man slithered from the silent shadows. He, too, wore a concealing hat. In his hands was a sawed-off shotgun. The hit man pointed the barrels at the base of my father's spine, and pulled the trigger.

BOOM!

I saw the flash, heard the echo, and the startled birds roared helter-skelter from the trees above. In one sick motion my father dropped to one knee and snapped his face toward the sky. Smoke rose and a sudden hot gush of piss ran down my leg. A scream got tangled in my throat.

The man with the smoking sawed-off spotted me across the street—I was trembling between the cars. Our eyes locked.

Am I next? I thought. *Is this our secret?*

The shooter froze inside my gaze. But his gold-toothed accomplice did not look in my direction. He snatched the shotgun from his partner, pointed the barrels at my father's head, and pulled the trigger.

BLAST!

I saw a spray of flesh and was knocked unconscious by a tidal wave of grief.

The earth swallowed my father's coffin. My mother suffered his demons, but she prayed and wore black in the unflinching sun. I prayed, too, and hoped he was going to God, though I feared that he was going to the other place. I'd seen my father's partner stash reefer, money, rum, and a gun in the casket before they closed it.

The títere patted my father's stiff shoulder before the lid went down. "Everything you gonna need for the next life, Negro." He looked at me. "Ven acá, nene."

I went to him.

His Puerto Rican accent was thick with alcohol. He rolled his *R*'s. "You father was a good man. ¿M'entiende? Un hombre verdadero."

I nodded.

"Acuérdate de él."

As if I could ever forget. I tried to pull away, but the man held me in place.

"You gotta be a tough guy now, little man. Unnerstand?"

My lip trembled, but I nodded, and I swallowed all that pain. It was a jagged rock inside my throat, but I swallowed it. My father was dead and so was my innocence. I was ten years old.

PART I:

WINDY CITY SHAKEDOWN

CHAPTER 01:

MONEY AIN'T A THANG

Getting out of prison felt different this time. Not that tired, ex-con bullshit about flying straight and keeping legit. Fuck that noise. I mean, I had a strategy, a definite plan, and it was simple. Legal too. Legit even. It involved forming a corporation, keeping books, paying taxes. But that didn't mean I was a good guy now. Why would it? I wasn't a born-again Christian, a Muslim, or even just tired of crime. It was that the rackets had never been that good to me. Not enough to justify the sacrifice. The rackets hadn't been practical.

Don't get me wrong: I had my moments. Scores where you hauled so much cash your eyes watered. Hell, I had one five-year era where the crib was sweet, the rides were mint, and the green just kept on flowing. I juggled females and got backslapped by every bouncer in every hot club.

But that turned out to be a mirage. Mostly, my life of crime had turned up dust. I was slipping through my thirties and the only thing I had to show was a criminal record, scars, and some dirty stories to tell. That, and a little over forty thousand dollars in cold, hard cash that I'd stacked running reefer out of my cell during the second half of a dime, a ten-year bid at Stateville Correctional Center, in Crest Hill, near Joliet, Illinois.

The forty large was strapped to my body, my gut. It felt like a part of me. I intended to walk out of the main gate, find my way to Miami, and invest it all with a friend who was starting a record label. We were gonna make salsa records. Good ones. Not the commercial crap that's been killing the genre.

First I had to sneak the money out of the prison compound. It wouldn't be easy. Hiding a nut like forty thousand when you're incarcerated is like trying to cover an elephant with a washcloth. Somehow I pulled it off.

I checked the mirror and gave the money belt one last tug. It didn't show. Not under my shirt and my new army field jacket. I winked at my reflection to get the nerves down.

The final pat-down on my way out was the main hurdle. I'd already undergone a strip search and retrieved the money belt after dressing.

My escort arrived. He was a new guard I hadn't gotten to know yet.

"Thanks for coming, Officer."

"Save it, skell. Move."

New guards always feel they have something to prove. I picked up my small suitcase, breathed, and took that final march.

The red-haired guard, who I knew too well, chewed gum, lazylike. It was still morning, but already he sounded tired.

"Arms up, Santiago." He began a slow pat-down.

I held my breath. The red-haired guard had been greased, and so had his supervisor, but you never know. Red let his pudgy fingers linger over the money belt.

"What's this?"

I swallowed.

"Put on a couple pounds, did we?" He flashed his bleeding gums. "Must've been all that high living you did at the taxpayers' expense."

"Yeah," I said. "Nothin' but juicy steaks and red wine up in here."

"Save the sarcasm, Santiago. Turn around."

I did.

Red finished the charade and gestured to the guards behind the mesh. "This one's clean."

They buzzed me through. One guard was busy putting up Halloween cutouts of witches and black cats with arched backs. I said, "It's a little early for that," but she ignored me. A corrections officer with a receding Afro went down a checklist:

"Santiago? Eduardo?"

"Yes."

"Recite your number."

I did.

"Eye color?"

"Brown."

"Hair color?"

"Brown."

"Height?"

"Six even."

"Weight?"

"Two-fifteen."

He looked me up and down.

"All right, two-thirty-five," I said.

"Better. Stand over there. Toes on the line."

I stood up straight.

"Look at the red dot. Smile if you want."

I didn't. The flash went off.

"Good," he said. "Talk to Hanks while this thing prints."

Another guard handed me my discharge papers. He spoke without looking up. "Don't lose these, Santiago, these are important. Department of Public Health info, so you can get an HIV test." He examined the next one. "Says here that you been ID'd as alcohol and/or substance dependent. Did those Pre-Start classes help?"

"I feel more reformed already."

"Anyway, this form is a referral to a treatment program in Chicago. Highly recommend you follow up with that."

I glanced at the heading on the form and nodded.

The guard inspected everything in front of him. "All right, Santiago, the rest of these forms are self-explanatory. Any questions?"

"None you can answer."

He smirked.

The photographer handed me a warm piece of plastic. "Here's your ID then."

Issued by the Illinois Department of Corrections, it identified me as discharged from state prison. The photo showed the beginning of wrinkles. Little bags under the eyes. Padding under the chin. It had been a while since I had my picture taken.

"You need a better flash for that camera. I look washed-out. Like I got no color."

The paperwork guard closed my folder. "It's a temp, Santiago, take it to the secretary of state within thirty days. Cough up a dollar, they'll give you a state ID. Maybe that one'll capture your pretty side. Now come on. Sign here, here, and here."

I did.

And that was it. My debt to society? *Paid*.

Outside it was the Midwest in autumn: cool air, decaying leaves, clouds, drizzle—the smell of these mixed together. I scanned the parking lot.

A glossy candy apple red Cadillac, one of those long, wide monsters built in the late seventies, idled. It crouched and kept its distance from the prison structure. Heavy metal pulsed behind its tinted windows. I walked toward it.

Antonio Pacheco, aka "Little Tony," my oldest friend, slid out from behind the steering wheel. Short and thick, he was dressed all in black. The belt of his leather jacket hung loose. He wore driving gloves and black wraparound shades cocked up on his head, even though the clouds were heavy and gray.

Tony whistled. "What up, dawg?"

"¿Qué pasó, loco?"

We hugged, then looked at each other. I hadn't seen Tony since his release, a couple years earlier. Standing up close now, I noticed his chin was also thick and visible, even though he wore a goatee. He had new wrinkles too. And his hairline headed for the hills. But he still had the dark, serious eyebrows, the deep-set eyes. He smiled. The fucker still had dimples.

"Looking good, kid."

"Me?" He squeezed my bicep. "How about you? What the fuck have *you* been doin', man? Breaking rocks?"

"A little bit."

A dark green spider clung to the side of Tony's neck. I flicked it.

"Wicked tattoo," I said. "Still a gangster, huh?"

"You know it."

I was happy to see Tony. A month earlier he had sent a messenger, a fine young Negrita who popped her gum and told me Tony needed to see me in Chicago when I got out. He needed my help on something. I had a contraband prepaid cell phone inside, and Tony had the number, but evidently *this* innocent request was something he did not want a record of. The girl he sent didn't say shit either.

I was focused on Miami then, and hadn't planned a detour to Chicago. But I owed Tony enough to listen. Plus, I figured it wouldn't hurt to spend a couple of weeks roaming the city, reconnecting. Seeing Tony outside the gate now made me feel satisfied that I'd made the right decision.

I smiled. "Tony, did you get my letter?"

He reached in his pocket, pulled a set of keys, and tossed them. "Got you a room in the old hood. Close to North and California. Near the park."

I looked at the keys and pressed the teeth into my thumb.

"Tell you the truth," he said, "I don't know why you spend the money when you can just bunk at my place."

I pocketed the keys. "Man, I been sharing space for a hundred years."

"Understood." Tony grabbed my bag. "Is this it? Where's the library? I know it don't all fit in this little thing."

"I donated most of my books," I said. "Those pigeons inside need 'em more than I do."

"And the congas?"

"Gave those away too."

Tony said, "You committing hari-kari or something?"

"Naw, man, I just felt like I needed a clean break."

Tony nodded and dropped my bag in the trunk. I read his bumper sticker: GAS, GRASS, OR ASS. NOBODY RIDES FOR FREE.

I tapped the Caddy. "You look to be doing all right."

"I manage." He produced a pack of Marlboros and shook one toward me.

I put my palm up. "Got nine months free of them shits."

"Word? Wish I had the balls." Tony flipped the square into the corner of his mouth, a trick I'd watched him practice a thousand times when we were teenagers, and later, a million times in the yard, the prison laundry, the kitchen, and his cell.

He smoked and squinted at the thirty-three-foot wall that surrounds Stateville. "The fucking *ass* of hell, huh?"

I nodded. "Remember when you compared it to our version of a frat house?"

"Hey, I was delirious from lack of pussy, all right? I ever say anything like that again, slap me."

We stood there, in silence, and stared at the top of the wall. Tony got the shivers. "Let's pull up," he said. "This place is stomping on my buzz."

Inside, the Caddy was clean and shiny. It smelled of a coconut-scented air freshener, which was too sweet. A miniature Puerto Rican flag hung from the rearview mirror. On the dashboard a small statue of Saint Judas, the one with the horn, kept watch.

Tony horseshoed the sunglasses around the little statue, made the sign of the cross, and dropped the transmission into drive. The tires slipped and squealed. I gave Stateville the finger as we fishtailed off.

After a minute I said, "It feels strange to ride in a car again."

Tony said, "Everything in the free world is gonna be like new to you."

We got on the interstate. I kept checking the speedometer, certain the car was pushing one hundred, but the needle never moved past seventy.

Tony threw Fat Joe on the system and sparked a blunt. "Cuida'o," he said, handing it over. "This ain't that bunk you been smoking in Roundhouse."

I hit it. "Please, Tony, who taught who how to smoke weed?"

But Tony was right, the shit was flame, and more banging than anything on the market inside. Two tokes and the music got tasty, the sky became infinite, and the road stretched to some unseen point beyond the horizon.

Tony slapped my leg. "How the brothers doin'?"

"The same, I guess."

"Probably gonna cut each other to pieces, now that you're gone."

I shrugged. "I don't know. I sold my reefer business to Múcaro."

Tony shook his head. "I give that bug-eyed motherfucker a week before he catches another case behind it."

"Yeah, or lets the Aryans muscle him out."

"Exactly."

"Fuck it," I said, toking. "That's his problem now."

I turned the music down to listen for the wind. It was silent, but visible in the leaves and the flocks of birds that ricocheted like molecules in the turbulence.

Tony glanced over. "So what's up with your drums, bro? You don't play no more? I thought I was gonna hear your tumbao."

It was my intention to buy new congas as part of my business venture. Like an expense. Part of me was eager to tell Tony all about it. But I knew it was too soon. I looked at him.

"I'll probably pick up some new congas, once I settle in somewhere. I didn't wanna carry all that weight around. But how about you, Tone? What're you up to?"

Tony licked the corner of his mouth. "Me? Not much. Got a little crew goin'. Young bucks. You know, can't tell their tongues from their assholes, but they do the trick."

Like most men we knew, Tony and I had fallen into gangbanging early on. We started by hanging out with friends from the neighborhood, and before we knew it, we were a crew slinging nickel bags of weed on the corner. Most of our operations had been fairly small-time.

Ever since those early days, it had been Tony's dream to make the shit more sophisticated, like a Latino version of La Cosa Nostra. Part of it was that Tony was a born schemer and a natural thug. Another part was his fetish for all things Italian. The only book he ever finished was about Lucky Luciano. At least half of Tony's eight or nine illegitimate kids were, as he put it, "half-Guinea and part Wop."

I asked Tony a direct question. "So what exactly are you slinging these days?"

"A little bit of everything. Mostly H-ball."

"Really? You cutting heroin now?"

"Yep. Got a smooth operation going. You'd be surprised: the Hot Corner still gets traffic. I call my shit *cornuto*. Italian for 'the horn.'" Tony glanced at me. "Don't front like you don't know what's poppin'."

Tony knew full well that most of what happens on the street winds its way to the prison grapevine.

I grinned. "You know them hags I did my stir with. Nothing to do inside but gamble, gossip, and smoke."

"Uh-huh. And talk shit about niggas too." Tony paused, but I acted like I didn't realize he was waiting for me to say something.

He cocked his head at me. "So?"

"So what, Tony?"

"What did you hear?"

"About you?" I turned to get a good look at him. "Nothin' much. Just a couple rumors."

"Lies, you mean?"

"I don't know. You tell me, Tone. I heard a really wild one about how you muscled in on Roach's cut."

"Oh, *Roach's* cut?" Tony nodded like he absorbed it all. He took one last annoyed pull off his cigarette, then ground it into the ashtray. Smoke escaped from the corners of his mouth. "Let me tell you something, Eddie: that business fell into my lap. You understand? I didn't muscle nobody outta nothin'."

"No?"

"Fuck no." Tony shut the music off. "I don't know what them tricks inside been telling you, Eddie, but—"

"Forget about what you think I heard, Tony. Just tell me the truth."

"Don't I always?"

I did not change my expression.

Tony shifted. "Roach must've got a bad shipment of Pitorro."

"What?"

"Pitorro. Puerto Rican moonshine."

"I know what it means."

"Well, that's what Roach calls his dope: 'Pitorro.' Maybe he stepped on it with something toxic, I don't know."

"Why, what happened?"

"Junkies started droppin' like panties in a two-dollar whorehouse."

"ODs?"

"Yup."

"Only Roach's customers? Not yours?"

"Nope. Four or five a day, for like a week."

"A bad batch of Pitorro?"

"Looks like it. Bucketheads on the street started calling it 'Da Holocaust.' It was all over the news."

I knew the news accounts. I read the *Sun-Times* every day. "You know what I don't understand, Tony?"

"What?"

"How Roach's junkies going belly up add up to you walking away with his clientele."

"Do the math, Eddie."

"Whyn't you do it for me, Tone?"

"Junkies wanna live too. Roach's clients needed a place to cop. Someplace safe. They didn't wanna drop Pitorro anymore, not if they could help it. Everybody out here knew you shoot that, it's Russian roulette. Roach tried to rename it, but everybody knew it was from the same source and looked for another shop."

"So you set up your own franchise?"

"Hey, it's a free country."

"Cornuto to the rescue."

"The fuck you want, Eddie? I saw a market."

It was exactly what I expected Tony to say. I looked him over. No sweating. No shifting. Tony was a killer at poker.

I sucked my teeth. "So you got no idea who spiked Roach's supply?"

Tony knew exactly what I was asking. He sniffed. "C'mon, Eddie, you know I don't play dirty pool."

I let out a sharp, one-second laugh.

"All right," said Tony. "*Sometimes* I play dirty pool. But not this time. You know I'd tell you."

I wondered. Long as I'd known Tony, I just couldn't be sure.

"So? How's the money?"

Tony slanted an eyebrow. "In heroin?"

It was a stupid question.

Tony flicked the gold necklace that hung heavily around his neck. "Like a sweet piece of ass on a Sunday morning."

Tony's cell phone rang. He fished it out and flipped it open, secret agent–style. "Yo. Yeah. Yeah. Uh-huh." He glanced over at me. "Whenever I get there. Quit breaking my balls." He shut the phone.

I said, "Girlfriend?"

"What?"

"Who was that on the phone?"

Tony hesitated. "Nobody. Customers. Where was I?"

"You were telling me about your business."

"Right. Anyway, the thing is, right now I got a chance to invest in some serious weight. Brown stuff, the good sticky shit. So pure, you can step on it and restep on it. I'm getting it from some Sicilians. Profits'll be through the roof."

"Yeah, Tony? And what about Roach?"

"What about him?"

"How you gonna deal *him* out?"

Tony tilted his head. "The old-fashioned way, I guess."

Not smart, I thought. With a big drop in business, Roach was certain to be desperate and more dangerous than ever.

I shook my head. "Tony, aren't we a little senior for this?"

"For what?"

"Street war. You got beef with Roach right now, and I mean I got your back and everything, but—"

"Hey, Eddie, do I look like I'm asking you to fight my battles?"

"Yeah, Tony, as a matter of fact, you do. I was all set to ride to Miami."

"Miami? To do what?"

"That girl you sent said you needed my help on something."

"I do."

"She made it sound important."

"It is. But it ain't got nothing to do with this other shit about Roach. That's *my* business. But how come you gotta be so serious? We ain't seen each other in two years."

I already knew that Tony had crossed into Roach's turf. Even a donkey could see that equals street war. For me, it was the most logical thing in the world to expect

Tony to ask me to back him up on that. Now it appeared he wanted something else.

"I just wanna know the scheme, Tony. Why did you send for me?"

Tony nodded. "OK. You have a right. But keep an open mind, 'cause this? This shit is over the top." Tony licked the corner of his mouth. "I need you to muscle with me on another heist."

"Another what?"

"A heist, bro. A stick job. You, me. Couple other cats. Shotguns and balls. Like the olden days."

And that's just how he said it. Like he was talking about baking a cake or putting up some drywall. I should've told Tony to drop it right there. To take me to the airport, the bus depot, drop me anywhere. Hell, if I'd have jumped out of the car at seventy miles an hour, I'd have been better off.

But then Tony said, "Listen, we're talking about a fuckload of money here, papa," and it was hypnosis. Like seeing your fat aunt's humongous tit, the dark brown nipple, that time she forgot to lock the bathroom. Or a cat with its guts hanging out.

I licked my bottom lip. "How much is a fuckload?"

"A million. Maybe more."

"Bullshit."

"Per man, Eddie. A million dollars per swinging dick on this job."

"Tony, you been smoking too much of that happy stick."

"Naw, kid. How you think I'm getting the buy money for that shipment I told you about? That's at least three quarters of a mill right there."

"Three quarters of a mill?" Tony had grown up on welfare like the rest of us. Even in our heyday as burglars and coke dealers, we never pulled a six-figure job. And we spent every penny without ever investing. "Tony, who the fuck you know that's got that much paper lying around?"

"Casinos."

"Like Las Vegas?"

"Uh-uh. Joliet. Shit's full of 'em now. Right down the block from Stateville. Big-ass boats on the river."

I almost laughed. "Tony, you ain't heisting no friggin' casino boat."

"You bet your brown ass I am. Pelón's got a foolproof plan."

My jaw muscles tensed. "Pelón? He's in on this?"

"Of course. He's the mastermind."

I took a second to make certain I heard Tony correctly. "Tony, are you telling me you still deal with that prick? Even after that shit he pulled?"

"Like he had a choice? C'mon, you were there, the bullets were flying. You can't hold that armored-car thing against him forever."

"Just keep him away from me."

Tony said, "I ain't asking you to lick his twat. The man generates paper, and I want in on that."

"Tony, you do what you want, but do it without me."

"I told you to have an open mind, Eddie. Pelón's got a surefire plan this time. He's cased the boat. He knows which way to go. Wait'll you see his crib."

"Tony, you really think you're gonna walk out of a casino with their loot? Them places got security up the ass. Cameras watch everything."

"That ain't stoppin' us."

"No? What, Pelón figure a way to make your ass invisible?"

Tony didn't come back.

"Fill me in, Tone. What's this master plan?"

Tony kept silent. The wipers ticked and a thousand beads of rainwater streaked across the surface of the windshield. Tony shifted in his seat.

"I can't do it, Eddie."

"You can't do what?"

"I can't give away the store like that."

Tony lit a cigarette and blew a thick stream of smoke, which crashed against the windshield and spread in an uneven circle. Then he turned on the radio and flipped through the stations.

I looked at him. "Tony, are you holding out on me?"

He looked over. "You know that ain't how it is. Pelón said mum's the word. Not unless you come on board. I already said too much."

I knew this made Tony uncomfortable. He was sentimental, and he thought of me as his best friend. He probably worried that I felt betrayed.

I shook my head. "Pelón's jerking your chain, kid."

"No he isn't."

"Sure he is. You're buying his loada crap, and you don't even know what's underneath."

"You think I'm that stupid, Eddie?"

"Aren't you?"

It was a left jab, light, but square on the chin, calculated to shake Tony loose. Maybe he'd spill more info. But he didn't flinch. I had come prepared to discuss a street war. To let Tony know that I wasn't gangbanging anymore, how much it bored me. I was not prepared to talk about a heist of any kind. I retreated.

"Tony, this is silly. Let's just drop it."

"Good."

"I'll take it up with Pelón myself. If he's got the guts to face me."

"That's fine. He wants to talk to you."

"I'll bet he does. But like I said, he's feeding you a load."

Tony scrunched his shoulders. "¡Coño, man! I thought the shit was dropped?"

We rode in silence for a while. Tony sparked another joint and switched the CD to a classic, *Lo Mato* by Willie Colón. I thought about the wild things that poured out of Tony's mouth: Pitorro. Cornuto. Money. Big shipments. Shotguns and balls.

But then I got high again and all I could think about was the poetry of the lyrics, the menace and melancholy of the music, trombone, the spell-casting voice of Héctor Lavoe.

And that's when it hit me: I was out. I was outside. I was in the open. I was free. No bars. No walls to contain me. I could choose my own direction. I was not restrained. The emotion of that moment rose. I shut my eyes and let it swell.

After a moment Tony said, "Yo, I know you must be ready to bust a nut, though."

I opened my eyes and smiled. "Brother, it's been so long, I get solid if I blink too much."

Tony laughed. "Relief is on the way, maestro. Chicago's a pussy buffet."

"I ain't sweating that."

Tony smirked. "Yeah you are."

It was true that a strange feeling had begun to invade me in the months prior to my release. Not the raw lust that Tony was talking about, although that was always there. Something else. A hunger maybe. Consciousness of emptiness. The sense that I had missed out by never getting married, never starting a family, never letting a woman get close. The day that I received Tony's messenger in the visiting area, I saw another inmate kiss his wife with such passion, it almost hurt. It was their one weekly visit, their only weekly kiss hello, and they meant it. I realized then that there had always been something unnatural about being alone. Like Adam by himself in the Garden. I didn't say any of this to Tony.

I cracked my knuckles. "Yeah, I'm sure there'll be plenty of skirts to chase. Right now I'm just looking forward to being able to go for a walk."

We rode in silence. After a while the skyline came into view.

Tony nodded. "My kind of town." He switched the CD to "When the Levee Breaks," by Led Zeppelin. "Still my first love," he said. "Rock and roll."

Ahead of us, Chicago spread like a multicolored fire on the plain. Giant buildings reached for something they could never know. And above them were the black and purple clouds. They hung like bunting over the unsuspecting city.

CHAPTER 02:

SAGITTARIUS (DEEP INSIDE)

Tony pulled up to the curb and pointed to a bar with a lit Old Style beer sign. "One of my accounts."

The place was empty except for an old man sitting at the far end of the bar watching the Bears struggle on TV. The bartender sat on his own stool, chin in hand, fixed on the game. He watched the third down and the punt before he ambled to where Tony and I leaned on the bar.

Tony made the peace sign. "Two cold ones."

The bartender opened two sweaty bottles and placed them in front of us. He took Tony's twenty from the bar.

Tony raised his bottle. "To you, brother. The Man tried to break you, but you held it down. Welcome back to the real world."

We clinked our bottles. The beer was cold and it chased away the cotton mouth. The bartender returned Tony's change, which Tony pocketed right away. He downed his beer. I left most of mine. We split.

Once in the car, we drove until we hit a stoplight.

Tony reached in his jacket pocket, pulled out the change, counted it. Two hundred and twenty dollars.

I rubbed my nose. "Didn't you pay with a twenty?"

"Good eye, Eddie. Every week I go there, I collect two bills."

"For what?"

"Protection."

"That old racket?"

"Two hundred a week, from that Polack alone. Plus a free beer."

Next we stopped at a Mexican panadería, where Tony pulled the same stunt. He ordered a bagful of pastries, paid with a twenty, got back a couple hundred, plus the original twenty.

I bit into a cherry empanada. "How many of these accounts you servicing right now?"

"Right now, only eight. But yuppies keep moving in. They already own the whole other side of Western. This area's getting more commercial." A light dusting of powdered sugar decorated Tony's goatee and shirt. He talked with his mouth full. "I figure I'll grow with the neighborhood."

We parked in front of a hot dog stand with a faded picture of a Vienna sausage.

Tony brushed himself off. "One more quick stop."

"I'll wait in the car."

"What, and miss all the fun? C'mon."

The place was a dump. It looked like you could use your finger to trace your name in the grease that coagulated on the walls. Fly tape swung from the ceiling, peppered with dead flies. In the seating area the only customer, a large black woman, sat and began to unwrap her food. Behind the counter a young Korean man in a fresh white smock put his newspaper down and wedged a cigarette in the ashtray.

"For here or to go?" said the Korean, without an accent.

Tony looked past the man at the Korean woman, no doubt the young man's wife, washing and cutting vegetables by the sink. He looked back at the Korean cashier. "For here, chief. Let me get some fries."

The man began to bag French fries for Tony from under a heat lamp.

Tony pointed at the deep fryer. "Naw, man. Fresh ones. Who knows how long them turds been sitting out there?"

The Korean kept bagging fries. "Sir, these fries *are* fresh."

Tony raised his tone half a notch. "Hey, do I know you?"

The Korean stopped bagging and turned to stare at Tony.

"We don't know each other, do we? Let me get some *fresh* fries."

The man dumped the bagged fries back under the heat lamp, then threw a handful of frozen ones into a wire basket and lowered the basket into the bubbling oil. Steam rose.

The Korean said, "Anything else?"

Tony placed the twenty on the counter. "Naw, friend, I already ate."

The Korean rang up the order, took the twenty, and replaced it with Tony's change.

Tony looked at the change without picking it up. "Yo, what the fuck is this?"

The Korean blinked. "Excuse me, sir?"

Tony pointed at the change on the counter. "This. What is it?"

"Your change."

"Right. Where's Kim?"

"Kim?"

"Kim, the owner. Call him. Tell him to get his ass down here pronto, like instant noodle. What the fuck does he think this is? Some kinda game?"

Understanding flooded the Korean's eyes. "Kim? Oh! *Mr.* Kim. No, he is not here anymore. I just bought this place."

Tony said, "You bought it?"

"Yes."

"From Kim?"

"That's right."

Tony looked at me. I shrugged. He turned back to the Korean.

"Listen, what's your name?"

"Soo."

"Sue? Is that short for Susan or something?"

"No," said the Korean. "*S-O-O.* Soo."

"Oh. OK. Listen, Soo, Kim and I, we had, like, an agreement."

Soo narrowed his eyes. "An agreement?"

"Yeah."

"You mean like…a contract?"

"Something like that."

Soo tightened his lips. "Are you a supplier?"

"Sort of. Basically, I come here every week. I order something from the menu. I pay with a twenty, like the one I just gave you."

"Uh-huh?"

"Now, when you bring back the '*change*'"—Tony emphasized the word by saying it slowly and making quotation marks with his fingers—"I want the same exact twenty that I handed you, OK, Soo? Plus two hundred-dollar bills on either side of it. You got that?"

Soo made a face like he didn't follow. I noticed then that Soo's wife had stopped chopping and was watching us with her hands on her hips. The knife was in her right hand. I glanced over at the lone black diner as she bit into her cheeseburger and left a perfect half-circle.

Tony grinned. "Look, Soo, it's not like you won't get your money's worth." Tony lifted the countertop and walked behind the counter.

Soo contorted his face. "Hey, mister, you cannot come back here!"

Tony made the "silence" gesture with his index finger to his lip. "It's OK, Soo, it's all right. I'm just gonna show you what I can do."

Tony walked past Soo, toward where Soo's wife stood next to the sink and the chopped vegetables. In one slick move Tony had the woman by the right wrist. The knife fell from her hand. She screamed as Tony spun behind her, grabbed her hair, and restrained her.

In a soft voice Tony said, "Scream again, bitch, and I'll cut your tongue out and drop it in the fryer."

Soo's wife swallowed the next one. Tony kicked the knife under the sink, beyond anyone's reach.

I looked over at the black woman. She began to get up to run with her food in her hands.

I pointed straight at her and spoke firmly. "Sit. Do not move. Turn your face away."

The customer eased back down and did as I said.

Tony dragged Soo's wife to the fryer. Soo had his hands out in front of him, like he was bracing, but he did not move. His wife's pleading eyes made me wish that Tony would just let go.

The husband's hands shook. "Sorry, mister. Look, look. Money." He hit the register, opening it. "Take it. Take the whole thing."

But Tony didn't stop. He extended the woman's hand to just above the bubbling oil. She emitted a low sob, and you could see her strain, but she was no match for Little Tony. Droplets from her wet fingertips sizzled as they hit the surface of the hot oil.

Tony held her in place and looked at her husband. "Please, Soo, focus. I don't want to get ugly here: The routine is, I pay with a twenty. You give it back to me with two hundreds kissing either side. Capische?"

Soo fumbled through the cash drawer, rattling coins. "I have only one hundred-dollar bill," he said. "The rest in twenties."

Tony paused as if considering. "Fine, Soo." He released Soo's wife, and the woman jumped away, clutching her hand to her chest. "I don't wanna be too much of a hard-on, but from now on, Soo, make sure it's in hundreds, OK? Too many bills makes my wallet hard to fold. It throws my balance off."

Soo paid the ransom.

Tony counted it. He looked Soo in the eye for a few seconds. "Listen, don't hold it against me, all right, partner? Let's start fresh. I just needed you to understand."

Soo remained still, but his mouth twisted.

Tony snagged one of the fries that Soo had originally tried to serve him from under the heat lamp. He popped it in his mouth, made a face, and spit it into a napkin. "You see, Soo? I told you them shits is cold." Tony looked at me. "How 'bout you, Eddie? You need anything?"

"I'm all right."

"Good. Now you ready for some real fun?"

We passed beneath two giant metal sculptures of the Puerto Rican flag, with its lone star, arching across Division Street, Paseo Boricua. We headed west, then drove zigzag patterns up alleys and side streets. Eventually, we came to Tony's intersection.

Streetlamps lit the rest of the city, but not this part. Someone had cut the power to the streetlights, throwing a black veil over the entire spot.

I shifted in my seat. "Looks like yuppies haven't quite discovered this block, have they, Tony?"

"Not yet they haven't."

Even if you've never been to the city, or you steer clear of low rent, you know about these pockets. You've seen them in movies, or on the news. Maybe you've dreamt that you made a wrong turn somewhere and got lost there, turning in circles, a breath ahead of the Minotaur. Tony parked next to a hydrant and pointed at the opposite corner.

"La Esquina Caliente," he said.

I knew the spot. Back in the day we stood there in parachute pants and zipper jackets, moonwalking, laughing, staving off cold, selling small bags of marijuana, and making out with rebellious girls. We never imagined we would ever be anything other than cool.

A new crop of teenagers stood with less energy now. They wore circus-tent jeans slung low on their asses, big hooded sweatshirts, and unlaced boots. They leaned a lot, shot dice, sucked 40s, and puffed weed like it was a chore. I would say at least half had their ears pressed against a cell phone.

I took a deep breath. "What are we doing here, Tony?"

"One last bit of business."

"Whyn't you drop me off first? I'm tired."

"Relax." Tony powered his window open. "You're back in Chi-town now. This is my turf."

A skinny punk with a heavy gold medallion ran over to Tony. "What up, T?" The skinny kid glanced at me, then back at Tony. "I thought you wasn't coming by till later."

"Yeah, well, I'm here now. You got my money?"

The kid pulled a small canvas bag from his waistband.

Tony snatched it and weighed it in his palm. "Feels light, Moco." He looked inside, then shot the kid a look. "Yo, Moco, what the fuck're you assholes doin' out here? Jaggin' each other off?"

Moco said nothing.

Tony shoved the bag under his seat. "Come 'ere."

The kid took a step toward the car.

Tony reeled him in with an index finger. "Down here, Moco. Close to me."

Moco leaned until his face was within Tony's reach. In the dark the orange glow from Tony's cigarette made a jack-o'-lantern effect on Moco's sharp features.

"Tell me the truth, Moco. You pinching my stash?"

"Naw, bro."

"Adding any cut to my shit, Moco? I know all the tricks."

"No, Tony, I swear."

"What the fuck is the problem, then?"

"We ain't been able to sling."

"Why not?"

"Them narcs keep rolling through here, breaking everything up."

Tony said, "Coltrane and Johnson?"

Moco nodded. "I tried calling you, T, but it keeps going into voice mail."

Tony's face went south. "Jesus! Why can't those pigs keep their snouts out my goddamn business?"

Moco shrugged. "They're crazy, bro. Johnson punched JJ in the eye. Almost knocked him out."

Another skinny punk swaggered over. He removed his hood to verify Moco's story. A purple lump of flesh stretched the rim above his eye so that his eyebrow looked like a black caterpillar feeding on a soft dark plum.

Tony examined the wound. "Man, ain't this about a bitch?"

The kid with the shiner stuck his chest out. "Yo, T, I can take whatever them pigs got."

Tony waved him off. "Shut the fuck up, JJ. Get back on post."

JJ flipped his hood and swaggered back to his spot next to the fire hydrant.

Tony turned to Moco again. He thumbed at me. "Moco, you see this man?"

Moco eyeballed me.

Tony said, "This is my boy that I was telling you about. Remember?"

Moco nodded. "Palo, right?"

"Call me Eddie."

"Eddie, yeah." He shook my hand. "Bro, you a straight-up legacy around here. Everybody knows about you. I been hearing about you ever since I was a shorty."

I barely nodded.

Tony said, "Moco, make sure everybody on the block knows he's my boy, all right? He comes by, you give him whatever he wants."

I said, "That's OK, Tony."

Tony ignored me. "You talk to him, Moco, it's like you're talking directly to me, you got that?"

Moco said, "Got it."

"Good. Now let me get a deck."

Moco looked up and down the block, then whistled. Another kid broke from the pack and hustled to a gangway, the cell phone still pressed against his ear. He disappeared into the gangway, then reappeared and hustled back, handing Moco a small bag, all the while chatting. Moco looked up and down the street again before leaning in. He handed Tony the bag.

It was a tiny glassine envelope with a small amount of white dust in it. Tony lit the Cadillac's interior.

"I wanted you to see my product."

Tony held it up. The small plastic Baggie was stamped with an image of a bull's head on it, like a cheap imitation of the Chicago Bulls logo. Tony pointed at the horn. "You see that? Cornuto."

"Congratulations, Tony. Now can we break the fuck out?"

Tony said, "What, you got a hot date or something?"

"I just ain't feeling this."

"You're paranoid, right? Like the COs are just about to walk in on you. You keep expecting the old 'face the wall and spread your butt cheeks' routine. I went through that when I first got out."

"It's not that, Tony. It's just—"

Suddenly, a skinny man emerged from a gangway across the street and shuffled toward us, with his shoulders hunched and both hands in his pants pockets. He was bony, but he had a thick, uneven beard and a head of hair grown wild.

Tony tossed his cigarette. "Great. Here comes buzzkill."

Moco pulled his sleeves up. "You want me to get rid of him, boss?"

"Just chill, Moco. Post up."

Moco x-rayed the intruder with his eyes as he walked off.

The man stepped to Tony's window and saluted. "¡Capitán!"

"Don't start, B."

The skinny man grinned and nodded. "How you doing, papi? Everything tight? How's your moms?"

Tony said, "You really peel yourself from the gutter for small talk?"

The man's grin widened. He was missing several teeth and the dark spaces staggered between the remaining ones meant his smile resembled the keys of a piano. There were dark circles under his eyes. He scratched his head.

"It's that, um, you know, Tone, I'm gonna get my Social Security check next week, and, um, how do you call it, as soon as I cash that, I was, um, I swear on my mother, I was gonna get straight with you, right? My hand to God. You know I'm good for it, right? But, today, I—"

Tony said, "Beto, stop trying to cop over here without cash, aw'ight? Go talk to Roach. I ain't carrying you no more. And where's your manners? Don't you see who this is sitting next to me?"

That was when I realized that I knew Beto. I mean, I *really* knew him. We went to high school together and dropped out around the same time. We ran in the same crew, hung out in the same clubs, pulled capers together. During our heyday we called Beto "GQ" because of his dapper style. The ladies loved him.

Beto looked at me. He appeared to be about half of his original size. His yellow eyes widened. He slapped his hands together. "Oye, pero, look who it is!"

He came around to my side of the car. I got out. Beto hugged me and I noticed that he stank mildly of urine. He felt real thin under his wrinkled shirt, which was damp. His face was sweaty.

Beto tugged at a knot in his beard. "Palo, wow, what a trip. The 'Man with the Plan,' huh? Wassup, gangster? How long you been out? You was still inside, right?"

"Until today. But you can call me Eddie."

"Eddie, yeah, that's good, papi, that's good, you look good. ¿La buena vida?"

"Something like that. What's up with you?" I said, and felt embarrassed the instant the words tumbled out of my mouth.

Beto bit his lip, scratched, and tilted his head forward enough to suggest that I take a good look. "Holding on, papi. You know how it be. I—I got the virus and everything. Fucked myself up."

"Sorry to hear that, Beto. I been reading they're working wonders with the drugs for that now."

"Yeah, so they say. But that shit costs. Anyways, you know me. Can't be on no kind of program."

I nodded.

Beto rocked in place and rubbed his forearm. "Yo,

Eddie, you know—I wanted to thank you, you know? For never ratting me out on that thing."

"Forget about it."

"You could've done yourself a solid by stabbing me in the back, and I really, I just…" He leaned in and gave me a quick half hug. "De corazón, bro. For not opening your mouth."

"Never thought of it, Beto."

"That was never your style." Beto flashed his piano keys. "Eddie, you think, you know, for old times' sake, maybe you could hit me off with just a couple dollars? Just for a few? I'm solid for it. I get my SSI check—"

"Well—"

"Remember ladies' night at Eddie Rockets, bro? Erik's North? Prime and Tender, back in the day?" Beto began singing the chorus from Exposé's "Point of No Return." He launched into a dance move called "the Running Man." "Remember, Eddie? When we used to battle?"

"I remember."

Beto froze the dance in midstride, with a leg in the air. "We used to be tight, Eddie, remember?" Beto popped back into action for a couple more steps, then froze. "I'll get the money back to you with interest, Eddie, I promise."

"That's not it, Beto—"

He popped back into song and dance for a wild breakdown, then froze. "C'mon, Eddie. You can call it money in the bank." He moved again, pop-locking and doing the chorus, then froze. "I'll never bother you again." Beto hopped and repeated just the chorus until he ran out of breath. He bent with his hands on his knees, huffing. "Remember, Eddie? The good times?"

"You always were the best dancer." I began to reach for my wallet when Tony piped in.

"Yo, Eddie, you givin' this títere legal tender? You may as well light that shit on fire."

Beto begged with his eyes. "C'mon, Tony, why you gotta be like that?"

"Beto, the guy just got back. Already you're hittin' him up with your pity party? Show some respect."

I waved Tony off. "I'm all right, Tone."

"I know you are. That's your flaw. You're soft. Beto! Here!" Tony tossed the sack of heroin he showed me out the window onto the street.

Beto jumped on it.

Tony snapped his neck for me to get in the car, which I did.

Beto leaned in to Tony's side with a bigger grin. "See, Tony? You always come through. Man, you got a heart of gold!"

"Stop counting on it, Beto, this ain't welfare."

Beto slapped Tony's shoulder and looked at me. "He's a good man, Eddie. Solid. A prince. He's gonna go far, this guy."

Tony lit a cigarette. "Why don't you go back to the methadone program like I told you, Beto?"

"I am, Tony, I am. I'm planning on it. It's my New Year's resolution, I swear. But you know, right now it's the holidays and everything. I just wanna celebrate."

Tony started the engine. "The holidays, Beto? It's a month to Halloween."

Beto nodded. "I know, right? You noticed the shit starts earlier every year? It's getting too commercial."

Tony shook his head.

Beto began to launch into more gibberish, but Tony powered his window up and cut him off. Beto waved like a kid in a home movie about to jump into the ocean and took off toward the gangway with his stash.

Tony slumped as if contemplating another shift at the mill. "The shit you go through to make a living these days. Anyway, let's stop at the crib. I got something I wanna show you."

Tony's place was a couple blocks away. A rear apartment on the second floor of a two-flat. We parked in the alley. Tony nosed the front bumper right up to a utility pole, next to the back fence, which left barely enough room for him to get out.

The backyard was dark, overgrown with brush, and full of garbage. It reminded me of the lot where I once saw a kid jump ten feet after getting bitten by a rat. I moved across the narrow sidewalk quickly to the back porch.

The back of Tony's gray building was scarred by graffiti, most of it gang-related. The porch creaked like an old woman's bones. The door to Tony's apartment was covered with a metal gate. The lone window had bars on it.

Tony worked the locks. "I'm staying here to save money right now. Once we pull the caper, I'm buying a condo on Lake Shore Drive."

We entered through the kitchen. The room was barely lit by a single low-watt bulb. It needed a paint job. The walls were yellow with grease, and years of dust caked the molding. There was a table surrounded by four mismatched chairs and the hardwood floor was painted plasma red. The sink was empty. A pot, one pan, and two dishes were stacked neatly on the counter. Music poured in from one of the other rooms.

Tony padlocked the gate behind us. He shut the door. "Anybody in?"

Two teenage girls bounced into the kitchen from the living room. If they were legal, they were barely legal.

Tony grinned, removed his shades, and tongued the dark-haired, olive-skinned one like he had just gotten back from the war. He whipped his leather off in a practiced style and hung it on the back of a chair, revealing thick forearms and a menagerie of tattoos.

I recognized the dark-haired female as Nena, the girl Tony had sent to Joliet to speak to me. The other girl was cream-colored. A green-eyed Puerto Rican who looked almost like a white girl with light brown hair.

Tony grinned so you could see his dimples. "Eddie, meet Sweetleaf."

Tony's girl, Nena, said, "We call her that 'cause she smoke a lotta weed."

Sweetleaf's white jeans were so tight, they were like a fine glaze.

I smiled. "What's your real name?"

"Nieve."

"Pure as the driven snow, huh? Your mother must have taken one look at you and come up with that."

Nieve opened her green eyes wide. "How did you know?"

I smiled. "Intuition."

Nieve asked for my jacket and carefully hung it on the back of a chair.

Tony wagged his eyebrows. "Yo, let's set this shit off."

We sat around a card table, boy-girl, boy-girl, and played drinking games. Nieve broke weed and rolled it into a cigar leaf. Tony did impressions and told jokes. The boom box went through a repertoire of freestyle and house, most of it from the eighties. Tony repeated, "Remember this? Remember this?" during almost every song.

Nieve held in smoke, but smiled when our fingertips touched as she passed the blunt.

Tony snapped his fingers. "Damn, I'm snoozing." He went in the bedroom and returned with his kit. "Almost forgot the yayo."

Therapists warn against this: hanging out with the old crowd. Scenarios that set off craving as predictably as ringing a bell. Your only thought becomes, *Do coke, do coke now!* Sometimes you don't know the trigger. Other times it's a lock. Like watching your old running buddies do blow. That'll get you thirsty every time.

Tony cut lines on a little mirror. He sucked them with a metal straw.

My nose tingled. "Where's the bathroom?"

They all pointed.

Tony thumbed at the cocaine. "Walk in the park first?"

"I'm straight."

"You positive?"

I smiled and hustled to the can.

Tony said, "Try not to stink up the joint, huh?" and the girls laughed, but not as hard as Tony.

I locked the bathroom door. My heart galloped. I needed to stick my mind on anything other than the coke rush. I splashed water on my face and looked in the mirror over the filthy vanity. My eyes were close.

After a few minutes Tony banged on the door. "Yo, kid, you fall in? Need a life jacket?"

"Tony, can you get away from the door?" I sat on the toilet and closed my eyes. I imagined Miami. The beach.

Hot sand. Women in thongs. I ran my fingers over the money belt under my shirt.

There is no doubt about it: cocaine can devour forty thousand dollars faster than the IRS on a rampage. I whispered the Our Father, said a couple of Hail Mary's, and the craving began to settle. I splashed water on my face again and walked out.

Tony blew a big cloud of reefer smoke. "Yo, E, you find the toilet paper under the sink? Or'd you go with the hand on this one?" Tony cracked himself up, but the girls laughed in a way that felt like they were only humoring him.

"I could use some candy or gum."

Nena was on Tony's lap by then. She offered bubble gum.

Nieve flicked her hair. "Yo, so how youse two know each other?"

Tony slapped the table. "Me and this nigga? Girl, since the seventies. Grammar school."

Nena said, "The *seventies*? Ho shit, I wasn't even born yet!"

Nieve and Nena were teenagers. This was prehistory to them. Their parents' generation. Tony recounted the first day, in fifth grade, when he was the new kid, a transfer student, and how I was the first boy in the class to befriend him during recess.

I smiled again. "Tony conned the teacher into believing he was such a little gentleman. Kept answering, 'Yes, ma'am. No, ma'am' to every question. Yet all the while I can see him giving the old bag the finger under his desk."

The girls giggled.

Tony sniffed his middle finger. "Cunt was onto me within a week."

"Yeah, but what a week."

We bullshitted like that for a while, recalling childhood adventures, like shoplifting comic books at Woolworth's and changing ratty old gym shoes for new ones at Gold-blatt's and just running out. We talked about other times, in our twenties, when we shared an apartment, a loft, and threw wild parties, like one where we dressed as the Blues Brothers, and another where we dressed as KISS—Tony was Ace Frehley and I was Gene Simmons. We ate magic mushrooms until they kicked in and Tony tried to do a back-flip off the couch and stumbled into our TV, breaking it.

Tony said, "The next day we stole a bigger one from the Polk Brothers warehouse."

The girls told us about a time they cut class to do acid and walk around Water Tower mall, laughing in people's faces.

Tony said, "Good times. That's what life is all about." He looked at me. "Now we're gonna make some new memories."

He took Nena's feet into his lap, removed her shoes, and began to give her a foot massage. Nieve poured Alizé into my cup. We kept on chatting.

Eventually, all talking stopped. Nena climbed in Tony's lap again. They humped, laughed, and made out. She rubbed him over his pants. Nieve and I sat in silence and pretended not to notice, but I was getting stiff.

Tony got up and grabbed the boom box. "We're going in the bedroom. Front room's all yours."

I swallowed. "Ain't you taking me home, Tony?"

"Later." He staggered toward the bedroom. Over his shoulder he said, "Talk to Sweetleaf, will ya? She looks lonely."

I followed him to the bedroom door. "Tony, I don't feel like small talk."

Tony looked at me with bloodshot, watery eyes. I could see over his shoulder as Nena spread herself on the bed. Tony whispered, "Don't be nervous. It really is like riding a bike." With that, Tony slipped into the bedroom and closed the door.

I went back to the table and sat in silence. Music pumped out of the bedroom. Before long we heard the bedsprings, muffled voices, laughter. Then the headboard banged slowly against the wall.

Nieve stood and headed for the living room. "You wanna watch TV?"

We sat in the curtainless room, on opposite ends of a soiled couch. Tony's weights and bench took up most of the space. Nieve offered me the remote.

I waved it off. "Watch whatever you want."

Nieve flipped through stations and stopped on a show about a California high school. Teenagers put on a play.

Nieve tilted her head. "You like this show?"

"I don't care."

"I can put a movie on if you want."

I shrugged.

Nieve got up and pressed play on the DVD player, then sat down again, closer.

We sat in silence as a set of woman's lips, a blonde, pumped up and down, machinelike, on a giant black cock. The camera pulled back and changed angles. The couple worked through an itinerary of positions. Freestyle music bounced in from Tony's bedroom and mixed noisily with the synthesizer porn score. Tony's headboard continued to bang against the wall.

The camera closed in and pulled back on the action. It focused briefly on the word "Sagittarius" tattooed in a cheap green cursive on the woman's back. Her ass was thick for a white girl. She looked right in the camera and said, "Deep inside, baby. Pay those bills."

By then, my dick was like cobalt. Nieve touched my hand, but did not hold it. She slid a little closer, leaned without a word, and started kissing my neck. I was too embarrassed to look her in the eye. I focused on the action on-screen.

Nieve unzipped my jeans and pulled it out. Her hand felt small. Her stroke was awkward. Still, it was warm. And soft. I don't know where Nieve imagined it was going, but there was no time. A heavy load bubbled out.

Nieve held it as it shriveled up. I'm not sure what she was waiting for, but the couple in the porno kept going, and Tony's headboard slapped the wall.

After ten seconds that felt like ten minutes, Nieve released. "I better wash up," she said.

I zipped so fast, I almost pinched myself. Nieve disappeared into the bathroom. After a while she returned, and we avoided eyes again. I felt like telling her that I hadn't been with a woman in a very long time. Maybe we could try again another day. I could get her number. Or maybe we could wait a few minutes.

But I didn't say a word. Nieve shut off the porn and sat Indian-style on the floor to watch the show about the California high school. The students' play was in trouble. Then somebody fixed everything by saying the show would go on.

*   *   *

The bedroom door creaked open. Tony came down the hall less urgent than before. His belt was undone. He wore a dago T, a wife beater that showed off his biceps and even more tattoos. The ones I remembered looked a little faded. Tony was sweaty, but not out of breath. He flashed a big tacky grin.

"What up, *pimp*?"

I didn't say a word.

He looked at Nieve. "You two getting along?"

Nieve looked at Tony, then at me. "He's really sweet."

"I told you."

I got up. "Ready to go, Tone?"

He looked at me. "Do I look out for my boy or what?"

"Just give me the address, Tony. I'll find my new place myself."

Tony waved me off. "Don't get your panties in a bundle, stud."

He went back to the bedroom and came back fully dressed, down to the driving gloves. Nieve got up from the living-room floor and joined Nena in the bedroom.

Tony had one hand behind his back. "Close your eyes and stick out your palm."

"How many times I gotta tell you, Tony? I'm ready to roll."

"Just do it. I got a surprise for you."

I felt stupid, but I closed my eyes and put my hand out. Tony slapped it with cold metal. I opened my eyes and saw a .38 Special. Chrome. As polished as Tony's car.

I handed it back. "I don't need this."

"Why not? This heater's a classic."

"I don't run in your crew, Tone."

"It's for security."

"I ain't that insecure. And I sure as shit ain't looking for no weapons rap."

Tony held the gun like he didn't quite understand. "Suit yourself." He tucked the chrome into his waistband and grabbed weed and coke off the table. "I thought it might come in handy."

We left without saying good-bye to the girls. Once in the car, Tony slipped the reefer, the coke, and the .38 under his seat. I was ready to get to my new place, take a hot shower, and spread out on some clean sheets.

Tony started the engine. He looked in the rearview mirror. "Fuck!"

"What's wrong?"

Tony opened his mouth to answer, but was cut off by flashing blue lights, and the unmistakable peal of a Chicago police siren tearing through the night.

CHAPTER 03:

JURISDICTION

Blue and white lights bounced off every surface in that alley like bottle rockets. My heart did the same.

Tony punched the dashboard. "Shit! It's Coltrane and Johnson."

"Who?"

I looked back at the unmarked squad. A white light flooded us, but I could see that they had snuck up and pinned the Caddy to the utility pole, which left no way out.

"Tony, you know these humps?"

A bullhorn blared: "All right, Pacheco. Get out."

Tony looked back. "We're stuck."

The horn: "Outta the vehicle! Now!"

Tony shut off the engine.

I caught his arm. "What're you gonna do?"

He jerked away from me. "Pull it together, Eddie. These leprechauns don't play."

Tony climbed out with his hands in front of him. Even if I made a run, they'd recover my suitcase from the trunk and ID me from what they found inside. It wasn't worth a bullet in the back either. I followed Tony into the spotlight.

Two plainclothes officers hopped toward us with their guns drawn. They doubled us over the hood of Tony's car and shackled our hands behind our backs, but didn't bother to pat us down.

One cop was black, the other was white. Their outfits were standard issue: blue jeans, windbreakers, baseball caps. The black cop wielded a round gut. A thin wedding band pinched his sausage-link ring finger. The white one was lanky, and tucked his jeans into skinny cowboy boots.

The black cop breathed raw onions down my neck. "Stay down, big man."

I did not resist.

The white cop flexed a deep rasp of a voice, with a slight Southern accent. "You too, Pacheco, stay down."

For reasons known only to him, Tony flopped like a marlin on a hook. The white cop unholstered a big metal flashlight and jabbed it into Tony's ribs. Tony tensed like he'd been stunned with an electric current.

The white cop reholstered the flashlight and looked at his partner. "See that, Johnson? Still breaking 'em after all these years."

Tony flared his nostrils and said something nasty about the white cop's mother. The man's pockmarked face almost cracked in two. He grabbed Tony by the collar and the back of the pants and shoveled him into a garage door, making a loud percussive *thump* and putting a dent in the thin door metal. The cop then picked Tony up and rammed him into trash bins, knocking them over like bowling pins. Garbage bags spilled. For a finale the tall white cop swung the point of his cowboy boot in a sudden, perfect arc, right into Tony's gut. Tony yelped.

The cop bent down and grabbed Tony by the wisps of his receding hair. "Don't you never say nothin' about my momma!"

Tony's face sagged. If he had anything else to say, he swallowed it. The black cop, Johnson, did nothing.

Coltrane let go of Tony and turned his square jaw at me. "And who the hell are you?"

I cleared my throat. "Santiago. Eddie Santiago."

"Santiago, why are you polluting my jurisdiction?"

"Excuse me?"

"Speak up!"

"I'm from around here."

"Around where?"

"This neighborhood."

"*Where*, Santiago? I want an address."

I didn't even know where I lived.

"By the park. I just moved here."

"You don't know your own address?"

"I'm new in town."

"Where from? My patience is growing thin."

There was no use hiding it. Coltrane could simply punch my name into the computer and it would all pour down. Or he could check my wallet and see my newly minted Department of Corrections ID.

I cleared my throat. "Stateville. I just got out."

Coltrane raised an eyebrow. "Now we're sharing."

Johnson crinkled his nose. "I *thought* I smelled convict."

Coltrane took a comb from his back pocket and raked

it through his oily, dirty blond head. "Fresh from the peni-
tentiary, and already itchin' to get back."

Coltrane put the comb away and dug a tin of chewing tobacco from his breast pocket. He pinched a wad and
stuffed it between his cheek and gum. He looked at his
partner. "Let's investigate, Johnson."

They frisked us, Coltrane on Tony, Johnson on me.
Johnson immediately felt my money belt. My throat
tightened.

"What's this?"

The chemicals in my stomach churned.

Johnson yanked my shirt open and the buttons flew.
His eyes widened. He removed the money belt and
unzipped it. "Aw, hell naw!"

Coltrane leaned and eyeballed the money without a
reaction. He rubbed his chin like it was an unanticipated
turn of events. Finally, he thumbed the cash.

"How much?"

My gears jammed. I couldn't process the words.

Coltrane's pitch rose. "Are you deaf, Santiago? I asked
you a question."

My voice almost cracked. "It's a little over forty
thousand."

The cops looked at each other, paused, then burst out
laughing.

"Let the good times roll," said Johnson.

I tried to weigh them down. "I worked real hard for
that."

Coltrane stopped laughing on a dime. "Hey! Santiago!
Blow it up somebody else's ass. Them prison jobs don't pay
but a couple cents an hour. We know you didn't earn this."

Coltrane took the money belt from Johnson's hands,

zipped it, slung it over his shoulder like it was the championship belt. "Keep your eye on the suspects, Johnson, while I check what else we got."

The black cop ordered us to our knees.

Coltrane went straight for Tony's stash. "Aha! Johnson, look at this jackpot. We got marijuana…a white substance that appears to be"—he sniffed it without snorting—"powder cocaine. And, oh yes"—he held up the .38-caliber revolver—"we got ourselves a peashooter."

Johnson leaned toward us. "Boy, you dumb fucks really stepped in it with that one. We coordinate with the feds on one of them RICO joints? You're talkin' mandatory minimums. So much time, you'll learn to suck your own balls."

Coltrane examined the gun. "That is, of course, unless CPD Forensics is looking for this." He looked right at me. "In that case it gets serious, doesn't it?"

Coltrane opened the .38's chamber, ejected the bullets into his palm. "Hollow points. Fat stretch right there." He sniffed the barrel and reacted like it was rotten milk. "Dang thing's been fired recently too."

Coltrane closed the chamber, put the bullets in his breast pocket, and tilted his head at me as he tucked the gun into his waistband. I looked at Little Tony, but he played "Keep Away" with his eyes.

Coltrane found my suitcase in the Caddy's trunk. He laid it on the pavement. "What's inside, Santiago?"

"Personal property."

"You claiming it?"

I knew from all of my jailhouse lawyering that I should never say or admit anything to a cop other than my pedigree information—name, address, and birthday.

Whatever else you say will never be used to excuse you, and will only be used to screw you. I said, "Everything in that suitcase belongs to me."

Coltrane opened it and shook everything onto the wet, dirty pavement. Then he pulled a bowie knife from his boot to pick through my stuff. I only had a couple of books left in my collection, but Coltrane said, "Brace yourself, Johnson. Another convict who loves to read."

Johnson shook his head. "Nigga, you a straight-up cliché."

Coltrane resheathed the knife in his boot. He opened a jewelry box and the one thing contained within it fell onto the clothes on the street. Coltrane's hand moved slowly toward it. He held it up.

"Is this a genuine Purple Heart?"

I did not say.

"Answer me, Santiago. My pappy earned his getting blinded while killin' Red Chinese. How's a sperm bag like you get one?"

"Be careful with it."

Coltrane stepped closer. I could smell the tobacco and saliva on his breath. "You serve in the military?"

I was a veteran of too many wars, but not in the way Coltrane meant. "No."

"Hmm. Figured this couldn't be rightfully yours."

Coltrane put the Purple Heart into the same pocket where he kept his chewing tobacco. Then he flipped through my mother's Bible. Rose petals preserved between the pages for nearly thirty years came loose and fluttered lifelessly to the pavement. I wanted to kick Coltrane's yellow teeth in.

For a second he appeared to read one of the passages.

He shut the book. "Santiago, you one of them jailhouse converts?"

I clenched my teeth. "Put my things back as you found them."

The flame in Coltrane's fading gray eyes sputtered, and I got ready for the flashlight in the ribs. But he turned the heat down.

"Perp, you ain't worth the sweat." He looked at Johnson. "Let's wrap these two in a bow."

Johnson shoved Tony into the backseat of their unmarked squad, while Coltrane tossed my things back in the suitcase, then tossed the suitcase back into Tony's trunk. He put the gun, the coke, the reefer, and my money belt into the trunk of their squad car and said, "Official evidence" as he slammed it shut.

Johnson folded me into the backseat. "Looks like you dildos just fell into a hole."

My throat constricted. "Where are you taking us?"

Johnson curled his lips. "Like you don't know."

Coltrane jumped behind the steering wheel and looked over his shoulder. "You belong to us now, Santiago."

He shifted the machine into drive and took off. My stomach flipped. We turned onto the street that leads to the station, and sped the rest of the way.

My heart squeezed against the walls inside my chest. We were a couple blocks from the station. Coltrane turned toward us as he drove.

"Got you girls shittin', don't I?"

He smirked, cut the wheel, and burned rubber down an alley, away from the precinct. I didn't know what to think. Obviously, we weren't on our way to the lockup. If we did not go to the precinct, we would not be processed. No process, no judges. No DAs. No indictments. No prison.

My pulse came down a little. I realized the whole thing was some kind of shakedown.

My money was in the trunk. My number one object became to get out of the vehicle and away from these assholes with as much of my savings as possible. I wondered whether I should speak up. I'd witnessed many power plays and it was usually the guy who shut his mouth the longest who came up aces in the end.

But not always.

I cleared my throat. "Where are we going?"

Coltrane and Johnson ignored me.

"Are we under arrest?"

Their body language portrayed nothing, no movement. They were like a still life of the backs of two heads.

I raised my voice a little. "Officers, I demand to speak to an attorney—"

Johnson turned. "Boy, if you don't shut that blowhole—"

I cut him off with, "Detective, I demand to speak—"

Johnson cut *me* off with a solid right hook to the side of the head. A black shroud dropped over my frontal lobe. I was knocked out.

When I came to, we were parked someplace quiet, and dark. My head felt heavy. Everything was dim. Tony and I were alone in the car. Coltrane and Johnson hovered above us like ghosts. I closed my eyes. Everything spun.

When I opened my eyes, I saw Coltrane and Johnson again, only now they stood on a loading dock next to the car. A sign behind them read, WHOLESALE MEATS.

Tony sounded far away. "You up, Eddie? Can you hear me?"

"Whut?" It hurt to talk.

Tony whispered, "Are you all right?"

It felt like I'd had too much to drink, only a lot worse. I had to concentrate because Tony was on some kind of time delay. His words only made sense a few seconds after he spoke them. The pain spiked inside my head.

"Goddamn. Where are we?"

"Meat market."

I had no clue. I looked around. The area seemed deserted.

"What are we doing here, Tony?"

"Coltrane stopped at a pay phone while you were zonked. Made a quick call, then drove straight here."

Tony looked out the window, away from me, away from the dock and from Coltrane and Johnson. "I think we're up for sale."

"For sale?" Maybe I was punch-drunk. "What'd you just say?"

"Roach."

"Roach?" It took me a second to recollect who he meant. "You mean...your street war?" It took me another second to realize what Tony was getting at. "Are you saying they'd turn you over?"

"Turn *us* over."

"They know you got beef with Roach and his crew?"

"Of course they do. And they know Roach'll pay."

"Don't they know what he'll do if he gets his hands on you?"

Tony turned to me. "Eddie, for a price, these niggas'll do it themselves."

"You're outta your mind." The pain shifted from my head to my stomach. "These guys are cops!"

Tony rolled his eyes. "Whatta you think we're doing out here? Look around. Nobody knows we're out here."

I looked up at Coltrane and Johnson, and again felt the impulse to run. I scouted a route, but the car door was locked, with no way to open it from inside. No key in the ignition. Kicking the glass out and trying to jump through was too many steps to complete before Coltrane and Johnson'd be off that dock and on top of me.

At some point they would open that door, to get us out. I determined that at that exact moment I would hoof it, even with my hands shackled behind my back.

Johnson looked down on me from the loading dock. It was like he'd read my mind. His eyes said: "I'll shoot you in the fuckin' back, punk."

I turned to Tony. "Think we can negotiate?"

"With what?"

"My money. We can give them some."

"They already have that."

We were in wet cement. "Ain't you got something saved, Tony? What about that cash you picked up at the Spot?"

"Man, that was just a couple G's."

"Nothing in the bank?"

"Nope."

"I thought you were rolling. Where's all that cheese you been grating?"

Tony said, "Wake up, Eddie!" He hard-whispered: "If they wanted to deal with us, they would. Obviously, that ain't why they dragged us to bumfuck."

Tony left no doubt: I was without a partner and without

a chance. And if the line between love and hate is a thin one, the one between hope and desperation is even more so. I crossed it.

I shrank farther into the seat. My chest tightened. I envisioned Roach leading us to some dark place to cap us, or maybe hang us from some pipes. At once, an image of my dead mother flashed, looking pasty, waiting for me at the end of the tunnel with her droopy eyes. Blood drained to my feet.

Just then, a long white limousine flew out of the mist. It slid to a stop in the gravel next to us.

Tony sat up. "Oh shit! It's Pelón! That's his ride!"

"You're lying."

Tony thanked God, Jesus, and the Virgin Mary out loud.

The limo driver got out, waddled to the back, held the door open. I saw the sheen of a white suit against tough dark skin. Pelón, who was in his mid-sixties now, peeled himself slowly from inside. He still shaved his head, and it still looked like a giant coconut.

Pelón poked the gravel with his cane, and worked like a newborn foal to find his posture. Once he got his balance, he moved quickly to the foot of the dock.

Tony kept thanking God under his breath.

I watched Pelón deal with the narcs. I hadn't seen him in over a decade. He looked older, of course, with more lines in his face. The black handlebar mustache of his middle age was gone, replaced by a thin silver mustache, which ended at the corners of his mouth. His eyebrows were salt-and-pepper, and his face was otherwise as clean-shaven as his skull. He looked thinner than when he was younger and into lifting weights. The cane was a new addition as well.

Pelón and the cops agreed on a price. I began to feel the noose loosen. The narcs jumped from the dock to the hood of Pelón's limo to make noise and demonstrate how agile they still were. Pelón cursed at them in Spanish, but he fished cash from an envelope.

Tony showed his dimples. "I told you the man was proper."

The cops yanked us out and undid the cuffs, which let blood rush back to my hands. Johnson licked his lips.

Coltrane flashed his yellowed smile. "Be careful where you walk, Santiago."

They hopped in their car. My money belt was still in the trunk.

I took one step toward their car with my finger raised. "Hey!"

Johnson looked right at me with his black hand on the door.

I nodded at the trunk. "My money."

Johnson crinkled his eyes. "Fuck you, Santiago." He slammed the door shut. "You bring that shit up again, I'll chop you in the fuckin' throat."

Coltrane punched the gas and they sped off, kicking up gravel.

Like a statue of an easy mark, I stood there and watched their taillights disappear into the mist. After they were history, I suddenly picked up a rock and threw it.

Tony spit. "Thank God they're gone."

Pelón grunted. "Them cochinos ain't gone nowhere. They just on ice."

I stared at the spot where the cops had entered the fog. My money was smoke. Florida? The salsa label I was going to invest in? Vanished.

Pelón coughed into a monogrammed handkerchief. I saw for the first time that his right hand had only the thumb and index finger. The missing fingers made his right hand look like a claw. He extended it.

"Bueno, Eddie, hace mucho tiempo."

I looked at the claw and did not take it.

Pelón looked at his hand, then back at me as he lowered it to his side. "You found a little trouble, eh?"

I had a lump in my throat. "My money."

Tony let some air out. "I just can't believe they gangstered it like that."

Pelón said, "¿Cuánto fue?"

I held my tongue for a second, then said it. "Forty. Forty thousand dollars."

"¡Diablo!"

I looked at the ground. "I got nothin' left."

Pelón shook his head. "Don't look at it like this. Is only money."

I looked at Pelón and wondered how he could possibly say that with a sober face.

We stood in silence for a second. I felt really lost.

Pelón put his claw on my shoulder. In Spanish he said, "Sometimes life hits hard to awaken us." He opened his envelope again and, with his claw, quickly counted twenty-five crisp one-hundred-dollar bills. "Toma. Take this until you get on your feet."

I looked at the money.

Pelón held it closer. In a Puerto Rican accent he said, "This ain't time for pride."

My whole life I've known guys like Pelón. They pretend to be stand-up compadres in order to gain advantage. For these types a couple of dollars always means leverage.

I took it. "You know I'll pay you back, Pelón."

"Who's keeping track? We do these things for our friends."

Pelón clapped his hands. "Bueno, vámonos. I got an appointment. But I take you home first, no?"

The fat driver held open the door. We climbed in and glided off. Inside the limo was very cold. The air was on full blast. Pelón had Tony fix him a drink.

"Later this week we make a little party," said Pelón. "The three of us." He touched my knee. In Spanish he said, "We must celebrate our friend's liberation!"

At that moment the only thing that I could think about was my money.

Tony sat up next to me. "Pelón, can we do something high-class?"

Pelón flaunted a perfect smile. "Ya tú sabe' que I don't do it any other way." He looked at me. "And you, Eddie? Don't you worry about them pennies. Squash it. Forget about it. Pelón gonna take care of everything."

As it turns out, he did.

CHAPTER 04:

MAESTRO (THAT LATIN STRUT)

I craned my neck up at my new apartment building: four stories of faded green aluminum siding that seemed to lean a little. Not like an old man who needs a cane. More like a tree that's begun to go away from its center. It reminded me of a teacher's explanation of the difference between potential energy versus kinetic. How a boulder on the edge of a cliff equals potential energy, while a falling boulder equals kinetic. The façade of my new apartment building was faded and quiet and grim. And it leaned just enough to give a hint of its potential.

Tony pointed to an empty window with the lights out. "Top floor's you, kid. The penthouse," which was his attempt at making things light.

Tony grabbed the suitcase out of my hand and went in. The hallway was a mix of roach spray, patches of worn, musty linoleum, and plaster from shit-colored walls that came off in chunks. Tony lugged my suitcase up the steps like a bellhop in one of those old black-and-white movies where white people travel by train and fall in love.

"Sweet location," he said. "Close to the park." Tony looked over his shoulder as he inserted the key. "You probably remember the 'L's pretty close, when you need to zip around."

Tony unlocked the door, stepped in, pulled a string in the center of the room. A circular fluorescent bulb fluttered on with a buzz. I remained in the doorway. Tony occupied the center of the room.

"I know it's tight," he said, "but it's just a spot to hang it for a while. Come in."

I traveled the length of the room in three steps. It had a small low bed, a scratched dresser, a mirror with the silver backing peeling off. The card table had a tiny refrigerator tucked under it. In the corner was a rickety chair.

"Smells like moldy clothes."

Tony forced open the window. "So you buy some incense."

The vomit-pink carpet was sticky, like it wanted to gum up the soles of my boots.

"Is there a toilet somewhere?"

Tony pointed toward the hallway. "You share with the other rooms on this floor."

"A kitchen?"

Tony cocked his head. "Get real."

I sat on the piss-stained mattress. Empty hangers dangled in the doorless closet like a previous tenant's bones.

I sniffed the air. "Did something commit suicide in here?"

"What the fuck did you expect for five hundred clams? You think this is 1986?" He pointed an unlit cigarette out the window in the direction of downtown. "At least you got a view. And you ain't locked in. This is by the week. You're good for a solid month."

Tony dragged the chair to the window and sat. He propped his heels on the sill, and tipped the chair back on two legs.

I rubbed my temples. Handcuffs, right hooks, and evaporating money morphed into a cinder block inside my head. "What the fuck happened out there, Tony?"

"With the narcs?" He leaned to flick ashes out the window, but got them on the windowsill. "Nothin'. Just another night in the business. They must've staked us out."

"Don't you mean they staked *you* out, Tone?"

He inhaled tobacco smoke. "If that makes you feel better."

I began to get heated. "Tony, how'd they know where to find you?"

"They're cops, Eddie. They probably followed us from the Spot."

I said, "When you picked up the money? We ran into Beto?" I replayed the tape in my mind of when we stopped at Tony's dope spot. "Didn't I tell you to take me home first?"

"You gonna blame me now?"

"You refused, didn't you?"

"Eddie, how the fuck was I—"

"You blew me off, didn't you, Tony? Every time I wanted to go, you made an excuse."

He narrowed his thick eyebrows. "You driving at something?"

"I'm out forty G's behind this."

"You saying I had something to do with it?"

"Didn't you?"

"Measure your words, Palo."

"Tony, you knew I'd be holding."

"So?"

"You knew business was good, and that I'd save. That's why you cooked up this stew. To rip me off. I wouldn't be in this if it wasn't for you."

Tony fake-laughed.

"You were real secretive on the phone."

"Eddie, you're paranoid."

"Who fired the gun?"

"What gun?"

"The one you tried dropping on me, not two minutes before the heat popped in."

"Coltrane lied about that. Did you forget how it is when pigs try to shake you?"

"You got my fingerprints all over that chrome. Why did you do that?"

"I was trying to give you a gift."

"Yet you handled it with gloves."

"My driving gloves?" Tony pulled them from his pocket and held them up like a trial lawyer. "We were going back to the car, remember?"

"You got a reaction for everything, don't you, Tony?"

"Eddie, if I was half as clever as you're making me out, I might have tried it."

Tony turned his attention back out the window. He smoked and shook his head, with the chair angled, and his feet back up on the sill.

"I'm gonna forget about this, Eddie. You just got sprung, you're tripping. And it's true that you have suffered a terrible shock. You ain't thinking right. Besides, you always had an active imagination."

I stared at my empty hands. Finally, I got up and walked across the room, took off my army field jacket, and hung it up in the closet. On the way back to the bed, I surprised Tony by kicking the chair's hind legs out from under him so that he fell hard to the ground. I jumped on top of him with my knee in his gut as I dug my forearm under his chin. Tony's face turned red and his eyes bulged with surprise.

I spoke through clenched teeth. "I want my money back."

Tony's windpipe sounded distressed. "I—I didn't take it."

"Liar! You set me up!"

In one swift move Tony threw me off and rolled out from under. In another move he was up on his knees, with his fists in a boxing position. His face was red. He breathed like a stoked engine. "I oughta pop you in the mouth."

I was a little out of breath too. We stood up straight, pupils locked. Tony lowered his fists.

"Eddie, c'mon—"

I startled him with a hard slap from the right, before throwing a quick hook around his neck from the left and yanking him into a headlock. I squeezed.

"Where's the money being dropped?"

"Sto—" He couldn't get the word out.

I shouted, "When do you get your cut?"

Tony bucked and threw me into the empty bureau. We knocked my suitcase on its side, but I didn't release. I squeezed Tony's head with my biceps, and kept my weight above his. Suddenly, the image of Tony's neck snapping spilled across my mind and I released to catch my breath.

Tony stood upright. His face glowed. His eyes watered and two lone tears spilled in long thin streaks to the bottom of his face. He sucked the mucus into his nose.

"Eddie, we been friends a long time. Don't you trust me?"

"Go tell whoever's got my money now to give it back."

The muscles in Tony's face turned slowly downward. He moved to the door. His shoulders slumped. "I'd hang myself before burning you."

Tony waited with his hand on the doorknob.

"You got the message, Little Tony. Gangster. Go deliver it."

Tony left. I listened to him hustle all the way down, keys and change jingling in his pockets. From the window I saw him jump in his red Caddy and rip a loud, squealing U-turn. Tire smoke rose into the yellow streetlight. It tainted the atmosphere with the smell of burnt rubber.

"Fucking asshole."

I picked up the chair and righted it. Tony's cigarette had flown and landed on the carpet, where it burned a small hole. I flicked it to the street, then pulled the window shut.

I jammed the chair under the doorknob to hold off intruders, and noticed a small illustration taped over the door. Saint Michael the Archangel. He flew down with scales and a sword upon a cowering Satan and knocked him into a lake of fire.

I counted the twenty-five hundreds Pelón loaned me, and divided them into three piles, which I hid under different sections of the carpet. Then I bent a wire hanger into a shank. If anybody came through the door, I would open negotiations by taking his eye out.

I grabbed my field jacket from the closet, folded it into a pillow on the bed, and hid the shank underneath. I pulled off my construction boots, placed them by the bed in a way that would make them easy to slip on in a pinch. I lay down to stare at the ceiling and to dwell.

My problem was the money. I toiled for it so long, staked so much on it. Losing it felt like an amputation.

I needed that cash to go into the salsa business with Chiva down in Miami. Chiva was to be my business partner, but he was also my mentor, my padrino in more ways than one. Neither one of us would be happy if I showed up without the seed.

I thought a lot that first lonely night about the past, especially my partnership with Chiva. The way it all started when he stopped for weed one day at my cell.

I'd seen Chiva before, hanging around with some old-timers in the Yard. He was a skinny black Cuban in his late fifties, with a salt-and-pepper goatee that he stroked a lot as he talked. He kept his kinky gray hair pulled into a short, stiff ponytail.

Chiva looked up and down the passageway when he came to score that first time. "Gimme two dimes."

I heard the man's order, but didn't move. "You a Cubano?"

Chiva said, "What the fuck, chota, you work for Fidel?"

"What's up with those hands?"

He made a face. "What kind of questions are these?"

"Your hands look calloused. They get that way from jerkin' off?"

Chiva balled up his fists. "Maricón, who the fuck is you to talk about my love life?"

Chiva was all of a hundred thirty pounds. I was two decades younger, and outweighed him by a hundred in solid muscle.

I said, "Relax, Manos de Piedras, I'm just curious."

Chiva tossed the money on the cot. "Just get the herb, cotorro. Stop putting on a show."

"You used to play congas?"

Chiva looked at me with his lids half-lowered and paused. "The proper name is tamboras."

"Your hands remind me of my father's."

Chiva said, "Wow, a sentimental marijuanero. You see everything in this place. Send me a postcard on Father's Day. For now, get me my dimes, OK?"

I smiled.

Chiva waited. Then he finally looked at his own hands. "You right, I play. But they're getting soft. I'm out of practice."

"Why'd you stop?"

Chiva raised his skinny arms to indicate the cell. "The fuck I'm gonna play in here? And get these faggots on my culo?"

"Think you're that good?"

"Mira, I didn't come here to stretch my tongue. Give me my yerba."

I got Chiva his weed and he split. For days, all I could think about was the sound of the drum. Finally, I greased a couple guards and imported two: a conga and a tumbadora.

The next time Chiva came to my cell, I stood next to the drums like a kid who brings home a ribbon. Chiva's almond eyes went round.

"¡Congo mulence!"

"What you think, Cuba? Think you can still play?"

Chiva stroked his goatee and looked at the drums. "You should've got a quinto."

"Part the Red Sea *and* carry you?"

Chiva grinned. "Rólate un tabaco."

I rolled a fat joint. Chiva inspected the drums. He looked them up and down, walked around, but did not touch or take his eyes off them. He turned them over and looked inside their hollow bodies. Then he set them upright and got down to their level to peer across the surface of their skins with one eye closed, the way a golfer or a pool player lines up a shot. I had no clue what Chiva looked for, but he impressed me that there was something innate about the instruments, something in their natures to sniff for, the way a dog confirms one of his own.

Chiva arrived at a conclusion. He sat on the edge of the cot, pulled the drums close, one between his legs, cracked his knuckles, and warmed up.

He slapped the leather. Tuned it with a wrench. Slapped it some more. Tuned it. We burned a big bomber. Then Chiva was off and drumming.

Beats ricocheted around the cell with the rumble of mythic stallions. Without thought, I yelled, "¡Camina Cubano!" like I heard on a record once. Black and Latino inmates gathered in and around my cell, and jammed with us, playing tin cups like cowbells, and even tapping out rhythms and melodies on the bars. Chiva's calloused hands made like jackhammers and butterfly wings all at once. He grimaced as he caressed and punished the drums. And when he smiled on certain high notes, his white teeth shone.

Over time I learned how Chiva studied percussion his whole life. He'd grown up with it, from his mother's overturned pots and pans, to some cheap bongos he got for Christmas once. As a teenager he scored the full-sized drums from money he earned shining shoes in the Capital. As he grew, he traveled the world in pursuit of certain teachers, certain experiences to call out the drummer within. He even returned to Cuba once and holed up at a relative's house in Oriente for months. They lit candles and channeled spirits with the help of rhythm, tobacco, and rum. Chiva studied percussion from an old man who actually invented a widely imitated variation of an ancient rhythm.

"In Cuba music's more than just to party. Is spiritual. Like a way of feeling the voice of the earth, the universe, and everything that lives."

I knew that Chiva believed it. He made me believe it. He told me stories about New York. How he strutted all over the Big Apple in the sixties and early seventies, hustling on the Lower East Side, Spanish Harlem, Brooklyn, the Bronx.

"Living the life," he said. "Smoking weed. Bebiendo ron. Eating steak in Times Square. And poosy? Olvídate. Boricua, Cubana, Colombiana. Dominicans? Asses as big as the moon." Chiva held his rough hands out wide enough to demonstrate. "¡Brutal!"

In those days Chiva played on the street, on the Brooklyn Bridge, in Central Park, in a thousand nightclubs. He heard the great ones play live too. Joe Cuba, Mongo, Candido, Patato. Even Barretto. Chiva witnessed a heyday through the skin of his drums. And he began to teach me the craft of it early on. The history. And the mythology too.

We started with the clave. "It's everything," he said.

"For the music you wanna play. The heart of it." Chiva clapped it out, and made the sound with his mouth: "Ta-ta. Ta, ta, ta. Ta-ta. Ta, ta, ta."

I clapped along. At first I didn't quite feel it. I was on time. I had the rhythm, the tempo. But I couldn't quite feel what was so special about this 2/3 beat. Until one day, when I was practically meditating, going through the exercises Chiva made me do on the drums. The clave surprised me. It came from inside, like a secret from another dimension.

After that, I practiced everything Chiva taught. Especially tumbao. And guaguancó, which seemed more spiritual to me.

One day Chiva looked kind of depressed as he went through the lesson. I asked what was wrong.

"These drums. I don't know. They get us through the night, but—"

I braced myself. I really did not want to hear that Chiva was finished with our studies.

He stroked his beard. "You know what? It's that if you want a drum that's really gonna speak to you, you gotta make it youself."

"You mean build it?"

"Sí."

"What difference does that make?"

"That's how you know it got a soul."

A couple years passed and Chiva's sentence was almost done. He'd be out about a year before me. I knew I would miss him, so I never raised the subject of his release. One day he brought it up.

"Bueno, niño, what you gonna do when you get outta this hole?"

I kept drumming. "Back to Chicago, I guess."

"I thought you got no family up there."

I didn't respond.

"No woman, no kids, right?"

"Nope."

"Your friends there are worthless."

I shrugged. "It's the only place I know."

Chiva stroked his goatee for a long time. He corrected something I did on the drum, then spoke as he studied my hand placement. "What about Miami?"

I stopped. Miami was where Chiva was headed. Like every Cuban, he had family there.

"Don't fuck with me, Chiva." I practically heard the surf in my eardrum.

"¿Cómo te parece?"

"What the hell would I do?"

"I bring you into what I got cookin'. I gonna start a business with some cats from my New York days. Musicians, music industry people. We gonna start a record label. Something like Fania. Make real salsa dura. Heavy shit. Not like these comemierdas."

Chiva and I often shared our disgust with the state of salsa from the eighties coming forward. The way light-weight salsa romántica had all but killed the market for what we considered salsa, the sound that I grew up with in the seventies.

"A record label, Chiva? I don't know shit about that."

"Listen, you making a little money here. You just invest. Be one of the owners. We gonna start small, so you can buy in with thirty, forty thousand."

I raised my antennae. Chiva had been a con artist his whole life. In his early teens he escaped the communists by bullshitting his way onto an American cruise ship, pretending to be the son of a Cuban diplomat. By Chiva's own admission, he had defrauded people, governments, and institutions all over the Western Hemisphere. In fact, the crime that landed him in prison involved a complicated insurance scam that resulted in Chiva's ripping off his own ex-wife and former mother-in-law, and then his ex–brother-in-law getting hot about it and "accidentally" getting "bumped" out of a seventh-story window. Still, in my heart I believed that, with me at least, Chiva had always been straight-up.

I took a breath. "You wanna be business partners with me, Chiva? You don't know that side of me. I can be fuckin' ruthless."

"I'm counting on it. And let me tell you, Eddie. Miami got so much delicious poosy, you pinga gonna write me a thank-you note."

That first night after I was released from prison, after my seed money got swiped by Coltrane and Johnson, after my scuffle with Tony, I lay in bed and let the gears crunch in my head. The scenes leading up to me getting ripped off replayed in a continuous loop:

Tony leading me by the nostrils. Coltrane slinging my money belt over his shoulder. Johnson punching me. Pelón's extended claw.

Around two in the morning I accepted that I couldn't sleep. I got up, laced my boots, and began to pace the small room. The yellow streetlight poured in and hung itself in abstract patterns on the ceiling and walls.

I felt a little guilty about the dustup with Tony. The way his face sagged as he stood by the door. But forty thousand dollars had sprouted wings, and it was very possible, likely even, that Tony played a part in that. No way I could just let that pass.

Either way, the narcs had my money now. And I had no clue how to get it back. Being cops made them untouchable. Sort of. Fucking with them would be very high risk. They obviously didn't give a shit about boundaries. How do you get an edge on hoodlums that carry the law around inside their wallets?

I leaned against the window. At least Tony was right about one thing: the view from my room was a clear shot of the Chicago skyline. I took my boots off and lay on the bed again. There was no point in staying up all night.

I certainly had enough cash with the two and a half G's that Pelón lent me that I could jump a bus to Florida. I could catch up with Chiva, let him know what went down. Chiva would understand. I could work, start over, deal from zero again, stack paper until I had my share of the investment. Chiva and I could still do our thing. There was no real need for me to stick around Chicago looking for trouble.

But then, that wouldn't be me.

I stared at the ceiling as I made my decision. Fuck running. Fuck taking it up the ass. I was determined to get my money back. No matter what.

PART II:

MOTIVES

CHAPTER 05:

SEPARATE WAYS (WORLDS APART)

Some mornings when I was a kid, my father would stroll in after one of his all-night romps. My mother would either curse or ignore him, and he would grab his keys and say to me, "Let's go before I do something wrong."

We would walk to the sounds of early traffic and birds, always to his favorite diner. I'd swamp pancakes in syrup—my mother only let me use so much. My father would drink black coffee and stare into his cup.

That first morning after my release and return to Chicago, I woke up with a headache. But my room was colored by the purple sunrise and that made me want to be outside. I sat by the window and spied on the city as it began to stir.

For an hour and a half, I tried to stand, walk, leave the room. Something pressed me down. Not fear, exactly. Discomfort. Unease. The knowledge that the free world was governed by alien rules, and that a long quarantine downstate had converted me into a stranger. It wasn't my first reintegration into society. I did other bids and came home. But this time it had been so long. The air itself felt different. Charged somehow.

The incident with the cops still stung. The ease with which they'd snuck up on me was a shock. Plus, the fact that trust was now an issue with Tony. And Pelón's convenient reappearance, the vanished money. It all supported this feeling, as light and formless as fog, that the world was upset with me somehow, out of balance.

My head hurt, but my stomach grumbled. And the sidewalks looked tempting, regardless.

I washed up best I could without touching anything in the moldy bathroom. I changed into new jeans and a never-before-worn World Champion White Sox sweatshirt, courtesy of the Department of Corrections. I dug up half the money Pelón had loaned me from under the carpet. I concealed the wire-hanger shank inside one boot, and tucked most of the stash into the other. I put walking-around money in my front pocket and a little bit in my wallet.

From the window I checked the street one more time, but saw nobody suspicious. Tony had called me "paranoid," which is better than "easy mark." But there was no logic in hiding. On my way out I locked and unlocked the door several times, like a caveman discovering fire.

Out on the street I waited for green lights before I crossed. I stayed within the lines, made sure cars came to a complete stop before I stepped off the curb. I kept my distance from other pedestrians, and let my hands hang loose, out of my pockets, in case I had to swing on someone.

The sun felt good on my face as it climbed, though the air was autumn brisk, the way it gets in Chicago. Everywhere you looked, you saw new buildings, all new construction, mostly expensive-looking condos. Lawns looked trimmed and the leaves, which were beginning to come down, had mostly been gathered up and taken to a dump somewhere. The sidewalks were neater than I remembered.

I saw white people everywhere. Not like the hillbillies, Polish, Italians, and Ukrainians that lived around my neighborhoods when I was a kid. These new whites had come from somewhere else. They carried giant cups of coffee, talked on cell phones, and accompanied anxious-looking dogs. I snagged a copy of the *Sun-Times* out of a newspaper box and headed for my father's favorite diner.

The place looked and smelled as I remembered. In the future Formica might survive a nuclear war. For a second, when I first entered, I thought I saw the apparition of my father seated at the counter, with his collar up, hunkered over a steaming cup of coffee, the cigarette between his fingers burning slow. My insides tingled and I wanted to run to him, to touch him, to ask what he needed.

But he faded. I sat on a stool next to where I thought I'd seen him. The waitress took my order and poured coffee. I dug into the news.

The coffee was weak, but the pancakes were decent. I slathered them in syrup, though not like when I was a kid. I started with the sports section and laughed out loud when one columnist said that you can usually tell that it is pennant season in Chicago when the Cubs have been out of it for a few months. The Bears were off to another lousy start. The feds investigated corruption at City Hall, again. Celebrities were rumored to be fucking other celebrities. And the weather would remain cloudy and gray.

Finally, one headline made me put my fork down: GANG MEMBER SHOT IN HUMBOLDT RESTROOM. The subhead read: NEW DRUG WAR FEARED. I gathered the details: A Hispanic male, nineteen years of age, a reputed gang member, shot several times while standing at a urinal in Humboldt Park. No casings recovered, but errant pieces of a .38 slug from a metal stall suggested hollow-point bullets. No witnesses came forward. Few leads, but detectives from Gang Crimes emphasized that it was still early. One department source speculated that the shooting was part of an escalating drug war, saying that "all hell's fixing to break loose." The article mentioned the victim's gang, which I knew to be Roach's set.

I concluded the obvious: Tony's crew had drawn first blood in the latest heroin war. I looked around to make sure no one watched. Then I ripped the story out, folded it, put it in my wallet, and asked for the check.

I caught the subway at Division and Milwaukee, the Blue Line, and headed downtown. The train announced its arrival with a musty wind that rushed out of the tunnel. Newspapers flipped like tumbleweeds on the tracks. I jumped on. The voice that announced upcoming stops was more computer than conductor, and I wondered if it was friendly, if it had moods, and who, or what, actually drove.

Tony stayed in my mind. His fucked-up schemes. His need to invite society to shove a big black firecracker up its ass. It was obvious from what I'd read in the paper that Tony and Roach were caught in a blood feud. What had once been only a rumor of war was now confirmed. Roach had lost turf. He'd lost customers. Now he'd lost a soldier. He really had no alternative other than to strike back. The air around Tony had become more hazardous.

I got off the train at State Street and walked around. Women were everywhere, in every size, every shape, every color. My eyes were not fast enough to capture them all. They mesmerized with their curves, their soft hair, the waves that rippled through them as they walked. Everywhere there was a calf, a bosom, an exposed knee. Boots and high heels clicked on sidewalks. Lipstick glistened. Earrings jingled, and so many perfumes, you wanted to float. Every once in a while, for one or two seconds, I managed eye contact. And occasionally a smile.

Out on Wabash the elevated trains shrieked and spit sparks. I walked and listened and stared at everything. So much color and motion. Horns and braking cars, bike messengers with whistles, shouts over construction, ringing cell phones, a million snippets of private, mundane conversations.

At Wacker Drive, on the Chicago River, a high-masted sailboat floated regally inland as the bridges rose and bowed after, slowly, gracefully, mechanically, one after the other, ringing their bells. I stared up at the buildings and felt enveloped.

Over on Jackson, the Sears Tower loomed. Enormous, black, and solid, like a figment of science fiction. It surprised me that it still looked brand-new. I tilted my head up from the base. Clouds passed. I walked over to Michigan Avenue and caught the 151 Sheridan bus heading north.

*   *   *

I felt better just to go around the city, and to look at it, to drink it in. The people, the landscape. Chicago looked different, newer, fresher, cleaner, with more trees, less garbage, less graffiti. It was enough sometimes to make me forget, for a moment, about double crosses, street wars, cash flow, prison, and the things that had been lost. But only in moments.

I jumped off the bus at Addison, by the totem pole, and made my way across the park to the water, over by the giant rocks that challenge the water's edge. Lake Michigan is immense. I once read that it's just a humongous block of melted ice from a previous age. If you've ever jumped in it, you have no problem believing that.

I watched a man fish off the rocks. He didn't seem to notice the waves crashing in foamy bouquets, threatening to pull him in. He appeared so sure-footed. I envied him.

I sat there for a long time, looking at the vast, undulating body of water, looking to the horizon, thinking of Tony. The way we grew up. Chicago was a different city then. Dirtier. Uglier. Yet somehow more real. Maybe it was just my memory. Or the fact that I had not given myself time to adjust. The modern city retained enough of its former self to remind me constantly of my youth, when Tony was my perfect friend.

The Lake especially reminded me of him. It was our spot. Especially this one summer, we practically lived there. We were in our early teens. I carried a boom box and played the cassette of Journey's *Frontiers,* over and over, convinced I understood the difference between illusion and true love. Sweaty females strode around in cutoff denim shorts, sliced high and tight, and bikini tops, which showed the contours of their stiffening nipples when they came out of the water.

I peeped a really busty one and gave Tony the elbow. "Mira esa."

Young Tony licked his lips. "Bro, I'd eat ten feet of her shit just to see where it came from."

I laughed, even though I'd heard that one before. By puberty Tony had a hundred lines to describe how fine he thought a female was. Like, "Damn, she's so fine, a priest'd spit out Communion just to watch her take a dump," or, "Fuck, she's so fine, I'd smash my nuts with a mallet just to sniff her crotch." Another approach was to imply that he'd already fucked the girl in question. Like, "Dude, she got the whitest teeth I ever come across. Get it? *C-U-M?* Like, I *came* across her teeth?"

"I got it, Tony."

"You understand what I mean, right?"

"Yeah." I pointed at a woman in her early twenties. "How 'bout that one? I bet an older woman like that really knows what to do. She can buy beer too."

"No shit. Friggin' bitch is so hot, I'd—" Tony froze in mid-setup and cocked his head to get a better look. "Wait a minute." He stood and shaded his eyes.

"Hot stuff, right, Tone?"

"Shut up, Eddie, you fuckin' pig. That's my sister!"

I had known Tony since the fifth grade. "Your sister, Tony? From the foster home?"

"My biological sister."

I was clueless. Tony took off across the hot sand. I followed him, carrying the boom box.

Tony cupped his hands around his mouth. "Yoli!"

The young woman shielded her eyes to look. When she recognized Tony, she screamed and jumped to give her brother a hug.

I looked her up and down. She was thin, but sexy in a black bikini that matched her dark hair. She had a mole near the corner of her mouth and a rose tattoo on her hip that peeked from behind the bikini string on her lean hip.

"Oh, my God," she said. "Toñito, how long has it been?"

Tony kicked the sand. "Like, five years?"

Yoli smiled. "What a trip. And I just saw Papi the other day."

Tony's smile faded. "You saw my father? I thought he was in PR?"

"He's been back for a while. He lives on Claremont. Right up the street from Clemente."

I was confused. "Tony, I thought your father died in Vietnam?"

Tony turned toward me, without quite looking, and shrugged. He turned back to his sister. "I ain't seen him since the sixth grade."

Yoli tilted her head and raised her hands out to her sides, like, "Oh well, that's our dad..."

Tony said, "How's he look?"

"The same. Got a few gray hairs coming in. Living off some woman. Lo mismo de siempre."

Tony nodded.

His sister reached into her purse for a pen and paper. "He ain't got a phone, though. You want his address?"

Tony and I went that same night. We stood on the sidewalk half a block away and Tony combed himself in the side mirror of a parked van. In those days Tony sported so much hair, he actually considered Gallo as his street name.

He looked at me. "I look OK, Eddie?"

"Dude, you could be in Duran Duran."

We slapped each other five. Tony had carefully ironed his clothes, but he was overdressed for a humid Chicago night. Sweat pearled and slid down his forehead.

"Here." In those days I always carried a bandana in our gang's color. "Keep this in your pocket to wipe your face," I said.

We moved toward the house.

Tony said, "Thanks for walking with me through enemy turf."

"This ain't *The Outsiders,* motherfuckers, this is *The Warriors.*" I pulled a butterfly knife from my back pocket and flipped it open, like I practiced all those nights selling nickel bags on the Hot Corner. "Anybody want a slice of life?"

"Good one."

I put the knife away.

Tony's father answered the door. He looked a little like Tony, except older, with a black mustache and gray streaks, like Yoli had mentioned. He did not look so much like Tony as Tony had said, and I decided that Tony looked mostly like his natural mother.

Tony's father seemed surprised, but not stunned. "Ay Dios, mira que milagro."

He shook hands with Tony, then decided to hug him.

Tony introduced me as his best friend. His old man gave a weak handshake, but invited us in. He introduced us to his girlfriend and her two kids. The kids disappeared into their room, where we could hear them playing Atari.

The girlfriend went to the kitchen. Tony and I sat in the living room as his father watered and pruned plants.

"Antonio, you look a little skinny." He spoke with his back to us. "You don't play sports?"

Tony shifted in his seat. "A little. I've always been thin."

"You got that from your mother."

"We like lifting weights," I said.

Tony's father did not offer an opinion. He snipped leaves like a barber.

Tony said, "Actually, I'm into bikes. BMX."

"Bikes cost and are always breaking down. Some desgracia'o always steals it. When I was your age, I played baseball. You don't like that?"

"It's all right. You gotta depend on everybody else to win."

Tony's old man pruned and spoke without looking at us. I leaned over and gestured for Tony to wipe his forehead.

Tony's father began to spray the plants. "You got a bike then?"

"They stole it off the back porch."

"Seguro. Your mother always keeps you in bad neighborhoods."

"Actually, um..." Tony seemed embarrassed. "I'm not living with her right now. I'm in foster care."

"See what I mean?"

Tony's father's girlfriend returned with a tray of champagne cola. His father put down the spray bottle and shared a drink. He sucked soda out of his mustache.

"Entonces, how much one of them BM-whatever bikes cost?"

Tony glanced at me, then looked at his old man. "BMX? A lot. Like two hundred bucks."

"Two hundred? That's it? Come back in two weeks, I'll give you the cash."

"For real?"

Tony's old man said, "Hey, what's a man work for if not to give his kids the best, right?"

We had dinner with the family. White rice, red beans, and fried chicken. For dessert we wolfed down birthday cake left from a party for one of the kids.

When it was time to leave, Tony's father put his hands on his son's shoulders. "You got bus fare?"

"We hoofed it."

Tony's father smiled. "Independent. You got that from me."

Tony smiled. "My mother says the same thing whenever we fight."

Tony's father chuckled. "Remember then: two weeks, I give you the money. But you can't spend it on anything but that bike, OK? I'm gonna trust you with it."

"I promise."

In Spanish the girlfriend said, "And don't forget, you have family here. You're in your house now." She gave Tony a sincere-looking hug.

For two weeks Tony talked up the bike. How he was gonna hook it up. Learn every trick. We joked about him letting the bike have his bed while he slept on the floor.

The two weeks dragged, but finally it was time to collect. We went to the house.

Immediately, we could see that something was wrong.

There were no curtains in the windows. We walked up the steps and leaned over to look inside. The apartment was empty. The only thing left was a small cactus that had apparently been knocked over on its side, spilling the soil. Tony checked the houses on either side, but there was no mistaking. The mailbox still read: PACHECO.

Tony stared through the curtainless window. "Something must've happened."

"Probably an emergency or something."

We avoided each other's eyes, and walked back to the neighborhood in silence. Along the way Tony picked up a stick and started hitting every tree, every parking meter, every hydrant. Not violently, but just enough to let the thing know that he was there. We never again spoke about the bike or his father's disappearing act.

A couple weeks later, Tony turned up in the neighborhood on the back of a shiny, red aluminum Mongoose, back then a very exotic bike. The boys asked him about it.

"Yeah, you know, my old man had it delivered to my house and shit."

Every one admired the bike and envied Tony.

When we were alone, Tony said, "Ain't you gonna ask me how I really got it?"

"I was wondering."

"I was by the Lake. Fucking white boy comes riding up on it all slow. All of a sudden, I was like, '*Bam!*'" Tony acted out a slower, more ferocious punch than any you'll ever see in real life. "Fuckin' white boy goes down like a sack of flour, holmes. All dazed and shit. I just jumped on the bike and took off."

"Ain't you afraid they'll catch you?"

"On this thing? I'm too quick." Tony popped a couple wheelies and bunny hops to show his control. "Wanna take it for a spin?"

I did, but it was time to go. "My mom's making chuletas."

"You can borrow it and take it home."

"I better not."

Tony nodded. We shook hands, the way you did back then when you were best friends.

I don't know if Tony ever saw his father again; he never mentioned it. Come to think of it, I can't recall what ever happened to the Mongoose either. Tony probably just outgrew it.

Sitting by the water now, so many years later, reflecting on young Tony, the tough breaks I knew life had handed him, it took the edge off my anger toward him regarding my forty thousand. It didn't do anything about my missing loot, but that was a problem that I was going to have to work out over time.

I continued to watch the sure-footed fisherman as he balanced on the rocks and cast his line, unconcerned, it seemed, by the fact that most times he reeled in nothing. Once in a while he did pull in a fish, and one time it was big enough he didn't have to throw it back.

Waves rolled in at precise, irregular angles and exploded against the rocks. Above the water big white birds, some gray, some white and gray, cawed, floated, dipped, and traced patterns in the air, like musical notes. I watched the sky turn lilac, blue, pink, red, orange, even yellow, randomly and all at once in swirls. A purple ribbon stretched along the fine clean line of the horizon and rose slowly.

The great cosmic curtain raised and covered the earth in black lace, and the fisherman finally packed it in.

I accepted that I had something painful to do, and that I could not put it off. I crossed the dark park and walked over to Broadway, hopped a cab, and had him drop me off a couple blocks from the cemetery.

I walked alone and prayed. The sign read, CLOSED AT SUNDOWN. I jumped the fence and took out the small map I'd kept for years.

The moon was not strong enough for that dark. I heard cawing again and feathers ruffling in the shadows. The friction of weighty takeoffs and landings. I imagined big black crows balanced on branches and headstones, watching me. Staring.

Were they laughing? I wondered. *Do they cry?*

I hunched my shoulders and pulled the collar up on my jacket. The wind stirred leaves and breathed melancholy across the ashen cemetery landscape. And it was not as good to me as it had been to the birds.

CHAPTER 06:

BEHOLD THIS GOLDEN CHARIOT

Some stains are so ground in, there ain't no way to remove them. I scrubbed the thick yellow paste below the waterline in the community toilet bowl, and it broke apart and flushed. The faint smell of piss lingered, despite all the air freshener.

My own room was better. I got it to smell like artificial lemons. But the sticky carpet had no remedy. I wrapped a new bedsheet around the knotty mattress, and loaded a new pillow into the matching pillowcase. I didn't purchase curtains on account that they would disrupt the sunlight.

I plugged in my new boom box and flipped through a small collection of CDs still wrapped in cellophane. Several Ray Barrettos, two Eddie Palmieris, plus *De Ti Depende* and *La Gran Fuga*. Nuyorican salsa. I unwrapped *Que Viva La Música* and slipped it in. Barretto ignited his congas like an octopus con soul. The "Puerto Rican Elvis" Adalberto Santiago dropped lyrics.

I took my new hot plate out of the box and set it up, boiled two cups of water in the olla, added oil and salt, two cups of rice, stirred, brought the heat down low, and covered it like my mother used to with aluminum foil and an upside-down plate. I put a skillet on the other burner and heated sardines with tomato sauce and onions in olive oil.

When the food was ready, I switched to Eddie Palmieri, *Recorded Live at Sing Sing*. He broke open with ten minutes of pure psychedelic salsa, "Pa La Ochá Tambó." I sat by the window, ate, drank beer, and tried to let the music penetrate.

But I kept thinking about my money. The events surrounding its disappearance. And the fact of Pelón's sudden reappearance on the stage. To me there was zero chance that Pelón's presence on the margins of a stickup could be a coincidence. No way. I simply knew him too well to believe that.

The day Pelón introduced himself, he was encased in a giant, fancy white car that had its top down. It was the mid-eighties, but the car had an ornate 1930s styling, with large curving fenders, running boards, bug-eyed headlights, an elaborate chrome grille, and bugle horns over the front bumper so that when he punched the steering wheel, it sounded like a brass quartet announcing the queen's arrival.

Tony and I were in our teens. Our crew had been selling weed on the street for a little while by then. Pelón pulled right up to the corner in his fancy car, blasting Raphy Leavitt, "Jíbaro Soy," on the tape deck. He was in his early forties, and still solid, muscular under his white guayabera. He wore a black handlebar mustache down to his jawline then, like Oscar D'León from around the same era. He wore a large hoop earring in his right ear, and he already shaved his head. The hand that would later become a claw was still intact.

Tony whistled and eyeballed Pelón's vehicle. "Hey, mister, what kind of car is this?"

Pelón turned down the music. "Excalibur. Phaeton. Don't get any fingerprints on it."

Tony inspected the lines. "Shit, man, this looks like something Capone would've rode."

Pelón winked. "Only if he knew what was good for him." Pelón looked at me. In his Puerto Rican accent he said, "What you boys throwing out here?"

I didn't know this asshole from the chief of police. I said, "Excuse me?"

"Aquí. ¿Qué es lo están vendiendo?" He rolled his *R*'s. "¿Marijuana? Coca? Crack?"

I made a confused face. "Sorry, mister. The government taught us to just say no."

Pelón smiled. He took his time to light a humongous cigar, really puffed it, creating lots of smoke. "Nene, if you too stupid to know who a cop and who not a cop, how I'm gonna know I can trust you with my business?" He pulled a knot from his pocket and peeled off ten hundreds, like they were singles. "You gonna tell me you no holding pasto?"

Tony sprang up. "Weed? Hell yeah, we got weed. Will nickel bags do?"

Pelón answered Tony, but directed his voice at me. "One at a time is two hundred bolsitas. I'm buying bulk now. Make me a better offer."

I shot Tony a look. "Sir, my friend don't even know what you're talking about. We're church people."

Pelón blew a fat cloud of smoke. "You really gonna let me drive away with a thousand dollars? And you call yourself a businessman?" Pelón started the Excalibur. "They got pendejitos like you humping corners all over this town. I find someplace else to leave my spinach."

Tony said, "Hold up, hold up."

Tony pulled me to the side. "Bro, that's a couple days' work in one shot. What if this cocopelao becomes a regular?"

"Yeah, Tony, and what if he's an undercover cop?"

"Get real."

"What you think, Tone? Think the government'll send someone who looks like a preppie? Watch *Miami Vice,* bro. Fuckin' cops and rats lie so much, they forget what side they're on."

"Eddie, that's TV. This is real life. What about this deal?"

"Too risky."

Tony crossed his arms. "If he's a narc, I'll take the rap. I'll make the exchange. You don't touch nothin'."

"You really that confident?"

"Look at him." Tony gestured at the back of Pelón's shaved head. "He's one of us, just all grown-up."

Tony made a deal for 250 bags, which was four dollars a nickel, which we figured as three in profits, since each bag cost us a dollar when we bought in bulk from a fat guy named Flaco, who ran a spot out of a tire shop. We weren't clever enough to calculate the hours spent copping, bagging, standing on the sidewalk, selling, making change, and getting into arguments with potheads, but that was only labor and we had no way of appreciating its value. The first deal with Pelón went easier than ordering drive-thru.

Tony sniffed his cut of the money. "See that, Eddie? No problem. Now let's pull up to the Centrium. They don't card there and they got girls from Wells High School who dress like Madonna."

"Sweet." I folded and pocketed my share of the loot. "So, did your new idol say anything?"

"Yeah, he called you a chocha."

"Fuck him."

Tony laughed. "Man, I made that up. Nothin', he didn't say shit. Just that he thinks it's the start of something new."

Thinking too much about my history with Pelón was bound to ruin my appetite, and the sardines and rice was the first meal I prepared for myself since getting out of prison. I made it a point then to actively think of something other than scheming-ass Pelón as I served myself and sat by the window of my little room to eat alone. I savored the salty fish, the sweetness of the rice and sauce, the privacy. I tried to recall the women I'd seen on the streets of Chicago that day. There had been so many.

The music coming out of my new CD player filled my little room. Palmieri wrapped up his concert for the inmates at Sing Sing with a funky rendition of an early hit, "Azúcar," which he delivered in two parts. My new neighbor banged on the wall. I turned the sound down, but not so much that I couldn't imagine being present at the actual performance.

From the window I saw Tony's Cadillac roll up and park quietly across the street. He jumped out and hustled toward my building without looking up. I listened as he took the stairs, two at a time, and waited for his knock.

Tony stood outside my door for a short while. His knock came soft. I put my empty plate on the table, turned the music down, opened the door without speaking, and returned to my spot by the window. Tony closed the door. He stood with his hands in his pockets.

I gestured toward my makeshift kitchen. "Serve yourself."

Tony nodded and quietly piled rice and sardines, and sat on the edge of the bed. For five minutes all you heard was the sound of his fork hitting the plate.

"Pretty good, Eddie. You learned a thing or two in that prison kitchen."

I got up and pulled two Coronas from the little fridge under my table, opened them with my shiny new Windy City bottle opener, the one with the image of the giant Picasso downtown, and handed Tony a cold one.

He thanked me and, almost as an afterthought, took a paper bag out of his jacket pocket. "I got you some incense."

I put the bag on top of the dresser, and sat next to the window again to drink. Tony emptied his plate and downed his beer. He took my plate and fork off the table, grabbed the dishwashing liquid and sponge, and disappeared to the bathroom. He returned and placed the clean utensils on the corner of the table. Tony stood in the center of the room.

"So . . . you look settled in."

I didn't say anything. Tony walked over and studied my new book collection. He checked out the CDs. "Can I put this on?"

"Sure. But don't scratch it. They're sensitive."

Tony took it back to Barretto, only this time with Tito Allen. He found a crack in the molding around my door where he could jam a couple sticks of incense. He lit them. They poured sweet red smoke.

"Strawberry," he said. "They come in different flavors."

I barely nodded.

Tony lit a joint, but I passed. He stood in the middle of the room to smoke by himself. When the joint was half gone, he said, "Eddie, I'm real sorry about what happened to your money."

I stared out the window.

"You know I'd get it back for you if I could."

I turned to look at Tony.

He didn't avoid me. "I'm hurt about it too, Eddie. You know that."

I downed the rest of my beer, but did not let Tony out of my sight. Then I stood, opened the dresser, and fished out the clipping about the shooting in Humboldt Park. I handed it to Tony.

"You making news again, gangster?"

Tony looked at the clipping and put it down on the table without reading. "I saw it on TV," he said. "So?"

"That was one of Roach's boys, wasn't it?"

"I heard he was from their set, yeah."

"Don't front, Tony. The paper says they used a .38."

"It gets the job done."

"The paper also said it looks like the killer used hollow points."

Tony said, "They do make things go splat."

"Any chance that's the same .38 you handed me last night, Tony?"

Tony paused. "Now, why the fuck would you think that?"

"Tony?"

"Why would I stick you with a hot piece, Eddie? Are you nuts?"

"Am I?"

"That gun I handed you was clean, Eddie. Never been used. I kept it in my own crib, up on the kitchen cabinet. Nobody even knew it was there."

"Tony, nowadays people carry nine-millimeters. They don't carry .38s."

"Don't be so sure. Work like that? Nine-millies tend to jam. Revolver? Functions every time."

"But it's a bit of a coincidence, isn't it, Tony? You handing me that .38. Getting my fingerprints on it the way that you did. Then me reading in the paper how somebody used a .38 on one of Roach's baggers?"

"Coincidence is all it is, Eddie. Nothing more."

I looked Tony right in the eye. He didn't flinch.

I pointed at the article. "Tell me you offed that kid, Tone."

"I would if I did."

"Did you order it?"

"Uh-uh. But that doesn't matter, does it, Eddie?"

"Why not?"

" 'Cause Roach is gonna think that I did."

There was no doubt about that. I said, "So, Tony, what're you gonna do?"

He shrugged. "Deal with it, I guess."

The smell of incense filled the room.

Tony took a deep hit of reefer. He did not say a word, but I thought I saw a shadow of the same unease that I saw the first time I urged him to shoplift, in the sixth grade.

I gestured for Tony to pass the reefer finally. "You gonna watch your back on this one, Tony?"

Tony passed it. "I'll sleep with one eye open."

I inhaled.

Tony kept his hand out. "So you and I still homeboys then?"

I looked out the window, then back at Tony. I'd come to a decision about him. The only one that made any sense. I blew the smoke out.

"To the end," I said.

We shook on it.

We went to the basketball court at Eckhart Park. You can play there at night because of the streetlights on Noble. Tony stretched like a professional dancer, very methodical. He delivered a lecture about muscles, joints, tendons, and the effects of aging. When he was through, he lit a fat joint and cracked open a forty.

I laughed.

"What?" he said. "Malt liquor's the food of the gods."

Tony got drunk and stoned, but, of course, it didn't matter. He was short, but a helluva ball handler and a monster on the boards. Once he got in the zone, only a brick wall could stop him. He walked through me for three easy victories.

I dropped to the ground, out of breath. "Damn, Tony, twenty years of drugs and alcohol, and you ain't lost a step."

Tony flashed his dimples and the wrinkles around his eyes. He dribbled out beyond the three-point line.

"Of course I've lost a step, Eddie. It's just"—Tony paused to release a perfect rainbow arc of a shot that was all net—"I'm so fuckin' good, I'm the only one who can notice."

Tony dropped next to me to smoke a cigarette. I stared at the halo around a streetlamp.

"Tony, I wanna ask you something."

"Shoot."

"What about Pelón?"

"What about him?"

"You think he may have set me up to get rolled?"

Tony made a face, like he wished I would drop the subject. "Eddie, why would he do that?"

"He knew that I was coming."

"So?"

"He must've figured that I'd be holding cash."

"I doubt it. Besides, the guy's banking off legitimate shit now. All kinds of real estate and shit. No offense, Eddie, but to him forty G's don't even qualify. And like I said, he wants to use you for that big casino job."

"Yeah, like that's really gonna happen."

"Bank on it."

"Tony, Pelón probably just made that shit up to get you to draw me to Chicago."

"No way. And I don't think he planned a job on your money either. Why bang you like that, when he needs you?"

"To throw me in the skillet is why. Put me on the defensive. Maybe he really is casing a big job, and he figures if I'm desperate enough, I'll jump at a chance to roll with him. I don't know. Don't you think he was quick with that loan?"

"Maybe he believes in hookin' a brother up."

"I ain't his brother." I paused. "You ever know Pelón to do business with cops before?"

"Of course. CPD is the biggest gang out here. They're corrupt as shit."

"Right. So it's possible Pelón worked with them on my money, isn't it? Just drop a dime, at least? Let 'em know I'm coming?"

"I doubt it."

"I'm saying it's possible, Tony."

"Yes, it's possible. But not likely."

My bullshit detector didn't register any clicks. It was possible that Tony really bought into Pelón's line and believed what he was saying.

I toned it down a little. "So what, you *work* for him now?"

"Sometimes."

"Is he backing you on this beef with Roach?"

"No, that's *my* business."

I thought about that. "You saying you don't kick up from the heroin?"

"It's not like he's a capo or a don, Eddie. He's just a businessman flipping real estate. Pelón owns a couple bodegas. He throws weed out the bodegas, but nothing hard. He don't want hypes on his premises."

"Does he run numbers?"

"Of course he does. Shylock too."

"So then *he* must be giving a percentage to someone. I can't see a cripple like Pelón, all past his prime and shit, collecting vigorish and not paying tribute to somebody to actually lay down the muscle."

Tony shook his head. "You'd be surprised, Eddie.

Pelón keeps his shit down low. The paisans don't even know he exists."

"So how's Pelón collect when the payments don't flow?"

Tony flexed his bicep. "I told you I ran errands, didn't I?"

I wasn't sure where I was getting. Tony was on the brink of war with Roach, yet he didn't seem worried. What he told me about Pelón's business didn't quite add up.

I took a real good look at Tony. "Ever think about leaving Chicago?"

Tony said, "And go where? Miami?"

"Why not?"

"When?"

"Soon."

"Not before the heist," he said.

"How about before Roach unloads buckshot in your ass, Tone?"

"Nigga, please." Tony leaned forward. "But listen, what would we do in Florida? Coca?"

"Nothing like that. Chiva's down there. He's making drums."

"Drums of what?"

"Congas, actual drums. Batá. Chékere. Cajones. Afro-Cuban."

"You mean like, to play? Is that a business? You don't know anything about that."

"Chiva's gonna teach me."

"Any money in it?"

"Enough to live on, I think." I didn't feel confident yet to tell Tony about the real venture, the record label.

Tony dragged on the cigarette and shook his head. "Dude, I can't go running off to make voodoo drums. I got too much going on in Chi-town right now. And it cost me too much to build my shit up. It's just about to start rolling."

I looked at the ground between my gym shoes.

Tony pulled up a hocker and spit it into the grass at the edge of the basketball court. "Besides, Eddie, I ain't too wild about scrounging around for a dollar. Not anymore, I'm not. And I ain't about to work no bullshit-ass job neither. You know that. I already did that when I came out on parole, and that shit just ended. Niggas had me steam-cleanin' uniforms from all over and pissin' into a cup."

I got to my feet and picked up the basketball. I dribbled as I talked. "Tony, ain't you tired of all this shit?"

"All what shit?"

"Like you said, never being able to let your guard down."

"It goes with the territory. This is the life we chose."

"Come off that movie script, Tony. There ain't nothing glamorous about what you do. Maybe it's time for something new. Where's this shit gonna end?"

Tony killed the cigarette and tightened the laces on his jumpers. "You know what, Eddie? All my foster mother ever says is 'Grow up. Get a regular job.' The other day I start thinking, maybe she's right. Maybe I oughta get myself another regular gig, like working security this time. Delivering pizzas maybe. I like bikes; maybe I'll be a bike messenger."

Tony lit another cigarette and blew smoke, which flew off on a stiff breeze. "Then I get the urge to check my

Caddy. I look out the window and there it is, all washed, waxed, and shiny. My mother's piecea shit's collecting dust across the street. And I'm like, 'Punch a clock for this? Fuck that!'" Tony twisted his face. "I'll leave that for some other mope."

"It was just a suggestion."

I dribbled the ball again, pulled up to the three-point line, where Tony launched his rainbow. I counted off the last seconds of an imaginary championship game, "Three, two, one!" and launched it. I knew from the release that the game was lost. The ball clunked on the rim with an ugly, pointless *twang,* and bounced away from the net.

Tony laughed. "Not making the highlight reel with that one. I guess I gotta keep schooling you."

Tony jumped up. He pummeled me against the ropes for a few more grueling rounds. It was easier than conversation.

CHAPTER 07:

LOVE TUMBLES DOWN

The following evening was boys' night out with Pelón. Tony told me to spruce it up, so I bought a black rayon shirt and black dress pants, some shiny black shoes. I took the hair down to sandpaper level by using the clippers without the guard. I shaved, but for fun I left myself the beginning of a goatee. I slid into the passenger seat of Tony's car.

He pretended to file his nails on my head. "Damn, Rambo, you sign up for the marines?"

"I got my game face on. No way to dress up this army jacket, though."

Tony smirked. "Don't worry, you make it look good."

Tony sported the leather with the hanging belt over a red dress shirt, black slacks, black shoes. The shirt was open at the neck, but Tony kept his gold necklace inside. He wore small diamond stud earrings and a gold pinky ring shaped like an eagle's head.

I touched the beak with my fingertip. "Tony, you punch somebody with that thing, you'll leave a puncture wound."

"That's the point."

We parked in front of a run-down bar on Ashland.

I put my hand on the dashboard. "Don't tell me this is the high-class joint Pelón's taking us?"

"Don't trip. Just picking up a little cash for the old man. Wanna wait in the car?"

I'd learn more if I got closer to Pelón's circle. "I'll come in for a drink."

We stepped through the door, and it was like we crossed a border. Immediately, you saw the red, white, and green, the eagle and conquered snake of the Mexican flag. There was a set of bull's horns over the mirror, velvet paintings of Pancho Villa, Montezuma, and the Virgen de Guadalupe. There was also a faded color poster of a middle-aged Vicente Fernández standing next to a horse. The men milled and postured in boots, belt buckles, holstered knives, and hats cocked at varying angles.

I spoke under my breath. "Órale."

"No shit." Tony did his best John Wayne. "Muchos hombres with grandes cojones."

We stepped over to the bar. Everyone took a good look at us and went about their business. The jukebox discharged brass, percussion, accordion, and strings in large rounds. The singer lamented lost love, but especially a longing for his beloved ranch back home.

Tony addressed the bartender by name. "Chino, dos tequilas por favor."

The pudgy bartender poured two shots that burned on the way down. Tony gestured at the curtain behind the bar.

"¿Tu patrón?"

Chino's eyes passed over me for a second. He shook his head.

Tony waved him off and patted me on the forearm. "No te preocupes. Este es mi carnal."

Chino didn't give a fuck whether Tony vouched for me or not. He reached under the bar so that we couldn't see his shooting hand.

Tony half-turned toward me, but did not take his eyes off the bartender. "Looks like I gotta go up alone. Wanna wait in the car?"

That was the second time Tony asked me to wait outside. "Go handle your business. I'll hang around down here."

Tony threw a twenty on top of the bar and barked at Chino. "Get my man whatever he wants. And buy yourself a mess of enchiladas with the change, you fat fuck." Tony scooted under the counter and disappeared behind the curtain.

Chino pulled his hand back in sight and waited for my order. I gestured at the poster of a smiling señorita holding a beer. "Carta Blanca, por favor."

Chino opened the beer and slammed it on the counter, making it foam. I took it and spun on my stool to watch the crowd.

Men gathered in the back around a pool table.

Near the front there were small round tables next to a small area that served as a dance floor. A man slumped over one table and clutched a near-empty tequila bottle.

On the dance floor there were two couples. The two women were the only females in the room. They were middle-aged, maybe even past middle age. They had leathery faces caked with makeup and the impression of long years of alcohol. They wore modest dresses and high-heeled shoes. The men who served as their partners were short, in their early twenties, and appeared so drunk that the women were forced to lead.

The music stopped. One of the women swayed over to the ladies' room. Her young partner pried the tequila bottle from the passed-out man's hand and took a swig while he waited for his lady to return from the toilet. The other woman fumbled through her young partner's wallet. She found money and went to the jukebox to select songs.

The music kicked in with a gust of passionate yodels. The other woman tottered back from the bathroom. A long piece of toilet tissue stuck to her shoe and dragged behind her like a tattered wedding train.

I drank and watched the four of them dance. They swayed, and despite their drunken imbalance, they were on time, on beat, and it was clear that they all felt the music. The tequila and the first sips of beer warmed my mood.

Suddenly, one of the men made eye contact with me. He stopped right on the dance floor.

"¿Qué miras, güey?"

I pointed at myself to be clear he meant me. "¿Cómo?"

"¿Tienes algún problema?" He stepped closer and put his hand on the knife in its holster on his belt.

My stomach tingled. In Spanish I said, "I'm just sitting here, drinking my beer."

In one deft move the little Mexican pulled the knife and flipped it open. "¿Quieres que te corte los pinches huevos, cabrón?"

I may as well have been a side of beef. I focused on the tip of the weapon, fully conscious of the point as the part that I most had to avoid. It was like the metal emitted a current that locked all joints in place. Maybe I could've smashed my beer bottle against the bar for a makeshift weapon—when I was a kid, Italians called that a "nigger knife." But the way the little man opened that blade, there'd never be enough time. Acid pumped to my throat.

I did my most soothing, Mexican-sounding Spanish. "Easy, friend. I simply appreciate the way you and your woman dance."

The man's eyes widened. "You want my woman?"

He raised the blade, but just then, a baseball bat swung and made contact with the little Mexican's forearm, snapping it. The knife flipped through the air, landed, and stuck upright in the wooden floor, like an exclamation mark.

Chino, the bartender, vaulted over the bar in a gymnastic move that seemed impossible for a man of his size. He still held the baseball bat.

The Mexican clutched his mangled forearm. "¡Aaay, ay ay!!!"

Chino bent over and pulled the knife from the ground. He threw the knife and the baseball bat behind the bar, then grabbed the Mexican by the scruff of his shirt. Chino looked at me like, "You want a piece?"

I shook my head. Chino led the man to the door and shoveled him out.

I looked around. Everyone had stopped their action. The song on the jukebox ended and left nothing but awkward silence. Then a new song began. The woman whose dance partner was just bounced was the first to move. Without taking her eyes off me, and with the toilet paper still dragging behind her shoe, she walked over to the vaquero slumped next to the half-empty tequila bottle. Defiant, she pulled on his arm so he regained enough consciousness to stand, put his hat on, and lean against her on the dance floor. Slowly, everyone returned to dancing, cursing, and stumbling their way through another loveless night.

I went back to my beer, and watched everyone around me without looking anyone in the eye.

Tony emerged from behind the curtain. He slapped me on the back. "Let's pull up."

Outside, the little Mexican was plopped on the sidewalk. He cried and held his mutilated forearm as he looked up at me.

"¡Hijo de tu chingada madre! ¡Esta me la vas a pagar!"

Tony looked at me. "What's his problem?"

"He ran into a Hall of Famer."

"Not yet he ain't." Tony started toward him.

I grabbed Tony by the crook of his arm. "He's harmless, bro, c'mon."

Tony pointed at the Mexican. "Merry Christmas, nacho."

We jumped in the car. I gave Tony the one-sentence synopsis of what went down.

Tony shook his head. "Damn, Eddie, I can't leave you alone for five minutes. You a straight-up *magnet* for trouble."

Little Tony, convicted felon, said this with such a complete lack of irony, all I could do was laugh.

Tony removed an envelope from his jacket pocket and tossed it between us on the seat. "Ten G's, right there, kid."

"Pelón's?"

"Minus my ten percent," he said.

"You get ten points just for collecting?"

"Kosher, right?"

"And Pelón gets paid to do what?"

"Vigorish. Bar owner's from Durango. Reefer importer, but also takes bets, then brokers some through our boy. Fuckin' Pelón got at least twenty accounts like that, that I know of."

I nodded. "Pelón must need capital sometimes. Dime bags in bodegas don't account for this level of movement."

"I told you, Eddie, the man's been lucky in real estate. He was buying two flats in Wicker Park when they were wort'less. With all these yuppies movin' in? Values're going through the roof. You seen all the new condos goin' up."

"Yeah, but if Pelón's pimping like that, why risk a heavy count with this casino job?"

"They say you can never be too rich or too thin."

"You learn that from watching cable?"

Tony smirked. "Wasn't it you who said, 'Careful planning and quick action eliminate risk'?"

"You remember how that worked out?"

Tony shook his head. "Listen, Eddie, I ain't never going back to prison, OK? That ain't even an option."

"What are you gonna do when they corner you, Tony? Go out, guns blazing, like Jimmy Cagney?"

"Fuck that shit. At least the terms'll be all mine, I'll tell you that much. But listen, don't bring up the casino job tonight. Let Pelón talk about it if he wants."

I wiped my mouth. "I just love it when anyone tries to muzzle me."

"Seriously, Eddie. Just let Pelón feel you out. Don't be so pushy."

"Pushy, Tony? How about I push my heel through the back of Pelón's throat?"

"See? Why you gotta go there?"

"Let me find out Pelón had a piece in me getting ripped off."

"Madon'!" said Tony. "Let's change the subject." He put the radio on The Loop FM, but low. After a while he said, "You wanna hear something funny? But you really can't tell Pelón that I told you."

"Scout's honor."

Tony paused. "About a year and a half ago, Pelón goes to PR on business, right? He meets this woman. Young as shit. In her early twenties."

I whistled. "Man, that fuckin' Viagra really is a little miracle."

"Quit fucking around and listen. So Pelón comes back. He tells me he got married."

"Married? With papers and everything?"

"That's what he said. Said she was beautiful. From the hills. Real clean-cut jíbara type. Pentecostal-looking. Don't speak no English."

"I never figured Pelón for the religious type."

"Of course not. He probably just figures a church girl ain't smoked too much cock. Anyway, he tells me all about what a dream it is to meet her at a time when he finally wants to settle down. Said the kicker was how her cooking reminded him of his mom's. So I go to his crib to meet this goddess, right?"

"Let me guess: hairy legs. Them Pentecostals don't believe in shaving."

Tony made a face. "Worse." In Spanish he said, "Uglier than a kick in the balls."

I winced.

"Skinny? Dude, she was all bones. Teeth like a chip-

munk. Anyway, we sit to eat. It was like she poured a
bucket of salt on each chicken wing. I'm looking at Pelón
like, 'Shit, if this was the way *I* grew up, I'd be copping
amnesia.' But I don't say shit. I figure the man's got a right
to whatever curls his toes, right?"

"Word."

"So a few months go by. Pelón's crazy in love. Every
time you see him, he's like, 'Ay, que mi negrita pa'aquí.
Que mi negrita pa'allá.' Buying flowers and shit. Wearing
cologne. He even got himself a new set of dentures. Then
one day I get a call from Cook County."

"Jail?"

"No, hospital. It's Pelón."

"Food poisoning?"

"Naw, man. Get this: the bitch tried to execute Pelón."

"Come again?"

"She tried to off him, bro."

"How?"

"In the bathroom. The way Pelón put it, he was
in the tub waiting to get his groove on. Got the bubble
bath going. Radio tuned to slow jams. Champagne's all
poured."

"Casanova time."

"Precisely. So his wife comes in. She's fully dressed.
Except she got a look in her eye like Pelón ain't never seen
before. He's like, 'Pero mamita, ¿qué te pasa?' And she's
like, '¿Tú quiere saber lo qué me pasa? Hijo de la gran
yegua.' And without warning, she snatches the radio."

"Oh shit. Don't tell me—"

"That's right," said Tony. "Playa's in a bathtub full of
water."

"So what'd he do?"

"Pelón jumps up and starts wrestling with his bride, trying to stop her from dropping the radio. The guy's naked, in a foot and halfa water, screaming, 'What's wrong, mami? ¿Qué pasó?' Finally, Pelón slips and slams into the marble outside the tub, just as she tosses the radio into the water."

"Goddamn."

"Yup. Nigga broke his hip."

"So that's why he needs the cane now."

"Exactly. According to Pelón, the radio in the tub actually knocked out all the lights. Now he's on the floor, in the dark, stunned from the pain, naked."

"So what'd she do next? Slice him?"

"Uh-uh. She grabs Pelón's nut sac."

"Oh fuck."

"Squeezes the man's quenepas until Pelón thought his shit was gonna pop. He's begging, 'Mamita, no.' She leans in and whispers, 'That's so that you never forget me.' She reaches in ole boy's mouth, pulls out his new dentures, holds 'em up. 'Te llevo conmigo.' "

"Psycho bitch."

"No doubt. Fuckin' creepy even."

"So what'd she do next?"

"She leaves him on the floor, naked, shivering. With a broken hip and no teeth. Throws his cell phone in the tub. Yanks the house phone outta the wall, so Pelón had to drag himself to the hallway of his condo and wail until one of his neighbors came out and called 911."

"Pelón told you all of this?"

"He was freaked out. Rambling in the hospital."

"That is some crazy shit. Did Pelón ever figure out what got into her?"

"He says bilongo."

"Bilongo? You mean like the song?"

"Witchcraft. A potion or something."

"Get the fuck out."

"Hey, I'm not telling you I believe it, Eddie. I'm telling you that's what he told me. I mean, the guy was hallucinating from the medicine, I think, so I'm not even sure he knew it was me, you know? But he talked about a bruja. Said she used to read the cards for him and tell him everything. From what Pelón said, she burned in a fire. Wasn't around to warn him away from the psycho jíbara."

I made a skeptical face. "You really think Pelón believes in all that?"

"I don't know. I will tell you this: the man was munching the saltiest, bitterest chicken wings and diggin' them like they was T-bone. I could see if she was one of these bitches make a nigga wanna climb some walls and shit. But *this* bird? One eye bigger than the other, a pig nose—"

"I get the point."

"You should've tasted them chicken wings. Miss America couldn't get away with serving me that. I'd break her tiara and shove it up her ass."

"Was Pelón embarrassed?"

"Heartbroken. He thought it was true love."

I nodded. After a minute I said, "How 'bout you, Tone? You fall for anybody since you been out?"

"Every day. Today I was infatuated with a couple strippers up in *Black Tail* magazine."

"C'mon, Tony, I mean on the real."

"What, the way bitches are nowadays? They're all frontin'. All of 'em. They're always after somethin'. The only thing they give a fuck about is money. You can't trust women, Eddie, don't fall for it."

"Tony, you got the balls to say that? With all them females you knocked up and never paid a dime to?"

Tony paused. "All right, some of them are more special than others, I'll give you that. I remember this one bitch. I didn't have a ride yet; this is when I first got out. So I waited on a bus stop in January in the middle of the fuckin' night. Windchill was like a thousand below. I thought my dick would break off like an icicle. When I got there, the bitch was on her period and hadn't even told me. I still fucked her."

"Not exactly throwing yourself on a grenade, Tone. Or even tolerating a salty chicken wing."

Tony smoked and thought about it. We crossed over the Chicago River and I noticed again the majestic skyline. Acres of new construction sparkled. Balconies had become standard in luxury apartments, and I guess because Tony and I were speaking of romance, I imagined myself sharing a glass of wine with a woman and watching the sunset from one of those balconies. In my mind I did not see the woman's face. She was more like a presence, a vague form who was there for a second, then evaporated.

Tony died his cigarette. He was ready to come clean. "Actually, about a year ago, Eddie, I saw this girl, a woman now, I guess. I knew her years ago."

"When?"

"Before I dropped out of Clemente." Tony said her name.

"I don't remember her." I thought I knew all of Tony's conquests from back then.

He shook his head. "You never met her. I never mentioned her. That was that summer you were sent to juvie. There was nothing left to report by the time you got back."

"Short and sweet," I said. "What happened?"

Tony curled his lips. "Foster care sent me to this summer camp. There were kids from the city there, but also white kids from the suburbs, mixed. I think they were supposed to be a good influence on us."

"It didn't work."

Tony ignored my joke. "This girl had red hair. Freckles. She didn't look like nobody from back in the hood. Remember that honey from *Sixteen Candles*? Like that, bro. But prettier. Her father was an actual doctor."

"Did you hit it?"

"Naw, man, we were kids. Sneaking away from the counselors to hold hands and talk. One time we saw all these lights going off in the sky and she told me it was a meteor shower. You never see those in the city because of all the lights and pollution."

I wondered about the sentimental pitch in Tony's voice. When Tony was only twelve years old, he had a foster sister who was stacked, sixteen years old, and she sucked Tony's dick every day after school because the foster mother was never around. A running joke for Tony then was that I could stop by for "sloppy seconds" any afternoon I wanted. By high school Tony had been getting blow jobs for at least two years straight. Now he was waxing poetic about talking and holding hands with some suburban cherry pie.

I nodded. "So what was so special about this one chick you didn't need to bang her?"

Tony took a deep breath. "I'm not sure. She was, like, excited about life. Really looking forward to it. She talked about colleges she was thinking about. How she didn't want to get married until she had a career. Her family traveled a lot. She was innocent. I remember she said she wanted to go to India by herself and just walk around taking pictures. Crazy, right?"

"So what happened?"

Tony squinted. "Bad luck. The first time I got the balls to kiss her, we got caught. Behind a tree. Her parents came down the next day and removed her from the program."

I smiled. "Real Romeo-and-Juliet shit, huh?"

"If you wanted to exaggerate. Anyway, I never saw her again until just last year."

"Where?"

"Downtown. I'm down there picking up a Garrett's cheese and caramel corn. I walk out the store munchin' and I see her pass right in front of me, like the girl that time forgot."

"How'd she look?"

"Good. I mean, great. Older, heavier, but nice."

"You sure it was her, Tone?"

"Oh yeah. It was her."

"Did you talk to her?"

"Naw, man. She was with her kids, two boys, redheads like her. They must have been about twelve or thirteen. The way they were dressed, you could tell they had money. Carrying all these bags from expensive stores. They could've been in a catalogue."

"Was her man around?"

"No. Probably a doctor or something too, like her old man. Doing surgery and shit, saving some asshole's life. Playing golf. Too busy making loot to be with his wife and kids."

"So what'd you do, Tony? Did you talk to her?"

Tony lit another cigarette. "I followed her. They walked

into an expensive-looking restaurant for lunch. I stood outside for a while, holding my popcorn like a fucking jerk-off."

"C'mon, Tone, you weren't tempted to just walk over and ask whether she ever made it to India?"

Tony's mouth went flat. The light turned yellow and he didn't speed up or stop and we ended up rolling through a red. Tony grabbed his shades from around the statue of Saint Judas on the dashboard and slipped them on, even though it was already dark out. Then he pushed a Guns N' Roses CD into the player. He cued a long ballad and cranked it. It was a clear enough signal that the discussion was over.

I thought about my own love life. Tony didn't ask, but if he had, I would have told him that I once dug a girl who confessed that she played *Purple Rain,* the entire album, in her head, every time we made out. There was another, a smart one. We never kissed, but she smiled like she wanted me to. Then there was a third, one who Tony knew. She stuck around. She visited often during those early years at Stateville, and I thought of her almost as a wife. But even she eventually grew tired of waiting and married somebody else.

And that was it, those three. They were the closest I had ever come to anything real. To this day I can't say whether any qualified as true love.

CHAPTER 08:

TUMBANDO CAÑA

The old man lived in a high-rise on Lake Shore Drive. The doorman announced us. Tony and I rode up in the elevator.

"See?" said Tony, warming up. "The man's pimping. Wait'll you see his crib."

Pelón answered the door in white boxers with red hearts all over. He wore a dago T and black nylon socks pulled up to his bony knees. A heavy gold medallion nestled in the gray forest of his chest: Christ crucified on a ship's anchor rather than a cross.

Pelón flashed his dentures. "Llegaron los invitados." He wore no jewelry on his two-fingered claw-hand, but his other hand was adorned by a thick gold bracelet and a diamond pinky ring. Tufts of shaving cream behind his ears indicated that we'd interrupted him as he shaved his head. His pencil-thin silver mustache was gone.

"I'm trying to look a little younger. But I no ready yet." He waved us in with a big cigar. "Están en su casa." He excused himself to the bathroom. "Make youself at home."

A female guard who I used to bang in Stateville used to bring me old copies of *Architectural Digest,* and that was the only place I ever saw cribs like Pelón's. The ceiling was low, which gave it a cozy, if somewhat boxy, feeling, despite all the square footage. Virtually everything gleamed. Things like the coffee table and shelves were made of green glass and chrome. The carpet was plush white. The entire space was centered around a huge maroon leather couch.

Tony pointed at the floor-to-ceiling windows that formed the eastern wall. "Yo, those face the Lake. Let's peep the view."

I walked over. Navy Pier was right there, scrubbed up and renovated. The giant Ferris wheel turned at a subtle rate, like the hands of a clock. I remembered when the pier was abandoned. Tony and I and our crew once climbed through a hole in a fence and hiked out to the end, where it gets real windy. It felt like we were at the end of the city. We smoked weed and watched the passing boats and fantasized about owning them. Tony performed jokes that he memorized from Richard Pryor, Rodney Dangerfield, and Cheech and Chong tapes.

He joined me at the window and we relived those moments. "Remember when we used to go to the platform at the other end there, over the water, and dive in?"

I squinted to make out the spot. "You had to get the arc just right to land between the rocks. Beto broke his arm."

Tony scanned the panorama. "Imagine bringing a honey up here to watch fireworks over the water."

I smacked my lips. "Probably *all* Pelón does: imagine."

Right then, Pelón returned from the bathroom. His

brown shaved head reflected the low light. He leaned on his cane.

"You should see the thunderstorms."

Tony pointed at the entertainment center. "Pelón, how many inches is that plasma?"

"No sé. Too many to count."

Tony inspected the old man's collection of DVDs. "How many movies you got?"

Pelón blew a breath, like he might have to count them all that very second. "Five hundred maybe? I collect classics." Pelón smiled. In Spanish he said, "Nothing else for an old man to do but sit and watch TV." He held up the cane. "Especially now that I can't dance like I used to."

He pointed his cane at a black-and-white print on one wall. "See that?"

I took a closer look. It was a print of a jíbaro bent over some sugarcane, his machete held high, about to deliver the lethal blow.

I cocked my head. "¿Tufiño?"

Pelón made a face. "How you know that?"

"I worked in the prison library."

Tony said, "Nigga even had secret Internet."

Pelón twisted the cigar in his mouth.

I pointed at the print. "Is that an original?"

Pelón grinned. "Does it matter?"

I dropped myself onto the plush maroon leather couch and sank in. "I guess not. This cow feels real. How much you drop for this?"

Pelón sniffed. "I always like style, you know? Class? Price is not the issue."

He pointed at a strange-looking chair. "Por ejemplo, esa silla. Design by a famous architect for the World's

Fair. Ten years before I was born. The king of Spain sat in that same chair."

Tony lowered himself onto it. "You saying my culo is now in the same spot where the king once farted?"

Pelón waved him out. "Zángano. In a *copy* of that chair." He plopped in it. "Is not so comfortable, but it makes me feel, I don't know—"

"Like a royal ass?" I said.

Pelón held his smile. "Something like that." He opened the humidor on the end table and passed it to Tony. "¿Habanero?"

Tony took one. I did too.

I puffed until the ember glowed. "So, Pelón, who's the famous architect?"

"¿Cómo?"

"The chair. Who designed it?"

Pelón rolled the cigar over his tongue. "See? That's why I no do so good in school." He slapped his hands once and rubbed palms. "Bueno, Antonio. You have somesing for me?"

Tony tossed the envelope on the coffee table. Pelón opened it, brought the cash close to his face like he needed thick glasses. He counted the ten thousand quick, with his two-fingered hand, then looked up like a cat with feathers in its mouth. He waved the money, rolled his *R*'s and softened his *V* to exaggerate and mock his own hick Puerto Rican accent: "I not a *Rree*publican, but the *Prr*esident is doing a *behrry* good job!"

I laughed at Pelón's caricature of himself, despite not wanting to encourage him.

Pelón peeled off ten hundreds for Tony. He looked at me.

"You friend got a easy life, no?"

I aimed for a smug tone. "God bless America."

Pelón hobbled over to the bar, where he lined up three etched glasses. He cut a lime into wedges. "You know, I did not wear my first pair of shoes until I was eleven?" He looked up at us. "Is true. We lived up in the mountains. En el monte. My old man cut sugarcane. Like that man in the picture on the wall over there. Caña that was used to make this." Pelón held up a bottle of Puerto Rican rum. "What you think about that? Swinging a machete all day in that hot Caribbean sun."

Our host dropped ice in each glass. He carefully poured Bacardi so that the ice cracked, then poured Coca-Cola. He squeezed and added wedges as he talked. "In that time nobody knew what it was like to have a luxury like meat. Eggs? Cheese? Sometimes. Almost never. We lived off things you pull from the ground. Yuca. Batata. Yame. De vez en cuándo un plátano."

Tony patted his stomach. "That's the shit. My foster mother makes that on Christmas."

"Try eating it every day."

Pelón placed the three drinks on a tray and balanced it on his five-fingered hand. He hobbled with the cane in his claw, but didn't spill a drop. We each took a drink.

Pelón rubbed his nose. "Sometimes my father, when he got paid, he would come with a live chicken under his arm. My brothers and I, we would see him on the path and run down to escort him to the house." Pelón laughed at the memory. "In those days we never heard of Thanksgiving. But every time we saw my father with a chicken, we make a parade." Pelón laughed even harder. I didn't see any tears, but he dabbed the corners of his eyes.

"Bueno. One day my brothers and I, we play in the back of the house. I don't say 'yard.' It wasn't. It was just, how you say? Selva. Jungle? You been to Puerto Rico?"

I shook my head.

Tony said, "Once. When I was a kid. It rained a lot. And the roosters in the morning don't let you sleep."

"There's a lotta jungle. Pero muy moderno. They got highways now. Refrigerators. You go to parts of PR, you think you right here. Not in those days."

Pelón shook his head and sipped his drink. He paused so long, I thought he was finished.

He continued in Spanish: "My brothers and I, we played outside. Francisco, my middle brother, we called him Chico. He fell. Nothing special. He just tripped, the way boys do. His head landed in a bush. When he got up, he made a face and held his head, but he looked OK. So we kept on with our game."

Pelón seemed for a moment to drift off into a private memory. He didn't really look at us.

"That night Chico woke up crying. The three of us shared a room. We all slept on one blanket, on the floor. When Chico woke up, he woke me and my other brother. I told him, 'Cállate, Papi's asleep. He has to work in the morning. Don't make him mad.' Pobrecito. He cried to himself. Me and my other brother went back to sleep."

Tony and I sipped our drinks. Pelón stirred his with his pinky, the one with the huge diamond. He slowed his tempo.

"The next day Chico didn't wanna play. He kept complaining that he had a headache. We told him to sit and watch as we went about our games. Then I noticed that Chico was on his back. My other brother and I ran to him.

Chico was passed out. My brother went to get Mami and she ran. She slapped Chico and said his name. He moved a little, like he wasn't totally out. Looked like he was having a bad dream."

Pelón took a sip. His expression curdled a bit, but I couldn't tell if it was his ancient memory or the overwhelming bite of alcohol. In Spanish he said: "My mother examined Chico all over. She dug through his hair and screamed, 'What's this?' She found dried blood. And a thorn. Like the head of a nail. It stuck out the top of his head."

Pelón pressed his thumb against the one-inch mark of his index finger to dramatize the image of the thorn poking out of his little brother's crown.

"Mami screamed, 'Mother of God! Help me!' She leaned and took the thorn between her teeth and slowly pulled it out. Pus and blood bubbled out of the hole."

Tony winced. "Nasty."

"My mother carried Chico to the house. She made medicine out of rompe saragüey. You know this?"

Tony shook his head.

I said, "Is that a plant? I heard it in a song."

Pelón nodded. "She dipped a cloth in it and began to squeeze out pus and rub the wound. By the time my father came home, my brother was in a fever. My mother tried to convince him to take Chico to the hospital." Pelón deepened his tone to imitate the boom of his father's voice in Spanish. "'Woman, you know how much that costs? It's too far, I'll never make it back by sunrise. Who's going to cut the sugarcane? Boys get fevers all the time. In the morning he'll be running around.'"

Pelón stopped there. He got up and walked across the

living room to the bar again. He added a little rum to his Cuba Libre. Still at the bar he leaned on his cane.

"My mother didn't sleep that night. She was up washing my brother's face. She put the medicine. Lit the candles. Prayed to all the saints. My father went to the colmado to play dominoes."

Pelón noticed then that his cigar had gone out in the ashtray atop the bar. He left his drink on the bar and lit the cigar and leaned on his cane and used the cigar to punctuate his words.

"In the morning my brother burned. My father finally agree to take him to the hospital. He snap at me and make me run to the neighbor's to fetch a horse. A tobacco farm a couple miles away. You believe that? I never rode a horse in my life. Who sends an impoverished child to get a horse in an emergency?"

Pelón looked deeply into the ember of his cigar. He turned the volume down. "I'm not gonna lie. I was excited to ride the horse. I was mad at my brother that I had to go straight home. In my mind I imagine running the horse down to the river. Jumping. Flying. But when I got on the horse, it went where it wanted. His name was Pelota. 'Pelota, Pelota, let's go! This way, Pelota, vámonos!' I don't think that goddamn horse spoke Spanish! I got off and ran back with it, I had to lead it, to pull this giant animal. Goddamn thing slobbered all over the back of my neck. So hot and sweaty. I was covered in mocos from the horse's snout. Probably the first time I actually wanted to take a bath."

Pelón stared into his glass before downing what was left. He spoke slower than ever. "By the time I got to the house, my father, he stood out front. Dressed in his white guayabera. Smoking his cigar with that serious look. Like a big shot. Like he was there to meet the mayor. My other brother sat on a rock by the side of the path with his head in his hands. My father said, 'Why did you take so long?' I let go the horse and ran in. Chico was stretched on my parents' bed. Probably the only time his back ever touched a mattress. My mother was on her knees next to him. She said his name and wrapped a rosary around his hands. I started to cry. Chico was the only one who looked at peace. The mattress soaked up his nightmares."

Tony and I were silent. We stopped sipping our drinks. Pelón looked at us. The tension in his crooked posture made it seem that he struggled to keep something in. Then he stood straight and grinned.

"So *that* was the first time I ever wore shoes. My mother bought them for me and my other brother to wear at the funeral. They were the wrong size. She bought them big so they would last. First time I ever wore underwear too. I'm sure my father protested. But after my mother let him win the argument about Chico and the hospital, she never let him talk her down again."

Pelón lowered himself into his special chair. He cleared his throat. "You boys need to understand something about this country. We have everything. De todo. But nobody's going to give it to you. And nobody's going to let you have it either. You gotta reach out with your own two hands." Pelón showed us his hands. The one with the gold and diamond pinky ring. The other with the missing fingers. "Reach out and grab it," he said. "Take it. Make it yours. That's the only way it's going to happen for you. These people've been running things in this part of the world for five hundred years. You think they gonna stop *now*?"

He poked the cigar between his dentures, leaned back, and spoke out of the corner of his mouth. "Understand what I'm getting at?"

Tony nodded. I did not say a word. There followed an uncomfortable silence where it seemed that Pelón looked right into me in an effort to read something.

"¿Sabes qué, Eduardo?" Pelón focused right on me. "You remind me of Brando."

Tony perked up. *"The Godfather?"*

"No."

"Where he plays the boxer?"

"Tampoco."

"I know," said Tony, "with the motorcycle gang. *The Wild One*."

Pelón wagged a finger. "Ever see *One-Eyed Jacks*?"

Tony shook his head.

I said, "Is that where he bangs the French chick?"

Pelón twisted his mouth like, *You wish*. "It's a Western. Brando plays a robber who gets double-cross by his best friend. He spends five years in jail in México, then comes back to California to kill the best friend. But the best friend is a sheriff now. He's got the police on his side."

There followed an abrupt silence, and I wondered whether Pelón figured my suspicions about Tony, about himself, and about my forty thousand. I wondered whether he meant to taunt me.

Tony seemed to pick up on this. "Yo, what is it about Eddie that reminds you of *that* guy?"

Pelón left the charge in the atmosphere by stalling. He grinned and turned the cigar in his mouth, like a true puppet master. "The way he watch everybody. Like he waiting his turn. A hungry young cobra waiting for blood. No te ofenda. Is a compliment."

Pelón's words hung for a second over the glass-topped coffee table. I let him watch as I finished my Cuba Libre and licked my lips.

I said, "So, Pelón? Does Brando kill the best friend?"

Pelón bit his lip. "Think I gonna spoil it? Watch it all the way to the end."

Just then, the phone rang.

Pelón excused himself. When he answered, his eyes darted over to me and Tony. "Sí, sí, espérate." He covered the receiver.

"Private call?" I said.

Pelón made a face like he appreciated that we understood, and gestured toward the other room. "Vayan a jugar billar."

The pool table was sleek, black, the slate dressed in green felt. Tony racked, I broke. Nothing went in. I went to the floor-to-ceiling windows. Cars sped below on six lanes along the shore. Beyond the lights the Lake was an immense cauldron of black ink.

Tony worked the table. *Crack. Crack. Crack-crack.* I'm confident that Tony never recited one law of physics, but he manipulated several with his cue stick.

Each of my balls was still on the table. "What the fuck, Tony, save some for me."

He pointed the stick. "Maybe in the next life. Eight ball, corner pocket."

He soft-banked it at an impossible angle. Of course it rolled in.

I high-fived Tony. "You're a genius."

Tony blew blue chalk off the tip like a gunslinger. "My secret is logical: I spend way too much time in bars."

I placed the balls inside the triangle. "Pelón lays it on thick, huh?"

Tony chalked the tip again. "What you mean?"

"I smell a snow job."

"He's just making conversation."

"Bullshit," I said. "When's he gonna get to the point?"

"Meaning?"

"The heist."

"Eddie, I told you he was gonna feel you out. Slow your roll."

Just then, Pelón interrupted: "Stick 'em up!"

He stood at the entrance to the room and pointed his cane at me like a tommy gun. He was fully dressed in a pin-striped navy suit, pink shirt, red silk tie, polished shoes. On his head was a navy fedora, tilted to the side. There was no way to know exactly how long Pelón had been standing in the room, listening.

He winked. "Let's go."

We followed him.

Tony popped his gum. "So what's on the menu?"

Pelón smiled. "No te preocupe. You find out when we get there."

We stopped by the elevators. Pelón gave me that same look from earlier. Like there was something that we were both in on. I had no instinct as to what it was. He held me in his gaze long enough to make me wish that he would stop. Then he used the tip of his cane to call the elevator. The little arrow pointed down.

CHAPTER 09:

SLINGSHOT

We rode in the limo to the suburbs.

"I taking you boys to the track."

Tony mixed drinks. "I don't know shit about playing the ponies, Pelón."

"Don't worry, I teach you." He snapped his fingers. "Pay attention."

Pelón took out the racing form and went into a long lecture about win, place, and show, across the board, daily doubles, exactas, trifectas, and superfectas. He talked a lot about the history of certain horses, their jockeys and trainers, and whether they liked one type of track or another. His tone was scientific. Especially when he unspooled the string of equations for eliminating risk.

In Spanish he said, "You get all that?"

If Tony and I had been cartoons, our eyeballs would've been pinwheels.

Pelón laughed and slapped his own knee. "Listen, tonight the only thing to remember is Curly-Q to win in the fifth."

I raised my eyebrow. "Curly-Q?"

"In the fifth."

Tony crunched an ice cube. "That a special horse or something?"

Pelón leaned back. "The trainer's a friend. Curly-Q come from a strong bloodline. But he had a little accident."

Tony said, "He peed himself?"

I chuckled, but Pelón said, "No seas tan pendejo." He continued: "After Curly-Q fell, people thought he finished. The trainer, he look in the animal's eyes. You know what he saw?" Pelón tapped himself in the chest. "Amor. Hierro. Corazón. He knew that horse was gonna come back."

Tony sat up. "Don't they normally shoot jacked-up horses?"

"Not this time. My friend took the horse away. Let it recover. Took care of him with some special vitamins. You know what? The beast is faster now than before. More confident."

Tony whistled.

Pelón said, "The trainer's no fool. He bring that horse back, but he tell the jockey, 'Aguántalo.' Go dead every race."

I said, "You mean, hold the horse back?"

"Sí."

"Why?"

Pelón looked at me like, *You really don't understand caca, do you?* "To drive up the odds. Curly-Q race eleven times since he come back. He move like his balls weigh fifty pounds. Everybody think it's because of the accident. Tonight the jockey gonna let him fly. El dinero está twenty-one to one."

The scheme took shape in my mind. Except for Pelón's role.

"Why's the trainer telling *you* all this, Pelón? What do you contribute?"

Pelón rolled his eyes. "I gotta explain everything?" He looked at his watch. "We gotta get to the window and post."

It was a long ride to the track. Pelón looked out the window and checked his watch every three minutes.

He tapped Tony on the knee. "¿Y tú, Antonio? What's gonna happen with this revolú?"

Tony sounded like a scolded teenager. "You see a mess anywhere?"

Pelón said, "You think I don't hear? I'm here, but I see what happen here, there, and over there. I got eyes that see backward and forward and to the side."

I said, "You're like a fly, ha, Pelón? All up *in* the shit."

He pretended not to hear.

Tony shifted. "Listen, Pelón, if Roach wants a piece of me—"

Pelón interrupted Tony by asking him outright: "¿Quie n mató a ese muchacho?"

"The little soldier in the park? I don't know. I didn't punch his ticket. None of my people did."

Pelón said, "That's not what I heard."

Tony shot back, "You shouldn't listen to gossip."

Pelón said in Spanish, "I don't understand why you in this business right now. You make enough money with me."

"Hey, school's out, Pelón, OK? Whyn't you go back to lecturing about horses?"

"It don't make sense, Antonio. With this thing we got coming up? Why risk it? You gonna earn more in one night than that business gonna bring in five years."

And there it was. For the first time Pelón himself put the casino heist in full view.

Tony focused on himself. "Look, Pelón, Roach is gonna come after me, regardless. It's war now. This is what I do."

"Do it smart then. Negotiate for territory. Maybe you make peace with him and you two put in together, you and Roach, buy in bulk, lower you own costs. You can even agree to keep the prices up. That's the way the big companies do it. Why you think gasoline costs so much? Use your head. Make a monopoly. Start collecting more money and forget about the pistolas."

"Number one," said Tony, "there ain't enough corners in the hood no more. Yuppies gobbled up so much turf, and the narcs keep baggers off their blocks, so it's almost all gone. Customers been squeezed off. It ain't like the eighties where you could throw product from any corner. You drive by Humboldt Park in the morning now? All you see is white people jogging."

I jumped in. "Don't they get high, though?"

"Of course. They just don't tolerate street pushers. You need a whole 'nother network to get to them. And I'm working on that, but right now the street is my bread and butter."

I said, "So what's number two?"

"Huh?"

"You said number one was not enough turf and street junkies left to share."

"Right."

"So what's number two?"

"Oh. Number two is: fuck Roach. He can eat a dick. I been in and out of this game before that faggot was jerkin' off his first nickel bag."

Pelón said, "Coño, Antonio, pero you never make nothing out of it. Let's face it. What you got to show for all them drug deals? And you too old now to play cowboys and Indians."

"It ain't about that."

I finished my drink. "Pelón, you're telling a dog not to lick his own balls."

Pelón shook his head. "I know." In Spanish he said, "The affliction of youth." He checked his watch and pushed the button to lower the partition and addressed his driver. "Oye, Gordo, if we don't make post, I swear to Lázaro, I gonna leave you face in a pile of horse shit."

Pelón raised the partition and rattled the ice cubes in his glass. Tony refilled it with gin and soda. The limo driver found a hole in the stream of traffic and took off.

It was natural in the cushy backseat of that limo to reflect on my history with Pelón. We had known each other a long time and done things together we both wanted to forget.

After the first deal that Tony made with Pelón in the mid-eighties, Pelón became a regular customer. Every month or so he'd stop by for two hundred, three hundred, or five hundred dime bags of weed. For me and Tony and our crew, it was always a fat, unexpected jump-off when Pelón rolled through in his fancy gleaming white Excalibur.

One day, about a year or so into our relationship, Pelón rolled up with a bag of breaded Ricobene's steak sandwiches.

I licked my fingers. "Damn, you could write a poem about these."

Pelón smiled and wiped sauce from his handlebar mustache. "You boys don't leave the neighborhood much, do you?"

Teenage Tony talked with his mouth full. He glanced down at his jacket, which was in our gang's colors. "Too many enemies."

Pelón shook his head. "There's a whole universe out there, and you putting up a cage. Finish eating. I gonna show you something."

We rode in the Excalibur with the top down. Pelón steered it up Lake Shore Drive past condos with views of the water. He drove to some North Shore suburbs. Huge mansions lined the coast. On the street people stared at us, and I couldn't tell if it was the wild car or the strange fruit inside that intrigued them.

Pelón pointed at a house barely visible behind the trees. "Some houses got swimming pools inside. Saunas. A private beach just for the house."

I wanted to see that. I asked Pelón how he knew this.

Pelón chuckled. "They got a lotta nice things too. Paintings, silverware, jewelry, cameras, stereos. Easy things to carry. And sell."

I adjusted my Super Bowl XX baseball cap. "You got a point, Pelón?"

"I'm saying this is a easy place to go shopping."

Tony wiggled his fingers. "Five-finger discount?"

"Better. I'm working on a deal. These people, they *want* somebody to rob them."

Now I *knew* Pelón must be full of shit. "Pelón, these

people been sniffing glue? Why would they want you to steal their shit?"

"Because they smart. Is between them and the insurance company. They no gonna be home. They let me know which window they forgot to lock. We comin' in a van dressed as painters. One, two, three." Pelón snapped his fingers.

"Why would we do this?"

"Because I gonna pay you five hundred dollars each. Plus, I let you take one thing from the house. Is gonna be fun."

Five hundred was a nice chunk. "What happens when we get caught?" I said.

"We won't."

Tony said, "Make it a thousand dollars."

Pelón shook his head. "Are you crazy? Six hundred."

"Eight-fifty."

Pelón took a deep breath. "Yo no sabía que tú era judío, Antonio. Seven-fifty, that's it."

Tony and I looked at each other. They shook hands.

I looked at the house. "Do your friends got an alarm?"

"Is broken and they no gonna fix it."

"Do they have a dog?"

Pelón grinned. "These people got so much money, they take the freaking dog on vacation."

We pulled the white van right into the driveway and up to the front entrance. Pelón bought the three of us coveralls that he splattered with different colored paints to make it seem like we worked in them. He went around the back while Tony and I waited in front. In a minute Pelón opened the front door.

"Unload the equipment," he ordered. "Move."

The three of us took a bunch of empty five-gallon paint buckets from the van into the house. We brought in some tarps, and shut the door.

We stood in the foyer and looked up at the chandelier in the high ceiling.

Tony whistled. "Who are these people?"

Pelón got right to business. "We gonna be organized how we do this. We start upstairs and work down. Focus on things that fit in the bucket. There's some paintings and a couple of carpets that we can disguise with the tarps and some blankets, but that's it for big things. Remember, it all has to fit in the van."

We started in the master bedroom. As we tossed every drawer, we found things to take, like a jewelry box full of rings, cuff links, earrings, necklaces, bracelets. We found passports, a gold watch. Pelón made sure he was in the room the whole time. He rifled, but kept an eye on us as well. He wrapped a small statue of an armless woman in a towel and put it in a bucket.

Tony sprayed himself with different colognes. He found a vibrator in the table next to the bed and tried to buzz first me, then Pelón, in the ear with it.

Pelón shooed him away. "Déja la jodienda. Get to work."

I found an envelope with cash in the back of a panty drawer and Pelón took it and put it in his pants pocket, under the coveralls, without counting.

Tony dug in the bedroom closet. "Shit, look at this." He held up a gleaming revolver.

Pelón took it. "Children shouldn't play with these." He put it in his back pocket. "Help me with this rug. Es oriental."

We rolled it up, wrapped it in a tarp, carried it down-stairs, then moved on to the other bedrooms. The daughter had a lot of stuffed animals and posters of unicorns. She also had a small TV, a stereo, and a Commodore 64 computer, which ended up in buckets. The son had an electric guitar.

"Snap!" said Tony. "I'm taking this ax. And that amp."

Pelón shook his head. "That's no gonna fit in a bucket."

"Fuck that," said Tony. He put the guitar in its carrying case, pulled the bedsheet off the bed, and began to wrap it. "I'll get you a backstage pass when U2 opens for me and Van Halen at the Rosemont."

Pelón looked at me. "What the fock he talking about?"

I put my hands up. "Can't stop a rock star with a dream, Pelón."

After that, we were warmed up. We went through the family room adorned with pictures of the balding husband, blond wife, daughter, and son. The kids smiled less in the pictures where they wore braces. We removed a reel-to-reel deck from the wall, and other components of a sound system, but sadly left the speakers, which Pelón said were too big. We took a portable TV, a VCR, an early Nintendo, a Sony Walkman, and two portable phones that were the size of small toasters. Pelón removed a painting of water lilies and wrapped it in a blanket, and did the same with another painting in the same style, this one of a small bridge.

In the office Pelón held a small statue of a blindfolded woman with scales and a sword. He held up the statue and said, "La Justicia," in a mocking tone, then wrapped it and put it in a bucket.

I noticed the man had a golden pen and pencil set displayed on his desk. I looked at Pelón.

"Take it."

I put just the pen in my pocket. Pelón found more cash in a drawer, which made him laugh out loud. Tony flipped through the man's collection of *Playboy* and *Hustler*. On the wall was a picture of the man of the house shaking hands with Ronald Reagan.

I pointed at it. "Pelón, you better be right that this friend of yours wants you in here. He looks pretty connected."

Pelón came over, looked at the picture, and smirked. "Mira, you donate enough money and politicians'll let you take a picture of their daughter with your finger up her ass, OK? Let me show how I vote." Pelón took the framed picture off the wall, let it drop to the floor, and smashed the glass with his heel, really dug it into the President's face.

In the kitchen we loaded the silverware, of course, but also a blender, a juicer, a coffeemaker, a milkshake maker, an automatic can opener. Tony helped himself to a beer.

In the garage we picked up all kinds of power tools, which we would never know how to use. Much of it was organized into toolboxes, which was convenient. We carried everything to the foyer.

Pelón sized everything up. "First we gotta get that rug into the van, along one side; then we carry the tools, the buckets, and finally we put the paintings in on the side. This has to be in and out; we can't give the neighbors too much time to notice."

We moved like an assembly line. The last painting was loaded and Pelón had his hands on both back doors, shutting them, when we heard a woman's voice from the front of the van.

"Excuse me, gentlemen? Señores?" She said it in that accent that white people have when they learn to speak Spanish in school.

We all froze. Pelón whispered, "¡Puñeta!"

Tony said, "What're we gonna do?"

The three of us remained hidden behind the van.

The woman's voice got closer. "Pardon me? Hellooo?"

Pelón looked at me. "Háblale."

My stomach turned. "And say what?"

"Get her to leave. Si no, we gonna have a lotta trouble."

I looked at Tony.

"Do it," he said. "Be smooth."

I went around to the front of the van. "Can I help you?"

The woman walked slowly up the long driveway. She had a Rottweiler on a leash. The dog's head was massive.

"Do you speak English?"

"Yes, ma'am."

"Are you housepainters?"

I looked down at my coveralls with its array of staged paint stains. "Um, yeah."

"I didn't know the Knutsons were having work done."

"Yeah, um, it's a surprise. I guess he, um, he—he wanted to surprise his wife."

"Really? Wish my lump of coal would think like that."

I smiled. I kept my eyes on the dog. It sniffed.

"We need some fixing too. Harold keeps promising to find some Mexicans, but he never gets out of his La-Z-Boy. Do you have a card?"

"A card?"

"You know, with your number? You're not union, are you?"

I shook my head. "I forgot to bring my card today."

"Are you union?"

I wasn't sure what she meant.

"Do you have a number?"

I swallowed and tried to think of one. "Yes."

"Can I have it? Actually"—she turned toward the front door to the house we just burglarized—"let me just go inside. Madge keeps a notepad and pen by the phone in the kitchen."

I put my hand up. "Don't go in there!"

She stopped in her tracks and looked at me. "Anything wrong?" The dog did not make a move, but it peeled its upper lip enough to show choppers.

"It's just we're not supposed to let anybody inside."

"I go in there all the time." She held up her key ring. "See? Got my own set. Who do you think waters their plants when they're in Boca?"

"It's not that. It's just, there's, um, there's a lot of fumes and everything. From the paint. It'll make you dizzy. You could get very sick. The dog too."

"Oh?"

"Yeah. We practically had to run out of there ourselves."

The woman pointed at the windows. "Well, then, how come those windows aren't open? Shouldn't you air the place out?"

"Yes, yes, you're right." I remembered Pelón disappearing around to the back when we first got there. I said, "We left the windows in the back open. We left these up front closed because we don't want nobody to see from the street and climb through."

"That's good. You can never be too careful. We've had a lot of break-ins lately."

"Right. Let me get a paper from the van. I'll write the number down for you."

"Wonderful."

I went to the front seat of the van, where I left the copy of the *Tribune* that I read on the ride up. I ripped a corner off one page and used the golden pen from the office to write "Painter." For the number—I was so nervous, instead of just inventing one, I wrote the only number that would come to mind, Bella's Pizza on Chicago Avenue.

I handed her the number. "There you are. Just call when you want us to start."

"Don't you wanna come across right now and see what it is? It'll only take a minute."

"Oh no, I, um, we—we got another place to paint. Right now. We're already late."

"At this hour?"

"We work a lot." Out of nowhere I said, "My kid needs braces."

"Seems every kid in America nowadays got a mouthful of crooked teeth."

"Tell me about it."

"You seem awfully young to have a child old enough for braces though."

I smiled. "I kinda messed up."

"Que sera, sera."

She turned and led the Rottweiler down the driveway. The dog looked back at me as it walked. Once they were off the property, I went around to the back of the van. Pelón stood with the shiny gun from the closet in his right hand.

"What the fuck were you gonna do with that, Pelón?"

He looked at the gun almost as if he were surprised to

see it there. "Nothing. Scare her. Take her inside and tie her to a chair."

"You think that humongous Rott was gonna let you get away with that?"

Pelón raised his eyes from the weapon and looked into mine. He lingered as if working his way through a decision.

In Spanish he said, "Let's just thank God that it didn't come to that."

I studied Pelón now, so much older, in the back of his limo, on our way to the track. Pelón was no longer the cocky, muscular home invader that he had once been. But he still emitted that same macho air that he carried all those years before when we executed that first burglary together. It was true that Pelón had wrinkled some. He had lost fingers, and picked up a cane since then. But he still filled his shoes like he could stomp somebody at any moment.

He smiled at me. "We almost there. You gonna see how the air at the track works a miracle on my mood."

It appeared to be true. Even with the cane, and the bad hip, Pelón seemed taller, almost peacocklike once we arrived at the track. That lasted until Pelón checked the stats for the fifth race. Curly-Q's odds had dropped to sixteen to one.

Pelón cursed in Spanish. In a hushed tone he said, "Maybe the word got out and there's a lotta people betting my horse."

He stepped to the window. "Fifth, nine thousand on thirteen to win."

I said, "Pelón, did you just bet nine thousand dollars on a horse?"

He wiggled his eyebrows.

Tony said, "Can I bet?"

"Por supuesto, pero avanza. I wanna get to the stands."

Tony took out the thousand Pelón gave him earlier.

I said, "You're not gonna drop that whole G, are you, Tone?"

"It's a sure thing."

Pelón took the thousand from Tony's hand. He looked at me. "¿Quiere un pedacito de pan caliente?"

"Too rich for me."

Tony told Pelón, "Go ahead and split the G in half, Pelón. Five for Eddie and five for me." He looked at me and winked.

I put my hand up. "That's all right, Tony. I'm just here to watch."

Pelón said, "Jódete entonce." He placed Tony's bet and we headed for the stands. Pelón noticed that the odds were now twelve to one. He cursed in Spanish. "They gonna drive the goddamn thing all the way down."

The smell of horse shit permeated. Pelón watched the other races through binoculars. "Is no fun when you got nothing on it."

I ate popcorn. "I don't know. The circus is fun even if it ain't your head in the lion's mouth."

Pelón shrugged. Horses raised dust with their hooves. People around us mostly lost, tore tickets, and made lazy comments to each other about balls that bounced and cookies that crumbled. Pelón spoke but did not lower his binoculars.

"Bueno, Eduardo, are you working?"

I leaned back in my seat. "I'm on sabbatical."

"I don't know such big words. But I got a lotta friends that need help, if you looking for a job."

"Yeah, Pelón? Maybe your trainer friend can get me started cleaning Curly-Q's stable?"

Pelón said in Spanish, "Why do you always have to make a sarcastic remark?"

"No offense, Pelón, but I really don't feel like going around collecting vig for you or your friends."

Tony said, "Good, 'cause that job's taken."

"Eddie, you ain't working for me. You tongue too loose right now. You could work as a bouncer. I got a friend who run a titty bar on the South Side. He needs help with the horny customers."

Tony's ears perked up. "Working at a strip club?"

"I think we can get you two hundred a shift." He threw in the bonus plan: "Plus, all the free toto you can eat."

"I'll pass."

Tony looked at me. "Are you crazy?"

Pelón said, "What're you gonna do for money? Shit gold?"

It was risky, especially since I still didn't know which way was up, but I said, "Don't wet your hanky over me, Pelón. I got forty grand stashed."

Pelón turned his ear. "Forty thousand? ¿Dónde?"

"Your friends, the dirty cops, Coltrane and Johnson. They're holding it for me. I'm getting it back from them."

Pelón lowered the binoculars. "You gonna do *what*?"

I repeated. "I'm getting my money back. From the narcs."

Pelón looked at Tony.

Tony shrugged.

Pelón cocked an eyebrow at me. "Is you been smoking the crack pipe? They not gonna give you that money back."

"They're not *giving* me anything, Pelón. I'm taking it. It ain't theirs to give."

"And how you gonna do that?"

"Don't know yet."

Pelón made a gesture with his lips that meant, "Bullshit." He raised the binoculars. "Mira joven, no hable tanta mierda. You want my advice?"

"I live for it."

He paused. "Forget about that money. And stay away from those cannibals. I might not be around next time to bail you out."

That felt like a threat. "You wanna talk jobs, Pelón? How 'bout we talk about this casino job, finally, huh?"

"Shhhhh!" He dropped the binoculars to his chest and looked around to see if anyone heard. "Why don't you put it in the newspaper?"

"Talk."

"This ain't the place, Eduardo. Squash it."

"Don't talk to me about no two-bit hump tossing boners out of a strip club, Pelón. Two hundred a shift ain't shit. I came to this city holding forty large, and I ain't leaving without it. I don't care whose wig I gotta peel."

Pelón looked at me like he wanted to slap the bold right out of my mouth. Then he raised the binoculars. "Antonio, your friend got a dangerous tongue."

Tony put a hand on my shoulder. "Come on, bro, chill."

I shrugged him off. The old man focused, or pretended to focus, on the track again. It seemed to me that there were many pieces left in the match between me and Pelón. But by my estimation at least a couple of pawns had just gotten lost.

The horses came out for the fifth race.

Pelón said, "¿Dónde está mi numero trece?"

Curly-Q was the last to come out.

Pelón checked the board and cursed. "Coño, eight to one. And he's gonna get the outside post. Maldito sea. Number three's the favorite, six to five."

The other horses went into the gate. Curly-Q acted like he didn't want to go. The jockey nosed him in, but Curly-Q backed up, like he sensed something invisible to humans.

Pelón watched through binoculars. "C'mon, papi. Métete."

The horse finally went in.

Pelón thanked God. He looked over his shoulder. In Spanish he said, "For a second I thought he stuck it up our ass."

Tony winced. "That woulda hurt."

Pelón went back to the binoculars. "C'mon, caballito. Win this one for papa Pelón, OK? No me engañe."

Tony clapped. "C'mon, Curly-Q. Fuck them other horses up."

The herd roared out of the gate. In half a second Curly-Q was in the middle, on the outside, away from the rail. There appeared to be nothing wrong with him. Whatever spooked him at the gate was over. His only visible problem was that half the other horses were out in front.

Tony held his chin. "That don't look good."

Pelón said, "It's early," although he already sounded less confident than a second earlier.

The horses rumbled round the first turn.

Pelón said, "Number three's on the rail."

Curly-Q began to fall back.

Tony said, "Shit!"

Curly-Q remained on the outside. He was still with the pack, but in an apparent battle to avoid dead last.

Tony made a face. "This blows."

Pelón slapped Tony's shoulder with a mangled racing form. "You mouth is bringing us bad luck! Shut up!" He followed with the binoculars, urging the horse with a whisper. "Suelta, caballo, suelta."

The pack went into the last turn in a cloud of dust.

"Suelta."

The race was in its final seconds.

"Dale, dale, dale."

And that's when it happened. The curvature in that final turn acted as a slingshot. Curly-Q began to move.

Pelón raised the volume on his whisper. "Dale, Curly-Q. Aquí viene."

Tony grabbed my forearm.

Curly-Q unleashed the thing that had been buried in its heart. It beamed ahead of the pack to challenge the favorite.

Pelón hopped. "¡Qué lindo!"

The horses pounded next to each other in a magnificent whirlwind. The jockeys spanked ass.

"¡Vuela caballo!"

And Curly-Q obeyed. From where we stood, it seemed that his feet did not touch the ground. The leaders crossed the finish line right next to each other. Tony's nails dug into my forearm.

Pelón grabbed Tony's other arm. "It's a photo finish!"

We watched the board. Number 13 came up the winner.

Pelón, the senior citizen with a fractured hip, jumped like a teenager. "My baby did it by a nose!"

Tony said, "We won? We won!"

The winners jumped and hugged and laughed.

"Sweet mother of mercy," said Tony. "We fucking won."

Pelón informed him, "And at eight to one! Not bad." He looked at me. In Spanish he said, "So how does that look?" He nodded at Tony. "Let's collect."

Back in the limo the winners glowed. Tony fanned himself with his eight thousand dollars. Back at the track, when he cashed in, he offered me a thousand, for the fuck of it, but I shook my head and said something about not having earned it.

Pelón was not impressed. Now, in the limo, the seventy-two-thousand-dollar champion pulled deeply on his cigar. "Don't you wish you put a little something on old Pelón to win?"

It would be a lie to say that I wasn't jealous. It occurred to me then that if I were to choke the life out of the old man right at that instant, I could get my forty G's back, plus a fat piece of interest. The only problem was what to do with his driver. And how would Tony react? Plus, there had been all those witnesses that saw us together at the racetrack. And the track must've had cameras too. Once they found his body, my mug shot would be all over the news. Killing Pelón in that instant was not practical.

"I'm happy for you, Pelón. You had a big night."

Pelón bit the cigar. He shook his head and grinned. "You got balls of ice, don't you, Santiago?" He pointed the wet tip of the cigar at me. "Pero no te preocupe. Tonight was chump change. You'll see."

Just then, the limo began to wheeze. It sputtered and the engine died. The driver coasted us to the shoulder. A honking semitrailer came so close, it rocked the limo.

Pelón lowered the partition. "Gordo, ¿qué carajo está pasando?"

The driver looked embarrassed. Pelón's pockets were flush with Curly-Q money. But Pelón's limo, his driver informed him, had just run out of gas.

CHAPTER 10:

WORKING-CLASS DOGS

Pelón was right about one thing: I could not shit gold. The cash I scored from him that first night would not last. My room was paid one month in advance. I'd already used about half a week. I sure as shit didn't want a longer stay than that. But it *was* possible that I would need more time, and definitely more cash to hold me over.

I checked the want ads. Everybody wanted credentials, experience—and was unwilling to pay shit. One warehouse needed someone to do heavy lifting, and I wasted no time getting to a pay phone. The woman who answered must've been sick of interruptions, because before I got two words out, she squawked, "It's filled!" and hung up. I threw the paper in the garbage and decided to pound the commercial areas and just fill out applications.

Every application looked pretty much the same: WORK HISTORY? None. EDUCATION? None. EVER BEEN CONVICTED OF A FELONY? Oh well. Most times they ask this, they leave space for you to explain. I doubt there's anything you could fit on that one line, or in the narrow rectangle they sometimes provide, that would make them overlook violent felonies. I figured they'd check my record anyway, so I answered honestly. A manager or someone would then take the application, eyeball it, smile, extend a hand, then tell me they'd keep it on file. Naturally, it didn't take too many such encounters for me to rethink the gig at the strip club.

But I didn't want to get any deeper with Pelón. I pounded the sidewalk.

On Hubbard Street, just north of the railroad tracks, workers from some kind of plant collected around a lunch wagon. They ate, smoked, and cussed. I asked if their plant was hiring.

They locked their faces like I'd said, "All right if I bang your wife?"

No jobs, they said. Not hiring. No hay trabajo.

I paid for a tuna salad sandwich and an orange juice and asked the lunch wagon man if he knew of any place hiring.

"The Polack say he fire a dude yesterday. On account of his drinking."

"The Polack?"

"He run a small ink shop down here. Near Oakley."

I memorized the approximate address and description, and headed west. The juice was warm. The bread was soggy. I wolfed it as I walked.

Blutarski was a big-chested man who wore his shirt open to the sternum, even though gray had overtaken most of the wheat fields that once waved across his chest. The hair on the top of his head was still a dark yellow, which looked as if it came from a bottle. It was thick. He wore it Bryl-creemed into a pompadour. He smelled strongly of body odor and did not bother to stop rolling fifty-five-gallon drums into a corner of his shop. His tone was skeptical.

"Ever mix ink?"

"No, but I could learn."

"You drink?"

"Almost never."

Sweat beaded on Blutarski's upper lip. "I don't mean when you're out trying to get some you-know-what. What a man does in his off-time is his business. I mean while you're at work. I don't need no lush falling into my machine."

"Not a problem."

"I ain't insured for that. You sue me, you ain't gonna get squat."

"I hate courtrooms."

"You mind getting dirty?"

"Wouldn't be the first time."

Blutarski nodded. "It's long hours on your feet." He looked at my boots. "Those things may as well be tissue. You'll need a pair of steel-toes."

"I been wanting to get a pair."

Blutarski breathed heavy through his nose. He stood next to a fifty-five-gallon drum full of ink and tapped it with a long spatula. I got the sense he sifted his memory of the work to find the right questions.

"How good are you at arithmetic? Simple fractions?"

"I got my GED. And I like to play with numbers."

Blutarski cleaned the spatula with a solvent, wiped it on his smock, and spoke without eye contact. "I can see how good you are with numbers, you coming to me sniffin' for a job." A bead of sweat wound over his pale white temple. He pointed the spatula. "Grab that smock over there, let's see how you stand."

The job title was assistant mill hand. Basically, all I did that first day was watch Blutarski mix ink in different proportions. So many parts this, so many parts that, voila: you got something new. Near the end of the day, he handed me a box with some small cans of ink and asked me to deliver them to a nearby print shop.

"After that, go home."

I hung the smock where I found it. Blutarski counted out half a day's wages, clocked at ten dollars an hour, cash.

"I open up at seven in the morning. Wear something old, 'cause you'll be into the ink. I don't pay you to nod."

I told him he wouldn't be disappointed.

"Somehow, I doubt that."

I delivered the cans and caught the Western Avenue bus. There were plenty of empty seats, but I rode on my feet, all the way home.

An ugly kid in need of skin care slid the tray with my burger, fries, and Dr Pepper across the counter. I sat in a corner, away from the other diners, and settled in with a paperback. When I left the story, the woman told the man, instructed him really, about the differences between love, skin hunger, and temporary kindness. I picked it up again and read only one paragraph before a black hand yanked the book away.

Coltrane and Johnson, the dirty cops who stole my money, stood in front of me. They grinned. Johnson, the African-American with the big belly, cocked his head.

"We cut in on a good part?"

Acid sloshed in my stomach. I snatched the book, though Johnson didn't try to keep it. His other hand held a cone of soft-serve vanilla ice cream. He licked it.

Coltrane, the white narc, nodded at the food on my tray. "You better make that order to go, Santiago."

"I ain't going anywhere."

Johnson put his free hand in his pocket, almost as if to restrain himself.

Coltrane amped his insincere grin. "It wasn't an invitation."

I had practiced what I might say, how I might react, if I crossed these two again. I narrowed my eyes. "Drop the routine, Coltrane. I ain't impressed."

Johnson took his hand out of his pocket. "You want the bracelets again?"

I looked Johnson in his bulging eyes. "You forget I've seen your best shot."

Johnson took a half step toward me. Coltrane put his arm out and stopped him.

Johnson got up on his toes. "I'll shove this ice cream up your ass, Santiago."

"Yeah, and your wife'll lick it out."

His eyes bulged even more.

Coltrane chuckled and pushed his partner farther back. He turned to me. "You're lucky I don't let him mop this room with you. All's we wanna do is talk."

I gestured. "The floor is yours."

Coltrane looked around the fast-food joint. "Not in here."

"Too many witnesses? I ain't getting in your car." I thought for a moment, then pointed across the street. "Over there. In the park. Under the streetlamp."

*   *   *

The two cops spread out on a bench. Coltrane stretched his long legs, and pretzeled his cowboy boots out in front of him. Johnson's gut was like a beach ball wedged beneath his tits.

Johnson spoke to his partner. "We shouldn't be doing this out here in the open."

"It's his neck, not ours," said Coltrane.

I stood in front of them on the sidewalk and held my dinner in a paper bag. "The clock is ticking."

Coltrane looked at his boots. He untangled and rewove them, which shifted him from one heel to the other. "You been catching up with your friends?"

"I was at work all day."

"On what?"

"Making an honest living."

Coltrane smirked. "Fat chance. How's 'Cueball' doing?"

"Pelón? Living large. As far I can tell."

"Is that right? We hear he's broke. His debits have overtaken his credits, and he owes the wrong people."

Johnson licked his ice cream. "Your boy's bleedin' like a stuck pig."

"He ain't my boy."

I flashed to the image of Pelón sprawled in the back of his limo, his pockets bulging with seventy-two thousand dollars' worth of racetrack money. Now these two were saying he had money problems.

"What the fuck do Pelón's finances have to do with me?"

Coltrane said, "He told you about any irons he's got in the fire?"

"Meaning what?"

"Any big plans?"

Right there, I figured the cops knew about the casino. "You got Pelón's number. Whyn't you call him and ask?"

Johnson shook his head. "We're asking you, smart-mouth."

"I don't know shit about Pelón's business. He don't tell me squat. Why would he? I hardly know him."

Coltrane studied me. He no doubt looked for signs, tics, gestures, to reveal when I lied. I breathed naturally and didn't turn away. But Coltrane was a patient inquisitor. He went through a ritual where he dug out the tobacco tin, broke off a piece, wadded it like a gumball, tucked it between his cheek and gum, put the tin away, and spit without ever speaking or taking his eyes off me. Finally, he said, "What about your friend Pacheco?"

"What about him?"

"He mention anything?"

I blinked. "About what?"

Coltrane smiled. "You tell me."

I remembered the reckless way Coltrane shook the dried rose petals from my mother's Bible. I rubbed my nose. "Listen, Detectives, my food is getting cold."

Johnson put the last tip of the ice-cream cone in his mouth and leaned forward. His belly shifted on its axis. "Santiago, you think Pacheco's got your back? That he's your homeboy? Y'all did time together and all that? He ain't no friend to you."

"What's that mean?"

Johnson began to say something, but Coltrane cut him off.

"Santiago, you know Pacheco better'n anyone."

"And?"

"Connect the dots."

I felt the vise again. The one that squeezed both temples the night my cash vanished. "Coltrane, are you making a specific allegation?"

Johnson slapped his knee. "You must've learned that kinda talk in the prison library."

Coltrane spit. He paused long enough to let the clouds above us make progress. "Santiago, you're the one who needs to get specific. Do you know who Paredes has been talking to?"

"Who the fuck is Paredes?"

Coltrane mangled all three pronunciations. "Wilfredo Paredes. Your man Pelón."

In all those years I had not known Pelón's full name.

Coltrane snapped his fingers. "Who's his Puerto Rican connection?"

I thought, *Puerto Rican connection? For what?* "I don't know shit."

Coltrane put his hands together. "What kind of an informant are you?"

"Informant?"

Johnson cracked his knuckles. "Please be the type I gotta slap around."

I made a face. "I'm not anybody's snitch."

"Yes you are," said Coltrane. "You're gonna be our confidential informant."

They wanted me to spy on Pelón and Tony and provide info. I took a second to let it resonate. "Is that why you have me out here on a busy street? Anybody can see me talking to you."

Coltrane said, "You were the one who didn't wanna go for a ride."

"You're trying to make me a marked man. Setting me up to get hit."

"You've watched too many movies. This is an investigation."

"Of?"

"A conspiracy to commit murder. Maybe you heard about that boy who caught a slug in the back of his head while he shook the piss from his wanger."

"I read about it."

Johnson said, "Punk didn't even get a chance to zip up. Force of the blast dropped him so's his face landed in the urinal. Chipped a tooth on the porcelain."

I held my reaction. I didn't want to give the detectives any reason to probe further. Of course they didn't need prompting.

Coltrane chewed tobacco. "You know, the culprit used a .38? Now, me and Johnson, we see that, we start thinking, 'Dang. Didn't we lift a .38 out here somewhere?'" Coltrane turned to Johnson. "Where's that heater at now, partner?"

Johnson thumbed over his shoulder. "Evidence locker, down at the station."

Coltrane said, "Maybe we should let forensics take a look? What do you reckon they'll find, Santiago?"

I wasn't surprised. Ever since I read about the caliber of the murder weapon, I knew the gun from Tony's Welcome Wagon would resurface.

I tried not to sound nervous. "Detectives, I got nothing to do with that."

"Maybe you never touched that gun," said Coltrane. "And maybe that wasn't even the weapon used to plug pee-pee boy. But the point is, Santiago, and you better listen: *riding in that Caddy with that pistol* equals *possession*. Period. We got you on a CPW, no matter what."

Johnson clapped once. "A felony for you, convict. Grand jury's gonna rubber-stamp it. Wait'll they hear about an ex-felon with a .38 just hours after being sprung. Especially one with your record."

The dicks painted a clear enough picture.

Johnson said, "You're gonna do as we say. Dig into your man's businesses and report every last nugget."

Coltrane spit and leaned back to his original position with his cowboy boots tangled out in front and his hands clasped behind his head. "Cooperate or it's back to the hoosegow."

I felt the hum that comes with the urge to do violence. "I don't think so."

The smile left Coltrane's face. "Excuse me?"

"If you had anything solid on me, Coltrane, you'd say it. You'd use it. You'd say, 'Santiago, we got X, we got Y, we got Z.' You don't. You ain't got shit. You got a gun recovered from someone else's car—"

"Possession—"

I raised my voice a little. "I'll do a possession rap jerkin' off. Possession won't mean shit inside but more juice than I had before I came out. Meantime, I bet the DA's more interested in hearing about two officers coming into a gun, possibly a murder weapon, and letting everybody walk in exchange for cash."

Their faces melted.

I continued: "So? Am I under arrest? When can I talk to the prosecutor? I got a confession to make. It involves bribing two cops."

Johnson's eyes widened. "You talk to anyone about either of us, cocksucker, I'll fucking—"

"You'll fucking what, Johnson? Shit in your pants and beg for a lawyer?"

Coltrane covered his lips with an index. "Grand jury'd never believe you, felon."

"Wanna find out?"

They looked at me. Johnson's mouth hung open.

I felt my blood surge. "Stay off my ass, both of you. You even think about fucking with me, get up early. Better yet, next time, bring my cash. All of it. Otherwise, stay lost."

I turned to walk away. In that moment, those first couple steps, I had the confidence to knock down every tree in the park.

Then Coltrane called after me. He'd regained enough composure to throw one last stone. "Fear of the Lord is the beginning of knowledge, Santiago. Look it up."

I can't explain it, but that one struck between the shoulder blades. I felt the eyes of the universe, and did not look back. I tossed my dinner in a garbage can, and ran to my room.

CHAPTER 11:

THE 1980s

The narcs really did a number on me. I lay in my room with the lights off, no music, not a sound. I was conscious of my breathing, careful to not make noise. My mind twisted upon itself.

Are they listening? Did they bug the room? Is there a camera somewhere?

I looked from my spot on the bed, got up, and with the lights off, I creeped around the tight space silently and looked and searched and felt under the table, under the bed, behind the little fridge, inside the fridge, inside the jamb of the closet door, beneath wherever the carpet was loose. Then I took my new butter knife and unscrewed the plate over the outlet, checked in there. I balanced on the chair, with the room still dark, and reached up to look and feel all around the circular fluorescent bulb. I found nothing. No cameras, no bugs.

They followed me, that much was obvious. They didn't just accidentally wander into that burger joint. I lay down again, quiet and still. My imagination filled that silence with voices I did not want to hear. I turned the radio on low, WFMT, the classical station. Sometimes I listen to this when I need to tone down.

I left the lights off and lay down again. It makes no sense, but I'll say it anyway: the violins in that second song were like sparrows. Some of the weight began to dissolve.

They didn't play fair, those narcs. They leaned on me with that .38 when they knew I didn't have shit to do with that homicide. If they thought they could pin a murder rap on me, they'd drop me in seconds flat. Unless, of course, they really figured me for more valuable on the street than in a cell. But I doubted that.

They said they wanted information on Tony and Pelón. But if they wanted Tony off the street, they had the .38. They recovered it from his car.

And Pelón? If they wanted dish on him, all they had to do was stake him out, tap his phone.

So what then? Why pluck *my* wings?

I lay on the bed and let it swirl. Beethoven surged out of the radio, loud, even though the volume was turned low. I took a break from detection and analysis and let the music fill me. The song crescendoed. I once read that Beethoven went deaf before he composed that piece, and I wondered as I listened, and became infected by its emotion, what is it in certain creatures that they perform better after they crash into a brick wall?

It was obvious that Coltrane and Johnson did not give a shit about removing criminals from the street. They had only one objective regarding Pelón and his big plans,

Tony and his big score, and me and my big mouth: another rip-off.

They said they needed me to be an informant. What they wanted was an unwitting accomplice. A runt to execute their insider trades. I give them details, the whens, the hows. They swoop in with their claws and snatch the goods. That was probably how they built intelligence on my stash. And now they wanted to use me to stick it to somebody else.

I got up and switched to WLS, talk radio, and threw myself back on the bed. This time I was able to shake the narcs. But they had already gotten fat off me once. And everybody knows what happens once you feed a stray cat.

That night I dreamt of the first time. It was the 1980s then, a couple years before Tony and I started burglarizing with Pelón. We lived in a neighborhood that had once been a white ethnic enclave of mostly Italians. Even though Tony and I both started life in Humboldt Park, we met in this neighborhood, where my mother and I moved after my father died, and where Tony ended up in a foster home.

Mexicans and Puerto Ricans, even some Ecuadorians and Guatemalans, had begun to infiltrate the area then, and the Italians could barely swallow it. Their gang had run this universe since the early fifties and they viewed the streets as their birthright. They clung to that turf by beating the shit out of whoever wasn't them. Sometimes they slashed your tires or burned your car where you left it. When they felt *really* proud, they would throw a kitty cocktail—a glass bottle filled with gas and stuffed with a burning rag—through your bedroom window.

Somehow Tony and I survived this environment, and

by the time we were teenagers, we cut our teeth on big Italian titties and ran around with their gang. At first it was nothing. Nickel and dime bags of weed. Every once in a while a dustup with other kids, decked in our colors. We would flash hand signs and shout meaningless slogans.

Our clubhouse was a basement in an abandoned building. We kept weights, dumbbells, and a ratty 'workout bench down there. We would jam to the Police and pump iron. One night Tony and I were down there when a couple of older gangbangers walked in. They were dangerous enough that even now, all these years later, I can't reveal their full names here.

"C" was a blond, blue-eyed Italian who styled his hair like Chachi from *Happy Days*. For a medallion he wore a big Italian cornuto, a horn that hung from the gold chain around his neck. C had a reputation among those who grew up with him for fearlessness. He was in his early twenties then and had already been to prison twice. One time I saw him inject steroids directly into his own neck.

"J" was a squat, American-born Mexican who prided himself on the fact that he spoke no Spanish whatsoever except for a few choice swear words. He referred to other Mexicans as "wetbacks." J had a pig nose and his main role since C's return from prison was to kiss C's ass and laugh at everything that C said.

When C and J walked into our weight room, Tony and I moved right out of their way. C and J pressed the weights we were working with like they were filled with helium.

C, the Italian, talked as he lifted. "You pussies warmin' up with this?"

Tony and I were at the peak of our workout, but I said, "Yeah, warmin' up."

C got up from the bench and punched himself in the chest. "Fuckin' A, eye of the tiger, baby! No pain, no gain, right, spics?"

They stacked weights. Tony and I tried to keep up, but the only thing we did was bulge our eyes and make red blowfish faces.

J, the Mexican, released his high-pitched laugh. "These spics are fuckin' lightweights, right, C?"

"Maron!" said C. "You girls lift like you got a friggin' salchiche shoved up your bungholes."

Tony and I did not want to let C down. But it got to the point where the weights did not move for us. Literally, I could not lift the bar to begin the exercise.

C shook his head and thumbed at me. "I think rubber neck forgot to eat his spinach."

J laughed. Then Tony laughed. Then I laughed, even though I was "rubber neck."

C adjusted the weight and began to do curls and admire his hair in the mirror. "What're you faggots doin' tonight?"

I put my hands in my pockets. "Us? Nothin'. Hanging out, I guess."

"Wanna hang with us?"

Right there, if I ever listened to my mother, the things that she told me to avoid, I would have made a beeline for home. Tony and I glanced at each other.

Tony picked up a dumbbell and started to pump. "What're you guys doin'?"

J produced a plastic bag of white powder. "You lightweights know about this?"

Tony and I did not know heavy drugs yet. The only thing we ever did was smoke weed. A couple times we got drunk on peppermint schnapps.

Tony put down the dumbbell. "What's that? Cocaine?"

J nodded. "Peruvian flake."

I told them that we never tried that, but I don't think they heard. J set up a line and snorted. C put the weights down and followed. Then he set up a somewhat smaller line. He looked at me.

"Your turn, rubber neck."

I looked at the line. It was soft and white. The most innocent-looking thing. I thought I knew what drugs did, that they were bad for you. I saw all the commercials and read the brochures. I was certainly old enough to know better. I snorted the coke.

Before that moment I thought inhaling cocaine might burn, and it did, it does, but not for long. A smooth, cool numbness rushed in to extinguish everything, like menthol, but a thousand times stronger. There was an instant spike in my chest. Parts of me began to tingle. I felt a sudden, instant happiness. I felt powerful. C took his time to line up another bump.

I fake-punched Tony in the arm to show my excitement. "Damn, Tony, you gotta try this shit." My lips felt like inner tubes and I figured that must be good. "Do it, Tone."

Tony's eyes drooped a little. In that moment my mind, my whole life, was a coke-fueled steam engine exiting the station. I wish now that I had left Tony standing there.

"Go on," I said.

Tony looked at me and I nodded. He leaned forward, took a hit, and came up with his eyes wide.

C clapped. "That's the shit, ain't it?"

Tony managed to say, "Uh-huh," and then sneezed.

"Smooth too, right, Tone? Must be some good shit."

C cut two more lines. Thick ones. He looked at me and Tony. "Go."

We snorted them. The shit hit directly in the sinus, and this time it hurt a little. Like a needle that pricks you in the brain. Or a brain freeze from a snow cone, again times a thousand. Tony wore a confused look. His nostrils reddened.

C said, "So?"

I wiped my nose. "Maybe we better slow down."

C laughed and J echoed his laughter.

C looked at J. "All right, brougham. Let's take that ride."

J pulled up in a Chevy Impala that I never saw before. C and I jumped in the back. Tony sat up front. There was a paper bag on the floor by C's feet.

I tapped J on the shoulder. "Whose car is this? Your mom's?"

"Naw, man."

C said, "We found it. Don't ask."

Nickel bags of weed was one thing, but I wasn't up for joyriding in a stolen car.

"I read in the paper that they throw hard time for grand theft auto these days."

C said, "You a lawyer now, motormouth? You see this, J? A Puerto Rican lawyer! Ha-ha!"

J slapped the steering wheel. "Yeah, right. This ain't *The Jeffersons*."

C looked at me. "Repeat after me, Rican. Loose lips sink ships."

"OK."

"Say it!"

"Loose lips sink ships."

"Don't ever forget."

We rode in silence for a while.

Tony said, "So where we goin'?"

I got excited. "We goin' to the show?"

Nobody answered.

"They got a double feature at the State Lake. *Trading Places* and they brought back *48 Hours*."

C said, "We ain't going to no movie, kid."

I looked at the paper bag between his feet. The power and control of the first shot of coke spilled out of me. My heart galloped like it wanted out of my chest. Suddenly, I felt afraid. Tony stared out the window.

"Guys, I think I better go home."

J looked in the rearview mirror. "What, are you high? Nobody's goin' anywhere. We're on a mission."

"Huh?"

C said, "You ain't going anywhere until this shit gets settled."

"What shit?"

C reached down between his legs and picked up the paper bag. He opened it and took out a gun. "Here."

I looked at the piece.

"Take it."

Tony turned to look. We eyeballed each other.

C pushed the weapon into my hand. "It won't bite."

I took it. The handle felt big, rigid, and cold. I'd never held a gun before. C grabbed another one out of the bag and handed it to Tony.

"Here you go, little man."

Tony looked at the gun. He looked at me. Then he reached for it.

I felt a cold sweat form. "What're these for?"

C blew up the paper bag and popped it. Then he tossed it out of the window. "Froggy got a flat over here. Couple porch monkeys jumped him and beat his ass with his own car jack. You believe that shit?"

Froggy was another gang elder, an Italian who had the reputation of being stupid but quick. He got the nickname of Froggy for dodging bullets in front of a disco on Grand Avenue one night after closing, then dodging more bullets a week later while still holding his Italian beef in front of Pepe's, just a few blocks away. As legend had it, Froggy never dropped the beef and actually ate it after the shooting was over.

J, the Mexican, said, "Them fucking coons put Froggy's ass in Cook County. Doctors say he might never walk again."

I felt the gun in my palm.

C cracked his knuckles and said the name of a black street gang. "You know we've always been at war wit them."

I knew that. We were at war. We had always been at war. The country was in a Cold War with the Soviets, the Middle East was at war with itself, and our gang was at war with pretty much every black street gang in Chicago. We were also at war with the Puerto Rican gangs, the Mexican gangs, and most other white gangs. I just did not know how all the wars got started or what the wars were actually about. I said, "So what're we supposed to do now, C?"

C rolled his eyes and the Italian came right out of him. "Maron, it's so easy. You see a nigger, you point, you pull the trigger. You see another nigger, you point, you pull the trigger. Simple." C made a gun with his thumb and forefinger, pointed it, and flicked his index finger to demonstrate just how easy it would be.

At that moment I was already a teenager. I understood that murder was not only illegal, but that it was immoral. I think I even knew that it was absurd, although I don't remember now. In C's universe Tony and I were ultimately spics, less than the dog shit on the bottom of your shoe, barely different from how he saw blacks or anybody else that wasn't him. Why had Tony and I sided with C about anything? I don't know.

I looked at Tony. Tony looked down at his gun. Nobody said another word until we arrived at our destination.

We rolled up on some projects, I won't say which ones. J shut off the lights and cruised quietly up and down the streets until we got to the block he looked for.

C practically whispered: "All right, here we are, get out."

I looked at C. "Why here?"

"This clique hangs up the block. We can't just roll up on them in this thing, they'll hear us."

I said, "So what's the plan?"

"Creep up on them until you get close. Then shoot."

J threw the car into park. C and J looked at me. Tony kept his face toward his lap.

"Don't worry," said C. "Once you start capping, we'll be right there to pick youse up."

J said, "Don't let go of the guns. Make sure you bring them back into the car. We'll get rid of 'em later."

Neither C nor J had anything else to say. The engine idled.

Finally, C leaned past me and opened my door. "Go on, Eddie. Earn those stripes."

I looked at Tony. He had his back toward me. I exited the car, shut the door soft, walked around to the passenger side. My knees wobbled. Tony looked up with those big, sad eyes.

"You coming?"

Tony slouched like a tired old woman. C patted him on the back.

"Go on, little man."

Tony opened the door, got out, and closed the door softer than I did.

J repeated his admonition about not losing the guns.

We walked down the dark, empty street, toward the courtyard. Up the street we heard music from a boom box, voices in an African-American Chicago accent, with its twinge of the South. Shouts and laughter echoed off concrete courtyard walls.

Tony and I crept across the street. We ground broken glass beneath our feet as we slithered and crouched behind parked cars to watch.

They were kids, all of them. Maybe thirteen to seventeen years of age. They wore their gang's colors, and lurked late, but they looked no more sinister than our own crew. A few collected around a cardboard box set up as a table. They sat on milk crates and played cards near the wall. Others gathered around a piece of linoleum and break-danced.

I looked at Tony. His eyes watered. I wanted to cry, too, but held it in. I tapped Tony on the leg and whispered, "What're we gonna do?"

Tony shrugged his shoulders. Snot dripped out of his nose.

I looked at the break-dancers. One of them did a move

called "the Snake," where he waved his entire body across the linoleum. It was Tony's signature move; he had nearly perfected it. In a time of peace we might have joined those kids or maybe battled them on the dance floor as friendly rivals. I thought about C back in the basement, the way he pressed our dumbbells like they were made of aluminum foil.

"Tony, we gotta do it."

He did not respond. I grabbed his chin. He looked at me. I showed him the gun in my right hand. He lifted his like it weighed fifty pounds.

I held up my left hand. Three fingers. Two fingers. One.

Headlights suddenly shone down the street, aborting our attack. A car turned onto the block and creeped in our direction. I put my hand on Tony's shoulder and we froze. We watched the car roll to a complete stop in front of us, maybe ten feet away. It was an Electra 225—a "Deuce-and-a-quarter"—loaded with black men. The driver powered his window down.

One of the dancers stopped in mid–pop-lock and ran to the Electra.

The driver had a deep voice. "What up, shawty?"

"What y'all need?"

"Ten nics."

"Dang, y'all finnin' to get high' 'an a muthafucka."

He reached in his pants and counted out ten nickel bags. The driver handed him the cash. "Stay up, shorty mac."

"Aw'ight."

The break-dancer hustled back. The Electra zoomed off. Tony and I were alone again.

I looked at him. There was no use waiting. I held up the three fingers again. Two fingers. One.

*   *   *

We crossed the street, entered the courtyard in short, quick steps. Most of the kids had their eyes on playing cards or dance moves on the linoleum. The music thumped. I pointed my gun toward the crowd of dancers and squeezed the trigger.

PAH!

The first blast was so loud, it kicked up my arm, stung my palm, and startled my eyes shut. I kept them half-closed as I gripped the handle, dropped the gun to position, and squeezed again.

PAH!

Somebody screamed.

PAH!

I heard glass break, more screams, and footsteps in a crazy pattern.

PAH! PAH! PAH!

I emptied the weapon and heard the echoes of the shots and terrified voices that fled as the music continued. I opened my eyes.

What I saw next will follow me to the Gates of Hell: two bodies. One kid facedown on the cardboard, his head surrounded by a fast-spreading halo of blood. Another kid, a card player, slumped against the brick wall. He still held his last hand, although he looked surprised, shot in the eye through the lens of his glasses. His homies had abandoned him at death's door.

All except one.

The kid who sold the nickel bags to the Electra pulled his weapon from his waistband. He raised it and pointed it right at me.

Fire flashed out of the barrel as his first shot startled

me, but missed. I didn't think to squeeze, and it would not have mattered anyway, since my gun was empty. I began to turn, to run, but his second bullet caught me right in the side, by the ribs, so hot and stinging that I landed on my back. The kid pointed the gun out in front of him and flew toward me with eyes of rage.

POP-POP!

The avenger dropped out of the sky and landed on the concrete next to me, a carcass. His weapon landed useless at his side. I looked up. Tony held his gun with two shaking hands. Smoke plumed out of the barrel. Tony's eyes were wide open. I realized instantly that I had not previously heard him fire a single shot.

The Impala screeched to a stop. C suddenly stood over me. He picked me up by the armpits, dragged me toward the car, and yelled at Tony to snap out of it. I remember thinking to hold on to the gun like J had said. They pulled me into the car. Blood was everywhere, wet and sticky. It pasted my flimsy T-shirt to my torso.

I was on my back in the backseat. J stopped the car on a bridge over the Chicago River and threw the guns over the rail. Even in my fever I heard the guns break the surface like turds in a toilet bowl. We took off again and the streetlights passed over me. I thought for sure that I was dying, and felt an odd acceptance about that as I drifted off.

It turned out that it was only a flesh wound. In and out, like an inoculation. I woke up in our basement hangout, stretched out on blankets. C treated the wound with alcohol, peroxide, and Mercurochrome, covered it with gauze, and it was fine. I was thirsty, dehydrated, but otherwise I was OK.

After that, mine and Tony's rank went up. Nobody treated us like peewees anymore, not even C. Froggy came out of the hospital dependent on crutches for a while, but it was never as grave as everyone said. Worse was the fact that he wasn't even sure that the gang we blasted was the one that beat his ass.

C bulged his neck muscles. "What the fuck are you saying, Froggy? Now you don't know it was them?"

Froggy shrugged and bit into his Italian sausage. Tony and I avoided eye contact. C called Froggy a degenerate hard-on.

My mother and I eventually moved out of that neighborhood, to be with our own kind, Puerto Ricans, near Humboldt Park again. Tony ran away from the foster home and came to stay for a time in my room. He eventually returned to his birth mother's house, which wasn't too far away, and we began to hang and make ourselves part of a different, more notorious Puerto Rican gang. History and loyalty in Chicago street gangs sometimes only travels a certain number of blocks.

C and J continued their careers in crime. Each went back and forth to prison on different raps over the years, each time growing more powerful and corrupt. I'm not sure where either of them is right now, but they are not in prison and they are very dangerous to be around.

Froggy, of course, as the joke became, lost the spring in his step after the carjack beating. Somebody who had it in for him saw him leave the shoe store in a new pair of Chucky T Converse All Stars. They followed Froggy and unloaded before he could get to Pepe's for a pizza puff. Every bullet found its mark. Froggy's funeral was closed casket, but according to legend he was buried in his gleaming new All Stars.

Me and Tony? We only had to live with what we did. I committed murder. Tony killed a kid to save my life. It hung between us, unspoken. And even now, all these years later, I don't think either one of us ever forgave me for it.

CHAPTER 12:

SNAKEBITE

The next morning was my first full day at the ink shop. Sweat collected on my upper lip as I walked in forty minutes late. I was prepared to get reamed. Blutarski cradled the phone, scratched on a notepad, and did not look up. He hung up, took more notes, stood without a word, grabbed a newspaper, and walked past me into the bathroom.

I hung around the shop clueless of where to begin. Blutarski ruffled paper on the other side of the thin plywood door. His long, sporadic farts were like a kazoo. I wondered if I was already fired and considered the door.

Finally, the toilet flushed. I didn't hear Blutarski wash, but he emerged with his golden pompadour greased and combed. The folded paper wedged under his wet underarm. A powerful stench wafted after him.

Blutarski hoisted his humongous pants. "Ed, you ever read the *Trib*?"

"Not so much since Royko died."

"That's a long time ago." He studied me through his

bifocals and tossed the paper onto the pile on his desk. He wrapped his belly in an ink-covered smock. "Suit up, Ed." He pointed at the safety goggles. "Put those on, you won't regret it."

I tied the smock and pulled the goggles over my head, relieved.

"Today we mix dark and light. Say you wanna make gray. What would you mix?"

"Half black, half white."

"The right ingredients, I'm mildly surprised. But half-and-half's for coffee. The proportions are infinite. One-fifth/four-fifths, two-fifths/three-fifths, et cetera."

I nodded.

"Now, when you mix dark with light, always begin with light. Always. Add dark as you go." He demonstrated with a little dab of white to which he added black and stirred. The black swirled and disappeared with the white into gray. "Never do it the other way. Add darkness a little at a time."

"How come?"

"The natural properties. Too much dark too fast overwhelms the lighter shades. You do it the other way, you hafta add way more light. To make it shine, I mean."

He collected two cans off the shelves and moved to a machine. He inspected the machine through both parts of his bifocals before he turned it on. Three large metal pins, lathes, like the ones in the old-fashioned washing machines began to spin. The sound was not quite dangerous. The rollers seemed heavy. Their spinning, or perhaps the turning of the gears inside, emitted a low hum that vibrated through the floor.

Blutarski breathed heavily as he inspected the machine. "You got an alarm clock, Ed?"

"I had a hard time waking up today."

Blutarski did not look at me. "Tomorrow you'll be on time, though, right?"

"The early bird gets the worm."

He looked at me over the bifocals. "And the early worm gets eaten."

The machine Blutarski used to flatten ink was a horizontal mill, also known as a three roller mill.

"You can figure out why." Blutarski indicated the three rollers the way a spokesmodel shows a product. "The purpose of these is to grind out impurities. The best advice I can give you, Ed"—he pointed at a certain section—"avoid getting any part of your body, any loose clothing, anywhere near that spot."

"Why?"

"That's the nip point."

"Meaning?"

"Too close and them rollers'll nip ya to pieces."

"Did you make that up?"

"Test it and see." Blutarski pointed out the safety controls and emergency stops. "Good for you to know where these are, Ed, but to be honest, if you get to where you gotta hit them buttons, your head's already under the truck."

Blutarski lectured about bases and agents, viscosity and dispersions, runnability and grind. He used a big spatula, which he called a knife, to dollop ink onto what he called the feed roller.

"Any asshole can read a color chart, can mix ink. It's the finesse, the patience. That's what lifts your ink to the proper level."

* * *

So it went for the rest of the week. Blutarski, the bottle-blond pompadour, worked his jaws. He talked and talked. I listened. He let me try my hand at mixing, sent me on deliveries. At the end of the day, I smelled of sweat, and felt depleted. The ink got under my fingernails. In the evenings I showered, sat around my room, ate, listened to music, and read.

I began to set my alarm clock for five. In the mornings I ran, stretched, did push-ups and crunches before work. I tried to not dwell on the situation with Little Tony, the narcs, Pelón, and my missing money.

But the frustration was there. The injustice. The anger. I couldn't see any angles. For me to figure a solution, it would have to come from somewhere deep. Right then, my rational mind was tapped out.

It was enough for me to focus on the job. A couple times Tony came around at night and whistled and honked his horn from the street. I pretended not to hear. Another time he found the downstairs door open, and came up to knock. I remained in bed with the lights off and was able to stay still and silent to fake like I wasn't there.

I listened to Tony run down the stairs. Shortly after, I heard him run back up. He slipped a piece of paper under my door and split. I waited until I heard him fire the engine and peel off before I got up to see what it was.

He left a note that read: *Hope you didn't leave town. Call me.*

I balled the paper and threw it in the plastic grocery bag that hung on my doorknob as a garbage pail.

*   *   *

It wasn't just that I was angry with Tony. I was also confused. It was obvious after Coltrane and Johnson's little visit that turning people against one another was exactly their style, their MO. That made it more likely that Tony had set me up. I didn't want to think that, but I did.

I knew I wouldn't be able to just cut Tony out of my life. If I kept him close, I could learn more than if I shoved him off. For me to recover my money, Tony would more likely play a part than not. I needed to bring him close again.

That Friday Blutarski paid me four hundred dollars in cash. "Taxes and all that other shit's your problem."

I thanked him and folded the money into my pocket.

"And don't spend it all. Next week I might not have forty hours for you."

I nodded. We wished each other a good weekend. The first pay phone, I dialed Tony's cell.

"Who is this and where the fuck are you calling from?"

"You always talk this tough?"

Tony said, "Coño, perdido, where you been?"

"Working."

"Pelón says he ain't heard from you."

"He hasn't. I got this job on my own."

"Doing what?"

"Mixing ink."

"I never heard of that."

"Me neither. It just came up."

"You like it?"

"It's all right. You going out tonight, Tone?"

"Say the word."

"Any live salsa in this town?"

"There's a couple spots. But you gotta dress. I'll come pick you up."

Tony knew which stores to go to at the mall. I looked at different pants, dress shirts, but the tags made me leave the best ones on the rack.

Tony said, "You don't like that shirt?"

I rubbed the tip of my thumb with my index and middle finger.

"Expensive?" He looked at the tag. "Eddie, that's what shit costs these days."

I told Tony how much I made at the ink mill.

"I don't know why you bother. Today, don't worry about price. This gear's on me."

"Tony, I can't—"

"Get over the humble act, bro. Prom night's over and you already got your first blow job. Let me spend. Otherwise, I'm just gonna grab whatever I want, and it might not be to your taste."

I tried on different pants and shirts. Tony picked out a couple suits for me. I checked myself in the full-length mirror. Tony helped me straighten the back of the jacket.

"How's it feel?"

"Smooth."

We both looked at my reflection.

Tony said, "Take that, it was made for you." He held up another suit. "This pinstripe too. *Sopranos*, papi. Now come on." He turned and walked toward the register. "Let's wrap it up before everyone thinks we're homos."

Tony bought me suits, dress shirts, ties, T-shirts, dress socks, underwear, and a couple belts. For a kicker he bought me a long black leather trench coat. I bought myself a black leather sport coat.

Tony shook his head when I tried on the leather trench. "I'm too short for that style," he said, "but you're killin' it."

We went to a shoe store. Tony asked to see a variety of Italian leather shoes in my size. Seven different pairs. The salesgirl went to the back.

I pointed at a snakeskin cowboy boot. "Tony, who's that shitkicker remind you of?"

"You want a pair?"

"No. We gotta talk."

"About?"

I looked around first to make sure we were alone. "Coltrane and Johnson."

Tony turned in his seat to face me. "What about 'em?"

"They came to see me."

Tony's eyes hardened. "When?"

"A few days ago."

"What'd they say?"

"They wanted to know about you, Tone. And especially about Pelón. What you guys are up to."

"Is that right?" Tony's eyebrows met in the center of his forehead.

"They asked about any 'big plans.'"

"What'd you tell 'em?"

"You gotta ask? I told 'em I didn't know shit."

"Is that exactly how you put it?"

"I told them I didn't know anything about you or Pelón. 'We're old friends,' I told 'em. That's it."

"Think they bought it?"

"Of course not. They know you and I got the same rap sheet."

"*Almost* the same. But what made them think you'd turn trick, Eddie?"

"They threatened me with that beautiful .38 you stuck me with. Said they're thinking about having it finger-printed. Maybe it was used to cap that kid in the park."

Tony's eyes didn't move. They didn't widen and they didn't turn away. He barely blinked. "They are blowing mucho smoke up your ass." He thought for a moment. "Did you ask them about your cash?"

"They didn't wanna talk about it."

"There's a surprise. How'd you leave it?"

"I told 'em I'd never sell out. They got a case, bring it. I got nothin' to say."

Tony tapped me on the knee. "You done good."

He nodded once to let me know that we weren't alone anymore. The salesgirl carried boxes of size twelves.

Tony said, "We'll take them all, honey." He pointed at the snakeskin boots. "And I'll see those in an eight and a half."

"I'll have to check to see if we have them."

"Please do. All of a sudden I'm in a shit-kicking mood."

PART III:

INTERLUDE: AZTEC GOLD

CHAPTER 13:

A TIGHT RED DRESS

We stood on the edge of the crowded dance floor, Tony and I, slick in our new threads, tipsy on Long Islands. A crowd of mostly Latinos swung their hips to piped-in merengue. On the low stage instruments waited.

I clinked Tony's glass. He didn't nod or wink or clink back. All night painted, curvaceous women spun circles, flicked their wrists, and flipped their hair on the dance floor, just two feet in front of us, yet Tony hadn't said a word.

"What's eating you? You been stewing since the god-damn shoe store."

Tony tipped his drink back. He'd already slipped to the bathroom twice to snort coke. I felt good that I hadn't been tempted to join him.

"You pissed about my run-in with the narcs?" I said.

Tony licked his lips and let his brown, sloping eyes drift over. He seemed slow, in spite of all the coke.

"What happens if they threaten to lock you up, Eddie?"

"They already tried that."

Tony turned back toward the crowd. "Yeah, but how you gonna do when they dangle your stash in front of you?"

"You sayin' our friendship has a price?"

Tony looked at me with dilated eyes. "Doesn't everything?"

"You worried?"

Tony slurred a little. "Shiiit. Muthafuckas out here gotta worry about me."

Tony looked in his empty glass. Then he lurched toward the bar. I watched him get swallowed by the crowd, and wondered why a guy I had always been straight with suddenly fronted like I might consider putting a knife in his back.

The live salsa band jumped into a set of covers, classics from the Fania-era. My blood rose. The conguero leaned over shiny black congas and made them chant. I felt a buzz, but at the same time a little jealous of his expertise.

Around the room it seemed no one in the club came alone. There were couples and groups and pairs of friends. On the dance floor men usually led women, although occasionally I saw a woman lead to make it seem that her partner was the compass. Many of the couples who faked their way through merengue were overmatched by salsa. Some men moved with confidence, on beat. The women at their fingertips spiraled like tops, and I was reminded of the times when Chiva and I smoked and danced in my cell. Not with each other, but at the same time, with invisible, imaginary females who followed perfectly.

My glass was low. I wound my way through the turning, writhing, gyrating bodies on the dance floor and leaned against the bar to order. That's when I noticed the woman in the tight red dress. She sipped a drink, and talked with another female.

We made brief eye contact; then she turned away, but not before I copped a smile. The red dress was low enough to show the tops of her big brown breasts. I ordered a shot of tequila, then looked again.

The woman in red was thick, the way I like. Hips like a stand-up bass. Brown, but not Caribbean brown, African, or even mulatto. She was Mexican brown. Mestiza. But not too Indian. Her cheekbones, the length and shape of her nose, the deep, silken blackness of her hair—every feature echoed Aztec ancestors.

The woman focused on her friend and did not look at me, but I could sense that she was aware of my up-and-down. My tequila arrived and I threw it back. After a while she looked in my direction again, looked directly at me, into my eyes, on purpose, for a solid beat, then turned away, this time without smiling. She talked to her friend, but flicked her black hair away from her face in a way that accentuated her elegant profile.

I tried to think of something clever to open with. I noticed that she was moving gently, almost imperceptibly in time to the music. I stepped over and cut into the conversation.

"Excuse me, trigueña, you wanna dance?"

She tilted her head slightly and blinked her answer, then placed her drink on the bar, and covered it with a napkin.

I leaned in her ear because of the music. "Why'd you do that?"

She touched my forearm and spoke close to my ear. "You never know when somebody might try to slip you something."

"That little napkin?"

"It's a deterrent. Plus, this way the bartender won't take it away."

She handed her girlfriend her purse. I took her hand and pulled her brown thickness to the center of the pulsating dance floor.

The thing about dancing salsa, it can be very instinctive. For some it's in the blood. Even so, if you don't practice, it can be very hard to feel exactly what you're supposed to do. The timing can be off. It's worse if you're a little drunk. That first step especially can be a tricky one.

I stood in front of her, resisting the urge to look down into her ample bosom. I held her hand and the small of her back, and stalled for a couple beats longer than I should have. The woman grabbed the lead and got us moving. I fell in step and she yielded the lead, which I felt in my hand. We moved back and forth in synch, a very basic step.

I spoke over the music. "You're wearin' the hell out of that dress."

Her smile had less volume than when she spoke to her friend, but it was there. She wore dark maroon lipstick, and eye makeup that reminded me of Cleopatra. "Can we not talk and dance at the same time?" she said.

I tried to turn her, but it was awkward and took us off beat. I would've felt embarrassed except that we jumped back on beat together, easily. I released her hand and she did some steps. I did my own, sometimes imitated hers, or added variations. A couple times she flashed a playful smile. She turned and I turned, and she turned and I turned, and we fell in step, together. No static. Just the eyes connecting in flashes, and a wordless conversation on the dance floor.

*   *   *

The song finished and we finished with it, on beat, but without too much flourish. The salsera in the red dress turned her smile down completely, businesslike. She fanned herself and lifted her hair away from her neck.

I asked if she needed a drink.

"Still got my Cosmo."

We made our way back to her friend.

I ordered a beer and introduced myself.

She told me her name was Xochitl.

"*So*-what?" I said. It sounded like she said *So-chee*. "Spell that for me."

She did.

"What kind of name is that, Xochitl?"

"Náhuatl."

"Does it mean anything?"

"If I tell you, you'll just say something corny."

Xochitl didn't introduce me to her friend—a black girl who looked bored—but I didn't care. I kept my eyes on Xochitl. She sipped her drink and watched the crowd.

I made a comment about how cool the club was, and Xochitl just nodded. I asked if she came often.

"Do they have a poster in the men's room with all the same questions?" she said with a slight, mischievous smile. "Let me skip ahead: I'm a Gemini."

"I can tell." Xochitl and I'd had nice communication on the dance floor. Now I was lost. "You're a pretty good dancer, Xochitl."

She thanked me in that way that people do when they're accustomed to compliments. I decided maybe Xochitl was a little stuck-up.

A guy on the dance floor led his partner and did fancy footwork. I pointed my drink at him. "You like that style?"

"He's all right. Kind of busy. Not a lot of people here dance on two, though. He must be from New York."

I was not sure what Xochitl meant by that, just a vague idea. While Chiva did occasionally count, his method of musical instruction did not involve as many numbers as you might imagine.

"I haven't danced in a long time," I said.

"It shows." Xochitl giggled. "I'm just teasing you. Actually, you have a pretty strong beat."

"Yeah? Maybe you can teach me some of your moves."

Xochitl crinkled her nose. "Better if you take a class."

I sipped my beer and tried to think of what else to say. Xochitl seemed a little icy, but a little flirty too. I might have walked away and looked for something easier, but I really liked the way she hugged the inside of her dress. She had given me just enough lead for me to keep circling.

Xochitl asked if I was Puerto Rican.

"To the bone," I said. "And you?"

She raised her fist in a Black Power salute. "Viva México."

"Figured." Her voice was a little nasal, feminine, but also a little husky. "You got a bit of a rough voice, Xochitl. I like that."

"My sister says I sound like Ana Gabriel."

I didn't know who that was. "You from the North Side, Xochitl?"

"My people are White Sox fans."

"South Side?"

She nodded.

I glanced at Xochitl's calves again. They had a nice big

shape, but not too big. Firm. And shaved, with no nylons. I wondered about the rest of her.

"How about you?" said Xochitl. "Where do you live?"

I wondered if that was a come-on. Like, maybe Xochitl was interested in leaving the club with me. I told her where I lived.

She rolled her eyes. "Ugh. I hate that neighborhood."

I could've asked why, or told her that the area had changed, but I didn't. Instead, I sipped my beer and looked around. It occurred to me to ask Xochitl where she learned to dance.

She sipped her drink. "I took lessons. That's why I recommend them."

We stood next to each other for a while, although not together. Xochitl drifted into conversation with her friend. I figured her for not interested. Another man asked Xochitl to dance, and she lazily refused. Then a Marc Anthony salsa came on, and she tapped me on the arm.

"C'mon, we can't let this one pass."

My heart didn't skip, but it did speed a little. I left the rest of my beer and followed her. Xochitl and I murdered it on the dance floor. We tore the song apart. By the time Marc Anthony emoted and the music rose, I felt warmed up, loose, in rhythm and in synch with Xochitl. It turned me on that after I made the first move, she now took the initiative to invite me back to the dance floor. The song finished and Xochitl and I returned to the bar.

"That was the best set of the night," I said.

Xochitl fanned herself. "You're pretty good once you get warmed up." She took some napkins from the bar and wiped my forehead.

I smiled at her. She smiled back.

Xochitl picked up her drink again. "So, Eddie, what do you do?"

I'd already spoken with a couple of other females that night and had practiced an answer. "I'm in the ink business."

"Ink? As in pens?"

"Printing. It's a real growth area."

"You wouldn't think so," she said. "With all the advances in desktop publishing."

"Yeah, well…how about you, Xochitl? You got a job?"

"I work in a law firm. Office administration."

I could've asked Xochitl what that meant, but I didn't care. The tight red dress was wrapped around the contours of her belly, and I had always liked a woman with a handful of stomach.

"You got a man, Xochitl?"

She lowered her lids a little and pursed her lips. "Right now, no."

I put my elbow on the bar. "That's interesting."

"Is it?" Xochitl sipped and looked around the room. She looked up at me with the short straw in her fingertips. "You know what I do have?"

"Tell me, Xochitl."

With a hint of Marilyn Monroe, she said, "A twelve-year-old girl, an eight-year-old boy, and a closet full of bills." She sipped her drink to watch my reaction.

I thought about saying how much I love kids, how excited I was about the idea of settling down, but I decided I'd appear more sincere by simply saying that it all sounded tough. "What are you trying to tell me, Xochitl? You drive a hard bargain?"

She smiled mildly. I watched her pick the cherry out of the bottom of her glass and bite it from the stem.

"You want another drink, Xochitl?"

"Water. I gotta drive."

We waited for the bartender. There was a large Art Deco mirror behind the bar. In it I saw a reflection of Xochitl standing next to me. I know I was a little drunk, but I swore that we looked really good together. Like a handsome couple. Our looks, our bodies, our colors, our features, matched and complemented each other's, as if by design.

I was just about to draw Xochitl's attention to our reflection when I noticed someone else watching us in the mirror. It was Pelón. He stood behind me and over a little, with his hands at his sides, smiling.

I turned to look at him. Pelón walked over, with the cane slung over his wrist. He wore a chocolate-colored suit with a crisp pink shirt and a pink-and-gray striped tie, a pink silk pocket square. He wore no hat, just his bald head reflecting the pulsing lights of the club. He also wore black-and-white wingtip shoes, real throwbacks that looked brand-new.

Pelón extended his hand. "Eduardo."

I didn't shake his hand. "What are you doing here?"

"Antonio tell me he was down here, so I stop by to say hello." He smiled at Xochitl. "¿Y esta dama?"

Xochitl introduced herself to Pelón and shook his claw-hand without reacting to it.

"Ah, Xochitl, yes," he said. "I know this word." Pelón did not release her hand. "Doesn't it mean 'beautiful flower'?"

Xochitl made a face like she was impressed. "Where did you learn that?"

Pelón batted his lashes. "An old man always has secrets. But even if I did not know, m'hijita, one look at you, and I would figure this out." Pelón kissed her hand. "Un placer."

Xochitl batted her lashes back, but I didn't feel that she meant it. She introduced Pelón to her girlfriend. The bartender came, and I ordered water for Xochitl.

Pelón slapped the top of the bar. "Water? Eduardo, these ladies are first-class. ¡Cantinero! Forget water. Bring us a bottle of your best champagne, eh?" He put his hand out to indicate both women. "I invite you beauties to a drink."

Xochitl said, "Champagne? How can we resist?"

The bartender collected Pelón's credit card to open the tab and hopped, popping open a bottle, which foamed. He poured four glasses. Pelón raised his glass to each of the women. "Para la belleza y la juventud. ¡Salud!"

The champagne was sweet, bubbly, and cold. Also, a little bitter.

A Colombian salsa came on. A historical song about a slave rebellion. Pelón said, "Oh no. This is my favorite." He put his glass down, grabbed Xochitl's girlfriend's hand, hooked his cane into the crook of my bent arm, and pulled the woman, without asking her, to the dance floor.

With almost no effort, Pelón led his partner through tight weaves, stops, hops, and turns. Not satisfied, he spun close to me and Xochitl on the edge of the dance floor and grabbed Xochitl by the wrist on just the right beat to make her fall along with the other woman into his groove.

Now Pelón, the senior citizen, led both women, one with each hand. He held his arms above his head and moved both partners merely by using his fingers, including the index finger on his claw, just twirling them. First one woman went one way, then the other went the other way. Then he turned them in the same direction at the same time, then counter to each other, crisscrossing his arms without knocking the ladies into each other. Pelón extended the women out to the end of his reach, then spun them to his chest, like he was romancing them. Sometimes he would release them and do a jig or something hammy like knocking his knees together, hot-stepping the black-and-white wingtips like Cab Calloway in a musical. This went on for ten full minutes as the DJ mixed Colombian-style salsas into one another, including "Llorarás" and "El Preso."

Finally, the mix was over. Pelón removed his pocket square and mopped his head as he flashed his dentures and took a little bow toward each female. The women came back fanning themselves.

I handed Pelón his cane. "What happened to your limp?"

"Se me mete la música." He raised his glass at Xochitl's friend. "And beautiful womans like this? Se me quita el dolor." He put his glass down. "¿El baño?"

I pointed Pelón toward the men's room and he limped off.

Xochitl's friend leaned into her ear and whispered. Xochitl nodded. She tapped me on the shoulder. "Eddie, we gotta go." She put her glass down.

"Don't you wanna dance no more?"

"I'm worn-out," she said. "Anyway, my friend and I came together and her babysitter needs to go home."

I took Xochitl's hand and leaned toward the dance floor. "Just one more."

She pulled her hand back, polite but firm. "I can't. Nice meeting you, though."

"You sure? My friend and I can drive you."

"I have a car."

"I don't mean the old-timer. I got another friend my own age. He can take your girl, get her home safe. I'll catch a ride with you, Xochitl. We can keep talking."

Xochitl smirked. "Yeah, 'cause you're so interested in conversation, right?"

I tilted my head. "Can I get your number?"

Xochitl smiled. "I already burn too many minutes on my cell."

"C'mon, I'll give you a call sometime. We'll meet up right here. Or wherever else there's music. I'm just looking for a dance partner."

After a certain point, for women who look like Xochitl, it must not impress them anymore how bad every man wants to bang them. She crossed her arms. "Why don't you give me *your* number and I'll think about it."

Now I was stuck without a precanned answer. "Actually, Xochitl, I thought I would be the one to call. I ain't got a phone right now."

Xochitl put up an index finger. "I know what that means. A girlfriend or a wife at home."

"That's not true," I said. "I'm just—"

"What? Can't afford a cell phone?"

"No, Xochitl—"

"See? That's why I don't mess around with mero mero machos. Or papichulos. And I *never* talk to married men."

"Xochitl, I'm single. How old are you?"

Xochitl made a coy expression.

"Mid-thirties?" I said.

Xochitl slapped me playfully on the arm. "¡Ándale! Grosero."

"Early thirties?"

She half-closed her eyes. "I've been telling everybody that I'm twenty-nine. Don't call me out."

"OK, Xochitl, so you're young, you're fine and everything, but you're not a baby, right? I can see that. You think I'm fool enough to try and slip something past a mature woman like you?"

"I don't know, Eddie, I just met you. I can't say yet how big a fool you are."

Xochitl sported a tough shell. But it was also clear from the way she looked at me that she was curious. I wanted to grab her full hips.

"Look, Xochitl, I just moved here, OK? I ain't hooked up my new phone yet, that's all."

"You just moved here? From where?"

"Downstate. I was out there with some family and I just decided to give Chicago another shot."

Xochitl angled one eye at me. "That true?"

"This is literally like my first night out on the town. I was planning on hooking up my new phone on Monday."

Xochitl's pursed, skeptical lips slowly gave way to an impish smile. "All right, mister. I don't know if you told a good one or not, but I'll give you my number. Just don't let me find out you're a liar, OK? You got a pen?"

I bit my lip. "Don't you have one in that cute little purse?"

Xochitl shook her head, but dug for one. I scored a book of matches from the bar. Xochitl wrote her name and number in a beautiful cursive on the inside cover and handed it back.

"Nine to five," she said. "Monday through Friday. But you better not be a stalker."

"Not yet, I ain't."

Xochitl pretended to pinch me in the ribs, which was almost better than if she had winked.

"You'll hear from me on Monday," I said.

"We'll see. Nice meeting you."

Xochitl gave a little wave and turned with her friend to make their way through the crowd. I took a real good look at her from the back. Xochitl had big curves right where I wanted them.

I pronounced her name again, *"So-chee,"* and buried the matchbook in my wallet.

Tony came back still tipsy. He had been watching me wrap it up with Xochitl and stood back. "You gonna hit that shit or what?"

I sipped my drink without looking at him.

Tony said, "C'mon, man, I'm sorry about before, OK? You know I trust you."

I looked at him. "You know what, Tony? You're a moody fuck."

Tony did not change his drunken expression.

"Did you see Pelón?" I said.

"He's downstairs in the hip-hop room trying to mack it to some young chinitas."

"Fuckin' asshole tried to cut in on my action. You call and tell him we were down here?"

"He saw my Caddy in the valet lot and called."

I poured the rest of the champagne into my glass and drained it. "Let's leave before he gets back and sticks us with the bill."

Tony shrugged. We headed out. The coat check girl handed us our leathers. We stood in the foyer and waited for the valet to bring the Cadillac around.

People walked in and out of the club. My mind was on thick, brown, curvaceous Xochitl. Just then, I noticed two guys, two cons I knew from prison: Chulo and Bulldog. They were Roach's boys. Chulo and I used to lift weights together. He still looked big and cut. They stood outside the glass door, on the other side of the rope. Roach came from behind and shook hands and chatted with the doorman.

I nudged Tony.

Tony said, "Mo-tha-fuck-er," and pulled his driving gloves on tight.

"Tony, you think there's a back door?"

"A back door for what? I don't run from no one."

The bouncer lifted the rope. Chulo, Bulldog, and Roach walked in. I made eye contact with Chulo. Recognition entered his face and he stopped short.

"Palo."

"What up, Chuló?"

That's when Roach spotted Tony, practically in front of him. Roach's face twisted. "The fuck you doin' in my spot, Little *Ph*ony?"

Tony didn't say shit.

Roach put his finger in Tony's face. I believe what Roach began to say to Tony was "Nigga, I'll peel yo' wig," but Tony blocked the completion of that sentence with an explosive open-hand slap to Roach's face. Roach tumbled backward like a preschooler, upending a table full of flyers on his way to the ground.

After that, it was a tornado of grabbed necks, punches, slaps, kicks, and shoves. Bouncers struggled to keep everyone apart. Eventually, Tony and I got pushed out the front door. Roach and his boys were pushed into the club as Roach pointed at Tony and shouted that Tony was a dead man.

One of the bouncers came outside and told us to get lost, but Tony shouted, "I'm waiting for my *fucking* car, aw'ight?"

The bouncer held his ground, but didn't push it.

The Caddy turned the corner. We jumped in without tipping and split.

I was out of breath. Tony had a bloody lip. He checked himself in the rearview mirror.

"Tony, you know they were about to go through that metal detector, don't you?"

"And?"

"Next time? No metal detectors."

Tony knew exactly what I meant and made a face like he didn't give a fuck.

"This is bullshit, Tone. You gotta make a truce."

Tony grabbed his nut sac. "I got their truce right here."

I shook my head. "This ain't gonna end well."

Tony tuned me out. We drove in silence. I couldn't wait to get to my little room, away from Tony and his crashing rocket. Suddenly, something dark, a blur, shot out from between two parked cars. Tony swerved and braked, but I knew before we heard and felt the *thump* that we would hit it. We got out and checked.

There it was: a cat with its guts hanging out. The tongue protruded and its eyes were wide, like its final thought was *Holy shit!*

Tony nudged the carcass with the sharp tip of his new snakeskin boot. He looked up at me with bloodshot eyes. "You know what sucks most about this?"

"What?"

"That's probably the only pussy I'm gonna see tonight."

CHAPTER 14:

MARGARITAS (WITH SALT)

I spent the rest of the weekend alone with the memory of Xochitl's face, her perfume, the shape she added to the red dress. I wanted to call her right away, the next morning, even though I'd read in countless magazines that women don't go for men who show that much interest. The number Xochitl gave was an office and she would not be there until Monday anyway.

On Monday, Blutarski split for lunch at exactly noon, which was his routine. I jumped in his chair, picked up the phone, and read Xochitl's work number off the matchbook. She answered with that rough voice, but in a businesslike tone.

I said, "Wassup, nena?"

"May I help you?"

"It's me, Eddie."

"Excuse me?"

"Eddie Santiago."

"With what firm, sir?"

"We met at the club?"

"Hold on."

Xochitl switched me to lame music. I squeezed the phone with my shoulder and pulled one of Blutarski's supersharp pencils from the cup on his desk. I drew large circles on a clean yellow pad.

Xochitl came back on the line. "Sir, may I transfer you?"

"Xochitl, are you trying to embarrass me?" I repeated my name and that we'd met at the club.

"Saturday night?"

"No. Friday."

"Which club?"

I told her.

"Hmm. Who did I meet?" She pretended to think out loud. "Oh wait! Are you the exterminator?"

"No."

"The accountant?"

"Uh-uh. We danced, Xochitl, remember? You said I had a strong beat?"

"I say that to everybody. Wait! Are you the guy who just moved from downstate?"

"That's me. The big guy with the goatee."

"You call that peach fuzz a goatee?"

I heard the phone ring in the background. I began to say that I could call back later, but Xochitl threw me on hold before I could speak.

She came back on the line.

I said, "Are we gonna be able to talk like this?"

"The mic is yours."

Just then, I drew a blank. There was a lull in phone calls, so we just floated in that artificial silence that happens when people listen to each other breathe over the line.

Xochitl dropped an abrupt laugh. "You're a regular poet, huh, Eddie?"

I smiled on my end. "Well, shit, now there's pressure."

"Do you suffer from performance anxiety?"

"What?"

Xochitl dumped me for another call. When she came back, I said, "C'mon, Xochitl, whyn't you let me take you out? This is silly."

"Where are you gonna take me?"

I thought about the bed in my little room, but said, "I don't know. Someplace where we can talk."

"Doesn't sound like you got much to say."

I said, "Maybe if I was looking directly at you, I would get inspired," which I thought was pretty good, but I think Xochitl had already dumped me for another line.

Suddenly, I smelled Blutarski. He stood over me. It was the first time since I worked for the man that he brought his lunch back to his desk. I was planted in his soiled chair, cradling his phone with my neck.

Blutarski gave me the "get out" signal with his fat thumb. "Hey, new guy, do I look like Illinois Bell?"

Just then, Xochitl came back on the line. "Sorry, Eddie, I gotta run. Call me tomorrow." She hung up.

The following day I called Xochitl from a public phone.

"You outside?" she said.

"Making a delivery." I'd forgotten that I told her I was in the "ink business."

"What is it you do again?"

I thought to change my answer to say that I was outside traveling to a corporate account. Instead, I said, "I work with my hands, Xochitl. I mix ink."

I explained a little about the process.

"Sounds messy. Do you like it?"

I began to say that it was all right, but Xochitl was already on another call.

When she came back, she said, "That was my daughter. How many kids you got?"

"None."

"Does that mean you don't claim them, you don't pay child support, or you just never gave them your last name?"

"None of the above. I never fathered any."

"How's that possible?"

"It just is."

Xochitl paused. "You never got a girl pregnant?"

"Not to my knowledge."

"Is there a problem with your sperm?"

"Boy, you don't hold back."

Xochitl giggled. "Are you gay?"

"Bite your tongue."

"Hey, you hear stories." Xochitl let the other line ring. "You never been married?"

"I never felt ready."

"At your age!"

"Maybe I just never found the right girl. But I think you've had your twenty questions, Xochitl."

"Something about you don't fit."

"You worried I'm a player?"

"Should I be?"

"Maybe I'm just mysterious."

"Or maybe you're hiding something."

"I guess you won't be able to figure that one out without getting a little closer, will you, Xochitl?"

"Apparently."

We let that one sit.

I said, "So? When are we going out already? I'm standin' in the friggin' rain."

"Invest in an umbrella. Call me tomorrow, Eddie. I gotta run."

An early-autumn chill settled over Chicago. The sky was overcast and gray. I stamped my feet, held the cool receiver to my ear, and wondered again whether Xochitl was worth the two quarters. I was getting tired of the phone. I dropped them and dialed.

"Xochitl."

"Hey."

"It's Eddie."

"I was waiting for your call. Wanna meet after work?"

I warmed up. "Tell me where."

She did.

"I gotta go home first, shower, and change," I said.

"Good. Remember to use deodorant." She said it in a way where I couldn't tell if she was joking. "And please don't be late."

I waited for Xochitl for over an hour. I dipped chips in salsa, nursed a strong margarita, checked and rechecked my new watch. Finally, I accepted that she wasn't coming. I paid the bill, left a weak tip, and walked out.

Xochitl was out on the sidewalk, in front of the restaurant, arguing into her cell phone.

I tapped her on the shoulder. "Looking for me?"

Xochitl signaled for me to hold, then walked away to finish her argument. I heard enough to know that the

other party hung up on her in midsentence. Xochitl re-
dialed and listened intently to the other end.

She left a voice mail: "Now you're afraid to pick up?
Think slamming the phone fixes things?"

Xochitl slammed her cell shut and walked past me.
She put her hand on the door to the restaurant and looked
back. "You need an invitation?"

"I waited over an hour, Xochitl."

"My babysitter fell through," she said. "Is that gonna
be an issue?"

Xochitl didn't wait for my response. Instead, she pulled
the door open. A cool wind hit her just before she stepped
inside, and even though Xochitl's eyebrows were knot-
ted in frustration, her black hair flew. I followed her.

The same guy who seated me the first time looked a little
peeved to see me again. He sat us at the same table. Xochitl
removed her brown leather overcoat. She wore a formfitting
tan turtleneck, a brown leather skirt, brown knee-high boots
with a nice heel. Her makeup was more sedate than it had
been at the club. She put the cell phone down on the table.

"Did you eat?" she said.

I was still a little peeved. "No, Xochitl. I waited for you."

Xochitl clucked her tongue and opened a menu. "Me?
I don't wait for no man."

In the better light of the restaurant, I was able to see
details of Xochitl's face and body that I hadn't noticed
in the low light of the nightclub. She had the very beginning of wrinkles around her eyes. Her face was slightly
chubbier than I remembered. And her hands, her fingers
looked a little rough, despite the manicure. Like maybe
they had seen a lot of work in a sink somewhere. But she

looked good. Real good. I inhaled her perfume and it softened my mood. The waiter asked for our drink order.

Xochitl kept her eyes on the menu and did not acknowledge the waiter. I'd read in some magazines that no matter what the official position, modern women still like for a man to take charge.

I said, "The margaritas are the bomb," and ordered two. The waiter took off.

Xochitl put the menu down. "Normally, I don't drink during the week," she said, "but I guess I could use one." She looked at her cell again.

"You seem distracted, Xochitl."

She put her phone down. "You're right, Eddie. I'm sorry. I shouldn't have made you wait so long. I honestly didn't mean to. I would have called if you had a phone."

Xochitl had a point. "Well, you look beautiful. It was worth the wait."

Xochitl thanked me with a smile that reached her eyes this time. I noticed her many gold rings. She wore a bracelet that had an image of the Virgen de Guadalupe. I reached across the table and let my fingertips barely skim the bracelet. "Gift from an ex-boyfriend?"

"Yeah, right. Some of us work for a living."

"Don't get testy. I guess I'm just wondering who's got you so hot and bothered over the phone."

"Listen, when you have kids with someone, you're stuck with them for life."

"Understood."

The busboy brought corn chips and salsa. Xochitl dipped. I noticed that her long nails changed color since Friday. They were pearl white now, with little gold accents. They matched nicely with her brown-and-gold motif.

Xochitl reached across the table and touched my chin. "So what happened to that fake goatee?"

I smiled. I had wondered whether Xochitl would notice that I shaved it off.

"Me la tumbé."

"Too bad," she said. "I kinda liked it."

The waiter brought our margaritas and asked for our orders. By then, I was not so sure that the magazines had it right when they expounded on women. I decided to let Xochitl order for herself.

The drinks were strong. The material of Xochitl's turtleneck stretched across her chest and hovered over the table. We talked about the fact that Halloween was around the corner, and how afterward the holidays would fly by. Xochitl went into a riff about the pressure she felt to provide at Christmas. I could not relate, but I pretended like I did. I agreed with Xochitl that our own childhoods had been more modest in comparison to the modern generation.

Piñatas hung from the restaurant ceiling in the shapes of burros and wild stars. I told Xochitl a story about the fifth grade, when we made a piñata for a Cinco de Mayo party, and how this blindfolded kid swung wildly with the stick and missed, hitting the teacher's face, cracking her glasses and giving her a bloody nose with one shot. I described how funny it was when the two halves of the teacher's glasses spun across the hardwood floor in opposite directions, and how her eyes looked bugged-out without the glasses. Xochitl covered her mouth when she laughed at my description of the teacher and said, "Pobrecita." She seemed a little rosy-cheeked from the margarita. I didn't tell Xochitl that the kid in the story was me, that the teacher was a bitch, and that I whacked her on purpose, that I could see beneath the blindfold the entire time.

Xochitl said, "Poor kid must've felt terrible."

"Ah, he was one of those kids that was always in trouble."

Xochitl nodded. She told one about a quinceañera where a spoiled girl waltzed in a ball gown, real sophisticated, then tripped and fell with her legs in the air. Xochitl was pretty mocking when she imitated the stiff upper body of the girl as she waltzed.

"When her heel caught that dress and she fell? Everybody saw her pasty legs and humongous ass. Not to mention her grandma panties. Some of us laughed. I mean the shit looked funny. Well, la princesita gets up and runs to the bathroom crying."

"That *was* a hard kick in the crotch for a fifteen-year-old."

"Let her learn. Anyway, they got it all on tape, right? So I keep telling them to send it to *America's Funniest Home Videos*. But the family didn't think it was as hilarious."

"Did everybody get cake at least? With the piñata we never saw the candy."

Xochitl dipped a chip. "You know what? She threw such a tantrum in the ladies' room, they called the party off right away, before cutting the cake. That pissed me off. I had already given my card with the money in it. So I just went over and cut myself a big-ass piece of cake, big enough for me and my kids, got the server to wrap it in aluminum foil, and took it home. We had it for breakfast the next day."

I grinned. "Tú eres mala."

"You never heard of, 'let them eat cake'?" Xochitl had a smile on her face that was the most unguarded so far. She looked right in my eyes as she sipped her drink.

"You," she said, sounding a little tipsy finally, "are a *very* good-looking man."

I resisted the temptation to lick my lips. "It's been a long time since I've heard that."

Xochitl blinked at me real slow. "You just moved here?"

"That's right."

"From where again?"

I paused. I knew Xochitl liked to ask questions, so I had prepared a backstory, just in case. Some women get hot for a guy who's been in a cage. But I figure the more ambitious ones will rarely go for it.

"I told you, Xochitl. I used to live downstate."

"Where specifically?"

"Joliet."

"Really? I got cousins who live down there."

"No shit," I said. "What do they do?"

"Oh, this and that." Xochitl mentioned a couple names.

"Never heard of them. But it's not exactly a small town."

"They're about your age. You grew up there?"

"I'm from Chi-town."

"What were you doing in Joliet?"

"Working."

"Doing what?"

"Odd jobs."

"Like?"

I ran through the résumé of assignments I had as an inmate. Kitchen detail became slinging hash at a diner. The law library became a bookstore. Maintenance became handyman at an apartment complex.

Xochitl sipped her margarita. "Joliet is kind of a strange place to move for that type of work, ain't it?"

I shrugged.

"You had family there?"

"I just needed to get away, Xochitl."

"From what?"

"Myself," I said, without thinking.

Xochitl raised an eyebrow, but let it go. She asked how far I made it in school.

"Not very. I hated homework."

"So your parents just let you drop out?"

"By that time my mother couldn't handle me."

Xochitl's eyes narrowed. "What does *that* mean?"

"Nothing. I just developed a mind of my own is all. I was hard to convince."

Xochitl nodded. "Wish I could say the same."

I asked Xochitl to tell me more about herself. She told me she went to an all-girls Catholic high school. She did well and got a scholarship to DePaul.

"I wanted to be a lawyer."

"What happened?"

"I got pregnant. Eighteen. My husband made me quit."

"You were already married?"

"You know how stupid an eighteen-year-old can be, right?"

"I have an idea." I put my drink down. "What happened with your husband?"

"I'm not sure."

"That's not exactly clear, Xochitl."

She looked me right in the face. "Neither are most marriages. But I don't think it's too smart to talk a lot about past relationships."

I nodded. "Now it's just you and your kids?"

"At one point I went back and tried secretarial school

for a couple months. Wanted to be a legal secretary. But my husband, we started fighting about it. I never went back."

Xochitl took another sip. Finally, she said, "This drink is too strong," and added water to dilute it. She looked at me as she stirred. "You know how it is, Eddie. Some things you just can't start over."

Halfway through dinner Xochitl looked up from her plate. "You been with a lotta women, Eddie?"

"Not a lot."

As an inmate I got an occasional slice. Friends and sisters of other women who came to Stateville to visit boyfriends and husbands and the fathers of their children. I would start them off as pen pals, then get them to visit and sneak me sexy Polaroids. We'd make out in the visiting room until I could get them to grease the guard for ten minutes alone in the bathroom. Over the years I'd lined up a handful of these—you have to, or you'd go insane.

I looked at Xochitl. "I thought you said you didn't wanna talk about past flings."

"I'm not asking for the whole sob story," she said. "I'm curious about lifestyle."

"I been with my share of women."

"Ever been tested for HIV?"

"Of course."

"Results?"

"Negative."

Xochitl ate fajitas like HIV was everyday conversation.

"You always talk so blunt, Xochitl?"

"We're getting to know each other."

I bit into my burrito. "And? What have you learned?"

"Well," she said, "you didn't think to ask me my own HIV status. I think *that* says something."

"Such as?"

"I'm not sure yet, Eddie. I gotta figure that one out."

After dinner I walked Xochitl to her car, a gleaming white Lexus with a tan interior. It had nice rims, and looked well-kept.

"Wow, Xochitl. They must pay pretty nice at that office."

Xochitl barely smiled, and did not offer an explanation.

The car had a sunroof. I said, "Wanna go for a moonlight drive?"

"I can't. I'm up early."

Xochitl unlocked the door and opened it so that it came between us.

I cocked my head. "Am I gonna see you again?"

Xochitl raised her crooked smile. "Call me at the office."

"When?"

"Whenever you want."

She got in the car, shut the door, and started the engine, then lowered the window and extended her manicured hand. I took it.

"Thanks for the company," she said. "It was nice to share a laugh."

I bent close and Xochitl pulled back a little.

"No good-bye kiss?"

Xochitl let her hand rest in mine and gave me the mischievous grin from the dance floor. "Mister, I hardly know you." She pulled her hand inside, powered her window up, and drove off.

CHAPTER 15:

LOVE'S LABOR

I called Xochitl the next day. It was too soon, I knew, but it would be the weekend soon and I did not yet have her home number or even her cell. If I missed her on Friday, the whole weekend would be lost. I explained all of this to her between being dumped for other calls.

She said, "You couldn't wait, huh?"

"I felt a connection. Give me a number where I can reach you after hours."

Xochitl put me on hold and left me there for a long time. I fed quarters into the pay phone and listened to an instrumental version of the Carpenters' "Close to You." Xochitl came back and almost caught me humming.

She said, "It's against my better judgment to give out my number, Eddie."

"Everybody needs to break the rules sometimes, right?"

"You got a pen?"

"You know I don't, Xochitl. But go 'head, give it to me, I'll memorize it."

"You'll forget it. Just call me at work on Monday."

"No," I said, "give it to me. I'll burn it into my brain."

Xochitl recited it. I repeated it. We went over the number until I convinced her that I had it on a mental tape.

"Give me a call tonight, but only if the spirit moves you."

I plopped down at the counter next to Blutarski. He'd invited me out to lunch.

"Big smile," he said. "Get lucky at the pay phone?"

"It's nothing."

"Usually is." He handed me a menu. "This is the best Polish food anywhere. Order what you like, I'm buyin'."

I had the chicken. Blutarski feasted on two huge pork chops smothered in gravy, potato pancakes with sour cream, and something called *goblacki,* which he translated as "cabbage roll." He ordered a beer. Then another. Then another.

I said, "Guess the secret of your health regimen's out."

Blutarski nodded and chewed at the same time, oblivious.

"You eat lunch like this every day?"

"Of course. You need a good meal in you to really work." He pointed a fork at me. "That might be your problem. You're not putting a good meal in your belly when it counts."

Blutarski mopped gravy with bread. With the other hand he held on to a pork chop bone.

I said, "When I was a kid, Italians used to call Puerto Ricans 'pork chops.' Like we were the only ones who ate them."

Blutarski grinned. "I bet that's not all what they called you."

We both chuckled. Blutarski ordered another beer and began to pick his teeth. "My wife used to cook this good. Even better."

"What happened, she retire from the kitchen?"

"She passed away."

"Sorry."

Blutarski grunted. "That's when I start coming here. I used to just go home every day. Twelve o'clock, every day, home for lunch. My wife used to make the best food. Her mushroom soup..." Blutarski's beer came. "It's tough when you get used to a woman's cooking."

"I'll bet."

Blutarski tipped his beer. "It's been four years. Sometimes, you know, I think..."

"What?" I said. "Say it."

"I dunno, Ed. Sometimes I think, maybe I'll go, I'll find myself a new woman. One of these old broads whose husband died and left her a house in Jefferson Park or something."

"Why don't you?"

"The truth? Romance. I ain't got the stomach for it."

"How's that?"

Blutarski squinted and almost frowned. "A woman, in order to really love a man, she needs to feel that you're passionate about her. That she's your everything. That's the only time a woman really releases everything what's on the inside, you know? In that place where she really lives. Behind the eyes."

I picked my teeth. "Boss, I didn't know you were this sentimental."

"That's not it. I've just lived so long now. I'm too selfish. I like too much quiet when I get home. I got used to that. The quiet." He sipped his beer. "I can't see how I could devote enough attention to any woman now."

The waitress, a fiftyish Polish woman with a hairnet, thick nylons, and soft shoes, stacked the plates. "OK, Janusz, anything else?"

"Just the check. And a couple pierogis to go."

The waitress held up the check and a paper bag with the pierogis, a step ahead of Blutarski. He paid and we left.

In the car he continued: "Looking into a woman, Ed, seeing who she is. Making her feel that she's my passion. I did that already, with more than one. I just don't think I have it in me for one more round."

On my way home from the bus stop, I played with the features of my new cell phone, and programmed Xochitl's number into the phone book. I was thinking about what I would cook for dinner, when I noticed Tony's Caddy pass. He noticed me, too, because he threw a manic U-turn and came to a screaming halt right next to me. I leaned into the passenger window and put my fist out for Tony to tap.

Tony didn't tap my fist. "Eddie, I need you to get serious."

I pulled my fist back. "About what?"

"Not here." He looked over his shoulder. "Get in."

"I'm tired, Tony; I need a shower."

He wrinkled his nose. "You stink."

"I been at work. You should try it sometime."

Tony bit the knuckle on his thumb. "I really need your help, Eddie, please. Let me talk to you."

Tony was sweaty. His pupils were dilated. I climbed into the car.

Tony peeled out and checked the rearview mirror. "They're all rats."

"Who, Tony? What's this about?"

Tony looked at me suspiciously. "Like you don't know."

He ripped down a side street and gunned it. He kept checking the rearview mirror.

"Tony, are we being followed?"

"Of course."

I looked behind us. "I don't see anybody."

"You wouldn't."

I was confused. "Why do you keep checking the mirror?"

"I wanna see if I still cast a reflection." Tony looked skyward and crossed himself.

"You wanna see what? How much blow did you do today?"

Tony laughed sarcastically and did not answer. We did laps around the neighborhood, intricate patterns that I imagined were meant to throw our pursuers off the scent. Tony spoke gibberish. His eyes darted. He checked the rearview and scratched himself. He flicked at himself as if to shoo away invisible flies.

"Right there!" He pulled over in front of a church. "In there, Eddie! Come on!"

Tony jumped out, crossed the sidewalk, and checked up and down the street like the Secret Service, with his hand inside his jacket, ready to draw. He ran up the steps, popped his head inside the church, popped back out, and waved at me to follow. I got out of the car and went up the steps, weary. Tony was already inside.

I stood in the back of the church as Tony walked the

aisle and checked the pews with his gun drawn. The church was empty save for a woman on her knees by the candles up front. Tony checked behind the three doors of the confessional. He walked up on the altar and looked up toward where the organist would sit. He put the gun away and tucked in his shirt, though he still looked disheveled.

He pointed at a pew. "You can kneel if you want."

I went to the last pew. "On my ass'll do. What's this all about?"

Tony passed me and went to the bowl of holy water near the entrance. He made a cup with his hands, scooped water, and splashed it across his face. He apparently emptied the bowl, because he went to the bowl on the opposite side and repeated the act, pushing his hair back with holy water, matting his goatee. He sat in the second-to-last pew, in front of me.

I studied his face in the light of the church. His pupils were very dilated. His nostrils looked raw.

"Seriously, Tony, how much blow?"

"Never mind that." He pulled his jacket off and tossed it. The gun was in its shoulder holster. He looked at me and tried to turn the tone of his conversation on a dime. "So, um, how you been, Eddie? You holdin' it down?"

"Whyn't you tell me why you brought me here?"

He rubbed his eyes, took a deep breath, and whispered to himself. Finally, he said, "They're watching me. They're probably watching you too."

"Who, Tony? Coltrane and Johnson?"

Tony sat up straight. "Are they involved in this too?"

"In *what*, Tony? What the fuck are you so worried about?"

He looked over both shoulders, then said it: "Vampires."

At first I thought he meant it as a metaphor. Like, Roach and his crew were such bloodsuckers they were almost *vampires*. Coltrane and Johnson roamed the night like *vampires*.

Tony said, "I'm talking about the real thing."

"Real?"

"Yes."

"Like vampires from Transylvania? With the fangs and shit?"

"Exactly. They been after me for the longest. They're jealous. I can feel their little yellow eyes."

Tony's dementia was in full swing. I looked at the giant cross up front. Jesus' face looked serene, despite the wounds.

Tony shooed invisible flies again. "They're even inside the porno."

"Where?"

"My porn. I watch it close. This chick is suckin' a giant schlong. Smokin' it like she wants it to fill her, right? Oh God!" Tony's eyes bulged at the horror. "Dude blows his load. And you know what she did?"

"What?"

"She stuck her tongue out. Tried to catch it all."

"Sounds like regular porn."

"You don't understand. That's when I saw it."

"What? Her sharp teeth?"

"Don't joke, Eddie! This is serious. I saw her mouth. The emptiness inside. A cave. Her insides were pitch black. She looked at me right through the camera, with those little yellow eyes. 'It's all for you,' she said. 'I did this for you.'"

Tony looked around and patted his pockets. "Christ, I gotta get some garlic."

"What you need is therapy. Detox."

Tony squeezed his head. He was on the verge of tears. "You don't know what I been through."

I put my hand on his shoulder. "It's OK. You're all right. The coke's got you—"

"Don't say that. That's not it." He spoke like a child who is afraid his mother will punish him. "Did you sell me out to Coltrane?"

"No."

"Tell me now, Eddie. Please. I need to know. It's OK. I understand. Confess to me here in the church. We'll go in the confessional!" Tony's voice echoed off the high ceiling. The woman by the candles stopped her prayer to look.

"Tony, you're bugging. You need professional help—"

"Tell me, Eddie. I'll forgive you."

"I *am* telling you."

"The narcs are trying to get to me through you, Eddie."

"They're trying to get to all of us."

"Whatta they want?"

"What do they always want?"

Tony squeezed his temples.

"Tony. Honestly. How much blow?"

Tony looked at me through his fingers. "Promise you won't laugh?"

"Of course not."

Tony counted out loud. "Seven, eight…maybe nine, ten grams a day."

"Goddamn, Tony. That's a small village in Colombia."

He bit his thumb knuckle again. "I'm bad, right?" He seemed to slump. "I'm gonna go to Hell for this."

"No, Tony, you just—you gotta come off that shit, that's all."

"I can't stop."

"Sure you can. I know that's what you think, Tony, but you have to gain control."

"Even now, Eddie. I'm twisting. I need a bump every fifteen minutes. But I'm afraid to do it in here." He pointed at Jesus on the cross. "He'll stop my heart and send me straight down."

Dilated as they were, Tony's eyes looked sadder than ever. I wondered if his birth mother had ever noticed all of that sadness in him. Maybe he inherited it from her.

"You gotta come off that shit, Tone. There's no way around it."

Tony made a face that was almost babylike.

"Get some counseling," I said. "Rehab. They got all kinds. Different techniques and shit. Support. You can't do it alone."

"Will you come with me, Eddie?"

"You gotta want it. I can't do it for you."

We looked at each other for a moment.

"Tony, listen. I bought a cell phone. Let me give you the number." I dug it from my wallet. "You get in a pinch, Tone, feel like you need to talk, you call me, all right? I'm here for you."

Tony looked at the number, then put it away. "Thanks, Eddie. You're the only one who knows."

The woman who prayed walked past. Tony watched her as she exited the church.

"This place is not safe," he said. "She'll tell the others."

Tony stood. So did I.

"No, you stay," he said. "We leave separately. It's safer that way. Anyway, it's me they're after. Wait ten minutes, then go, Eddie, all right?"

I began to say to Tony that maybe he should not be alone, but he moved so fast, and I really didn't feel like spending the night watching him come down.

At the door he spoke without looking back. "Eddie, listen to what I'm telling you, all right? It's not a game. These fuckers are slick. They been around for centuries. Get yourself some garlic."

He walked out.

Then he popped back in, genuflected, and popped back out.

I sat back down, alone in the infinite quiet of the church. I looked up at Jesus again, unchanged since my mother forced me through catechism all those years before.

I shrugged, and thought, *What can you do, right?*

The image of Christ appeared sympathetic, but it did not respond.

CHAPTER 16:

DAWN OF THE GILDED AGE

My walk home from the church was a lonely one. I kept thinking about Tony. So much poison had entered his body, it had polluted his thoughts and taken him off the wheel of logic to a place humans aren't supposed to go to, unless they are in a deep and fitful sleep. I thought about Tony's life, some of the things I saw him do to cut himself into his present state of mind. It felt like I was dreaming the past, even though I was fully awake.

I thought about that first burglary with Pelón again, in the suburbs, when that lady with the Rottweiler almost caught us, when we were teenagers. It seemed pretty harmless then. But it whet our appetite, and our sticky fingers. Pelón knew that it would. Before long, he rolled around in the sparkling white Excalibur again with a couple of Giordano's pizzas in the passenger seat. Our crew pounced on them.

Tony was really skinny then, even though he ate everything that was not already in somebody else's mouth. He inhaled his third thick slice and reached for another.

Pelón said, "Coño, pero you eating them like Tic Tacs. With an appetite like that, I soprise you no hustle more."

Tony pumped his chest. "What're you talking about, Pelón? We out here twenty-four, twenty-four."

Pelón looked at me. "And look how hungry I found you."

I said, "We know there's no free lunch, Pelón. So I guess that means you didn't come by here to feed the needy, right?"

Pelón picked his teeth and grinned. "Eduardo, you talk real direct. I like that."

"So?"

He looked at his toothpick. "You nenes feel like another trip to the suburbs?"

Stealing became a vocation for us. A thing that we did. Our practice. It was fun. Pelón would find a house and case it. We would strike when the people were away. We didn't know Pelón's sources of information, and we didn't care. If it was Christmas, we rode to your crib listening to *Asalto Navideño,* climbed in through the windows, and ripped all of the wrapping off everything under the tree to see what was worth taking. On every job the take was cash, never less than a thousand dollars apiece. And the freedom to help ourselves personally to various items.

Pelón did all of the fencing. Sometimes he would come back after a job and give us each an extra five hundred, a thousand, saying the take was better than he thought.

Tony and I shared an apartment then, a big, raw loft on Ogden. Before long, it looked like a flea market. We had all kinds of electronics, works of art, carpets, lamps, books, cassettes, LPs, CDs, picture frames, video games, golf clubs, Rollerblades, a huge vintage collection of *Playboy* magazines, and a complete, leather-bound, gold-leaf 1975 edition of the *World Book Encyclopedia* that I found in a house with an actual library inside.

Pelón never allowed us to keep any weapons, saying that he did not want to be responsible for any accidents, but one time I dropped a samurai sword in the bushes outside a window in Highland Park when Pelón was distracted. I went back for it later that night. I hung it over my headboard, which saw a lot of action in those days. Tony and I threw big parties and gave wealthy women's jewelry to the boricuas, italianas, morenas, and mexicanas who danced wildest for us. The way Tony and I saw it, the burglaries were easy, and the benefits were awesome.

One day Pelón combed his handlebar mustache and pursed his lips like he was considering something pitiful. "You boys don't have any real ambitions, do you?"

Tony put his hands in his pockets. "One day I'm gonna own a boat."

Pelón shook his head. "How you think that gonna happen?"

Tony blinked.

"You boys need to grow you business. Think big."

"What you mean?"

Pelón rolled his *R*'s. "Crack. Thees ees the new hot thing, no? And you boys wasting you time with marijuana?"

I said, "Pelón, the jail time on crack's heavier than any other drug. Even coke. I saw it on channel eleven."

"Sí, you right," he said, nodding like I'd made a point that he had somehow overlooked. "Coca the rich man's

drug. Uncle Sam no gonna fuck with his own kind, right?"
He looked at us both. "So, OK. You boys think you ready
for a real score?"

It was a whole new scheme, different from the walk-in-
and-take-it routine that we were accustomed to.

"This time we gonna rob a stash house."

Tony looked from me to Pelón. "A what?"

"Dónde guardan las drogas."

I said, "Pelón, we know what a stash house is. You
feelin' suicidal?"

Tony said, "Stash house gangsters are always strapped
with major firepower."

Pelón said, "Not always."

I said, "This ain't one of your insurance scams, Pelón.
Nobody goes on vacation and leaves packages of dope
lying around."

"I has a connect that gonna give us perfect intelligence."

"You and your connects are gonna get us all killed."

"Fíjate que no. I has a friend who tell me about these
white boys who run a transfer station in Skokie. Real
quiet. They never got trouble from nobody. To them is
just a business. They got a dude in a wheelchair, one guy,
a homo, he never leave the house. He in there full-time,
watching the stash. Nobody suspect a thing. He hold the
coca for a day or two. It comes from México. Then some
other people come down from Canada and take it the rest
of the way. Regular, every two weeks."

Tony said, "A dude in a wheelchair? How much coke?"

Pelón said, "Kilos."

I shook my head. "That can't be right."

He wagged his finger. "Eduardo, you know the story

about the drowning man? God send three people to help, but he push them away. Then he ask God, 'Why you forgot about me?' That's you."

"Is the sermon finished? What're we gonna do with all that coke?"

Pelón passed his hand over his bald head. "You let me lose hair about it. I give you five thousand each after I unload, and you don't have to do shit except come with me to scare this cocksucker good."

Tony and I looked at each other. *Five thousand dollars? Apiece?*

Tony looked at Pelón. "Scare him? Pelón, for five thousand dollars I could be the fucking Exorcist."

We recruited Beto to be the getaway driver. This was before Beto was known as GQ, and way before he fell completely into heroin and became just plain, deteriorated Beto. We knew young Beto from gangbanging, and he was not a cat who lost his mind when things got hairy. One time we raced against a carload of Indian punks on Lake Shore Drive. Beto was behind the wheel. When we hit the S curve by Oak Street Beach, our car swayed. The rear wheels skipped as we plowed toward a low concrete wall. Tony and I, as the passengers, screamed as we headed for a crash, but Beto simply countersteered, and stuttered his foot on the pedals in just the right way to recapture traction and torque away from the wall. Our tires screamed as we fell back into the curve, but the Indians behind us failed in that maneuver and smashed their car to pieces on the concrete wall. One of them died and it made the news.

On the day of the stash house job, Beto, the getaway

driver, pulled the van into the parking lot of the apartment complex.

Pelón leaned over Beto's shoulders and inspected the view. "Park where we can watch the apartment with the ramp in front."

Beto found a spot where we were partially obscured by a leafy tree. We watched the front door to the apartment for fifteen minutes. Nothing happened. Finally, Pelón said, "I think we ready to go with the plan."

The plan consisted of me going up to the door in a Commonwealth Edison uniform and pretending that I was there to read the meter. Once inside, I would evaluate whether Pelón's information was correct. If I found the invalid home alone, as expected, I was to simply overpower him, knock him out of his chair, signal the others, unlock the front door, and wait for Pelón and Little Tony to enter.

"After that," said Pelón, "we has to work a little, because this hijo de puta no gonna wanna tell us where the coke is, what the combination is if they keep it in a safe. Like this. That's why we prepare to go all the way, to scare him, OK? We gotta let this cocksucker know we serious. We make him think we cut his balls off and feed 'em to a lizard, but he gonna present us with the freaking coke. No other way about it. ¿M'entienden?"

Tony said, "Yeah, we got it."

I said, "Why do I have to be the one who goes in first?"

Pelón straightened my hat. " 'Cause you the best actor. Besides, this guy's a pato, and you the best-looking one. Remember to smile like you like him. You the one who gonna get us inside."

*   *   *

I stepped to the door in the uniform Pelón got me, complete with the ComEd hat, a clipboard, and a fake ComEd ID.

It took a long time for the man to answer. He spoke to me from the other side of the door without opening.

"How could you be here to read the meter again? You people were out here just two weeks ago."

I said, "Yes, sir, it turns out that reading was incorrect. It shows you used an impossible amount of hours. It has to be a mistake. If we don't correct it right now, the old numbers'll stand, and you're gonna get a bill for thousands of dollars."

The man paused. I was looking at a closed door.

"You don't sound like the regular guy. Where is he? Why isn't he here?"

"That's just it, sir. He didn't do such a good job, so he was fired. I'm on this route now."

The man waited a long time. Finally, he cracked the door.

"Let me see your ID."

I showed it to him. He looked at it, looked up in my face, and smiled.

"Will it mean anything," he said, "if I tell you what a terrible inconvenience this all is?"

I tried to smile the way Pelón said. "I understand, sir."

"You're so polite." The man opened the screen door. "Come in then, and do what you must."

I tipped my hat brim as I walked past. "This'll only take a moment."

I eyeballed the space. The man was white, but his artwork had an African theme. Statues of skinny men with big ones. I looked him over. He checked me out. He wore a paisley shirt.

"Beautiful apartment," I said. "You decorate this yourself?"

"With my own hands."

"Is that a real elephant's tusk? It's huge."

The man followed me in his wheelchair. "I'm not supposed to have it, it's contraband. A friend of mine brought it back from Kenya. Got it from a bona fide witch doctor. Do you believe that? Supposedly, it has amazing curative powers, if you just touch it. Take your gloves off and feel."

"My hands are still cold," I said. "This job has me outdoors a lot. Your apartment's more spacious than it looks from outside. Two bedrooms?"

"Wouldn't your paperwork show that?"

I almost stumbled over my tongue. "Oh, yeah, well. Part of the problem with the other guy, he lost a lot of paperwork. They say he was, you know—" I pretended to gulp from an imaginary bottle of booze.

"Hmm. He didn't seem like the type."

I tilted my head. "They say you can't always tell."

The man in the wheelchair stared at me. "The second bedroom's an office," he said. "I run a consulting firm out of there. That one over there is the lone bedroom."

I nodded. "You live alone?"

"Who's asking?"

I smiled at him.

He smiled back. "Exactly how much time do they give you to read these meters?"

I walked toward him. "Listen, mister, I'm sorry about this."

"About what?"

I grabbed him by the shoulders and pushed him over onto his back.

"What the hell? What are you doing?"

I pulled the chair away from him. His skinny, lifeless limbs slanted at disturbing angles.

"Christ, what is this? You don't have to rape me."

I quickly checked the other rooms. "I don't wanna hurt you, mister. But I got a couple friends coming in here now, and they won't blink to chop you into little pieces. Just cough up the kilos and we'll be out of your way."

The man screamed. There was no way that thin drywall would contain all of that noise. I bent over and smacked him once so hard that he stopped immediately.

"I'm not joking, mister. Put on a display like that and these guys'll bury you in the woods." I pointed at him. "Do not move."

I went to the blinds and did the signal that Pelón worked out, then yanked the phone from the wall. In fifteen seconds I heard a light knock at the door.

Pelón and Tony walked in with backpacks slung over their shoulders, like it was the first day of school.

The man was still on his back. "Who are you people?"

Pelón said, "You gonna find out who we are if you no give us what we come for." He threw his backpack on the couch. "Where's the coca?"

"I don't know what you're talking about."

Pelón looked at Tony. Tony bent over the guy and pulled him up by the hair into a seated position on the floor.

"Owwww! What do you want?"

Pelón said, "You gonna be quiet, maricón?"

"Fuck you."

"Where's the coke?"

"In the fridge, but I drink Pepsi, asshole."

Tony said, "You think this is a fucking joke?" and slapped the guy back onto his side. Then he grabbed him by the neck and pulled him up again.

"Help! Help!"

Pelón went in his backpack and pulled a pair of sweat socks balled into each other. Tony held the guy's hands behind his back while Pelón overpowered him to stuff the sweat socks into his mouth.

"¿Ya ve, mamáo? Cállate la freaking boca."

The man's eyes watered. He blew his cheeks out to breathe with the socks in. Tony bent on one knee behind him and kept him restrained. Pelón went in his backpack again and pulled out a straight razor.

"Aha?" He opened it and showed it. "You think we come to play?"

I clapped my hands together, once and loud. "Hey, mister! We can just tear your place apart looking for it. If it's in a safe, we're gonna need you anyway. You may as well cooperate."

The man's eyes pleaded. He began to really cry. I looked at Pelón.

Pelón said, "¡Basta! I didn't come here to do nothing but leave with all the coke." He looked at Tony. "Dame la mano."

Tony still held the guy by the wrists, behind his back. He forced the man's right hand in front of his face. Pelón slashed the man across the palm. The man's eyes bulged, but his scream was muffled by the socks in his mouth.

Pelón raised his eyebrows. "You see? Now you got a new life line, pendejo. I predict things no go too good."

The guy sobbed, and shook his head, defiant. Blood flowed from his palm.

Pelón raised the razor. "¡Oye! Cara de crica! I gonna use this to slice you face a thousand times, eh? I slice you eyeballs. Then I gonna grab a bottle from the bar over there, or maybe I find bleach under you sink, and I gonna put it on you face and you sliced-up balls, OK?"

Tony made an exaggerated face. "That's right, motherfucker! We'll pour the whole friggin' bottle down your throat."

Snot dangled from the man's nose; but his sobs began to calm down. He was trying to regain control.

Pelón pulled the socks from his mouth. "You gonna behave?"

The man caught his breath. "I don't think you know what you're getting into. These fellas are Sicilian, and—"

Almost as a reflex, like a bee sting, Pelón flicked the razor across the man's soft, fleshy cheek. He opened a four-inch gash, which bled instantly.

"Owwwowowow!"

Pelón replaced the socks in the guy's mouth. "I tole you. I gonna do that a thousand times. I don't give a fock *who* think they own this coke. Is *mine* now."

The man's eyes rolled out of synch with one another. Then he focused on Pelón and nodded. Pelón pulled the socks again.

"You ready?"

The man breathed. The muscles in his face sagged. He bled all over his paisley shirt. "The entertainment center."

"Inside?" said Pelón.

"Underneath. You gotta move the damn thing."

Tony released the guy's wrists and let him flop onto

his side again. He and Pelón grabbed opposite ends of the entertainment center and inched it away from the wall.

Tony said, "There's nothing but carpeting under here."

The man covered the gash in his face. "Find the square."

I looked over Tony's shoulder. Pelón was behind the entertainment center. He felt the surface of the carpeting. He found a straight edge and dug his nails to get ahold of the patch of carpeting and peel it back. Underneath was an eighteen-inch by eighteen-inch metal door in the floor. Pelón fingered the handle and pulled the door up. Underneath the door, inside the floor, was a compartment and inside the compartment were the magic kilos, stacked like soft white pillows. Pelón's grin blossomed.

"Antonio. Agarra las bolsas."

Tony grabbed the backpacks.

The wheelchair man spoke directly to me. "Think you can just lean me against the couch, please?"

He looked utterly helpless on the floor. Blood was everywhere.

I went over and pulled him up. "You wanna go back in the wheelchair?"

"Just lean me against the couch for now."

I pulled him to the couch and leaned him, careful to avoid the blood.

He looked at his sliced hand and felt the gash in his face. "You people are vampires. You're damned."

Pelón was still behind the console. "Coño, six kilos!"

Tony flashed his tongue. "Scarface himself only got *two* keys from the Colombians at the motel."

Pelón said, "And this is a lot better than the movies, niño. I can unload these tonight, unopen, for fifteen

apiece! That's ninety thousand right there! And if I break
it up and throw them on the street? ¡Olvídate! I can't even
do that much math. I pretty sure you boys gonna see a
bonus. Let's put them in the bags."

The bleeding man looked at me. His eyes looked vul-
nerable. "Do you think you can go in the bathroom and
grab me a towel for all this blood?"

I made eye contact with Tony, who held a bag open for
Pelón. He nodded. I went to the bathroom and grabbed a
towel off the rack. I looked in the medicine cabinet and
grabbed a bottle of hydrogen peroxide.

By the time I came back, ten, maybe fifteen seconds
later, the man had a pistol raised with his sliced, wob-
bly hand. I realized instantly from the bloodstains on the
couch that he had reached between the cushions to find it.
He pointed the pistol to the side of the entertainment center, where Pelón was just about to emerge with a backpack
full of coke. I leapt toward the man, shouted, and executed
a snap kick, which was the only kick I bothered to learn
in a class during the *Karate Kid* phase. The gun exploded
and flew out of the man's hand at the same instant. It fell
across the room. Tony grabbed it.

Pelón stood frozen and stunned. He looked me straight
in the eye for a long, silent moment, then touched himself
in the torso, as if looking for the spot where the bullet
entered his body. I pointed above his head. Pelón turned
and looked up. The drywall directly behind him had a
bullet hole the size of a quarter, about an inch above his
bald dome.

Pelón turned slowly toward the man. "¡Maldito sea!"
He grabbed the gun from Tony's hand and cocked it.

I said, "Pelón, no!"

Pelón looked at me with the gun pointed at the man's belly.

"Don't make this worse. That gunshot was heard by the neighbors. They already called nine-one-one. We gotta roll!"

Pelón looked at the gun. He nodded. He quickly ejected the bullets toward one end of the room and tossed the weapon toward the other. "¡Vámonos!"

Tony and I headed toward the door. Pelón was behind us. He said, "Espérate," and we froze by the door.

With a wild look, Pelón picked up the elephant tusk and swung it like a heavy baseball bat at the man's head. From our vantage point Tony and I could not see what precisely that did to the man, but blood exploded and his head rocked and hung to the side like his neck had become rubber. Blood splattered all over Pelón's pants and shoes.

Pelón dropped the tusk and lingered a second over the body to take a mental snapshot of his handiwork. Then he said, "¡Muévanse!"

We hustled out the door, down the ramp, into the van, which Beto had waiting right in front.

Beto pulled off without burning rubber or driving erratic. "I heard a gunshot."

Pelón said, "Nobody got shot. Freaking guy decided he wanna play rough. No fue nada."

Beto said, "Is everyone all right?"

Pelón said, "You see us, don't you? Stop asking so many questions and focus on the road."

Beto got us to I-94 and headed back toward the city. Nobody followed.

Beto drove with both hands on the steering wheel. "So how was it? Did you get the yayo?"

Pelón said, "Ha! Piece of bizcocho, nene. You gonna have a good time tonight."

After the score Pelón played with his hoop earring and offered us an opportunity to renegotiate our contract. We could either take our five grand apiece, as agreed. Or we could keep one of the kilos, break it up, and start throwing it on the street. Using it to make crack was another option.

Pelón said, "It all depends on how much you love money."

Tony and Beto looked to me to take a position.

I kept my finger to my lip as I thought. Finally, I said, "Why don't we keep it as flake and put it on the street in quarter bags. Crack's too political right now; we don't need that kind of attention."

Everybody nodded. So we walked away from the episode with a big brick of coke and a new business. That night we all sampled our supply and discovered that it was super high-grade material. I remember the way young Tony laughed when I told him that his nose looked like it was dipped in powdered sugar. We were each certain to turn a fat profit over the five grand "invested," and we all felt real good about that. Occasionally, I thought about the guy in the wheelchair, but then I shook it off. It was the beginning of a whole new era.

CHAPTER 17:

PORTRAIT

I sat by the window and dialed Xochitl's number. The night sky was clear, the moon was out, and across the miles, the Chicago skyline twinkled.

Xochitl answered.

"Guess who?" I said.

"How'd I know? I normally don't pick up if I don't recognize the number."

"You hiding from someone, Xochitl?"

"No," she said. "I just don't like to be bothered."

The lights were off in my room. The classical station was on low.

Xochitl asked what I was up to.

"Sitting in the dark, thinking," I said.

"About?"

"You, girl. That's why I called."

"What kinds of thoughts does a grown man have in the dark?"

I paused. "How 'bout I save those for when I see you in person?"

Xochitl laughed and the sound of her laughter made my blood flow.

We chatted about a lot of things, like the assholes Xochitl worked with and how much they did not appreciate her, finding time for chores, where we did our groceries, how her kids performed in school, her hopes that everything would work out better for them than they had for her. I mentioned that it must be nice to have someone to care for.

"It is," she said, sounding only half-convinced. "Actually, I know that's true, it's just—"

"You don't have to explain, Xoch."

"I know. Actually," she said, "I'm a little worried about *you*. You're the one who sounds a little distracted tonight."

I thought about saying it was nothing. "I'm a little down. I ran into a friend today. He's pretty messed up."

"Drugs?"

"What else? Coke's eating his brain."

"He's probably just depressed," she said. "Self-medicating."

"You read that in a book?"

"Just common sense. Sometimes the best you can do for someone is back off."

"Ever dealt with an addict, Xochitl?"

"Who hasn't? But I ain't even talking about that. I'm talking about human nature."

Xochitl told me about her sister who married an alcoholic. How he hit her. Controlled everything. Kept her from her family.

I tried one of my mother's lines. "El amor es ciego."

"That's not love," said Xochitl. "That's abuse. My sister was smart. She could have been something. Now she spends her day doing laundry, cooking, cleaning. All of that has its place, but... So many times I told her to leave; couple times she's actually done it. Then he cries, she takes him back, and it starts again."

"Change is a motherfucker, Xochitl."

"I know it. Believe me I know. And it's gotta come from within. How deep is your friend?"

I thought about Tony's anguish in the church. "Rock-bottom. Completely divorced from reality."

"That's too bad. But sometimes that's just what it takes to really see."

I wasn't sure what I thought about that. It *sounded* logical. Static interfered and I walked around the room to improve reception. I changed the subject.

"Must be hard on your family," I said. "To see your sister, I mean."

"You'd be surprised. I think my parents would be more traumatized by my sister getting a divorce than by her playing a punching bag the rest of her life."

"Is that how they reacted to you? When you left? You haven't said much about it."

"All you have to do is ask."

"So I'm asking."

Xochitl took a breath. "I'm separated, not divorced. The lawyers are still working on it. We have the children. Property to consider."

"Property? Sounds complicated. You the one who broke it off?"

"It usually takes two to drive a marriage into the ground. Can we change the subject?"

"Sure." I lay on my bed. "So what are you doing now, Xochitl, this instant when I called?"

"Watching a novela. Giving myself a pedicure."

"Mmm," I said. "Now there's an image. What are you wearing?"

She said, "Don't be a juvenile," but I could hear her warm up on the other end.

"You need me to come over and massage your feet, Xochitl?"

Xochitl brought her voice down to a purr. "That sounds nice."

We let a little silence pass.

"What about you, Eddie? I haven't heard you say anything about your family. Any brothers and sisters?"

"I'm an only child."

"Kind of rare in our community. You must be spoiled rotten."

"Oh, I'm rotten, all right. But I was never spoiled."

Xochitl said, "How come your parents had only one?"

"It wasn't by choice. My moms had a bunch of miscarriages. I almost didn't make it. Choked a little on the umbilical cord. My father said she didn't want me to see this world."

Xochitl made a disgusted sound. "Only somebody who's never carried a child could say something like that."

I didn't disagree. We were quiet for a second. I could almost hear Xochitl concentrate on getting the polish on her toenail.

"Where are they now?" she said.

"Who? My parents? Resting."

"Retired?"

"No. In the cemetery."

Xochitl's voice softened. "I'm sorry."

"It's been a long time."

"Do you have any other family here?"

"My mom has a couple brothers around. They got wives and kids and all that. I never got to know 'em."

"How about in Joliet? You said you stayed with family there."

"Oh yeah...that was this, um, this one favorite eccentric uncle. He passed away too."

"So you're basically alone?"

"Isn't everyone?"

"No," said Xochitl. "But is that the way you like it?"

"I don't know. That's just the way it is."

Xochitl waited a few seconds. "What are your plans now?"

"Whatta you mean?"

"Your goals," she said. "What are you working on?"

"Who talks like that, Xochitl? You been watching too much *Oprah*."

"Listen, there's nothing wrong with having a strategy for self-improvement."

"See what I mean?" The truth is I liked the way Xochitl talked. I let a few beats pass. "I don't know, Xochitl. Goals? I studied percussion. Hoping to get back into it."

"Music?"

"Uh-huh. Congas. Afro-Cuban rhythms. Salsa. Bomba, plena. All kinds of stuff."

"Aha! The secret of that incredible beat. You wanna be in a band?"

"Someday."

"You say you *used* to study. Did you quit?"

"I gave my drums away."

"Short on cash?"

"I didn't pawn 'em. I donated them. They were cheap. And they weren't handmade; I didn't make them myself. I just figured it was time for me to make my own."

"To build them yourself?"

"Yeah."

"Does that make them sound better?"

"That's what I hear."

I was tempted to tell Xochitl about my Miami plan, the salsa label with Chiva and all that, but I figured it was probably a bad idea to tell a female who I wanted to get with that my agenda included skipping town. I said, "I know this guy. A friend of mine. He's like a mentor. He knows how to make 'em. He's gonna teach me."

"Sounds like fun," she said. "I'd love to hear you play. Maybe I could dance for you."

"There's a pretty thought."

After that, Xochitl and I listened to each other say nothing over the line. I thought about her thick hips and big smile. I lay on my bed with the phone pressed against my ear. I didn't want to hang up, but it felt like we were at the natural end of the conversation.

"Guess I'll let you go, huh, Xoch?"

"It's getting late."

The silence extended.

"Xochitl, this is crazy. I don't even know where you live."

"Why would you?"

I changed my approach. "What're you gonna do once you get your toenails done?"

"I'm gonna stay on my couch and eat a pint of ice cream. I rented a movie."

"Yeah?" I pictured myself on the couch next to

Xochitl, watching her pull the spoon out of her mouth. "For the record," I said, "I like Rocky Road."

"Sorry, honey, all's I got is butter pecan. I got your number on my cell now, though. I'll call you tomorrow."

We said our good-nights. I was about to press the end button when I heard Xochitl say, "Eddie, wait!"

"Yeah?" I pressed the speaker to my ear and figured that I could be dressed and out the door on my way to her place in two minutes flat.

"A white T-shirt and pink cotton panties."

"Huh?"

"What I'm wearing. Remember you asked? I'm in a clean white T-shirt, V-neck, no bra, and soft pink cotton panties. Just out of the shower."

"Oh shit." The blood rushed to my center.

Xochitl giggled. "Sweet dreams, bad boy."

"Yeah, all right, Xochitl." I would have followed up with, "You don't play fair," but she had already hung up.

I met Xochitl on the front steps of the Art Institute, by one of the lions. She wore a navy skirt suit with nylons, beige pumps, a cream-colored blouse under a navy coat.

"You look official."

"One of the partners had a deposition today. He brought me to translate for our Spanish-speaking client."

We walked into the foyer.

"I usually come here Thursday evenings, Eddie. They open late and it's free."

"You do this often?"

"Every once in a while."

"You don't get bored?" I said. "Seeing the same old shit?"

"They have exhibits where they bring in new stuff, but no. The ones I really like look different every time."

We walked around quiet galleries, looked at paintings and other objects, liked them or did not like them according to our whim. Sometimes Xochitl knew things about the pieces, the artists, the movements.

I scratched my chin. "How did you get into this?"

"The nuns made us take art appreciation."

We walked around a little.

"How'd you end up working as a receptionist?"

"And part-time translator."

"Right. How did you get into that?"

"Like I told you, I thought about law, a million years ago, before I became a mother. Now that I'm finally on my own, I'm sort of thinking of going back to school and maybe picking up that path again. I figured it made sense to work in an office first. See if I like what lawyers actually do."

"Do you?"

"Too soon to tell. I know I don't wanna be a receptionist forever."

We came upon a picture of an old man with a guitar. He looked like a bum. Real strung out, on a curb. He reminded me of AIDS patients by the time they hit the ward, the way he leaned against a wall and held his guitar like it was the last pint of blood.

Xochitl said, "I have this idea that I wanna help people. But also, I need to make money."

"Does your office help anybody?"

"Yes, of course. But there's a big focus on making money."

"That's only natural."

Xochitl stood in front of a painting that was mostly just black geometric lines on white space. Maybe a spot or two of color.

I tilted my head. "Don't look like much."

"That's the beauty. It looks like nothing's happening. After a while you see the energy and movement."

I curled my lips. "Energy and movement? How 'bout just lazy painting?"

"No way. This painting's about balance and harmony."

"You're only saying that because you read the literature."

She put her tongue in the corner of her mouth. "Maybe. But that doesn't mean that it isn't true. It's about order in the universe. It takes a lot of work to make something look like that."

I shook my head. "The world ain't never that tidy."

"That's why they call it art."

We moved on to a large canvas that depicted a life-sized, very well-dressed couple from the horse-and-buggy era, arm in arm, on an evening stroll, protecting themselves from a light drizzle under an umbrella on a cobblestone street.

"*That*," I said, "that looks like something. They almost look real."

Xochitl nodded. "They say Paris is romantic, but I went there and didn't feel a thing."

"Did you go with anyone?"

"My husband and the kids." Xochitl got closer to the canvas. "Look how beautiful she is. I love the way they dressed back then."

Xochitl stared into the painting. I looked at her profile

and saw an angle on her that had not been visible before. I touched her cheek. She looked at me. I leaned in and kissed her.

Xochitl's lips were soft and warm and full. I eased my tongue into hers and it felt like two clouds melding into each other.

Xochitl bit her lower lip. "I've been waiting for you to do that."

I took her hand. We walked around some more. In one room was a collection of weapons behind glass. We saw two sets of armor next to each other, one full-sized, and one much smaller. The information said that the smaller one was designed for a youth.

Xochitl shook her head. "Isn't that crazy? Sending a kid that young into a battle, where he needs to wear something like that?"

"Maybe it was just responsible. A birthday present from his father. Like, 'Here, son, your first armor. Watch your back. And don't get your head chopped off, it's rough out here.'"

"That's one way to look at it."

We ended up in front of a painting called *Zapata*. The revolutionary enters the room all sombrero and cojones like the Angel of Death. You see a gun and bullets and there's a knife that may or may not be pointed directly at Zapata's eye, yet he's the dangerous one.

"Xochitl, there's something I should tell you."

She looked at me. She moved to the bench in front of the painting and sat. I sat next to her. I looked up at the painting.

"I been wanting to explain something. Thinking of how to say it."

"Coming straight out usually works best."

I didn't avoid her eyes. "I'm a convict. An ex-con. I just got out of prison."

Xochitl did not change her expression. She did not gasp. She did not get up and walk away, or run. Finally, she said, "I wondered."

"How do you mean?"

"I grew up in Little Village. I had cousins. I've seen convicts come and go."

"Is it that obvious?"

"No," she said. "It's not. But I knew there was some-thing. You have a certain walk. The way you look at people."

"That doesn't put you off?"

"How long were you in for?"

"Ten years."

"Híjole. Did you kill somebody?"

"I was young and stupid and was in the wrong place at the wrong time with the worst people. It eventually came back to me. Plus, my lawyer was a complete jerk-off and that's how I drew the time."

"Your lawyer messed up? Now you *do* sound like a typical con."

"I'm giving you the facts."

"Facts are always open to interpretation."

"I guess you *do* work with lawyers."

Xochitl studied the image of Zapata. "You must have seen some ugly things in there."

"Some."

Xochitl looked at me. "Thank you for trusting me."

"I figured you should know who you're talking to."

"I respect that."

She rubbed my leg over the jeans. We were seated next to each other. Her hair hung down.

Playfully, she said, "So, did they ever make you, um, pick up the soap?"

"No, Xochitl, my butthole's intact. But I did see some wild shit."

"Is it as dangerous as we see in the movies?"

"It can be." I told her about the time I saw a con use a sock filled with coins, how he swung it like a propeller at three would-be rapists until he left loose teeth scattered on the concrete. "That was my first week in."

I told her about another incident where an old man disfigured a young buck with a pork chop bone that he sharpened against the concrete floor of his cell. I described the way the skin from the young man's cheek flapped down.

"You could see his teeth through the hole in the side of his face."

"Ugh."

"It's really an alternate universe. Lots of rules and at the same time no rules. This? Where everybody walks around a museum and looks at things and whispers and acts like they're talking about real life? Two-dimensional. Inside? Everything is real. Even the gossip has consequences."

Xochitl nodded. I guess she felt the tension in my voice, because she touched my face and put her hand in mine. "That was a *part* of your life, Eddie, but it doesn't define you. Let's not worry about the past."

We looked in each other's eyes. I kissed her.

I said, "I really like to be with you, Xoch," which sounds immature now, not fully formed, and is not the way I would say it if I had that moment to live again. I don't know if Xochitl was about to say anything in return, but the guard announced that the museum was closing and that we needed to go.

Outside we stood on the steps and looked down onto Michigan Avenue. It rained so light that you didn't quite need an umbrella.

"You hungry, Xochitl? Wanna go for a drink?"

She made a disappointed face. "I have an appointment. Can I drop you off?"

I looked at her heart-shaped lips and thought about the intimacy of the car and that awkward moment that would happen when it was time to get out.

"You know what, Xochitl? It's such a nice night, I think I'll walk around, downtown. Catch a movie or something."

"Great."

"Listen, Xochitl, I learned some things today."

"Like what?"

"I learned if you slap together a few lazy lines, you can make people think it's about harmony and balance."

"Payaso."

"You know what else? I learned who got the softest lips in Chicago."

Xochitl smiled her crooked smile. We kissed one more time, on the steps, between the two lions, and I relished the way her tongue felt. People emptied out of the museum and flowed past us in a steady stream.

Xochitl waited. But then she separated and slowly went down the steps.

I watched her go down to the sidewalk, where she

bloomed open a floral-print umbrella that seemed at that moment like the only splash of color on the streets of our town. I watched Xochitl's movement, her flow, until all I could see was the top of her umbrella floating. I kept my eyes on her bouquet until it was completely out of view.

CHAPTER 18:

PRIME RIB

The elevator traveled ninety-five stories in less time than it takes to count that high. The doors opened. I stepped into an enormous restaurant in the sky.

The maitre d' led me to Pelón's table, which was right next to a floor-to-ceiling window on the southern side of the restaurant. Pelón chewed an unlit cigar and reflected the low light of the restaurant with his white suit. Tony sat across from him and stared into a beer.

I stood at the edge of the table. "What up, putas?"

Pelón took the cigar out of his mouth. "We was ready to order without you. Why you so late?"

I looked at Tony and pointed to the empty seat next to Pelón. "Move. I want to sit across from the two lovebirds."

Tony made a face, but moved next to Pelón. I took my seat and looked at the two of them, side by side. Tony should've looked good. He wore a fine maroon dress shirt. His goatee looked neat, and he'd gotten a cut and combed what was left of his hair. He wasn't jumpy like he had been in the church that day when he was sweating vampires. But the bags under his eyes were full. And the eyes themselves were empty.

I ordered a scotch on the rocks and grabbed a breadstick. "So, Pelón? You called for a sit-down. What's your big announcement?"

Pelón chewed the cigar tip. "Children always want dessert first. You know the most important people in this city eat up here?"

I dusted the shoulder on my black leather sport coat. "*I'm* here, ain't I? But this isn't a social visit."

"Tranquilo. Let's order dinner and have a little somesing to drink. I know you never seen a view like this."

We were at the northern end of the Magnificent Mile, ninety-five floors up, facing south. The enormous cluster of skyscrapers that form the core of the city dominated the night with their constellations. The metropolis stretched away in a flawless grid. I ordered a rib-eye steak, medium well.

When we were finished eating, Pelón leaned in and lowered his voice to a near whisper. "Antonio told you about the casino, no?"

"He mentioned you were putting something together."

Pelón grinned. "The plan is ready." His eyes creased. He rolled the cigar in his mouth.

I leaned in. "You need me to get a pencil or something? Shoot."

"You, Antonio, my brother, Cabezón, from Puerto Rico gonna be the crew. You go on a casino boat. It gonna take a cruise."

"A cruise? To where?"

"No place. Up the river. Is just an excuse to gamble."

"Then what?"

"The boat comes to a point where it turns to go back to port. The turnaround is always at the same spot, same location. The river gotta be deep enough. It's a pretty big boat. Happens at the same time too: one hour, twenty-five minutes into the cruise."

"Why should I care, Pelón?"

"That's the mark. Five minutes before the turn, you gonna get everybody's attention. You gonna announce the stickup."

"I am?"

"Yes. You, Antonio, and my brother gonna handle bags and guns. You each gonna show you weapons. They gotta believe you freaking crazy, like you looking for an excuse to shoot somebody. Everybody gotta know this is a stickup. My brother and Antonio gonna collect the money. This is gonna be a special cruise for high rollers. Average bet gonna be a thousand dollars a hand, minimum. Believe me, the cash gonna flow."

"What exactly is my role?"

"You gonna keep the peace, Eddie. That's you specialty, right? 'Cool Hand Luke'? You run the operation and keep everybody on ice."

"A babysitter?"

"You the boss on the scene."

"What happens once the bags are filled? We'll be out in the middle of the river."

Pelón smiled and wiggled his eyebrows. "You gonna love this. They got a little boat, a motorboat that hang off the back of the ship. They call it a dinghy. They use this thing to ride around the casino boat, when they tie the big boat to the shore."

"When they dock?"

"Exacto. You three gonna get on this boat and come to shore. I'll be in the car right there, waiting."

"We're just gonna jump into the little boat and ride it to shore?"

"Sí."

"Who knows how to work that thing?"

"My brother live his whole life on the Island," said Pelón. "Believe me, he knows boats. But there's gonna be a kid on board who really knows. That's this kid's job to lower the dinghy to the water, start it, drive it. He gonna do this for you."

"What if he doesn't wanna cooperate?"

"Por favor." Pelón used the two fingers of his claw to tip his martini glass and drain it. "If that boy say no to you, my brother gonna shoot that pile of mierda right through the palm of his left hand. After that, this freaking boy'll push his mother off a cliff just to please you."

I made eye contact with Tony. I turned back to Pelón. "How come you get to drive, Pelón, while everybody else does the dirty work?"

Pelón raised his cane to remind me of his condition. "With this hip? I slow you down. My brother, he's in good shape. He help carry the money."

I turned the ice in my scotch. "So that's it, Pelón? That's your master plan?"

"¿Cómo te parece?"

"Stupid. Destined to fail."

Pelón's grin fizzled. "How can you say that? You never even been on the boat."

"That plan'll never work."

"¿Por qué?"

"First of all, you know there's gonna be cameras everywhere. Even if you get away, your picture'll be all over the news."

"I gonna get you a disguise."

"What? Ski masks?"

"No," said Pelón. "We doing this on Halloween. They having a party on the boat. You gonna be in a Halloween costume."

Tony finally sat up. "Costumes? Really, Pelón? Can I go as Dracula?"

Pelón said, "Shhh! You wanna call the chief of police and let him know?"

Tony slumped like a dog that hears the door open, only to realize he isn't going anywhere.

I shook my head. "Halloween costumes? Where'd you get that idea? One of them stupid movies?"

"Is gonna work this time."

"No it isn't. The casino must have an alarm system. Armed guards? Two-way mirrors? Undercover officers? A safe or two where they keep the *real* money? Think about it, Pelón. Someone on the other end of that boat'll be on a cell phone with police before one penny gets put into one bag. It's too sloppy."

"Trust me, there's no cops close to where you getting off. Is out in the middle of nothing, nowhere. Farms. Woods. By the time police get there, we lost."

"And the armed guards?"

"They have none. I been on that boat a thousand times. I never see no armed guard."

"They must be undercover."

"There's gonna be one state trooper in plainclothes on that boat. That's it."

"How do you know this for sure, Pelón? Another one of your dingbats on the inside?"

"I do has a connection on that boat. She a black-jack dealer, but she no gonna be on that cruise, she on vacation."

"Remember how well your connect worked last time?"

"Nene, I don't gotta explain caca to you. Last time you wanted to do things you own way, and look what happened." Pelón held up his damaged hand and gritted his dentures so that we made no mistake that he referred to his own injury. "I'm telling you there's only one trooper on board that boat—one—and that's it."

Tony said, "Well, you know *he's* gonna be armed."

"That's true, pero his only mission gonna be for you not to hurt nobody. He no gonna care about nothing else, believe me. Eddie gonna take a hostage to start the show. With you gun pointed at somebody's head? And these other two, Antonio and my brother, waving guns too? Even if he think he's Clint *fucking* Eastwood, he no gonna make a move."

"Your plan depends on me taking hostages, Pelón?"

"Just for show, Eddie, take it easy. Is an insurance policy."

I shook my head. "You're so off, it's almost comical. I'm not doing that."

"Why not? You not gonna hurt nobody."

I looked at Tony.

Pelón made an annoyed sound. He turned his face toward the window and drew his hand to indicate the entire city. "Eddie, you see this? You see how straight this city looks? Perfect lines, back and forth, up and down? You think that happen by accident?"

"Save the politics, Pelón."

"You like details. That's smart. I always like that about you. That's why you gonna be perfect for this. But don't worry, nobody on that boat is gonna stop you. They got insurance for this. And when they see the cañones? That gonna be the only thing they worry about: to give you everything you want until you take you guns and go."

The waiter came and took Pelón's card. Pelón lifted the toothpick with the two olives from his empty martini glass and pulled the olives from the pick with his dentures. He made a big production of chewing, then spit the pits back into the empty glass, one by one. Finally, he dropped the toothpick in. "¿Bueno, señor? ¿Satisfecho?"

I leaned back in my seat. "Really, Pelón. I'll take a pass."

Pelón's face contorted. "¿Cómo? But why?"

"It sounds dangerous and stupid."

Pelón ground his dentures. "I just tole you. I really thought about this."

"There's eight million ways it could go wrong. None of us have the experience or expertise to pull this off. Besides, I'm still young. Maybe you forgot what that's like. I just got out of a dungeon. I got too much to look forward to."

"Like what? That piece-of-shit job Antonio told me about? You ain't going nowhere with that."

"Watch your mouth, Pelón."

His tone grew more forceful. "We need a fourth man."

"Find one."

"No." He shook his head. "It has to be you."

"Why?"

Pelón rolled the cigar in his mouth. His eyes dug in.

"You already know too much. We can't just let you walk away now."

I narrowed my eyes. "Is that a threat?"

"You should know by now, I don't make threats."

I looked at Tony. Either his mind was really on some other planet, or he did an excellent job of pretending not to notice the icicles forming over the table. I looked back at Pelón.

"I told Tony when he first mentioned this bullshit fantasy that I had no bones to make with either of you. You clowns wanna play stagecoach, get your fuckin' heads blown off, get locked up, be my guest. I wish you well. Somebody asks, I say squat. I fuckin' zip it. They get the rubber hoses out, the water torture, the little black box with the electric current, and I will take it. I already have. Tony knows I can keep a secret better'n anyone. So should you."

Pelón narrowed his eyes.

I focused. "But hear me, Pelón: if you think you're gonna get me to play your game by making threats, think again. And bring along something other than that cane. That ain't no elephant tusk. And I ain't in no mother-fucking wheelchair."

Pelón looked stunned. His mouth hung open. Tony stared out the window. Fireworks began at Navy Pier, and we had the strange advantage of seeing them from up above the explosions. Pelón searched for something to say. I stood to leave and was just about to wish the two of them a bon voyage when the waiter returned, looking embarrassed.

Pelón blasted him a dirty one. "What's *your* problem?"

The waiter returned Pelón's card. In a fey French accent, he said, "I'm sorry, sir, perhaps you have some other form of payment. Your debit card has been declined."

CHAPTER 19:

FLING

That night I had no problem putting Pelón and his stupid ideas out of my mind. I met Xochitl at a beautiful spot she knew called Coco's on Division Street, Paseo Boricua, a bar/restaurant where they had live salsa on the weekends. The crowd was mainly Puerto Ricans in their late twenties and up who danced, drank, and flirted in their own realm.

Xochitl waited alone at the bar when I arrived. She lit up when she saw me approach, got off her high chair, and greeted me with a smile and a peck on the lips. She grabbed a napkin and wiped the lipstick off my mouth.

"I got a tab open. Whatta you wanna drink?"

"Whatever you're having."

"Apple martini?"

"Make that a Corona."

The salsa band was taking a break and the DJ had the crowd moving to a nice bachata, a duet between a man and woman. Xochitl smelled incredible. We stood close.

I gave Xochitl the up-and-down. She wore black

Capri-length pants that flared on the bottom and reached past the tops of her black leather boots, which covered her calves. The boots had a solid heel. Up top she wore a white short-sleeved blouse that showed a mere hint of cleavage, yet emphasized her heavy bosom. She wore large hoop earrings, lots of thin, jangly bracelets on one wrist, and a big turquoise number on the other that matched her eye shadow. Xochitl's straight black hair came halfway down her back and could have been in a shampoo commercial.

"You want something to eat?" she said.

I pushed a lime into my beer bottle. "I'm just enjoying you right now."

Xochitl showed me her dimples. The DJ switched to some old-school house music, and Xochitl and I danced in place a little, finished our round of drinks, and ordered another. I hung my black leather sport coat on the back of her chair.

"You look good in that shirt," she said. "Shows off those broad shoulders and that chest. These other bitches must be going crazy."

"How long you been here drinking without me, Xochitl?"

She winked, then ran a manicured fingernail along my jawline to my chin.

The salsa band came back. They launched into "Muñeca" and Xochitl and I wasted no time. We were among the first to start dancing, although it seemed like most people there soon joined us. Xochitl and I were already in a groove, and I just turned her this way and that with ease. We were so connected, it was so instinctive, that at times I just flashed in my mind to what I wanted her to do, and she automatically did it.

When we stood by the bar to drink again, I kissed her, nothing too aggressive, but Xochitl slid her tongue across mine softly and I pulled her toward me by the small of her back. This time I wiped the lipstick off my own mouth.

"Deliciosa."

And that's how the night went: drinking, dancing, talking, laughing, holding hands, kissing, making eyes at each other, eating tostones and coconut shrimp by the bar. By the time I walked her to the car, I was so wound up, I could have picked Xochitl up and carried her up the four flights to my room.

But it was too soon for that.

We leaned against her Lexus, me pressed up against her, letting her feel me, holding her by the back of her head, kissing like teenagers getting their first shot. I moved to her neck and tasted her perfume. Xochitl tilted her head back and moved her hands slowly down along my back to my butt. I pressed into her.

Xochitl was at a near moan. "We better stop," she said.

I kissed her. "You sure?"

She kissed me back. "Yes." She kissed me again. "Let's stop before we go too far." She kissed me a third time, but grabbed both of my hands with both of hers and held them between us.

I licked my lips and tasted her. "Maybe you're right. If we go another minute, you won't be able to hold back."

Xochitl raised both eyebrows like, *No doubt about it*.

"You all right to drive?"

"I'm fine. I'll be a little distracted, but I'll survive."

I told her to take a cold shower.

"I need *some*thing, that's for sure."

She got behind the wheel and lowered the window.

I leaned in. "Call me when you get home safe."

"I will."

"When am I gonna see you again, Xoch?"

She popped a stick of gum in her mouth and looked up at me. "You like to bowl?"

Xochitl and I had fun at Diversey River Bowl, near Western, knocking over pins and flopping the occasional gutter ball. She had signed up for a league at her job and figured she wanted to practice before letting her colleagues see that she wasn't very good.

"They say networking is important. I figure this'll be a good opportunity to get to know some of the lawyers away from the office."

"I'm sure they'll like that. Maybe you shouldn't wear such tight jeans on game day. They ain't letting you get a full extension."

Xochitl popped a thigh at me. "They look cute with these bowling shoes, though, right?"

I winked and watched her line up, approach, and send the pink bowling ball down the lane real slow.

"A little weak there, Xoch. Keep practicing. I'll grab us something to eat."

I bought a couple of slices of pizza and soda. When I walked back, I saw Coltrane and Johnson standing next to Xochitl.

"Friends of yours?"

I put the food down. "What do you want?"

Coltrane sucked his teeth. "How you been, Eddie? Looks like you been livin' a life of leisure since we last met. Fancy restaurants. Hangin' out in bars. How come you don't invite nobody?"

Johnson picked up my bowling ball and stepped onto our lane. "Even met you a little señorita. This cat works fast."

"Watch your mouth, Johnson."

He ignored me, focused, and sent my ball flying on a curve toward the number one pin, landing a strike on his first roll.

Coltrane sat down. "Johnson here's the star of our detective union."

"This year we're gonna win that trophy." Johnson grabbed my slice of pizza and took a bite. He dropped it on the plate. "Ooh, that's hot." He gulped my soda.

Xochitl looked very annoyed. "You guys want this lane? We can leave."

They ignored her. She sat back down and looked at me.

I said, "You guys wanna take a walk and talk about it?"

My ball came back up. Johnson said, "I'm just getting warmed up." He lined up and looked over at Coltrane. "Don't take this the wrong way, partner, but I love this shit. Using this here heavy black ball to knock over them little white pins? Heaven. No offense."

"None taken."

Johson bowled another strike. He bit off another piece of my slice.

Coltrane said, "See you got a phone now, huh, Santiago."

"Is that a crime?"

"I bet you're makin' a lotta coochie-coo with this one."

Xochitl said, "Leave me out of your conversation." She grabbed her purse and looked at me. "I'm going to the ladies' room."

Coltrane and Johnson both stared at her ass as she walked away.

Coltrane looked at me. "Some like 'em feisty, I guess."

"Why don't you get to your point?"

"You got anything to report, Santiago?"

"Maybe. First we gotta talk about my forty thousand."

Johnson downed more of my soda and burped. "Man, you's a fuckin' one-trick pony."

Coltrane said, "Really, Santiago, you talk like you're the one driving the bus."

"Ain't I? Right now I'm the only one who knows every detail about Pelón's big score."

They perked up.

"That's right. I got the time, the place, the method. The dollar amount he expects to recoup."

Coltrane said, "Big money?"

"Your fuckin' pensions'll seem like pigeonshit."

Coltrane nodded. "And what makes you think you're my only source on this?"

"Look at how you're dressed. If you had a direct link into a whale this big? You wouldn't waste your time with me, Coltrane, let's face it."

Johnson said, "Ain't you logical." He grabbed my ball again and sent it down the lane. This time he left two pins.

"Fuck!"

The machinery wiped the fallen pins and reset the two that remained.

Coltrane whistled. "Seven-ten split, partner. The hard one." He looked at me. "So what's this big deal then? And when's it going down?"

"Get real."

"Are you really *that* inside?"

"I'm practically Pelón's gynecologist. Seen blueprints and everything."

"Do tell." Coltrane got up and dried his hand over the fan by where the ball came out. "But if this haul's so scary big, how come you're looking to trade for a measly forty thou?"

"Because that money you're holding belongs to *me*. I earned it. I saved it. And besides, I don't wanna do business with Pelón. I'm not into what he's into. It's too high risk. You, on the other hand, got no qualms, right? Let Pelón steal the jackpot, then steal it from him with no resistance."

Johnson shook his head. "Boy, you flip the script, and spin crap from gold. You think a jive-ass story like that's gonna shake two veterans?"

I brushed my hand across my mouth. "All's I'm telling you is I want my money back. Any scheme you come up with that don't include returning my cash falls into the don't-give-a-shit pile."

Johnson snapped his neck toward me. "I oughta slide your ass down this lane and knock these pins over with your forehead."

"Try it."

Coltrane said, "Relax, both of you."

My ball came back and this time Coltrane took it. He looked at me as if he might consider my offer. But then he shook his head. "No deal, Santiago. I ain't got nothin' I wanna trade. You're gonna serve up the goods to me for one simple reason: because it's the right thing to do."

"You're bugging."

"Maybe. Just keep reading that Bible. Now watch this."

Coltrane aimed and flung the bowling ball with such precision that it rode the gutter's edge like it should've fallen in, but instead knocked the seven pin on the outside so that it flew across the frame and smashed the ten pin into the wall. Coltrane pumped his fist and high-fived Johnson. "Yeah, baby!"

Johnson said, "I'm telling you, Herman, we're takin' that trophy this year."

Johnson dropped what was left of my pizza slice and killed my soda.

Coltrane pointed at me. "We'll call you."

"I never gave you my number."

"We already have it."

They walked off.

Xochitl came back from the ladies' room. "Who were those assholes?"

"My probation officers. They're kind of upset I been ditching them."

"You're still on probation?"

"Sort of."

Xochitl was smart enough to know that wasn't quite right, but secure enough to not need all the answers.

"Sorry, Xochitl. You wanna leave?"

"No." She bit her slice and picked up her pink ball. "We came here to do our own thing, right?"

CHAPTER 20:

AUTUMN LEAVES

Xochitl and I hiked along a trail through the woods. I looked up at the canopy of leaves. Two and a half seasons' worth of sun, wind, and rain had polished most into colorful autumn gems. Ahead of me, Xochitl walked in gym shoes, comfortable-looking jeans, and a denim jacket. Birds cooed and fluttered and the trees swayed in the breeze.

"Women at my office go to the spa, and I like that too. But I always feel like a nice hike slows the clock a little."

"Feels like we're not even in the city," I said.

Xochitl looked back at me. "Are you all right, Eddie? You seem a little low. Even in the car."

I was distracted by the fact that I still saw no solution to my missing forty thousand, but I smiled to let Xochitl know that I liked her attention and didn't need to talk. She turned to watch her step.

"When I was fifteen," she said, "I visited my grandparents in México. It's all mountains. You go away from the town and in a minute it's a little like this, but steep, up and down. I used to go for long walks."

"Ever get lost?"

"There was usually somebody with us. Sometimes I went alone. I felt so comfortable."

We came to a bend in the trail, where it turned to hug a slow-moving brook. There was a small clearing and a large tree that had fallen on its side. Xochitl put one foot on it, put down her backpack, pulled two water bottles, and tossed me one.

"How 'bout you? Travel much?"

"Oh yeah, all over the world, Xoch."

"Seriously. Ever left the Midwest?"

I took a sip of water. "I went to the Big Apple, once. As a kid."

"Family trip?"

"Sort of."

Xochitl sat on the fallen tree. "Tell me."

I sipped my water. "It was unexpected. One day in the fourth grade, I'm in class, daydreaming. Suddenly, I see my father's face in the classroom door. He flashes this huge smile, which he used just on me, I think. All teeth. Anyway, he gets real grim, comes in, tells the teacher he's sorry, it's a family emergency, but we gotta run. I'm gonna be out for a couple of days."

"What happened?"

"He wanted me to play hooky with him. So I grab my bag and he walks me out with his arm around me, like he's prepping me for the bad news. We get outside and parked out front is a tricked-out '72 Camaro Super Sport. Red with bright orange flames. Spoiler in the back, mag wheels."

"Your father just bought it?"

"He had it. He holds up the keys. 'Wanna ride to New York?' I'm like, 'Right now?' He looks back at the school.

'Unless you'd rather go back.' I'm like, 'Hell no.' We jump in. The car's got just one eight-track: *Rumours* by Fleetwood Mac. I go, 'Pop, whose car?' He pretends not to hear. When I asked if Mom was coming, he tells me, 'I left her a note.' "

"Communication *is* the key," said Xochitl, smiling.

"I wouldn't know. We gassed up in Indiana. Ate in Ohio. Whenever I got out, I looked at the car. It got more beautiful every time. Slicker. More muscular. We hit mountains in Pennsylvania, with the sun going down behind us, and everything ahead of us bronze. The trees, the road, the clouds, the tops of the other mountains."

"I love the light like that."

"Me too."

I made eye contact with Xochitl. She smiled and didn't pull away.

I bent and picked up a smooth stone. "Whenever we couldn't get the radio, I slipped in the eight-track. My dad liked 'The Chain.' I dug another song, 'You Make Loving Fun.' "

"As a fourth grader?"

"I didn't know what it meant. Maybe I still don't. I just liked the way it sounded. But by Pennsylvania, we both dug 'Go Your Own Way.' We couldn't get enough. He made me play it three times in a row. Anyway, at one point he pulls into a rest area. 'Wait outside the door.' I tell him, 'I wanna listen to the rest of the song. I'm big.' He looked at me for a second. He leaves the keys in the ignition and gets out. Then he leans in. 'Eddie, listen. Do not open the trunk. Whatever you do, don't look inside. You got me?' "

Xochitl widened her eyes. "Let me guess. As soon as he goes inside..."

"Believe it or not, no. I was afraid. And I didn't want him to catch me."

"What do you think was in there?"

"Something a ten-year-old should never look at."

"Did that make you nervous?"

"Yeah. But then my dad came back, he winked, and all that melted. It was late when we crossed into New York. My dad told me about his life there, when he first came from PR at, like, twelve."

"Did you stay with family?"

"We drove to the beach."

"The beach?"

"My father shuts the engine. 'Let's take a nap.'"

"In the car?"

"Yup. When I woke up, the sun was slipping over the horizon. My father was outside, on the sand, by the water's edge, smoking and staring at the ocean. I walked up to him. He looked down and put his arm around me. 'I used to swim as a boy in Arecibo.' He nodded at the water. 'Taste it,' he tells me. I smiled, bent, stuck my fingers in, then stuck them in my mouth. I gagged and said, 'Sala'o.' My father laughed and threw his cigarette in the sand. 'That's where we come from.'"

Xochitl wrapped her arms around her knees. "He sounds a little philosophical."

"Not to write an essay about it, but yeah, a little. We found a bodega and bought one serving of eggs, bacon, and toast with two forks. My father divided everything in half, and we dug in. 'That Camaro loves gas,' he said. But then he winked. 'I love this, Eddie. You and me eating out of the same plate.'"

"Cute."

I threw the stone I had been playing with across the brook. It skipped along the surface and made it to the other side.

"We ended up in Brooklyn. My father found an empty parking lot and let me drive the Camaro in circles."

"How old were you?"

"I could barely reach the pedals. After that, we drove to a garage. My father let me out across the street and up the block a little. He tells me, 'Wait here. I don't care what you hear, don't go near that garage.' He removed his watch and gave it to me. 'If I'm not back in fifteen minutes, find a cop and tell him that your father went inside and never came out. Don't go in with them. Tell them to come with their guns. You got that?' I repeated it. 'Good. Other than that, don't move for fifteen minutes.' "

Xochitl said, "Oh, my God. I would have been trembling."

"I was scared, but somehow I also knew my dad would come back. He drove up to the door, honked the clave pattern, and the door rose. He drove that smoking hot Camaro inside and the door came down. I checked the watch to set the time, but my father came out like ten minutes later, walking, light on his feet."

"Were you sad about the car?"

"I expected it. My father shows me a thick roll of hundreds. He peels the top one for me. 'You my little sidekick.' "

"A hundred was a hell of a lot of money back then."

"For a kid? Candy bars cost a quarter. Anyway, we rode the train to Coney Island. It was overcast, and we were practically the only ones out there. My father goes on this ride. The Hammer. Basically it just flipped you. I was afraid. My old man says, 'Wait down here,' and gets on without me. He's the only one on it. The thing spins him, flips him. I can hear him yell and laugh and scream my name when it flies past. At one point the ride freezes at the top, my father's upside down. Coins rain out of his pockets, through the metal cage, to the pavement beneath the machine. I waited for the ride to stop, 'cause I didn't want it to swing down at me. But then I ran for the coins."

"You were getting paid left and right that day."

I paused to look around the woods. I don't know what I expected to see. The trees did not move. And Xochitl listened. I wondered whether I should tell her the rest. I looked her in the eye again. She seemed wide open.

"So when the ride stops, I run over to pick up coins. My dad comes down the steps with that pícaro smile. Hair's messed up, shirt's all crooked. He sees me grabbing. 'Finders, keepers!' He nods. I see another quarter and go for it. But then a few feet away, I see a tiny plastic bag with brown powder in it. Then another. I reach for the first bag, and suddenly, my dad's like, 'Eddie, no!' He jumps down the metal steps and grabs my arm, I mean really squeezes it. He got in my face and pointed at the Baggie. 'Never touch that! You hear me?' He shook me. I noticed what looked like a rubber band half-hanging out of his pocket. 'Don't never let me see you touch that!' "

Xochitl made a sad face. "Did you cry?"

"That was one of only two times I ever saw real sadness in my father's eyes. He picked up the Baggies and put them in his pocket. We rode the train to the airport in silence. When we got to our stop, he looked up and down the platform and went in a public toilet by himself again."

"With you right with him?"

It was a question that had never occurred to me. "Later, as we walked toward the airport, he suddenly stopped. 'Espérate.' He spotted a garbage can, looked around, reached in his pocket, took whatever was left, and threw it in. Then he reached in his waistband and pulled a gun."

Xochitl said, "Wow."

"He wrapped it in a handkerchief and also tossed it in the garbage. 'Can't take that on a plane.' We bought tickets and waited at JFK until the last flight of the day back to Chicago."

Xochitl was still seated on the dead tree. She patted the spot next to her, and I sat.

She put her arm around me. "Did you guys ever talk about that again?"

"What would there have been to say?"

Xochitl shook her head and passed her hand over my cheek. "Tú eres *tan* humilde. That's growing up too fast."

I put my head on Xochitl's shoulder. We stayed there for a while and watched the brook flow.

Xochitl and I headed back along the same trail, trying to beat the rain back to the car. The gray clouds finally delivered a light shower.

"I don't think we're gonna get back before it gets worse," she said. "We'll be soaked by the time we get there."

The water thickened. Droplets popped against the leaves and stirred the smells of the forest. Lightning flashed, and seconds later the thunder. I recalled the trees that I had seen that day that appeared to have been struck.

"Maybe we should pick up our pace."

We hustled, but by the time we got to the car, it was

really coming down. Xochitl and I sat in the car, wet and cold and shivering, yet excited from the brisk walk. We drove for a while and held hands, without music, without the radio or conversation, just the sound of the windshield wipers, and the occasional moan of distant thunder.

Xochitl squeezed my hand. "You ever think about writing some of those stories?"

"Which ones?"

"Any of them. Like the ones you told at the museum. The guy with his teeth showing through the hole in his cheek."

I twisted my face. "People are sick of prison tales."

"How 'bout the one about your father and the Camaro? Maybe you should keep a journal."

"Why?"

"To preserve it."

"Sounds like homework. I told you I dropped out of high school, right?"

Xochitl turned the Lexus down Lincoln Avenue. Without warning, without putting on the signal, she pulled into a motel parking lot. My heart began to move. She shut off the engine and jumped out into the rain.

"Wait here," she said.

She ran into the office. A minute later, Xochitl came out of the office and headed for a room, but did not look in my direction. She let herself in, and left the room door wide open.

I exited the car and ran to the room, trying to avoid the puddles. I locked the door behind me. Xochitl was already in the shower. I sat on the bed, then got up and sat on the chair next to the small table. The walls were a queasy pink, like the carpet in my room, and the carpet was a very faded orange. The cover on the bed looked like something left over from *The Brady Bunch*. The bed itself was big. I wondered if Xochitl wanted me to join her in the shower, then figured she would have waited, or she would've come out by now and said so. I felt cold.

I changed the thermostat and the heat came on full blast. The room warmed up quick. I checked myself in the mirror. There was not much I could groom.

The TV got bad reception, except for channel 3, where two women did a 69. I flicked it off as soon as I saw that. The radio worked fine and I went up and down the dial, but found nothing that felt right.

I heard the shower shut off, killed the radio, and scrambled to sit in the chair and find a pose that said that I was ready, but that I did not expect too much. Xochitl came out of the shower with a white towel wrapped around her torso and another one fashioned into a turban on her head. She rushed over to the bed and jumped under the covers like she didn't want to be seen. She pulled the covers up to her chest and finally looked at me.

"Go take a shower."

Once in the bathroom, I saw that Xochitl had written the word "Hurry" in the water that condensed on the mirror. I let the hot water run over me, and soaped myself, and thought about the parts of Xochitl's body where the same bar of soap had been. My stomach stirred. I felt nervous, but something bold coursed through me.

I washed myself and dried myself more thoroughly than I ever had, and when I was through, I wrapped the towel around my waist and looked at myself in the fogged-up mirror. It would have been nice to have a toothbrush and toothpaste, but nothing is ever perfect. I walked out.

Xochitl sat on the edge of the bed now, wrapped in the white towel. Her hair hung loose as she dried it with the other towel. I stood next to the entrance to the bathroom.

"Ven."

I swallowed my anxiety and walked over and stood in front of her. Xochitl looked up at me with an expression that I had not quite seen since our first encounter on the dance floor. She put down the towel she used to dry her hair and stood in front of me. Her fingertips and nails traced over my arms and across my chest, light and slow. She followed the lines of some of my tattoos.

Heat licked up my spine and into my throat. I kissed Xochitl and pressed against her there, next to the bed, and the soft warmth of her exposure slipped across my bare chest. Our tongues were inside each other's mouths, as far as they could go.

Xochitl stepped back. Her eyes hooked into mine. She uncinched the towel around her torso, let it drop to the floor. She climbed into the bed without any shame about her nakedness. She pulled the bedsheet up to her nipples and looked at me with something other than a smile.

I stood wordless.

Xochitl tilted her head in that sly, cocky way of hers. "Quítate la toalla."

I removed my towel and dropped it.

Xochitl smiled. "Bueno," she said. "Now shut off the light."

CHAPTER 21:

AFTERGLOW

Our clothes were cold and damp from the rain, and we wore them over our musty bodies. Xochitl focused on the road. She switched stations on the radio, and pretended, it seemed, that I was not in the car. I reached over and touched her hand. She didn't remove it. But she didn't really receive me either.

I went through her CD collection and found one by Ana Gabriel. "This the woman your family says you sound like?"

"Supposedly. Sometimes."

I put it on. I think the song was called "A Pesar de Todos." The singer hit notes that roughened her voice a little and I understood the comparison. Xochitl's face seemed to grow longer.

"¿Qué te pasa?"

She bit her lower lip.

"Xochitl?"

"What?"

"You all right?"

"I'm fine."

"You seem far away."

She didn't deny it. The rain stopped, the night had fallen, and the rain-slicked black streets reflected dimly the artificial lights of the city.

I shifted in my seat. "I wish we could've stayed back there longer."

"I have to pick up my kids."

I looked out the passenger window. The landscape of the city's North Side scrolled past. I asked what I really wanted to know. "Didn't you like that, Xochitl?"

She let out a deep breath. "Please don't, Eddie."

"Don't what?"

"Don't be so typical. You were there."

I flashed to a moment at the motel when I was looking down at Xochitl and she was looking back at me with her mouth open. "So then? Why are you pulling back?"

"I'm not," she said. "Let's just let this be what it is."

"I have no idea what you mean by that."

She shut off the defroster. I killed the radio. It got very quiet.

I said, "Do you always carry condoms in your purse?"

"Do I need to justify myself to you?"

Xochitl was right that she didn't, but I did not have it in me to say so. Instead, I went through her CD collection. I found something that I thought might sugar the mood, but it made no improvement. I reached for Xochitl's hand and this time she pulled away. I left it alone and pretended to watch the road.

Xochitl pulled in to the White Castle on Milwaukee. She parked and asked if I wanted anything.

"Is it all right if I come too?"

"Fine." She slammed the door.

Inside, she ordered sliders, onion rings, and a Coke. I asked for the same and paid for both of us, which felt good. We took our identical trays and sat across from each other at an antiseptic-looking metal table, under fluorescent bulbs that felt more artificial than most. Under this light I noticed that Xochitl had washed off her makeup in the shower earlier. She chewed her little cheeseburgers slowly, as if she were so fatigued, she could barely raise her food.

"Is it really that bad, Xoch?"

"Is what so bad?"

I waved my hands around. "Whatever it is that's cramping you."

"Maybe you don't know me so well." She bit into a burger and looked away as she chewed.

I put my food down. "OK, Xochitl. You're right. I don't know you yet. Not really. But I want to. And I *do* know that you were in one frame of mind before we ... Now you just seem upset."

She looked at me. "You really wanna know?"

"I do. What's wrong?"

Xochitl bit into her burger and chewed slowly. She looked slightly away and fixated on an invisible spot in the space next to my head. "A long time ago, at DePaul, I fell for this boy. He was black."

"What did your parents think?"

"I tried to keep it a secret. He loved computers. Wanted to work for NASA."

I'm embarrassed to admit it, but I felt a twinge of jealousy. I knew that was silly, so I bottled it. "You were pretty smart yourself there, Xochitl."

"I was afraid to bring home a bad grade. One time in grammar school I got a D on this art project. My father beat me with a telephone wire."

"Damn. So what happened with this boy in college?"

"I started going to his dorm after class. Pretty soon I got pregnant. I agonized what to say to my parents. I was throwing up. My belly was getting big. Finally, I told my mother."

"How'd she handle it?"

Xochitl looked me right in the face again. "At first, nothing. Just nodding her head, looking to the side. When I told her the father was black, she lost it. It didn't matter that he was brilliant. She cried like someone died. Kept asking me why I had done this to her. How this was going to kill my father. And then she said there was only one choice."

"Shotgun wedding?"

"Abortion."

"Oh."

Xochitl lowered her head. "Before that, she always said it was a sin. Now, all of a sudden, she's telling me that God sometimes lets us correct our mistakes."

"You did it?"

Xochitl let the question hang long enough to make me wish I hadn't asked.

"She made me feel ashamed. Like I was trash." Xochitl looked me in the eye. "I never told her to stop. I never said that it was my choice."

"You were young. She was your mother."

"Maybe. Or maybe I just let her make the hard decision. I don't know anymore. She rode the bus with me to the clinic. Took me inside. I never said no."

I nodded and touched the back of Xochitl's hand.

"My parents wanted me to go to college. Meet a white boy or an educated Mexican. Get married a virgin. They never let me go anywhere. I couldn't stay at the dorms, even though my scholarship paid."

"They were protective."

The grown woman in front of me did not buy that.

"What happened with the astronaut?"

"I ignored him until he stopped trying to talk to me after class. I never told him."

Tears welled in Xochitl's eyes, but didn't roll. I offered her a napkin.

Xochitl took the hair out of her face and dried her eyes. "I don't know if God punished me. I fell off track right away. Started smoking pot. Cutting class. Making out with whoever. I fell behind and dropped out."

"How did your parents react?"

"I didn't tell them. I left the house every day like I was going to class. Killed a few hours. Came back when I was due."

"How'd you manage?"

"I roamed around for a few days. Went to some matinees. Window-shopping, daydreaming. But I had to do something. There was this man who my family knew. He was from the same town as my father. Pretty well-off. He had these restaurants on the South Side, taco stands that are always busy. It was known that he was looking for a wife. He was older, in his early thirties."

I chuckled. "Over-the-hill, huh?"

"Remember, I was nineteen. I saw him at family gatherings. As I got older, I caught him staring. He would look away, but I knew. When I graduated from high school, he came by the house and left a present. A gold necklace with a small diamond. My parents were so pleased. My mother especially."

Xochitl bagged her garbage. "I just looked him up. Called for him at one of his restaurants, found him, asked if he would come pick me up near the school, which, of course, he did. I started a relationship with him right then and there, on the spot, on purpose."

"You seduced him?"

"It wasn't hard. I told him I always liked him. That the necklace made me feel special. We went by the Lake and made out. I started doing this every day. Getting him real worked up, but never going further. He kept trying to spread my legs. I told him that was reserved for my husband."

"And he bought that?"

"He's still paying for it."

"How did it go with your family?"

"He went to the house and told my parents that we were in love. That he wanted to do everything with respect. I would never lack for anything. If I wanted to continue in school, he would not be against it. He promised to buy me a house. When he asked for my hand in marriage, my father got up, walked across the room to a cabinet, took out a dusty bottle of tequila reserved for baptisms and funerals. They did a shot and the deal was done."

"And now that's your soon-to-be ex-husband."

"The one and only."

"What happened when he found out you weren't a virgin?"

"Please. Men are so gullible."

"Why didn't you go to school? He said he didn't mind."

"We married that Christmas. I was pregnant by Valentine's Day. At that point he was like, 'Tesoro, a woman cannot go to school and work and be a good mother, ¿sabes?' He insisted that I would never need to make money because of his businesses, and so the baby had to become my focus."

"But after that, you had another child."

"Some years later. It was the natural order."

We tossed our garbage and went to the car.

"Did you love him, Xochitl? Ever?"

Xochitl looked past me, through the glass behind me, through the night even, like maybe the answer to that question existed somewhere near the moon. "I grew to appreciate him. He's a good man. Hardworking. Self-made. Obnoxious sometimes, but a good provider. We have a couple Laundromats now."

"But?"

"What do you want me to tell you?"

"The truth, Xochitl. Why did it end?"

She paused. Not like she tried to figure out an answer, more like she wondered whether I was worth saying it to.

"Was it the sex?"

"The sex was fine," she said. "He's very passionate. I just never felt like…I had to have him. And I came to a point where I thought maybe that was something I needed. And he as well. He deserves someone who feels the same."

Xochitl looked at me and smiled. Not the mischievous smile, or a flirtatious smile, or even the type of smile that indicates any happiness whatsoever.

"I'm sorry, Xochitl."

"For what? It wasn't your fault."

No. It was not. The world is full of compromises, stupid choices, and shattered dreams. Everybody gets a taste of that. Some more than others.

I touched her hand again. "You don't have to replay those old scripts, Xoch. It's OK to make something new."

Xochitl locked eyes with me for an instant, but didn't amen or even nod. Instead, she turned the defroster down, put the car in motion, and drove.

CHAPTER 22:

NURSERY RHYME

I listened to the Bears vs. Green Bay. The Monsters of the Midway trudged through a rough patch and it was hard not to think of my run-in at the bowling alley with Coltrane and Johnson.

Their eyes ignited when they heard I had dirt on Pelón, but they pulled back fast. Maybe they only pretended not to be juiced on my offer. Maybe their complete blow-off of information in exchange for my money was simply lowballing, a negotiation tactic. But the cockiness in Coltrane's voice, the look in his eyes, when he said I would serve up intelligence simply because it was the right thing to do? That made me wonder.

I spun circles around it in my mind. The seconds ticked off in the fourth quarter and the Bears resigned themselves to another unhappy ending. I heard a knock at my door.

I jumped off the bed and hustled to my table, where I picked up a steak knife. I moved quietly over to the side of the door. There was no point in pretending I wasn't home—my radio was on and the volume was up. I put my hand on the lock and asked who it was.

"I'm looking for a hungry man."

I tossed the steak knife on the table and opened. Xochitl held a pizza box in one hand and a shopping bag in the other. She handed me the pizza and kissed my cheek as she walked past. She placed the shopping bag on the carpet. I put the pizza box on the table. Xochitl removed her coat and held it in her arms. We faced each other in the center of the room.

"You should've called. I'd have cleaned up."

"I wanted to catch the real you." A purple sweater squeezed Xochitl's chest. Black leggings outlined her hips and thighs.

I nodded at my hot plate. "I could've cooked, at least."

She gestured at the pizza box. "What's the matter, you don't like Father and Son?"

I looked around the room. "Eating at the restaurant itself would've been better."

"Get over it." She handed me her coat.

I hung it.

Xochitl grabbed two six-packs out of her shopping bag and stacked the beers in my little fridge, except for two, which she handed me to open. She stacked two plates with sausage pizza, and moved with hers to the edge of the bed.

I dragged my lone chair to face her.

Xochitl spoke with her mouth full. "My feet are killing me." The same black leather boots from the other night wrapped her calves to the knees.

I put my plate down. "Let me help you with those."

She let me unzip each boot and place it neatly in the

corner. She pulled her legs under, Indian-style, on the bed, and had to bend way down to find her beer on the floor. We ate, drank, and listened to the postgame analysis on the radio.

Xochitl polished a Corona, then stood and went to the shopping bag. "Te compré un regalo."

She handed me a small gift-wrapped box. I put my plate on the table.

"Why?"

"What a question. Open it."

I unwrapped it. "A tape recorder?"

"That's what it says."

"For taping shit off the radio?"

"No. For recording your own voice."

"I don't sing, Xochitl."

"Talking."

"About what?"

She took the box and opened it. "I already put in batteries." She removed the tape recorder from the box and rewound. "Listen." On tape Xochitl recited "Mary Had a Little Lamb." "I had to test it. You should record those stories of yours. I know you can't see writing them. Maybe if you hear yourself, it'll do something for you."

I examined the tape recorder. "Think I got something to say, Xoch?"

"If you keep it real. The guy at the store said you don't have to crowd the mic so much. It'll record from across the room."

"Sweet."

Xochitl was on her knees, on the floor, in front of me. I was still in the chair.

"You gonna use the tape recorder?"

"Every day," I said.

"Will you let me listen to the results?"

"What would be the point of doing it if I didn't?"

A huge smile splayed across Xochitl's face. "I told you to be honest. But it's cute that you felt you needed to say that."

I leaned down to give Xochitl a quick kiss and my cell phone began to ring. I went over to the top of the bureau and checked it. Tony's name and number popped up.

I hit the reject button.

"Who's that?" she said.

"Remember that friend I told you about?"

"The one who's messed up?"

"He's been calling like crazy for the past few days. I don't feel like talking to him."

"Too much drama?"

"He's always trying to get something, and his mind is not all there. I'm sick of dealing with him."

Xochitl checked out the view of the skyline. "You can see more than I would have guessed." She went back in the shopping bag. "I'm glad you have a CD player. Look what I got you." She handed me a copy of *Rumours*.

I said, "I haven't seen this album cover in almost thirty years."

"Sorry, I opened it," she said. "I couldn't resist. I didn't know what kind of music you were talking about. I recognized some from the radio, though. Number six is my favorite."

I flipped it over. " 'Songbird'?"

She put it on and played it. I felt a very dim, distant recollection. Xochitl stood behind me at the window and put her arms around me. We listened to the entire song. I wondered if Xochitl was trying to tell me something. But I didn't have the nerve to ask.

"Did you learn anything, Xochitl?"

"Yes. We have different tastes in music."

I slapped Xochitl on the butt. She giggled. I took her face into both hands and gave her a succulent kiss.

"Is there anything that we *both* like?"

Xochitl angled her head, and we kissed again and found our way to the bed. I sat her on the edge and kneeled. I kissed her and let my hands travel. Her chest rose and fell. I moved to her neck, then down her neck. When she pulled off her sweater and tugged at her bra, I swallowed her brown nipple. I massaged her in slow circles over the leggings and felt her moisture through the cloth. Her breathing quickened. I kissed her stomach and felt the scar. Then I sank lower, peeled off her leggings and panties, and let my mouth go the rest of the way.

Afterward, we lay in bed, held hands, and stared at the ceiling.

Xochitl squeezed. "You have a soft touch."

I looked at my other hand. "You think?"

"Not the skin, the skin is tough. I mean your *way*. Tu manera de ser."

"Um. Is that good?"

"That strong beat comes in handy."

"I like *your* rhythm too, Xoch."

"So everybody's happy."

We listened to the cars on the avenue below.

"Xochitl, I been wondering."

She didn't say anything or gesture in any way for me to continue.

"If this is too sensitive, tell me."

"I will."

"What was it that made you feel so pressured? With your parents, I mean."

"Does it matter now?"

"Maybe."

Xochitl didn't let go of my hand. "I don't know. It was never a clear thought."

I listened.

Xochitl rolled over on her side to face me. She propped her head on her elbow and I took in her full stomach.

"I was an infant when we crossed the border. My father carried me. My mother and her brother carried the belongings."

"Your old man swam with you on his back?"

"It was supposed to be shallow. There were ten or twelve of us. Halfway, the river suddenly went to their armpits. My father held me above his head. Some people got swept away. The coyote himself went under. Those who made it were scattered along the riverbank. My parents and mother's brother found each other. They joined other survivors."

"Thank God."

"Most supplies got lost. The coyote was gone. No guide in the desert."

"That's fucked."

"They were supposed to meet others who would bring them to Amarillo. My father's buddy was taking us to Chicago."

"Underground Railroad."

"Without a conductor. We wandered in the heat. It was freezing at night."

"You remember all this?"

"I've heard the story so many times."

"Everybody must've been freaking out."

"Some men fought. Everybody got sunburned. They hunted possums, I think, but there was no water. My father says he thought about his mother a lot. On the fifth day my mother's brother died of dehydration. They had to leave his body."

"Poor thing."

"The next day they found a road. A passing trucker brought them to a hospital."

Xochitl and I lay on our sides, face-to-face. I brushed the hair away from her brown eyes.

"What a nightmare." I wanted to make Xochitl feel better, but didn't know how.

"My whole life, my parents, they lay it on how they came to this country for me. To give me and then my sisters, who were born here, an opportunity."

"Parents talk like that."

"My mother has this way. Like you never deserved her sacrifice. Like she might have *been* something."

"You felt guilty."

"She wanted me to. I don't know, Eddie. I never talk about these things."

Xochitl's eyes watered. I pulled her into my chest and kissed the top of her head. It felt good to feel the heat of her breath on my skin. We spent the rest of that Sunday in bed.

CHAPTER 23:

CONFESSION

After Xochitl left, I lay around feeling lonely. I thought of calling her, but knew that was desperate. I thought about recording something on the tape player like she wanted, but couldn't think of anything.

Around nine at night I heard someone climb the stairs, real slow, with a strange, almost unnatural rhythm to his step. I realized it had to be Pelón with his bad hip.

I opened my door and went to the top of the stairs. He was halfway up the last flight, but he rested against the wall.

"Diablo," he said, out of breath.

"What're you doing here?"

"I can't visit?"

I went back to my room, left the door open, stretched out on the bed with my hands behind my head. Slowly, Pelón hobbled the rest of his way up, then down the hall to my room. He caught his breath and grinned.

"Shut the door behind you."

He did. He turned and stood and leaned on his cane.

He was wearing glasses, and I remembered that he sometimes used to wear them in the past, but realized that I had
not seen him wearing any since I got out. His prescription
had gotten very thick. I didn't invite Pelón to sit.

He looked around the room. "Antonio say he no see
you no more. You don't return his calls."

"Are you his secretary now?"

Pelón pursed his lips. "Who bit you to put you in such a
bad mood?" He hobbled over to my window and nodded.

I knew Pelón would not leave until he got his point
across. "Help yourself to that chair."

He plopped in it, gritted his dentures, and released
a burst, like a machine that depends on compressed air
might do when it breaks down. In Spanish he said, "Bones
don't help like they used to."

"That's what you get for living so long."

Pelón creased his eye. "Think you can offer me
somesing to drink?"

"I got nothing."

"Not even a glass of water?"

I almost said no, but I got up, got a cup, went to the
bathroom, and half-filled it.

Pelón smiled. "This didn't come from the toilet,
did it?"

"Taste it and find out."

If that made Pelón nervous, he didn't let on. He took
a pillbox out of his breast pocket, and popped two of
them. "Percocet. Don't know how I could make it without
them."

"Why did you come here?"

Pelón nodded like, *Yes, yes, business.* "I wanted to talk
to you about the police."

"What about them?"

Pelón tapped his cane against the floor. "They dirty."

"No shit, Sherlock."

"No," he said. "They *real* dirty. Evil."

I don't know if Pelón paused to give me a chance to respond, but I waited for whatever else he had to say.

"They gonna try to turn you, Eddie."

"Turn me against what?"

"You own people. Antonio. Me."

"Who says I'm with you jerk-offs?"

"They want what I got."

"Why would they think they can leverage me against you, Pelón? Who the fuck am I to you?"

"You the fourth man, Eddie. I need you to get the job done, and they know it. They can smell these things. They want everything."

"Whatta you mean, 'everything,' Pelón?"

"Everything. La Esquina Caliente. They buying property around there."

"Real estate?"

"Sí. That's what they do."

"Coltrane and Johnson?"

Pelón nodded. "They buyin' lots of buildings. Houses."

I thought about that for a second. I didn't see what anything like that had to do with Pelón. Or with me, for that matter. "That sounds expensive. But why do I give a fuck?"

"That's why they keep this war going."

"What war?"

"Between Antonio and Cucaracha. That's why they like it. They know while everything hot around there, the values ain't gonna go too high. They can just buy, buy,

buy. Then when they own as much as they can, they clean up the block and the value goes up."

It sounded far-fetched. "What's your angle on all of this?"

"I'm the one who came up with the idea."

Now we skated way out there. Pelón just admitted that he was in business with Coltrane and Johnson. In Spanish he said, "Who you think poisoned Roach's material?"

"The cops?"

Pelón raised his eyebrows like, *Who else?*

"That's crazy."

"That kid in the park?" he said. "Who you think shot him? Follow the money."

I thought about the fact that the kid was shot with a .38 on the same night that the narcs had recovered a .38 from Tony's car. And how later they were real cocky about their ability to link that very weapon to the murder.

I said, "What could they possibly gain from all that?"

"I tole you. They keep the war going and keep the property values down until they can't buy no more. They tryin' to control the market. Tony's operation is on the corner, out in the open. Any enemy can drive by and spray bullets. Roach thinks Tony is his enemy. Tony thinks Roach is the enemy. They both just puppets."

"You got a wild imagination."

"I already ran this scam. Over there by Wicker Park. You remember how that was? Now for this piece, I brought in these two, and it was my biggest mistake. I was the bank, their name was on the deed with me, through some dummy companies. I thought it was perfect because they could give protection. That was my mistake. Now, these hijos de putas are X-ing me out."

"Why?"

"They don't need me no more."

I didn't follow.

Pelón's face began to sag. "Estoy pela'o."

"Huh?" It'd been so long since I'd heard it put that way, it took me a second to figure out what he meant. "You're broke?"

I thought about Pelón's apartment. His peacock's fan worth of hundreds in the back of the limo after the race-track. But I also remembered how the narcs had said he was "bleedin' like a stuck pig."

I said, "Tony said you own bodegas."

"I used to."

"A bunch of buildings in Wicker Park?"

"Gone. I lost it all."

"How?"

"Taxes."

"The IRS?"

Pelón made a face. "Uy. Don't even mention those animals. They're the ones who got Capone."

"Why didn't you pay?"

Pelón looked at the floor. "Everybody has a weakness."

"You spent all that money on hookers?"

"Gambling. Those goddamn casino boats. The freaking high rollers' table." Pelón shook his head. "I used to think that I was in control."

Pelón talked about the cycle. First he went for the fun, entertainment, with friends. Then by himself, because he was lonely and bored.

"I bet, and sometimes I win big. Then I bet more. That's how it sucks you. You put more on the table every time, trying to get back what you lost. You start chasing it.

Everything disappears down the little hole. Is like a slow fire."

"Your condo?"

"We in court right now. The bank is taking it."

"What about the money Tony brought to your house that night?"

"That was nothing. Just a loan. The Mexican is a shy-lock."

"Your winnings at the racetrack? Curly-Q?"

Pelón shook his head. "After I drop you and Antonio off that night, I went straight to a casino boat. I came home with eight hundred dollars."

"You blew seventy thousand in one night? How's that possible?"

"When the Devil is determined, he doesn't sleep."

"Jesus. What about your limo?"

"I bought that car used. Is not worth much. I had to lay off my driver. Now I'm driving it myself."

If I were more sophisticated, I might've thought that the way in which Pelón had an answer for everything was proof that he thought about it too much and was therefore lying. Somehow, instinctively, I saw past all that reasoning, and I took Pelón at his word.

I said, "So you're really busted. That's why you're so hot to do this job."

"They got a lotta money on that boat. A lot of it was mine."

I nodded.

"I know that boat inside out. I know every routine. The schedule, the movements. I ain't done nothing but think about this. Success is guaranteed." Pelón put his hand out. "You gonna be the fourth man."

I stood and shook his hand, the one with the missing fingers. "I wish I could say that everything is gonna work out for you, Pelón, but I don't think that's the case. For the last time, count me out."

Pelón's weak smile went straight to shit.

I went to the door, opened it, and kept my hand on the knob. "I'm sure I'll read about your adventures one day."

Pelón sat in my lone chair, in the middle of my tiny room, disappointed, not believing that he'd just been dismissed.

My posture left room for no doubt.

Pelón hoisted himself out of the chair slowly and hobbled up to me. "Sometimes the young, they don't know what's good for them."

"I'm not that young anymore."

"You should see yourself through my eyes." Pelón put his hat on, tilted it, and went out.

I shut the door and went to the window to watch. The limo was across the street. A long time later, Pelón emerged from my building. He hobbled slowly. Sure enough, he let himself in behind the wheel of the long white limo, and chauffeured himself to wherever else he had to go.

After Pelón left, I thought about the things that I knew about him, the money I knew that he made all those years before, when Tony and I were affiliated with him on the burglaries. The money he *tried* to make. Pelón always had his hand in something.

After the stash house job, where Pelón made like a raging elephant and crushed the wheelchair guy's head with a tusk, my crew and I avoided doing anything but routine burglaries with him. Mansion jobs where we were assured of nobody being home were a staple. Breaking into warehouses at night was fun too. My crew and I also made money flipping cocaine. We didn't need to do anything more dangerous than that. Eventually, Pelón came to our loft and spoke to me, Tony, and GQ about another high-risk venture.

This was in the mid-nineties. Pelón was in his late fifties then, but he still filled a shirt, wore a hoop earring, and kept the handlebar mustache dyed black. He said, "You ladies gonna wet you pantaletas when you see the money on this one." He looked around our circle. "The only thing, since this is more money, is gonna be a little complicated. We gonna disarm one guy."

Beto snorted a line of coke.

I shook my head. "Complicated, Pelón? You lose your marbles. Remember the stash house?"

Pelón's skin was dark brown, yet he clearly reddened. "Eduardo, I told you never to speak of this."

"We don't need any more bodies, Pelón."

Pelón looked at Tony and pointed at me. "Oye pero, mira este." He gestured around the loft. "You doing real good from all the business I send you. Maybe before you preach, you go to church and give the money back, eh?" He looked at Beto. "And you, GQ? You ready to give back the jewelry and the BMW?"

"Fuck that."

Pelón slapped Beto five. "Fuck that in the fondillo."

Tony said, "Pelón, don't be such a hard-on. Eddie's only sayin' we can't be offing people just for kicks, that's all."

"That's right. And we can't be risking that kind of time, Pelón. It ain't proper. And the money ain't worth it."

Pelón squinted. He leaned back. "Maybe what you say is true."

Nobody else said anything for about half a minute.

Tony said, "So what's this new gig, Pelón?"

Pelón sat up straight. "An armored car."

Tony and Beto looked at each other, then at me.

I turned my nose up. "The fuck you talkin' about, Pelón?"

"They deliver money to banks and check-cashing places."

Tony grabbed the rolled hundred from Beto. "They look like tanks. Ain't those things stuffed with Benjamins, like this one right here?" Tony snorted a line using the hundred-dollar bill. In a higher-pitched voice, he said, "Armored cars are like a fuckin'..." Tony searched for the words. "Like a money buffet, ain't they, Pelón?"

Beto laughed.

Pelón grinned. "Eso sí. Dinero para los pobres."

I said, "Bullshit, Pelón. Armored cars ain't nothin' but a party for anybody with a death wish. The name itself says it all. They got trained marksmen who'll blast you just for dreaming about it."

"No," said Pelón. "They train those guards to let the money go. Insurance pays for it. The company gets more headaches if they hurt somebody, 'cause then they get sued."

"The fuck you know about *any* of this?"

"Is true."

Beto sneezed and wiped his runny nose. "But, Pelón, where you gettin' your info?"

Pelón combed his handlebar mustache in mock humility. "I got a jevita on the inside. She a cashier at this check-cashing place. She watch them come and go, every week, every month. They come in, holding big bags of money. The best day is the day before the welfare checks. They stock up on cash. This spot we taking is the first stop of the day." Pelón rubbed his fingers together and worked his accent. "The bags gonna be fluffy and eh-stuffy."

Tony said, "Your girlfriend's gonna just give up the scoop?"

Pelón grinned. "I already got that from her. I don't even need her anymore."

I crushed a cigarette in the ashtray. "What happens when the cops grill her and she gives you up, Pelón? No offense, but our names'll be dripping from your lips the minute you see dicks in the showers."

Pelón slammed his fist on the table. "Freaking watch you tongue when you talk about me, Santiago! I never rat on nobody! You hear me? I eat time in Pontiac when you was busy sucking you momma's titty and sticking a finger up you own culo."

The guys held their place. Pelón came down several notches. He took a folded handkerchief from his back pocket and wiped his bald head.

"Listen. That girl's not gonna say a goddamn thing about me. She don't know me. She never see where I live. She don't even know my real name. I never let her see me in the same car twice. She nothin' but a little pendejita with a nose problem. I don't even fuck her, she just suck my bicho. After the job she ain't never gonna hear from me again."

Tony and Beto looked at me.

Tony said, "I don't know, Eddie. What if this broad's got good info?"

"What if she don't?"

Pelón screwed his eyes up. "This is simple. Two guards in one truck. They double-park in front of the store. The passenger gets out, goes to a door on the side. He open it, get the bags, and carries them into the store. That's it. The driver, he stay inside. He can't leave the steering wheel. This way nobody drives off with the truck."

Tony raised an eyebrow. "How the fuck're we gonna deal with their guns, though?"

Pelón waved him off. "When you sneak up behind a man and put a cañón in his ear, tell him you gonna spray the sidewalk with his brains? He let you take the gun, the money, the keys to his car, his girlfriend's toto, whatever you want. It ain't his money."

Beto cut coke on a mirror. "What about the driver?"

"I told you. He no gonna make a move. He's protected inside the truck and he cannot leave that steering wheel. Company rules."

I said, "What if he doesn't follow the rules?"

"That's why there's gonna be four of us. Number one, Antonio, he gonna cover the driver with a big gun so he don't get no ideas. Once he see that barrel pointing at his face? And he already behind bulletproof glass? Even if he Chuck Norris, he not gonna open that door. Me and Eddie, we take the other guard's gun, put him on the floor; then all three of us take bags and jump in the car. Beto gonna drive again."

I said, "What happened to your policy of never letting us carry weapons?"

Pelón bit the tip of his cigar and spit. "On this one we need guns for them to take us serious." He popped the cigar in his mouth and slapped Beto on the shoulder. "Everybody gotta graduate sometime."

Tony and Beto each had their fingers laced, waiting for my response. Their lust for money had been tweaked by the waves generated by that first stolen kilo we put on the street. We had grown that business over time and were all doing pretty well. We did carry guns sometimes when we made major deals or transported weight from one locale to another, but we had an agreement, a code, I guess, that the guns were just for self-defense. After Tony and I shot those kids in the projects, I never again wanted to be the first one to shoot. I led my crew in that same way. But Pelón's vision of money bags that we could just sneak up on and take with a simple show of force was impossible to ignore.

I took the rolled hundred from Tony and snorted a line. A hundred bedbugs marched, one by one, up my nasal passages and down my throat, into my ear canal, along the grooves inside my brain.

I looked up at the wooden beams that held up the loft's ceiling and fixated on a cobweb that I had not noticed before. "If we're gonna do this, Pelón, you gotta let me take the lead." I looked around the circle. "Beto, you're gonna be inside this time, on the set, with me and Tony. Pelón, you drive."

Pelón's handlebar mustache drooped. *"¿Qué-qué?"*

"That's it," I said. "No arguments. I don't want you anywhere near the action, Pelón. I don't want you near people. You are not to handle any weapons, especially not a gun."

"Oye, ¿pero quién carajo dijo que tú eres el que manda?"

"That's the bottom line, Pelón. It ain't a negotiation. We do this how I say, or not at all."

Pelón looked at Tony, then at Beto.

Beto said, "We're all in it together, Pelón. What does it matter who does what? Whyn't you hear Eddie out at least?"

Pelón looked at Tony, who just shrugged. He looked at me. "Fine. Tell me your great ideas, then, *jefe*."

I got up, grabbed paper and pen, asked Pelón a few factual questions, and sketched out the first draft of the plan.

I cased the check-cashing place on the days Pelón said. It was a few doors from an intersection. There was a diner on the corner and I sat there and ate a pepper-and-egg sandwich and watched the armored car as it came and went, per the schedule that the girl had given Pelón. I did this several times.

The uniformed guards' routine was the same each time. As Pelón said, the driver, always the same, a young black man, double-parked, threw on the hazards, and waited. The passenger guard, always the same, a large white woman, dismounted, opened a side door, unloaded a dolly, loaded the dolly with a couple small boxes of coins, then stacked packed bags of paper money on top. She would angle the dolly and walk the money into the check-cashing place, then walk out with the dolly empty. In and out, the whole thing never took more than three or four minutes.

The last time I cased the routine, I brought Tony along.

I said, "See that? We let the lady guard unload the cash. While her hands are occupied tipping back the dolly, you sneak up behind her, Tone, let her feel the barrel in her temple to freeze her. I'll come from the front of her, and once I see you connect with her, I whip out my piece to emphasize the point. I'll remove her gun from the holster and toss it. We'll have GQ cover the driver from the front, demand that he keep his hands visible, let the driver see the gun so he knows jumping out of the truck is pointless. Meantime, you put the lady guard facedown on the pavement. I'll jump into the truck with my piece trained on the driver—"

Tony said, "Won't the driver start shooting once you try to climb inside?"

"We won't give him a chance. GQ'll keep his eyes on him from outside, and the driver'll have his hands up, he'll be totally focused on G. I'll surprise the driver by hopping in through the side door with my gun out—remember, Tony, that side door's behind him. He won't have time to try anything."

"You're that confident?"

"In myself right now? Yeah. Anyway, I disarm the driver, then make him toss every bag down out of that truck. Pelón pulls up the van, Beto starts loading. Once the armored truck is empty, we get the woman up in there. I cover both guards, you help Beto finish loading, and when we're done, we jump in the van and drive off to the warehouse for the drop. Simple, right?"

Tony ping-ponged his head like, *Maybe. Maybe not.* "We gotta be quick, calm, cool, and collected."

I sipped my coffee. "Aren't we always?"

Tony said, "What if some cop drives by?"

"I already thought of that. When the operation starts, we can have Pelón park across the street there. From that position, because of that empty lot, he can watch the whole thing go down. He can monitor all directions, especially

north/south, since we basically got east/west covered. If
he sees blue lights on a roof, he signals with the car horn.
We'll hustle inside the truck until they ride by. In that scenario, same thing, if I haven't been in the truck yet and
disarmed the driver, we do it then. Beto keeps an eye on
him, I jump in, you follow with the lady guard. Beto goes
in last."

Tony mopped syrup with a big piece of French toast.
"What about if the cops don't come until Pelón moves to
the loading position? He won't be in the same position, so
he won't have the same view. He won't see cops coming
either north or south until it's too late."

"Well, he's not going to move those—what is that,
you figure—thirty feet? He's not gonna move those thirty
feet from that first position unless he sees that the coast
is clear, right? Once he pulls up next to us, it's gonna be
bam, bam, bam, ten seconds, fifteen seconds, the bags are
tossed in the van and we're ridin'. Like you said, we just
have to be quick and collected."

Tony mopped more syrup. "Sounds reasonable."

I looked sideways at Tony. "I have one concern."

"Shoot."

"Beto. You really think he can handle this kind of
drama? This ain't pedal-to-the-metal shit. This is looking
a man in the eye, communicating, 'I'll blast you,' even if
you don't mean it."

"GQ'll be a'wight."

"And you, Tone?"

Tony shoved in a whole wedge, with syrup and butter
dripping down his chin. He chewed and spoke with his
mouth full. "You know me, brother. Just take me to where
the action is."

*   *   *

We set up exactly as imagined. It was a crude plan, but we weren't knocking over Fort Knox. We had stolen a car two days prior, changed the plate, and parked it strategically on the same side of the street as the check-cashing place, two spaces behind where the truck usually made its stop. Fifteen minutes before the truck was scheduled to arrive, GQ popped the hood, and he and I stuck our heads under it and pretended to work on the engine. Tony was on a pay phone next to the door of the check-cashing place, shielding his face with the phone's box and pretending to have a conversation. Pelón sat in a stolen van, a fast one, with forged plates and the engine running at the intersection, facing south as a lookout.

The armored car came down the street headed east, right on schedule. As always, it double-parked right in front of the check-cashing joint. GQ and I watched the hazards come on, our faces shielded by the raised hood. The lady guard stepped down, went to the side door, opened it, took down the dolly, and began to stack. She had a red ponytail hanging out of the back of her uniform baseball cap.

GQ and I checked for rolling cops and bystanders, saw nothing, and pulled the nylons down over our heads. Tony hung up the phone, pulled his nylon down over his face, and made his move. Beto and I stepped quickly toward the truck. There was a second where the lady guard was oblivious to us descending upon her, and that was all that we needed.

Tony was behind her in a flash. He put a .44 Magnum to her temple and she froze. Beto jumped in front of the armored car, covered the driver, and shouted, "Freeze! Keep your hands where I can see them!" I pointed my

Glock between the lady guard's eyes and said, "Don't move, sweetheart."

The woman gulped and let me remove her revolver from its holster and throw it under a parked car.

"I have three kids," she said.

"So kiss the earth then, lady, and keep your mouth shut."

She hesitated. Not like defiance. More like she was paralyzed by fear. Her face contorted like she was about to cry.

I said, "C'mon, lady," and without another word to her, Tony smacked the woman over the head with the gun butt, hard enough that her eyes rolled up and she just dropped to the ground, collapsing into the dolly, keeling the thing over. The money bags thudded to the pavement next to her.

"Great."

Right then, Pelón honked the horn in the signal that meant cops in his rearview.

"Fuck, fuck!" I poked the woman. "Get up, lady! Inside!"

She was woozy from Tony's hammer shot. Pelón rehonked the signal.

GQ was getting antsy in front of the vehicle. "C'mon, fellas, let's move!"

I said, "Motherfucker! Tony! Let's toss these bags inside and grab her under the armpits!"

We quickly tossed the money bags into the open door of the truck, but had to tuck our guns and each use both hands to lift the heavy woman from the asphalt and shovel her through the door. We got her up high enough that she spilled herself inside.

Pelón honked again, real quick, like the cops must be

right up his ass. I grabbed my gun again and was about to hop up through the door and cover and disarm the driver, like we planned, but GQ was flaky, after all. He couldn't wait any longer, so instead of keeping the driver in his sights until I had him, like we had gone over a hundred times, GQ spun around and jumped ahead of me to be the first inside the truck. I was right behind GQ, reaching, thinking I would ream him about it later, when I heard him say, "Oh shit!" followed by a loud gunshot inside the truck that made me spring back.

GQ shouted, "¡Diablo!"

A third armed guard had been sitting inside the truck. None of us knew he was in there. None of us had ever seen him, so none of us were prepared.

GQ jumped right off that truck without having been hit by that first shot, and it turns out that GQ's gift for getaway driving was actually just a knack for getting away. He moved his feet so fast, it was like a scene out of *Benny Hill,* or a Charlie Chaplin flick, only faster. GQ was around the truck and out of my sight in the instant between my realizing that a shot had been fired and Tony shouting, "Let's bail!"

Tony and I both bolted in the direction where Pelón idled. Pelón burned rubber toward us, but seemed not to see us the way he revved the van's engine. I was just about to scream, "¡Para!" for Pelón to stop, when another shot spiderwebbed the van's windshield before I even heard it pop. I glanced back and saw the guard, a white man who'd been hiding inside, now crouched in front of the armored car in a shooting stance aiming at the getaway van. I looked again at the van as it flew past and saw the driver's-side window explode as Pelón had his right hand up to shield his face and a bullet lopped off his fingers with a spurt of blood. The guard shot at the van several more times as it flew, but Pelón just kept going.

Tony and I turned to run again, but the third guard's next shot pinged on the sidewalk next to us and we dove behind a parked car. We didn't know whether he had any bullets left. There was a moment's silence, but then we heard several more shots, this time from an automatic, and heard a scream that sent an electric shock down my own spine. It sounded like you might imagine a crazed chimpanzee or baboon's wail might sound, only wilder.

Tony and I had to look. We peered over the hood and saw Beto standing with the automatic in his hand, watching the white guard writhe on the pavement, hold himself, and howl from his wounds. I noticed then that the armored truck driver had indeed remained behind the wheel as Pelón had said, and figured he must now be on a radio calling backup, the police, whoever.

I shouted to Beto, "Run!" and he snapped out of it and took off down a gangway. Tony and I flipped around the corner, jackrabbited between parked cars, cut down an alley, jumped over a wooden fence, and we were gone.

Back at the loft Tony and I walked in circles, worried that we had been made, snorted gallons of coke, and considered driving to Mexico.

The news of the foiled robbery was all over TV. Me, Tony, and Beto were reported as unidentified white or Hispanic males, twenty-five to thirty, wearing nylons over our heads. Pelón, the getaway driver, was identified as a black or Hispanic male, no nylon over his head, but they got his age wrong, saying he was thirty-five to forty-five, when Pelón was already well past fifty. They showed a police sketch that didn't look that much like Pelón, got his mustache all wrong, but otherwise you could sort of see where they got it from. The getaway van was reported to be found blocks away, full of holes, with the bloody dashboard confirming that the driver had been shot.

The female guard that Tony had smashed over the head suffered a concussion. The black driver of the armored truck was unharmed. The white guard who maimed Pelón, the one who had surprised us by being inside the truck with a loaded gun, had died of his wounds.

"Sadly," said the reporter, "a company spokeswoman told us the third guard is not usually assigned to that route. Since welfare checks arrive tomorrow, check cashers in this part of town stock cash a day early. Company policy requires a third armed guard inside the vehicle on those days for extra protection."

I shut the TV off and looked at Tony. "Nice intelligence Pelón gathered, huh?"

Tony said, "We never cased the truck on a day before welfare checks hit?"

We hadn't. That had been my mistake. I said, "Pelón got shot in the hand, I saw it. If he goes to the hospital for that, Tone, they'll arrest him on the spot. We're fucked."

Tony said, "Maybe he bled to death."

"Not from that wound. Motherfucker never lost control of the van as he kept going either."

Tony said, "They got the FBI on this?"

"They're sayin' it's a federal crime."

"You think it's true what that lawyer on the news said?"

"What?"

"How that one guard dying makes this a death penalty case?"

I bit my nail and didn't answer.

We watched the news for days, ordered in, had some favorite girls come over, and never really strayed from the loft. Tony had a couple pit bulls then and walked them on the roof of our building just to avoid going outside. The FBI's lack of progress on the attempted heist and murder was reported less and less, later and later in the newscast. Eventually, it fell off the radar completely.

Pelón was AWOL. So was Beto. Tony and I stayed close to the apartment, but little by little, we began to go out on short errands. Picking up toiletries. Renting videos once we got sick of all the favorites in our collection.

Over a few days we went back to normal. Beto never popped up and we didn't look for him. We started tending our cocaine business again, but barely, only with well-known customers, and extra paranoid.

When Tony finally tried calling Pelón from a pay phone, just to see what the fuck ever happened to him, Pelón's phone was disconnected. Eventually, we heard a rumor that he was hiding out somewhere in the hills of Puerto Rico. Beto, nobody knew about; he had become a ghost.

Tony and I wanted to believe that we had cheated the system once again and we began to tell ourselves, in our own subliminal ways, I think, that the matter of the attempted armored-car heist was resolved in our favor. We were golden. It wasn't us who pulled the trigger. Things would soon be swinging again. We stopped worrying about the feds.

*   *   *

Tony's pit bulls were safely walked and locked back upstairs in the loft one morning when a tactical unit of the Chicago Police Department took me and Tony down in a snap, just as we were about to climb into Tony's racing green Jaguar and drive to Chinatown for some dim sum. In seconds flat detectives had us facedown on the pavement, our hands cuffed behind our backs. They called us scumbags and read us our rights.

The first thing I figured was that either Pelón or Beto or both had been in custody all along and one or the other had worked out a deal to finger us. But it's a good thing that Tony and I had the habit of not confessing too easily, since it turned out that the armored-car job wasn't anywhere near the reason that the cops had pinched us that morning.

It turned out that Tony and I were ratted out by J, the pig-nosed Mexican from our old hood who called other Mexicans "wetbacks," the one who had driven that night all those years before, when Tony and I were teenagers and shot those black kids in front of the projects. J had gone on to commit many other crimes during his career, but when he got pinched for two bodies related to his chop shop, he turned canary and rolled over on every accomplice he had ever witnessed commit a serious crime, which among many included me and Tony.

There is no statute of limitations for murder. Nearly a decade and a half after Tony and I tried cocaine and committed reckless homicides, our crimes had returned to claim their toll.

Tony and I moved from the front of our loft, to the back of a squad car, to the Thirteenth Precinct holding pen, to Cook County Jail, to Stateville Correctional Center, in a slow, but certain, migration. Tony and I each copped a plea and drew a decade. We each understood that we could have bought ourselves time by ratting others, especially Pelón and Beto, who had just been hot news with the armored-car fiasco. But each of us agreed that this was not our way, and I think now that in some way each of us had always expected that awful night to return.

We did our time in maximum security. Tony did his eight and out, due to perceived good behavior. Me? I did not see another moment of freedom for a decade. Not until the day that Tony came to Stateville to collect me and ended up telling me about Pelón and his intention of trying one more ridiculous stunt, the casino job.

CHAPTER 24:

THE COLD, HARD ONES

I pointed at the earrings. "Let me see those, right there."

The pawnbroker took them out and placed them on the felt mat on the counter, next to the other ones I already selected. They were all gold—simple, but pretty—very much like one another in design or style, and the only issue was to pick the right size. The pawnbroker appeared bored with the potential sale. He lazily pointed at other, more expensive jewelry.

"I'm all right with these." I picked a nice big pair, although not too big. "Can you gift wrap them?"

The pawnbroker made a face like, *Buy a clue, this is a pawnshop.* "I give you nice box. You wrap it on you own."

I paid about a day's wages, and couldn't tell, for lack of experience actually *paying* for jewelry, whether I'd been ripped off. I tucked the small box with the earrings into my jacket pocket and looked around the pawnshop again.

A pair of halfway-decent congas collected dust in the window. I looked them over and thought of the rush if I took them home, how big they would sound in my little room. I could play along with Barretto on "Indestructible" and "El Hijo de Obatala," and if Xochitl would get up and dance around the room while I did that, it would be bananas. The price on the congas was high, but I had it in pocket. I told myself that it would not be practical to lug those to Florida. That was half the reason I gave away my prison drums.

Immediately, the notion took shape in my mind that to leave Chicago meant to say good-bye to Xochitl. It should not have mattered. Xochitl was a fling, I told myself that. The earrings were just something nice for a friend.

But I felt a pull inside that wanted more. And I did not understand then, although I see it now, that the impulse to take those congas home was somehow related to my developing feelings for Xochitl. Like a secret desire to throw over an anchor and stay put.

What happens when you can't pull up?

I left those dusty congas where they were and headed out.

Tony hit me on the cell as I walked home from the grocery store.

"Where the fuck you been, dog? You don't check voice mail?"

"I been busy, Tony. What's up?"

Tony let the silence congeal. I figured him to be in one of his self-pity rounds. I was not in the mood.

"Tony, if you got something urgent, man, shoot. Otherwise, I'm on another mission right now." Xochitl was on her way over for dinner and I wanted to be finished cooking for her before she arrived.

Tony said, "They're after me again."

Great, I thought. *Vampires in your rice and beans?* "Tony, you need a doctor. I can't help you."

"No, Palo, I'm talkin' about Roach and his crew. I was coming out of La Pasadita with some chiles rellenos and tacos and—and these niggas must've been waiting. Bullets started flying. Glass was everywhere. All I could do was drop to the ground. Once I heard their car peel, I jumped to bust caps, but they vaporized. My car's a fucking basket case. They Swiss-cheesed it. And I fuckin' landed on top of my tacos, too, and crushed them."

"Is that it? Were you hit?"

"That ain't enough?"

"But you're all right?"

"Fuck no, Palo, I ain't all right."

"Stop calling me that. You sure it was Roach?"

"Who else?"

"Did you see him, Tony? Was it Roach or Bulldog or Chulo or anybody you know?"

"It was their crew."

"How do you know?"

"Instincts, nigga, instincts."

I didn't even respond to that. Tony played a game where he waited for me to say something that meant I was jumping in on his side. The silence between us fattened. I was at my building.

"Tony, the best I can tell you is to make a treaty." It was language from when we came up, when gangs were more formal and alliances were negotiated and approved by war councils. "Make a treaty and make this go away, Tone."

Tony said, "Shit, them niggas want beef, they found it. This shit is blood in the streets."

"C'mon, Tony, how's it worth all that?"

"I built this business. These niggas can't stop me."

I put my groceries down, dug for my keys, and looked for the way out of the conversation.

Tony said, "You in on this or what?"

I took a deep breath. The type of breath that goes into the receiver on a cell phone, flies up to a satellite, flies down to the other cell, and lets the attentive listener know you ain't feeling whatever he just said.

"Eddie, they tried to execute me."

"I heard. Your tacos got crushed." My grocery bags were on the sidewalk in front of my building. Inside those bags were the ingredients for dinner with a sexy woman. "You know what, Tony? You knew what this was. You knew the cold, hard facts about gangbanging and slinging dope. You wanted to check back in? You're in. You want this shit outta your life? Change your lifestyle."

"What?"

"You heard me. You wanna throw smack—this is it, Tone. You should ask yourself why you can't just walk away."

There was a deep silence on the other end.

I tried another tactic. "Look, Tony, if you want, I can talk to Roach. I know his boy Chulo real well. I could set up a meet. Someplace neutral. We can talk and squash this. But not without sacrifice on your end."

"Sacrifice? Is that all you got?"

"Right now, Tony? Yes. I'm offering you a solution." I tried to assure Tony that I was there for him, that I was still his best friend, and that this was the best option. Halfway through that spiel, he hung up.

The salmon I chose for Xochitl was pink enough to indi-cate freshness. I cooked it in a crazy coconut sauce the way Chiva showed me in Stateville. Chiva himself had learned to make it in Cartagena, a city of dark lovelies on the coast of Colombia. Chiva stopped there on tour once, and ended up living on a boat, fishing with a jealous woman, for seven glorious months.

I gave my salmon the nose: almost as good as Chiva's. The rice was fluffy the way I liked, the corn was buttered, and the wine cap was ready to unscrew. I checked the clock on my cell. There was just enough time to jump through the shower.

Xochitl called from her car. "You coming down?"

I looked from my window and saw her in the driver's seat. "Look up, I'm waving at you."

She didn't. "I don't feel like climbing those stairs."

"Come up, Xochitl. You gotta see the feast I made."

"I'm not hungry, Eddie."

"Xoch—"

"Fine. But I can't stay."

I unscrewed the wine and poured generous amounts, then unlocked the door and left it wide. Xochitl came down the corridor slowly. I locked the door behind her, and she stood in the center of the room with her hands in the pockets of her navy trench coat. I offered her the wine.

"Trade you for the coat."

She took the wine. "I'm OK."

"You cold, Xochitl?"

She sipped her wine. "I told you I can't stay."

I grabbed my own glass. Xochitl sat in the chair with her coat on. I raised my wineglass at her, then decided to scrap the toast.

"You usually work this late without warning?"

"I wasn't at the office."

"Where were you?"

"What's that smell?"

"Coconut salmon," I said. "Helluva job keeping it fresh this long. I thought you would come earlier."

"I'm not hungry."

I thought to say that I had made it for her, but didn't. Instead, I got up and served myself. I pointed my fork at the fridge. "There's more wine, if you want."

I went back to my plate. No other conversation happened while I ate. Xochitl finished her wine, but made no move toward the bottle.

I got up and poured more for myself and rescrewed the cap. "You don't like the menu tonight?"

"I told you—"

"C'mon, Xochitl. I call you up. I invite you. I cook you a nice dinner. All right, so the wine's cheap."

I stood and went to my dresser drawer, where I had stashed the gift box with the earrings out of view. I extended the box to her. Xochitl looked at it. It occurred to me then that she might think that it contained an engagement ring.

"Nothing *that* deep, Xochitl, don't worry."

She did not take it. "I gotta go."

"Xochitl, why're you shutting down again?"

"This is not—"

"What?"

"I can't do this, Eddie."

"You can't do what, Xoch?"

"I can't get involved with you."

So there it was.

"Xochitl, I'm not trying to nail you to the floor."

"There's always strings, aren't there?"

"Like?"

"My kids?"

"I like kids."

"I don't need you to like them. I don't want you to." Xochitl shifted her weight from one foot to the other. "I'm still married. Do you get that?"

The jewelry box was still in my hand. The landscape between us expanded.

"You told me you were separated."

"I am."

"So then? Aren't your lawyers working on a divorce?"

"You think it's that easy? Like you hire somebody to clean your house and that's it, the chores get done? He's my husband. We have an estate together, a marriage."

"So this is you having an affair then, Xochitl? Is that what this is? You having an adventure?"

Xochitl didn't avoid my eyes. "Right now I'm staying with my parents while I get an idea what I'm gonna do. My children stay with him."

"How long has it been?"

"A couple months."

I didn't know what else I wanted to know. I thought about the phone calls she got sometimes. "I pretty much figured shit was still brewing between you. I don't care about that."

"I do."

"Are you going back to him?"

"I need help with my kids, Eddie. Things cost."

"You don't love him, Xochitl. You told me so yourself."

"That isn't what I said. Don't twist my words."

"What about us, Xochitl? You could love another man, and do what we did?"

Xochitl half-closed her lids. "What you and I did is over, Eddie. I'm sorry."

Xochitl's hands were in her pockets again.

"I thought we were good."

"We were just being kind to each other, Eddie. That's all."

"Kind? What am I, a charity?"

"What did you think, Eddie? That we were going to fall in love and run away to a big house?"

What a cut. The jewelry box got sweaty in my palm. Xochitl walked past me and leaned to kiss me on the cheek, but I pulled back.

"Don't take it like that," she said.

She waited for a few seconds longer, then unlocked the door. She did not bother with a long last look.

I listened to Xochitl's footsteps fade down the stairs. I didn't go to the window and watch her go to her car, though I heard it start and heard her drive away. I put the unopened jewelry box on top of the dresser, then put my fist into the wall one time, hard. Plaster crumbled. I grabbed the rest of the salmon, the rice, and the corn and flushed it down the toilet.

PART IV:

GALLERY OF ENDANGERED SPECIES

CHAPTER 25

THE MOURNING AFTER

I arrived on time for work, but that didn't matter. Blutarski was bent when I got there, in the middle of a big mess. He lifted a fifty-five-gallon drum off its side, where it had landed in a violent splash that sent black ink in all directions. A couple of other drums were overturned in the same manner.

Blutarski cursed in Polish.

"What happened?"

He looked up at me, startled. "Some friends you got."

"Who?"

"I knew when you came here, with that hungry look—"

"Who did this?"

Blutarski shook his head. "I never liked police." He reached into his pocket. "Storm troopers in my shop. Here." He peeled off three 100-dollar bills. "A week's pay through today, Ed. Don't come back."

"But—"

He held up his bifocals. "Listen, kid, it ain't you." He

looked at the mess. "I depend on a certain routine, and this ain't it. Take the money."

Coltrane and Johnson were tightening the strings on their puppets. One little rampage, and they had canceled my work permit. Blutarski stood in front of me, reeking of body odor, with a look of defeat and defiance as he held my severance. I took the money.

"Can I help you with the mess at least?"

"Just go."

It was the end of my career in the ink business.

I took a quick account: The money I got from Pelón that first night? Gone. The money I made on the job? Spent. In my pocket? Three bills. Financial prospects? Fucked.

I walked east down Hubbard, past some old faded murals. Cut over to Kinzie and headed downtown. Wind sliced through urban valleys and whipped flags in a way that would eventually shred them. I thought about everything that went down, and about nothing at all. I walked for hours, until the sun disappeared. I had nowhere else to go.

I leaned my elbows on a railing on a bridge over the Chicago River. Night had taken over. The surface of the water reflected the lit city as a phantasm and my throat tightened. I wondered how deep the water went. How cold it might be. I put my face in my hands and saw the past as if it were a private movie.

I saw my reflection as a child, looking in a mirror, trying to get a tie to come out right. I was nine, and had never worn one.

"Hey, Mom, can you get this for me?"

In Spanish she said, "I told you to pick the one that clips on."

"But I like this one."

"You're just like your father." She tried to figure out the tie, but couldn't. "You're gonna have to bother him."

My father had brooded by himself in their room all morning. I stepped quietly and stood in the doorway. He sat on the edge of the bed and faced the wall with his back to me.

"Pop?"

He remained motionless.

"¿Papi?"

He turned his face toward me. The color was gone. All that remained was ash.

I held up my tie. "I don't know how to do it."

His eyes were almost blank. He swallowed. I walked over and stood in front of him.

He did not look at me. "Dame."

He took the tie, hung it around his own neck, and tied it. Then he untied it and looked me in the eye for two seconds. "Mira," he said. "Watch. Aprende."

He tied the tie again slowly, step by step, but did not pay attention to the tie itself as his eyes remained in some other, lonely universe. He untied the tie.

"Trata."

I tried to do it. He reached and guided my fingers until it came.

"Así está bien. You gotta practice."

The three of us rode in a taxi for the first time. My father wore all black, which included a leather sport coat and black shades. My mother wore one of her most somber church dresses. I sat between them. We pulled up to the funeral parlor and walked in.

The lobby was crowded with gangbangers. In the mid-seventies Puerto Rican and Mexican gangs in Chicago were organized and visible. They didn't just sport colors, they wore jackets and sweaters and vests with patches of their gangs' insignia. There were sets all over the city in those days, with names like the Latin Kings, Insane Unknowns, Imperial Gangsters, Spanish Cobras, Latin Lovers, Maniac Latin Disciples, the Gents, and Villa Lobos. I won't say which set my father's brother belonged to, but they came to the wake forty or fifty deep, all of them in their gear.

My father walked in, and there was this hush of recognition that spread through the room. First one, then another, then another gangbanger, expressed his condolences. My father only nodded. My mother signed the guest book and found a friend in a corner. My father asked for his own mother, and somebody told him that she was inside.

He looked at me. "¿Quiere' entrar?"

The truth is that I did not want to enter. I had never seen a dead body and I didn't want to start. But it seemed to me in that moment that my father was asking me to accompany *him*. I took his hand and we walked in.

His mother sat in one corner, and at first we went straight to her. My father bent and kissed her. Her eyes were swollen. She kissed me, although I didn't really know her. She lived in New York.

She looked at my father. In Spanish she said, "Go say good-bye to your brother."

I squeezed my father's hand as we made our way

toward the coffin. Some gangbangers who hung around
the body walked away. We stepped right up to the open
casket.

My uncle looked fake. Not real. Like a very lifelike,
sleeping mannequin of himself. His face was swollen, and
the makeup was thick, and not his exact skin tone. He was
a Vietnam veteran, a marine, and somebody had decided
that he should be buried in his dress blues, medals and all.
He lost his right arm when some kid next to him stepped
on a land mine, a story that he once relived in my presence. The sleeve of his service uniform was folded and
pinned to itself. I knew from my mother's gossip that my
father's brother had returned from the war addicted to
heroin, and also that he had fallen into gangbanging, she
believed, to prove that he was still a man. His death had
been spoken about in whispers, but I overheard that he
hanged himself from a tree.

I began to cry.

My father rubbed my back. "Get on your knees and
pray."

I did, but my father did not join me. I opened my eyes
and noticed the bruises on my uncle's neck, which were
poorly covered by the makeup. I looked up at my father.
Tears streamed from under his sunglasses. I stood next to
him and saw that he had his hand on his brother's mutilated arm, the stump. My father rubbed the part where his
brother's elbow had once been. Massaged it. He began to
sob and I began to cry again. I wanted to run, but I could
not let go of my father's leg.

When my father finally came down from the emotion,
he spoke to his brother as if the ears still worked.

"You was a very good brother, Paco. You was beautiful.

Thank you. Thank you for bein' my brother." My father continued to rub his brother's mutilated arm. "I'm always gonna love you."

My father looked at me finally. He removed his sunglasses and used a handkerchief to wipe his bloodshot eyes. "Eddie, I ever tole you that my brother coulda been a pro baseball player?"

I shook my head.

"We never talk about that no more. He was a pitcher at Tuley. He was the best. He throw that ball so hard and so fast, it make your eyes spin. One time he threw a no-hitter and it made the paper. I think the Cubs were looking at him."

I looked at my uncle's body in the box. He was a long way from the major leagues. My father bent, kissed his brother's forehead, really lingered on it, then whispered something in his brother's ear. My father stood, reached down, and removed his brother's Purple Heart. He pinned it to the center of my tie.

"This belongs to you," he said. "You a warrior too." My father took one last look at his brother. His mouth contorted. "Let's get outta here."

I removed my face from my hands and tasted salty tears. A slight gust kissed the surface of the Chicago River, and the city's reflection rippled. I reached for my wallet and found a quarter, which was buried deep inside. I flipped it, but did not make a wish. Instead, an ancient voice inside my head said this: *Do not make dreams your master.*

A heavy truck crossed the bridge, belched noxious fumes, and shook the bridge a little. I wondered what would happen if the bridge collapsed. Woe to the soul who finds out.

CHAPTER 26:

BACKSLIDE

The thugs were out there, as expected, on La Esquina Caliente. I went up to the kid who had shown Tony his shiner my first night back from prison, when Tony introduced me around. His black eye pretty much healed since then.

"What up, shorty?"

The kid looked at me a little distrusting.

I said, "What's your name again? JJ? Remember me? Tony introduced?"

"Oh yeah, yeah. What up, old school? Palo, right?"

"That's right."

The other kid, the skinny one, shook my hand. "What up, dawg?"

I pointed at him. "Moco?"

"Word."

I said, "Moco, I need a quarter."

"Weed?"

"Naw."

"Cornuto?"

"Naw, junior. Sugarcane. You carry that?"

"Bet."

JJ went over to what looked like a discarded beer can in the gutter. He looked around, picked it up, twisted off the top to reveal that it was actually a trick can, a container disguised as a beer can. JJ picked out a small bag of cocaine, brought it over, handed it to me.

I looked at the bag. "That's it? That's how much I get for twenty-five dollars?"

"That's how we bag 'em, G."

The thought *Just drop it, run!* passed through my mind. I had three 100-dollar bills in my pocket.

I said, "Let me get three more bags, then," and right there went a third of all my cash.

JJ went back to the discarded beer can. I looked at the others who stood around and noticed the two girls who had been at Tony's house the night I returned from prison. The dark-haired, olive-skinned one named Nena that Tony fucked in the bedroom, and the light-skinned, green-eyed one that had given me the hand job in the living room, Nieve. JJ and I finished our transaction. I walked up to Nieve.

I called her by her street name. "Sweetleaf, right, mami?" She nodded.

"You still like to party?"

Nieve smiled. She looked at Nena, then back at me. "You just cop somethin'?"

I patted my jacket pocket. "A little blow."

"I got weed."

"Perfect."

Nieve looked at her partner. "Can Nena come?"

I looked at Nena and calculated the chances of a threesome. But then I thought about sharing the coke.

"Why don't we make this a party for two—you know I don't bite."

Nieve did not seem concerned. We left Nena on the corner and walked toward my place. Nieve told me she was seventeen. She asked how old I was.

"You don't wanna know, girl. Remember when Carter was president?"

"Who?"

"Exactly."

"Age ain't nothing but a number, anyway," she said, which only proved how young she really was.

We walked past a bodega.

"Should we grab some forties?" she said.

"I spent my cash on the coke."

"I got a fin."

"Hurry up," I said, desperate already to get back to my room and put down a bag.

Nieve walked out with the 40s. We got to my place and hustled up the stairs. We threw our jackets on the bed. Nieve was dressed in tight white jeans and a hooded sweatshirt that didn't take anything away from her taut, young body. She cracked open her 40 and checked the view.

I emptied a bag onto a plate, cut it into two little lines, pushed one nostril closed, and sucked. It was so instant, it had to be psychological. I mean I just sat back for like half a minute, and I was like *soooo* happy. Ecstatic. I felt like it was a good thing that Xochitl and I broke up. Real good. And the job? Fuck the job. Hell, in that minute the coke popped like Independence Day. It gave me a thousand little hugs and I didn't even understand why I had been so upset earlier. Shit, now I could play the field.

I looked Nieve up and down.

Yeah, I thought. *Now I can fuck all types of females. Who needs just one?* Fuck being tied down. It was time to fly. Time to taste everything. To make life an adventure. And Florida! Fucking Florida. That was just like this big, wet, juicy papaya, waiting for me to put my tongue on it. How did Chiva put it? "So much delicious poosy, you pinga gonna send me a thank-you note?" Hell yeah.

I could make money doing whatever. Real money.

I floated on that first powerful rush. I said, "Nieve," and pointed at the plate. "Get busy, already."

Nieve did a line.

I patted her firm ass. "Good girl."

"Wanna smoke a blunt?" she said.

"Is the pope Catholic?"

She'd bought a cigar along with the 40s. I watched her cut it open and fill it with weed. I shoved a towel under the door. We smoked. Nieve giggled. I put on some Eddie Palmieri. Nieve didn't know who he was.

"You ain't got no reggaeton?"

"Hell no."

"Hip-hop?"

"Nope."

"Merengue, at least? Bachata?"

"Only salsa up in here."

"Can I put the radio on?"

"Just listen to this." I turned it up.

Nieve made a face.

I said, "We'll do another line, you'll get over it."

We emptied another bag. Palmieri broke into "V.P. Blues" and it sounded really good. Even Nieve said so.

I said, "You know how to dance salsa?"

We danced in my room. It felt stupid, since she had no

clue how to move to it and I did not know how to lead the uninitiated. The carpet didn't really let us slide. And that is not a song that lends itself to dance as well as others. My limbs felt heavy from the coke. We tripped into each other and Nieve laughed, even though it wasn't funny. Every two minutes she paused to grab the 40 off the table and pour malt liquor down her throat.

At one point she put the bottle down, but instead of dancing again, I said, "Come 'ere, girl," and grabbed her by the back of the neck and kissed her hard.

The kiss was sloppy and wet, but Nieve did not pull away. I pressed up against her and tongued her like it was passion, though it wasn't that at all. My heart beat too fast, and I told myself it was just the coke. I wasn't used to it. I squeezed Nieve's little tits over her sweatshirt, stroked her firm thigh, and tongued her like I wanted her to take me seriously.

At one point she pulled away and laughed. "Damn. I thought you was shy."

We made out some more. The natural thing would have been to proceed to the bed, but I didn't want her there. I wanted her on her feet, and as we kissed, I led Nieve toward the wall—toward the door, actually—and when we got there, I pressed her to the door and kissed her hard. She didn't resist.

Nieve tasted like spit, actually—that was one thing I didn't like. Like when you drool in your sleep and you wake up and your own spit has gotten all over and it's gone kind of stale. Whatever. I didn't give a fuck.

I reached down to undo the button on Nieve's white jeans and unzip them and pull them down over her white hips. I wanted to pull her panties down, too, just to the middle of her thighs, and expose her bush. I wanted to smell her, to find out whether she smelled different from Xochitl. I wanted to part her and stick my finger in abruptly, and stir up the juices until they filled the room with that strange, sour aroma.

Then I caught a glimpse of myself in the mirror with my hand on Nieve's zipper. I saw the lines in my face. The bags. The mileage in my eyes. And Nieve, with her eyes closed, and her head tilted back—not in ecstasy, but in something else. I thought about the crookedness of Xochitl's mouth, her pain when she talked about the abortion, and I backed off.

Nieve opened her eyes. "Are you all right?"

I went to the table to line up another bag. Nieve stood with her back against the door.

I snorted a line. "Shit!" I looked at her. "You shouldn't follow strange men to their rooms, Nieve."

Nieve did not seem to know what to make of that. "Are you OK? You want me to suck it?"

"No."

Nieve paused. "You got a bathroom?"

I did not look in her eye as I tossed her a roll of toilet paper. "In the hall."

I snorted the next line by myself. It burned my membranes and dripped down the back of my throat. My heart made like it wanted to bust a hole through my chest. Nieve came back and sat on the bed.

I sat at the table, and tried mentally to bring my heart rate down. I was breathing erratic.

Nieve said, "You got any more sugar?"

I had one bag left. "No," I said. "I'm out."

She said, "I'm gonna spark the rest of that blunt, then."

"Do what you want."

She stood by the window and smoked. I looked at her. She really was very pretty.

"Nieve, you see downtown?"

She nodded and held in smoke. I looked her over as she stared out the window.

"You ever been to the Art Institute?"

She shook her head. "What they got in there?"

I laughed to myself. After a while I stood and went to my dresser and found the box with the earrings. I handed it to Nieve.

"What's this?"

"For you, Nieve. But don't open it here. Take it home."

Nieve made a face that showed that she honestly did not get it. "Today ain't even my birthday."

My head raced from the coke, but I said, "Maybe it *is* your special day, and you just didn't know it."

Nieve looked at me, stuck out her tongue, and crossed her eyes. "You're a little freaky."

"You should go now."

Nieve nodded, but finished her blunt. Without being asked, she wrote her name and cell number on a napkin and left it on the table. She gave me one final kiss, and it still tasted like stale saliva, despite all her smoking.

Once Nieve was gone, I put the last bag of coke in the top drawer. I looked at the napkin. Nieve signed her name in big, round, childish letters. She dotted the *i* with a little heart. I tossed the napkin in the garbage and went by the window.

The skyscrapers in the distance had not changed their positions, yet somehow they seemed diminished. The coke was in the top drawer. I thought about washing up.

CHAPTER 27:

CONFUSION'S MASTERPIECE

I had a helluva time trying to fall asleep that night. The coke wound through me and I wrestled with the sheet on my bed until it was balled and pinned in the corner. My naked body scraped the rough fabric of the piss-stained mattress. I thought to go for a walk, but then a slight, coke-induced paranoia made me afraid of what I might find out there. So I just did circles on the mattress, with the lights and the radio off.

When I did sleep, I dreamt of raindrops in the forest and of splattered ink, of magic acts, and laughter that was not my own. The bed itself fell through the sky, through space and time, through clouds, until I was nauseous. When I awoke, it was still dark. I was thirsty. I wanted orange juice bad, and I didn't have any. I would have settled for coffee, but my milk had curdled. I remembered I had cocaine in the top drawer.

I thought to place the cocaine in the garbage or flush it, so I would not be tempted later, but then I thought, *What if I really want it later?*

I left the coke where it was, waited for the sunlight, then went for a walk.

I lay in bed most of that day and felt dreary and worn. It was that familiar drop in energy that follows a severe cocaine high. I thought about the coke in my drawer as the cure, but resisted in a way I had practiced in therapy and it worked. You just let the hunger sit for a minute. You live with the hunger until it doesn't hurt as much. In the end things like this always come down to willpower.

The next day came with the realization that I had reached the end of something. I had come to Chicago to see the city, yes, but I had mostly come because Tony sent word that he needed me. I reconnected with him only to find that he was probably beyond help.

I remained in the city to track my money down and to figure out a way to recover it, but so far there was no sign. Coltrane and Johnson wouldn't yield any leverage that could spring the money from their grip. They didn't go for the bones I tossed. And the possible connection between that hit in the park and the .38 they recovered from us kept them well beyond my influence. They squeezed me out of work like it was fun for them. Once Pelón's caper went bust, they would have a lot less use for me. I didn't want to see what that would do to their social skills.

Pelón didn't have any money, so there was no hope to recover my stash from him, even if he did have something to do with ripping me off.

And Xochitl was history. I was tempted to reach out to her, to fight for her, to try and recover a piece of that exquisite supernatural that I felt when I was with her.

But she had made it clear that her life was intricate, and I cared about her too much already to tangle her world up with mine. She had made the right choice.

So there really was no reason, no rationale, to remain in Chicago. I had about a buck-fifty left of the three I got off Blutarski. That needed to stretch to Miami. I called Greyhound. I could barely swing it. I'd make it there thin, seeing mirages from the hunger probably. Chiva would just have to come through.

So that was it. That was my plan. Pack my shit, go to the bus terminal downtown, buy the ticket in cash, be on the bus that same night. I felt a sense of relief that soon it would all be over.

Tony startled me in the hallway as I came out of the bathroom after my shower. I was in my slippers and wore only a towel.

"What're you doing, standing in the dark?"

Tony had his back against the wall. His eyes were bugged-out, almost blank. Even though I was the one just out of the shower, Tony was wet and shivering. He looked pale, although it was hard to tell in the low light of that hallway.

I ushered him to my room, shut the door, dressed in front of him, which we often did in prison. His eyes were gone.

"Tony, sit down, you're making me anxious."

He didn't. He just stood there in a defeated posture, eyes numb. Not a cocaine numb, but another, post-traumatic dullness.

"¿Qué pasó?"

He stared in the direction of the window. I went around and stood in front of him. He looked through me.

I snapped my fingers. "Yo, what the fuck? You need to go to the hospital?"

Tony's eyes finally found a spot on my chest and climbed slowly to my eyes. He began to tear. "I was just there."

"What? The hospital? With who, your moms?"

"Moco. JJ."

Tony's minions from his dope spot. I imagined the rest. "They been shot?" I said.

"Roach and his boys. Someone. I don't know." A single tear creviced along Tony's laugh line. "They fucking came through the block and sprayed 'em, Eddie. They cut those boys in half."

"They're both dead?"

Tony looked down again. "Moco's gone. JJ ain't never gonna walk again."

"Is that for real?"

"The doctor said it to my face."

I recalled the way JJ strutted the night we met on the Hot Corner.

"They fucked up Moco's face so bad, his mother won't be able to give him an open casket."

Tony began to cry. I put my hand on his shoulder, and he dropped right to his knees and sobbed. He howled so loud that it was almost unnatural. I hunkered next to him.

"You can't blame yourself, T." I put my hand on his back. I wanted to say that those kids knew what gang-banging was all about when they signed up, but then I really didn't know what I bargained for, when *I* first got started. Nobody does.

Tony remained on the floor. His breathing was out of control. I stood and got him some water, then sat on the bed and allowed him a shade of privacy. Eventually, he stopped crying. The room grew silent. I imagined an entire roll of cloud cover pass over us in the sky while we waited for the appropriate gesture.

Finally, I said, "My heart breaks for those kids and their families, Tone."

Tony looked at me. "Then help me make it right."

"Tony, I cannot—"

"Help me make a truce, Eddie. No more war. This whole thing happened because I was greedy. Those kids, they got shot because of me. Help me make it right. I can't live with this. I'm ready to tell Roach he can have the whole neighborhood."

"You're gonna get out of the business, Tone? You don't mean that."

"On my word. I just need to tell Roach. He can work the whole West Side. I wave the white flag. At least then my moms, my people, will be safe. I got kids running around all over, you know that. I don't wanna spend the rest of my life waiting for a piano to fall on top of us."

I was skeptical. "Just like that, Tony? What about that shipment you been talking about?"

"Fuck that. I don't want no more blood." Tony sounded as if he might begin to cry again. "I feel sick, Eddie. I need help."

I looked in his eyes and believed him.

"Just come with me to the meet," he said. "Watch my back. I'll do the talking. This is my mess to clean up."

"What if Roach don't wanna talk, Tone? What if he just wants to blast?"

"We'll do it someplace neutral, like you said before.

Someplace where we know everybody gotta check their gats at the door."

My suitcase was already packed. Miami was waiting.

Tony said, "I don't stand a chance without you, Eddie."

There was a bus leaving that very night. But then, they left on a regular schedule.

I said, "When do you wanna do this?"

Tony stood and went to the window. "As soon as possible. I don't want nobody else to get hurt."

I walked over to him. "I'll get word to Chulo and set it up."

He nodded.

"We still friends, Tony?"

He looked at me. We shook hands the way we did when we were seventeen.

The meeting went down at a spot called La Caverna, aka "Da Cave." It was an underground club, located in an industrial part of the city, on the far South Side, practically next to Indiana. It is the type of place that does not advertise, and isn't noticed from the street. You don't need a secret password, but you do have to know where it is, that it's there. From the outside it just looks like a low building in pale yellow brick. A small plant or a small factory of some sort. The windows had been filled in with bricks that were a different shade of pale yellow from the originals.

Da Cave was owned by a guy named Big Mike, aka "Bam-Bam," and he didn't get either nickname because of his size. He was a half-black, half-Mexican leader of a notorious Chicago street gang that had tentacles throughout most public-housing projects, and every major prison in the Midwest. Big Mike was known as the wrong nigga to fuck with. Nobody wanted to be in the crew that pulled a stunt at his personal club.

We walked up and heard the music pump from inside. Barely. It was more like something you felt. We walked in.

The bouncers inside the door patted us down. One waved a metal detector over us and it went off by my feet. I said, "Steel-toed boots," and he rapped each one with his knuckles. Satisfied that we carried no knives or guns, they let us pass through the black curtain into the club.

Inside the club a mix of black, white, yellow, and beautiful brown people bopped, stomped, ground, made sex faces, and grinned in a musical orgy of bumping house music. Tony led me to the back.

Roach sat and drank with Chulo at a little table in the farthest corner. Mirrors went all around the room, and Roach and Chulo sat with their backs against the mirror. There were two empty seats at the table. Tony and I walked over and stood in front of them.

Roach made a face and pointed at his watch. "Get yourself a rollie. Maybe you won't be late for business meetings."

We sat. Tony didn't flinch. Chulo and I acknowledged each other with a quick nod.

Roach began to talk. Actually, he shouted, but I couldn't make out a lot of what he said, because the music was so loud. I leaned in.

Roach repeated: "You niggas wanted to talk, so talk."

I shouted over the music: "Tony wants to say something."

I leaned into Tony's ear. "Just drop it straight, see how they react."

Roach waited. Chulo waited. We all waited. Tony did not speak. He seemed catatonic.

Roach sucked a cigarette until there was no tobacco left. "Listen, assholes, you called this meeting. You got me down here. Now speak."

Tony stared at Roach.

Roach looked at me. "Is your boy playing games again?"

I elbowed Tony, but Tony did not react. He kept his eyes on Roach.

Roach shook his head and blew smoke. "These niggas call me down here, talking truce. Now he's trying to pull that stare-down bullshit. Nigga, I already perfected that."

Tony licked his lips. "I gotta piss."

Roach said, "Don't forget to wash your hands after."

Roach and Chulo laughed.

I figured Tony went to the bathroom to snort himself numb. It was a lot for him to concede. While Tony was away, Roach talked about all of the trouble Tony had caused him. How much money he lost. How tampering with the business brought the heat down.

Roach said, "Palo, you're a reasonable man. You understand my problem, right? Before your boy fucked with my supply, everything was straight. Dope spots was blowin' up. Supply came steady. And the law was on ice. Now, all of a sudden, this nigga spikes my shit, my custies are fallin' off, and I'm like, practically outta business. I got narcs up my ass. And my suppliers are tripping because I can't move white or brown like I used to. How the fuck am I supposed to take that?"

"I understand, Roach, but listen. Tony didn't spike your dope."

"Bullshit."

"He didn't. And you didn't have to blast those two kids who worked for him."

"I ain't blasted nobody. Not yet."

I said, "You guys shot up Tony's car comin' out of the taco stand. And yesterday you did the drive-by at Tony's dope spot."

"None of that shit was me."

"C'mon, Roach. Everybody knows it was you. That's why we're here. That's why Tony's calling this truce. He wants this shit to stop."

"We'll take it however we can get it," said Chulo. "But that shit wasn't us. Tony's the one who's been fuckin' *our* deal. And he killed one of our youngest, most productive soldiers."

I looked at both of them. I could see no reason for them to lie. I wondered if Pelón had been telling the truth when he laid it all on Coltrane and Johnson.

Roach made a face. I saw Tony approach in the mirror behind them.

"Squash it," I said. "Here he comes."

Tony sat next to me. I turned to him and spoke directly in his ear. "Let's get this over with. Tell them you want out of the business and that they can take over your spot. You're retired."

Roach and Chulo leaned forward.

Tony said, "I want out."

His rivals waited to hear if there was anything more. There wasn't.

"Is that all you got to say? What's the catch?"

I said, "That's it, Roach. Tony's retiring, moving on. We're pushing to Florida. You guys can waste your lives chasing junkies. We're going to Miami to work on our tans. Tony's only request is that you lay off the rest of them kids that sling for him."

Roach knit his eyebrows together. "Don't tell me what I gotta do, muthafucka. Any one of them punks tries to pick up where this asshole left off is gonna find I do things lovely."

It was then that I saw, out of the corner of my eye, that Tony had something in each hand, at his side. He held each beneath the level of the table, out of Chulo and Roach's view. I strained to see through the flashing multicolored darkness of the club, the shadows that bounced off the mirrors, to make out the reflection of what it was. I suddenly realized that Tony was holding two wooden stakes. He must have stashed them in his snakeskin boots and recovered them in the bathroom. The metal detector wouldn't have picked up on them.

I yelled, "Tony, don't!" but it was too late.

He jumped up and plunged one supersharp stake right through Roach's silk shirt, cracking the sternum. A stunned Roach toppled backward into the mirror behind his chair with Tony on top of him. Tony pushed the stake into Roach's chest with all his weight and muscle.

"Die, motherfucker!"

The violence popped off so sudden and unexpected, that both Chulo and I just froze for one instant, two seconds, as Tony pistoned the other stake into Roach's gut. Roach rolled his eyes and slid down along the mirror toward the floor.

Chulo finally reacted. He grabbed Tony around the neck, yanked him off Roach, and tossed him backward to the floor. Tony scrambled to his feet with one bloody stake in his left hand. He switched it to his right, and he and Chulo faced off. People around us reacted like it was a regular club fight and started toward the action, but when they noticed the bloody stake and all the blood on Tony's face and chest, they exploded in panic. Women screamed over the music, and everybody scattered in a masterpiece of confusion.

Chulo charged Tony and avoided the stake to grab ahold of Tony's other arm and swing Tony into a wall. The mirror that covered that wall cracked into big pieces and Tony dropped to the floor, losing the bloody stake in the stampede. Chulo jumped on top of Tony and began to choke him. He was much bigger than Tony and it was clear that he would soon cut off all oxygen. Without thinking, I jumped and kicked Chulo in the temple with my steel-toed boot. He jumped up, grabbing his head. Chulo swung around and punched me so hard in the chest, the air went right out of me. He slapped me, and I fell to one knee, but then I jumped up and we traded blows.

Bouncers jumped on us and tried to bring us down like bulls. Chulo and I made eye contact. I don't know what passed through his mind, but I saw Tony's fist fly from behind Chulo and the bouncer who had Chulo tied up. The bloody stake was in Tony's fist. Tony popped that stake right through Chulo's neck like it was made of cellophane. The tip of the stake was on one side of Chulo's neck and the base of the stake stuck out the other side, like the bolts on Frankenstein's monster.

House music still pumped. The bouncer who held Chulo released him, jumped back, and screamed from the shock. Chulo did a little dance, a freak-out that I think meant his spirit was flying out of him in that instant, like static lightning. He reached for the stake, but couldn't raise his arms up to his neck. He dropped to the floor. I yanked myself away from the grip of the bouncer who held me back, and Tony and I scrambled for the exit with the rest of the crowd.

We flew in a car Tony claimed was a rental.

"Are you insane?" My heart was going a thousand beats per minute. "Why the fuck did you do that, Tony? What the fuck have you done?"

"Shut up, Eddie!"

"Tony, you stupid motherfucker... you committed two hits in public view! At Big Mike's! We're fucked! You signed our arrest warrants, you stupid son of a bitch! You signed our death certificates."

Tony said, "Moco was my nephew, Eddie!"

"What?"

"He was my nephew. He was my sister's kid. Yoli." Tony looked at me. "I was supposed to take care of him, Eddie. And look. Look what I did to him."

I remembered how Tony howled when he told me about the drive-by shooting and about his visit to the hospital.

"That kid was your family?"

"Yoli's son."

There was blood all over our clothes.

"Why did you have him out on the street, Tony? You killed two people over nothing. Roach didn't even do it."

"Bullshit!"

"You fucking sociopath. You're beyond help. And you threw the noose around my neck right with you."

"He was my blood."

"Then you should've been giving him a ride to school! Instead, you put him to work. You practically pulled the trigger."

"Don't say that."

"You're twisted, Tony. I'm sick of you."

"Stop it!"

"You're evil."

Tony screamed at the top of his lungs, "Shut the fuck up!" and pressed his foot on the gas as we got to the Dan Ryan.

I punched the dashboard. "Take the speed down to normal, you fuckin' asshole, before you get us pinched in these bloody clothes!"

Tony slowed down.

I didn't say shit else until we got to my apartment. I removed my army field jacket and flipped it inside out, to hide the blood. "Pull over."

I got out of the car and leaned down. "I don't ever wanna see you again, Tony. You hear me? Stay the fuck away from me."

I slammed his door. Tony sped off.

The bloody clothes went in a plastic bag, which I, in turn, placed in another plastic bag. I jumped in the shower. Pink water whirlpooled into the drain. I washed quickly, but thoroughly, toweled off, dressed, and headed straight for the streets again.

I moved like a big black cat, like a fly, hypersensitive to every movement, every sound. I made sure no one watched or followed. I slipped down an alley, made sure again that I was alone, and tossed the evidence in a garbage can. I quickly buried it under some other garbage.

It was too late to catch a Greyhound to Miami that night. I would have to camp out until morning. I hurried back to my room.

I pulled the chair next to the window and sat and watched every minor movement, determined to stay up all night, to keep vigil. I sat and watched, and it was quiet, but I concentrated on the exact location of every sliver of streetlight, over every dark spot, every shadow within view of my window. The changing of the stoplights—green, yellow, red, green, yellow, red—like the ticks of a cosmic clock.

It was a caterpillar's march to sunrise, and I didn't make it. I must have nodded off, because suddenly the Devil himself chased me through an empty house. I found doors and windows that led to other rooms, and kept barely getting away. Suddenly, I was in a room with no windows, no door save for the one I came through. The Devil walked in with a grin. My heart was atomic. I couldn't breathe. His teeth were black, and his body was black, lean and muscular. He was so black he was almost purple. But he spoke Spanish.

"You know what I'm here for, right?"

I felt piss run down my legs. I remembered suddenly that when I was a kid, my mother taught me that if I encountered Lucifer, to simply say Jesus' name. The Devil stepped slowly toward me. He grinned, and each tooth was etched with the live portraits of a thousand screaming souls.

"You ready to place your bet?"

I opened my mouth to say His name, but nothing came out. My heart was a flame inside my chest and I felt the metamorphosis of the condemned. My flesh burned and rotted. It felt so real.

The Devil slapped me. "Wake up, muthafucka."

I came to, abruptly.

Coltrane and Johnson stood over me. Johnson slapped me again.

Coltrane said, "Wakey, wakey, punk."

I looked up at them.

"Having a bad dream?"

I sat up in the chair. I would've asked them what they were doing in my room, but that would have been pointless.

Coltrane said, "The time for pussyfootin's over. Sit on the floor."

I sure as shit didn't want to place myself so easily within kicking range, but they stood over me already, and I believed Coltrane when he intimated that I had seen the last of the soft touch. I moved to the floor.

Coltrane sat in my chair, in front of me. He gestured at my packed suitcase. "Traveling somewhere?"

"Leaving on the Greyhound tonight. I won't be a headache for you any longer."

Coltrane said, "Oh no?"

Johnson kicked me in the chest and knocked me onto my back. He stood over me. "Ever been to an underground spot called the Cave, hand job?"

I sank. The floor could've opened up and sucked me in. It would have been a relief.

"I heard of it."

Johnson grabbed a plastic bag off the table and threw it in my face. My plastic bag. The one with the bloody clothes.

Coltrane said, "Here's one from OJ, dumb fuck: When you wanna get rid of the evidence, get rid of it. Burn it. Bury it somewhere where it can't be found. Get on a plane and go somewhere else and toss that shit in a river. Something. Don't just toss it in a garbage can five minutes on foot from where you hang your head, nimrod. Especially when you know you're under surveillance."

Johnson said, "You are tied up completely now."

"Not that it matters," said Coltrane. "But we got about fifty eyewitnesses ready to pick you from a lineup any moment we haul you in. Same goes for that turd you hang out with."

Johnson said, "You understand now? We make our careers if we bring you in."

Maybe, I thought. But they hadn't cuffed me.

I got up and rubbed myself where Johnson booted me. "So what's the scenario?"

Johnson looked through my empty drawers. "Don't talk cute anymore. What's this?" He found the last bag of coke. He held it up to the light. "You're so fuckin' weak." He tossed it at me. "Fix yourself, if you need to, junkie."

The bag landed on the carpet. I left it there.

"Go on," said Johnson.

"Fuck you."

Johnson moved toward me, but Coltrane froze him with an interruption.

"The *scenario,*" said Coltrane, "is what it's always been. You work for us now."

"Get used to taking orders, Santiago. You're our bitch."

I looked at the bloody package on the floor next to me. The plastic bag with my clothes, my hair, my skin fibers, my DNA, and the blood that sprayed out of Chulo's neck. It was that falling piano that Tony had mentioned earlier. And it had landed right on my neck.

I nodded. "What exactly do you need me to do?"

*　　*　　*

They told me that the day before, they had tracked Pelón to the airport. They watched him pick up his brother, who'd just flown from PR. They knew the brother had a rap sheet and that it wasn't a social visit.

Coltrane said, "We know whatever Pelón's got in the broiler's ready to come out. We need you to dig up every detail and inform us, minute by minute."

"And then what?"

"Performance first," said Coltrane as he stood and snatched the plastic bag with the evidence off the floor. "Then maybe we talk about what we do with this cherry pie you gave us."

"And don't even dream about running," said Johnson.

Coltrane pointed his pinky and index finger. "If we so much as imagine that you skipped town, we'll phone this homicide in and there'll be a nationwide manhunt. Won't be no place you can go. We'll find you. And then we'll drop you for murder one."

I swallowed.

"Don't look for us, we'll reach out to you," said Johnson. "And yo ass better be there."

They shut the door.

I picked up the leftover bag of coke and ran to the bathroom with it. Strange to say, but it looked like a tiny white orchid of some sort, the way it floated on the surface of the toilet water before it spun down.

I hit Pelón on the cell phone.

"¿Bueno?"

"Soy yo. Eddie. We need to talk. But not on the phone."

In Spanish he said, "Good news?"

"What you been waiting for. I'm ready."

"Good. Come over. We at the apartment now talking about it."

Pelón's hallway smelled of cooked liver, and when he opened the door, I learned his kitchen was the source. He broke into a wide, self-satisfied, friendly grin.

"I knew you was gonna wake up, Eddie. Pásate. I was just about to fix some drinks." He walked behind the bar and went about the complicated business of making mojitos. "My brother say everyone in the capital drinking this now." Pelón mashed leaves with a pilón. "Can you believe a drink with mint? And a pedazo de caña?" He looked up from the dicing. "You want one?"

"No."

"Don't look so nervous."

My stomach was forming ulcers, but I didn't think it showed. I wondered if Pelón really read me, or whether he just tested me. My decision to join the casino job should have been sudden from his point of view.

In an effort to show how at ease I was, I went behind the bar and grabbed a tequila bottle. "In Chicago we drink the hard stuff."

I poured myself a quadruple shot.

Pelón made a face. "Coño, nene. Slow down."

I gulped down half. Pelón finished making mojitos.

"What's different about your apartment, Pelón?"

"I got rid of some furniture."

I noticed then that the fancy "King of Spain" chair was missing. The TV was gone. His sound system. Even the big maroon leather couch.

Pelón had three mojitos on the tray. "Vámonos al otro cuarto. They in there shooting pool."

I followed Pelón into the other room. Tony stood at one end of the pool table. He studied the shooter and leaned against his cue. The shooter leaned over the pool table, lined up his shot. He flicked his wrist, the one with the thick gold bracelet. The balls cracked against each other in a way that made him curse.

The shooter stood erect, but his face remained twisted in frustration. He picked up his cigar.

"Let me introduce my brother," said Pelón. "¡Cabezón!"

Pelón's brother turned to him. He was bigger than Pelón, taller, broader in the shoulders, more muscular. He was just as black and just as bald, it seemed, because he wore a big toupee in a James Brown style.

"Cabe, say hello to our other companion. Palo."

Pelón's brother, Cabezón, squinted at me as he pulled a very long draw off his cigar. Muscles stretched the fabric of his lime green guayabera and his dark green slacks. The hand with the thick gold bracelet also sported a large gold pinky ring. Cabezón blew enough cigar smoke to shut down a room. He stepped toward me and extended his big hand.

"Encantado."

What I saw when Cabezón opened his mouth made my brain pop. It felt like someone smashed a hammer right into the top of my head.

In Spanish I said, "Excuse me?" to get Cabezón to repeat the word, any word, to say anything, but just to open his mouth. "What did you say?"

"Mucho gusto."

It was *him*.

My lip curled. My hand went numb as a reflex. Cabezón shook my hand and I let him, but I was in shock. His teeth were made of gold. I recognized him instantly. I almost whispered his name. Cabezón was Pelón's brother and we had just met. But I had seen him once before.

Cabezón was the monster I saw spray my father's brains against a brick wall.

PART V:

NIGHTFALL

CHAPTER 28:

THE FOURTH MAN

I was in a tunnel that stretched and contracted. Cabezón was at the other end of it. Beyond him there was haze or fog that suggested light, and between us there was only darkness and shade. The instinct that makes the mother bear slash at anybody who looks at her cubs vibrated like a supernova inside me. Somehow it got compressed.

Cabezón said, "Why they call you Palo?"

My stomach churned battery acid.

Cabezón looked at his brother. "Your friend looks sick."

Pelón chuckled like he was nervous. I opened my mouth as if to say something, and a little vomit shot out, unexpectedly, onto the bright white carpet, and onto Cabezón's crisp, lime green guayabera.

He cursed and wiped himself with a handkerchief. "¿Coño, pa' eso bebe?" He ordered his brother to take away my tequila. Pelón took my drink from my hand and said that if I thought I would be sick again, to please go to the bathroom.

I looked at Pelón. I immediately realized that if Cabezón was the gold-toothed killer in the gangway, then Pelón was likely the accomplice, the one who snuck up on my father and fired the first shot. I felt tremendous heat in the palms of my hands. Pelón's apartment spun under my feet.

"I have to get out of here."

Pelón said, "¿Cómo? You just got here."

I went out of the apartment, to the elevator, where I waited for what felt like an hour for the car going down. Pelón watched from his doorway. He asked if I wanted water.

"Go away."

The elevator opened. I hit buttons like it could never be quick enough. Downstairs I made it out the main entrance, and as far as the gutter out front, before my knees buckled and I threw up.

I waited for Coltrane and Johnson at Buckingham Fountain. I stared at the bronze sea horse and remembered a time when I had been at the fountain with my dad, in the summer. We came by the fountain to watch the water display and the colored lights at night, and when the water shot in the air, my father walked on his hands and did cartwheels to make a real show out of it.

There was no water display and no lights that night as I waited for the narcs to show. I saw them walking toward me and I waited until they were real close before I said their names out loud.

Coltrane said, "This is romantic."

"I chose this because it's out in the open. I'm not in the mood for your antics, Detective. We don't have time."

Johnson frowned. He licked a lollipop. "Like we give a fuck about your moods."

"There's a lot going down tonight. I need to get ready."

"A lot? What does that mean?"

"A heist that you never thought Pelón could pull off. Son of a bitch got an airtight plan."

Coltrane and Johnson looked at each other.

Johnson pointed his lollipop. "Spill it."

"In a second, narc. First I wanna set some ground rules."

"Say what?"

I spoke clearly. "You heard me. You too, Coltrane. Don't think the bully tactic is going to work this time. The way I'm feeling? A bullet to the head would be a relief. Prison's the only place that feels like home anymore. I'm more desperate than you think."

Johnson seethed a little, but Coltrane only nodded.

"Ground rules are for my own protection."

"Go on then," said Coltrane. "Speak."

"You're in it for the money, and that's what you're gonna get out of this, loads of cash. Only thing is: there has to be something in it for me."

Johnson said, "We don't negotiate with convicts."

Coltrane said, "Easy, partner. Go ahead, Santiago. Shoot."

"You agree? I'm entitled to get something outta this too?"

"What have you got in mind?"

I told them what I wanted, including which parts were nonnegotiable. I told them much, but not all, of what I knew. Enough juicy details about Pelón's plan to get them really stoked. I reminded them that time was running out.

"I'm not haggling. We can drop the whole thing right now. You really think you can pin a murder rap on me—then go ahead. Arrest me. Maybe you can get a little overtime out of it."

They were reluctant, but we agreed to terms. I'm certain they called me "sucker" and had a good laugh after I walked away. Any idiot should've known there was no way these two would ever honor our pact.

The crew met at Pelón's to eat ribs and go over every last detail of the plan for Halloween night. It was painful to sit near Cabezón as he smirked and licked barbecue sauce off his fingers. Pelón kissed his ass. And Tony acted as if he felt better than he had in a long time.

Cabezón talked about life in PR. Deep-sea fishing, scuba, snorkeling, the way he still picked up lonely American women in hotel bars in the Cóndado. I didn't pry or try to investigate anything more than what I needed to know, because there was no doubt that these were my father's killers.

There was no doubt, and there was no other way out of my predicament other than to play the game the way it was designed. I had a strong impulse for vengeance, and it was something that had been there most of my life, in the back of my mind, at my core, underneath all my thoughts. It was a poor substitute for the love that I once shared with my father, but it was all that I had. I clung to it, subconsciously, for all my life. And now it was at the surface.

What could I do? It would take great cunning—not luck—to escape from this. I wanted desperately to live. And I didn't want any more black marks on my soul.

So I prayed and went in to the meeting with Pelón and

his brother and Tony, and I ate with them, and I put up with Cabezón's jokes. When Pelón went over the plan, I paid close attention and stayed in character as the guy whose only interest was to pull off a successful job and go home.

I was the last to arrive on the night of the heist.

Pelón opened the door with a worried look. "You really trying to give an old man a stroke." He asked for my jacket.

"Just give me the costume, so we can get the fuck outta here."

He handed me the box that was on top of the bar. Cabezón and Tony were ready. Cabezón was dressed as a lion, with the big overstuffed headpiece, like a mascot at a college basketball game. Tony was dressed and made up in face paint as a happy clown. Pelón, of course, was dressed as himself, since he was the getaway driver, and no one would see him.

I took the box to the bathroom to change. Pelón had bought me a gorilla costume. It was a little big on me, which was OK. Actually, it was good. I put it on and practiced moving around in it. I struck poses in the large bathroom mirror like I imagined I would during the stickup. It was hot inside the costume. I took the mask off and joined the others.

"Looking good," said Cabezón.

I ignored him.

Pelón displayed our arsenal on the same coffee table where Tony had once spilled ten G's for him. We had two 9mm's for me and Tony. A sawed-off shotgun for Cabezón.

His weapon of choice, I thought, recalling how he used one before.

Pelón said, "I'm gonna repeat this: These weapons are clean. They're untraceable. No serial numbers. Never been used on any other jobs. Never shot anybody. You gonna make sure you wear your gloves every time you handle the weapon, and at all times while you on the boat. When the job is over, you got the money, you in the dinghy coming over to the shore"—Pelón slowed his tempo to emphasize—"you *drop the weapons into the water.* Do not bring these guns on shore or into the getaway car. We don't need to get caught with them later. ¿M'entienden?"

Pelón paraphrased what he'd said in Spanish for his brother. He looked at the three of us. "Any questions?"

Cabezón, the lion, Eddie, the gorilla, and Tony, the clown, stood mute.

"Bueno. Let's take this party on the road."

CHAPTER 29:

SLOW DANCE

The casino boat was full of people in costume, just as Pelón had said, except some of the scarier-looking ones had actually gone dressed as themselves. Everywhere people dropped money and appeared to have fun doing so. Slot machine bells and the sound of coins falling provided the constant illusion that the players—not the casino—were the ones who made money.

Cabezón, Tony, and I went our separate ways, since there was no need to stay together the whole time. Our appointed hour of announcing the holdup was an hour and a half later, at the halfway point in the cruise, as the boat turned, and by that point we would, according to the plan, have met in the men's room, which was located exactly where Pelón said it would be, on the schematic he had drawn for us, on the coffee table, back at his place. For the moment we didn't need to be together.

I walked around the casino and watched people gamble. I played a little slots and blackjack, like Pelón suggested, so the cameras wouldn't pick me up just hanging around, which might create suspicion. A woman at the slot machine next to mine had come as a slut. I wished that all I had on my agenda that night was drinking and gambling with an easy woman. A simple life never sounded better. The gorilla suit felt like a wool blanket. I moved to the deck for some fresh air.

I tried to bring my heart rate down, to enjoy the moment of relative quiet and stillness that existed out on that deck, but it didn't work. When I turned to go back in, I saw a couple, a man and a woman dressed as Tarzan and Jane, or maybe as cave people. They were out there in that cool night air, completely into each other. They tuned the rest of us out, and did a slow dance under the moonlight on the deck of that big boat, with no music. They didn't seem to notice or care about me. I left them to their private wonder.

The appointed hour was upon us. I made my way to the men's room. I waited outside a second and looked around to make sure that no one followed, or was onto us, but, of course, there was no way to tell. Abraham Lincoln and a pirate came out of the bathroom, laughing. If everything went according to plan, Pelón was out there, up the coast a ways, anxious to scoop us from shore. Coltrane and Johnson were on standby at their post, eager to stop the four of us and make off with the casino's money. There was no backing out now. I walked into the bathroom.

Cabezón pretended to piss at a urinal, which would have been impossible, since there was no zipper on the front of his lion's costume.

"Finally," he said in Spanish. "Where have you been? We're gonna be late."

I checked under the stalls. Nobody else was in there—except for the clown shoes in the far stall.

"Tony?"

"Yeah."

I turned to Cabezón. "Remember not to speak, don't say anything, not one word. We don't want to give them a clue who we are. Your Spanish will reveal a lot."

"Don't give me orders. And tell that other one to come out already."

"Tony, you ready?"

He didn't answer. Instead, I heard him snort a big hit. "Wooooeee!"

Somebody dressed as Napoleon came in and went to the urinal next to Cabezón's. I went into the stall next to Tony's, so as not to look like I was loitering in the men's room. Napoleon finished and went out without washing his hands.

I heard Tony snort another big hit. "Feeding time!"

"Tony." I spoke in a hushed tone. "You better relax." His clown shoes looked even more ridiculous under the wall of the bathroom stall. "We gotta do this, now, c'mon."

Tony flushed the toilet. I took out the 9mm I had stashed inside my gorilla suit, and took it off safety. I walked out of the stall. Tony came out of his stall still dressed as a clown, but with his wraparound shades on. The 9mm was in his right hand. He practically bounced. Cabezón saw that we brandished our weapons, and backed away from the urinal. Instead of holding his dick, he had been holding the sawed-off shotgun.

"¿Listos?"

I looked at Tony. He looked at himself in the mirror, held the gun up at his own reflection. "That's right, player haters! Rock and roll!"

We walked out of that bathroom, a motley crew, an unfit unit, ready to bring noise like nobody on that cruise ever knew. Even though we had our guns out, and people immediately saw that we carried weapons, they didn't react like they would in a bank or a liquor store, because it was Halloween. Many people were in costume, and it was easy to believe that our guns were fake, strange additions to our attire.

Cabezón put an end to all of that underestimation when he pointed the shotgun at a camera above a black-jack table, where we were to set up our base and do all of our collecting. He fired off an explosive round.

BOOM!

The camera shattered and people screamed, ducked, ran, scrambled, and scattered away from us as if by a sudden and powerful gust. Tony jumped up on the blackjack table, waved his gun, and shouted, "Everybody down on the ground, now! Quiet! Shut the fuck up! Down on the ground!"

He fired into the ceiling. *PAH! PAH!*

"Down, bitches!" By that time, five to ten seconds into it, everybody cowered, some whimpered, some prayed, but everybody was getting down. Except one very pregnant woman dressed as Humpty Dumpty. She screamed and waved her arms.

I made sure not to point my gun at her. "You, miss, come 'ere." I threw my arm around her neck. "You're gonna be my hostage." She screamed and I shouted, "Shut up!" I whispered in her ear, "Behave, I won't hurt you," but I don't think she heard, because she continued to cry.

I pointed my gun at the nearest pit boss. "You with the slicked-back hair! Get up! Fill the bags my partners are handing you!" I pointed at a dealer that had handed me good cards earlier. "Lady. Help him fill the bags."

They paused.

"Move!"

They were panicked, but their training was tight, because they jumped into the routine of collecting everything that was back there behind the tables.

Pelón had warned me not to get suckered by one of those exploding dye packs banks sometimes give robbers. They explode a few feet from the premises and cover you with dye that is almost impossible to wash off, so the police can track you and ID you after the job.

I said, "Don't give me any of that fuckin' bait money."

The pit boss was sweating. "No, sir, we'll cooperate. Please don't hurt anyone."

"Bring me the kid who knows how to operate the dinghy."

"We'll have to call him down on the radio."

"Do it!"

The pit boss was a class act. He got on his radio and called down for the kid, and did it routinely, like nothing out of the ordinary was going on, nobody pointed a gun, no robbery was being committed, just a dinghy that needed operation.

"He'll be down in a second."

"Finish loading the bags."

People sniveled and tried to stay off our radar. Tony was still up on the table, going over the room like a beacon, looking for that excuse to shoot someone. Cabezón stood sentry, five feet from me, shotgun at an angle across his chest.

"The bags are ready, sir."

"Where's the kid for the dinghy?"

"I don't know, sir."

"He has ten seconds to present himself before I shoot you."

The pit boss radioed whoever to send the kid down.

The report came back: "He's afraid to go down there."

The pit boss pushed his hand through his hair. "Negative. He must report down now. We need it lowered."

"Tell him he don't gotta get in it with us, we know how to run the boat. If we gotta go look for him, it'll be worse for everyone. Especially him."

The pit boss began to relay the message. Surely, an alarm had already been sounded. Surely, some cops were on their way.

I talked over the pit boss as he delivered the message. "The sooner he puts it in the water, the sooner we're gone!"

The pit boss spoke into the radio: "For the love of God."

The crowd cowered, but remained under relative control. Some cried and prayed out loud—all of which was made ridiculous by the fact that many were dressed as cowboys, big chickens, historical figures, ghouls, or cartoon characters. The pregnant Humpty Dumpty under my arm shivered from fear, even though I shushed her. It had not been three minutes since we announced the holdup.

The kid for the dinghy appeared at the far entrance and walked slowly toward us.

"Hurry up, we just wanna get outta here!"

He picked it up. Tony jumped down from the black-jack table. He grabbed a bag; Cabezón grabbed a bag; I grabbed a bag. The pimply white kid walked ahead of us toward the back entrance of the deck. I released my pregnant hostage and she threw herself on the ground to thank God.

I put my arm around the kid for the dinghy. As we exited, I turned and said, "Happy Halloween, everyone!"

Tony did one better and shot a slot machine, which made everyone scream and raise the volume on their prayers.

"Go 'head and follow us!"

We walked out on the deck. The kid said, "Climb in, hit that button there, it'll lower the boat. You unhook there and there."

"What's your name, kid?"

"Brian."

"Newsflash, Brian, you're coming with us."

His face reddened. "But you said—"

"Don't cry, Brian. We just need you to operate the boat. We're looking for our ride up the coast here. You take us to shore—after that, you do whatever the fuck you want."

"Please, sir—"

I motioned toward the boat with the 9mm. "Move. Fuck this up and you'll be sorry. Do as I say, and you'll be telling this story for the rest of your life."

The rest went without a hitch. We got in. Brian cried to himself, but he put the small motorboat in the water. We cruised across the surface in the direction we had sailed on the casino boat, just like Pelón had told us. The casino boat looked huge from the vantage point of the water, but it shrank and disappeared around a bend as we made our escape.

We saw the headlights, about where Pelón had said he'd be. He flashed them to let us know it was him.

"Over there, Brian."

The kid guided the boat to our rendezvous. We three bandits jumped into the knee-high water with a bag of money in one hand and a gun in the other.

I said, "Go home, Brian. Fuck the shit out of your girl-friend the next time you see her, all right?"

The kid turned the dinghy around and put it in high gear.

The three of us threw our guns out into the middle of the river, although I kept an eye on Cabezón and made sure he tossed the sawed-off before I flung the automatic. We hustled up the muddy embankment to the getaway car.

CHAPTER 30:

TODO TIENE SU FINAL

We snaked along a lonely, unlit back road. The woods that surrounded us were etched in black ink, against a deep purple backdrop. The blackness was speckled with silver moonlight.

Our headlights cut the path. Tony and Cabezón were in the backseat. Pelón and I were up front. Pelón drove. I was wet to my knees and cold.

It had been three or four minutes since we got away from the river, but I was still out of breath.

Tony said, "We fucking blanked 'em, Pelón. I can't believe they laid down so easy."

Pelón stiffened at the wheel. "Tranquilo, nene. We ain't done yet."

"Fuck yes, we are. They ain't stopping us now." Tony put his hand on my shoulder. "Ready to count some money, G?"

I pushed his hand off, but did not look back at him. I heard Tony lean back in his seat.

"Now it gets easier," he said. "I need a light."

Tony's elation turned the screw for me—the fact that

he could even pretend to be at peace and satisfied, so soon after the horror of what he did to Roach and Chulo. I don't know why. I twisted in my seat to look at Tony and say something. I don't know what. Maybe I meant to curse him. Maybe I wanted to blame him for my own actions.

When I turned, I saw Tony's greasepainted clown face all white, with the big red smile painted on, turned all the way up. The rock-and-roll shades were cocked at an arrogant angle on the top of his head. A celebratory cigar was pinched erect between his teeth. The depth of Tony's eyes was there, even in that dark interior, connected to me like we were fifteen again.

He said, "It gets easy now. Doesn't it?"

And that's when Cabezón pulled the trigger on a .357 Magnum that must've been stashed in the backseat. The fucking thing detonated like a whole universe being born. And poor Tony missed it. He never saw a thing. His brains burst out the other side of his head in the rough shape of a thick black rose in bloom. What remained of Tony's head snapped limp as the gray matter, which once contained his thoughts, smeared and peppered the backseat, the ceiling, the side and rear windows. The clown smile flipped upside down and the cigar dropped as Tony's face became a mask of instant self-grief.

I screamed.

Cabezón swung the Magnum at me. I threw my left like a boxer and jerked to the side just enough to swat the barrel away and feel the fire of a second discharge burn the back of my hand, the back of my wrist, my forearm. I felt the heat of it on the side of my face. The *POP!* was so loud, it cracked my eardrum. I grabbed the barrel with my right and pushed it away from me.

Cabezón pushed back and tried to point the smoking barrel. He cocked the hammer, and on instinct, because I'd seen it on TV once, I slipped my thumb into the space between the hammer and the firing pin. Cabezón gritted his teeth and squeezed. The hammer snapped onto my thumb. I winced, but the gun didn't fire. Then the Magnum jerked free from my grip. I fell back into the dash. I rebounded toward Cabezón, arms out, only to catch an explosion at an angle across my chest.

The pain was shocking, unbelievable and immediate, even as my body flew backward into the dash. Still, I understood that Cabezón was about to bring that Magnum back down, and point it at my forehead.

I flopped myself, with all my weight and all my pain, against Pelón, and the steering wheel flipped 180 degrees. The car cut across the road at an impossible angle, tires screaming over the double yellow line, across the edge of the road, over the gravel on the side, down an embankment. I think now that Pelón must have tried to throw the wheel back toward the road, because the car flipped like it had no weight at all. We rolled, turned, and crashed into each other like lottery balls.

Metal crunched. Glass turned to dust. Somewhere in the backseat the gun went off. I thought I saw Pelón fly through the driver's-side window, but then my head slammed into something, and everything was painted black.

It ain't like you think over there. Saint Peter doesn't wait by the entrance. Neither does Satan. I did hear music. Ancient, childish music. Simple, but not crude. I can't say if it was harps. But everything was crisp and clear, like when you try on prescription glasses for the first time. Except that isn't the sense I'm talking about.

I spun, like when you fall asleep, or maybe fall in love. There was fog. I recognized the music. I was going in circles.

I was at Coney Island again, on the merry-go-round. The horse was wooden, but it had a heart that pumped buckets of blood. The beast twitched between my legs.

I saw my father. He stood by the side and watched me go round. He still wore the suit that he was buried in, but he was not dirty, and there were no maggots. I wanted to call to him, to get off the carousel.

A poem formed on the blackboard of my mind:

Remember when I was a crow,
Perched at the end of a limb,
At the edge of a forest
Of headstones,
And you dropped to one knee,
Because you thought you were alone?

The merry-go-round spun faster. My father became a strobe. He winked. And then he was gone. The music got loud. The horse began to snort. It arched its muscles like a giant bow that would make an arrow out of me. The spinning got faster. I floated to the surface.

When I came to, I was facedown. My face pressed into what had once been the ceiling of the car. I was disoriented and did not immediately know where I was, what had happened, or, for that matter, *who* I was. All that existed was ignorant consciousness. Awareness of nothing.

But then, I felt something warm on the back of my neck, heavy and thick as ink. I tried to move, and it was as if my body did not understand what I wanted it to do. Finally, like some insect when it breaks its cocoon, I was able to move my arm. And then I touched what was on the back of my neck, and understood what it was. I didn't scream. It was too late for that.

Tony's corpse was on my back, bleeding onto me. I struggled out from beneath him, and pulled myself from the wreckage, through the tight opening that had once been the front windshield. I scraped myself on the twisted, jagged metal and shattered glass.

I threw up while still on all fours, heaving until I had nothing left, just air and acid that burned my throat in a way that confirmed that I was still alive. This was not Hell.

My chest hurt. I pulled myself up, leaned against the car like a drunk, looked around. Nothing. No bodies where they had been thrown from the car. No money bags. Pelón and his brother were gone, like true thieves.

There were no witnesses around. No sound of police in hot pursuit or an ambulance. Nothing. Nothing but the trees, and the sound and smell of the trees, and the stars, and the slight, faint, unhappy moon. Slowly, in excruciation, I peeled off the gorilla suit. It was heavy with river water, my sweat, and Tony's blood.

Beneath the costume I wore black jeans, a T-shirt, and a bulletproof vest Coltrane had given me as part of our deal. I removed the vest and looked at the Magnum-sized dent in it, felt it with three fingers, and dropped it to the ground.

I peeled my T-shirt up and looked at myself. A magnificent

bruise the size of a large grapefruit had formed on that part of the chest reserved for pledges, where a child believes his heart is. The skin was unbroken. I touched it. It was so tender, I almost yelled and had to gnash my teeth to absorb it. At least I was intact.

The knife I bought at the army/navy surplus store was still sheathed and fastened to the holster on my calf.

I got down on all fours again and looked inside the car. Tony, the clown, faced me, his sunglasses lost in the tumble, his eyes open, but lifeless, like stars gone black. His face was stiff already in the horrified expression of his final moment. I pulled him from the wreckage and it hurt, because of my injuries, because of his, because of the broken glass. A smell of shit and piss came from the corpse. I loved him so much.

I pulled Tony from the wreckage completely and rolled him onto his back so he could face the stars. Some of what remained of his brain leaked out of the opening in the side of his head into the wet grass. I kneeled by his body, and felt a new pain in my stomach, but I held it down with my eyes closed. I watered, but held it down. I put my mouth next to Tony's ear, near the entry wound that smelled of gunpowder, and burnt flesh, brains, and blood. I talked to him softly and told him the things I never said. I prayed a quick prayer for his soul, then kissed his forehead. I closed his eyes for him, and kissed his forehead again. I didn't want to leave him. He was my brother. But he was already gone.

I stood, a little stronger, and looked around. Tony's body was still warm, which maybe meant I had not been knocked out for very long. The killers might be close.

I walked up the hill to the road, and followed the path cut by the car, where it had disturbed and upturned the earth. Nothing in either direction, except dark horizons. It occurred to me that Pelón and his brother would not take the road, since police were certain to scour the area, and they would not want to be seen out here at night, in the middle of nowhere, carrying money bags. The wreckage would not be visible to any cars on the road, so unless some helicopter searched this particular area, the wreckage would remain undisturbed and unnoticed for a while.

I looked down the hill. Tony looked hopeless down there next to the car. Ridiculous in that clown getup. Not at peace. I looked along the line of trees that formed the edge of the forest at the bottom of the hill. I walked down the hill, searched the earth for some sign of the villains, some trail of blood or torn clothing. Footprints. Something. I found nothing.

I walked along the edge of the trees for a spell, where the forest began, and still saw nothing. It occurred to me that they could not have made so much headway, because Pelón limped, and the crash must have injured one or both of them. I turned back until I returned to where the car and Tony lay, and it was there that I realized they must have headed straight into the woods.

I cut into the trees, downhill, and strained my eyes in search of some evidence. The land sloped downward for a bit, then turned sharply up. It was hard to walk. Much of the land was covered by thorny bushes that grabbed and tried to ensnare you, cut you, slow you down. A fever grew inside me, and I did not tire. For the first time since childhood, I was afraid of nothing. The land sloped upward, and drew my sweat. I knew that if they came this way, the terrain would drain them. I picked up my pace, looked, and listened.

I felt strange. I realized that I could not hear out of my left ear very well. I heard ringing, but it didn't bother me; it didn't discourage me. My eyes were sharp and I saw in the dark. I felt like a bloodhound. Like I sensed my prey with faculties that I never knew I inherited.

I climbed the hill and looked, and as I neared the top, I heard something. I stopped and listened, and at first I did not capture it. I stood very still. I looked around. Then I heard it again.

An animal?

I listened. I recognized it now. Spanish. Coming from the right. I followed it and stopped when I saw Pelón's white suit reflect the diffused moonlight. Pelón was sprawled on the ground, his back against a tree, his head cushioned by a money bag.

Cabezón stood over him and argued that they needed to keep moving, that he would help. Pelón shook his head and cursed and held his leg. I saw that Pelón's leg was broken. A dry white point of bone stuck out from his bloodied pants.

I drew my knife and moved toward them, slow and careful not to step on any twigs or rustle any leaves. I saw everything in silver under the increasing wattage of the moon. I snuck behind a tree, right next to them. I could smell them. Their heat, the aroma of their sweat, the stink of their evil. I wondered where Cabezón's gun was. Certainly, he didn't have it out. I figured it must be tucked into his waistband. Pelón was incapacitated. The knife was in my hand, long and sharp. I listened as the brothers spoke Spanish.

"We have to tie it with something," said Cabezón. "We have to continue."

"That won't solve anything," said Pelón. "The pain is too great. We are cursed."

"I'll go find a doctor."

"Not even a babalao can help us now!"

Cabezón said, "Stop it with your voodoo!"

"We sealed our fate."

I jumped from behind the tree and rushed. Cabezón must have been descended from warriors, because he turned in time to see, then threw his forearm up to block me, which worked, because our forearms knocked into each other like two clubs, preventing me from stabbing him in the neck. He slapped me with his other hand in a way that he must have practiced on palm trees in Puerto Rico, because his hand was rough and hard, and the force was so powerful, it knocked the rest of the hearing out of my left ear. I went down.

Cabezón reached in his waistband for the gun handle, but I flung my right leg, caught him on the knee so that it snapped like a piece of hickory. I dove as Cabezón collapsed next to a fallen tree. The gun was in his right hand. It slammed against the trunk of the tree, and I was on top of him before he could raise it again. My left was on Cabezón's wrist, pressing it against the bark, trying to snap his forearm, so he would drop the weapon. Maybe it was instinct, but Cabezón used his other powerful hand to dig into the bruise on my chest, even though he could not see it under my T-shirt. I screamed, swung the knife down with fury, and drove the blade through Cabezón's forearm, nailing him to the fallen tree.

He cried, "¡Maldiiiitoooo!!!" and the Magnum flopped

out of his hand. Cabezón kicked and threw his free arm and legs like a cockroach that's been hit with the spray, trying to get to the knife handle, but I was on top of him with my knee in his neck. I pulled the knife from his arm and tossed it out of anybody's reach. Then I jumped for a rock that was about the size and weight of a heavy bowling ball.

Pelón said, "Eddie, no!"

I dropped my knee into Cabezón's chest before he could get himself up, and brought that heavy rock down upon his head. Again. Then again. Then again, as Pelón cried out and reached. The skull only cracked loud the first time. After that, each blow sounded like a *thump*. Cabezón's head became soft with every shot, like wet earth. Every time I lifted the rock, his face shone in the platinum moonlight and he looked more deformed, until the final blow, when he no longer looked human. He was transformed into a toupee-wearing monster. It was as if that rock revealed what was underneath. I rolled the rock into the dark downhill.

Pelón crawled onto his brother's corpse and howled.

In Spanish he said, "Look at what we did! Look!"

I jumped and grabbed the knife and the gun, but Pelón was not after those. Instead, he cried so deep, so hard. The sound was almost unnatural. It infected me. I fell to the ground next to the brothers and cried. I wept so hard it wrenched in a way that had nothing to do with the physical world. Pelón and I sobbed together, almost in harmony. After a time we subsided to just quiet llantos. The trees swayed and creaked in the breeze.

Finally, Pelón spoke: "I knew this day would come. I knew it that day we killed your father." He rubbed his face, his eyes. He nodded as if looking at a kaleidoscope of his life. "La bruja. She tole me. She say, 'The evil you seek you must not do.' 'Why?' 'The seeing eye will make you pay.' I say, 'Give me protection.' She laughed and said, 'There is none. The truth shines in the dark.'"

Pelón looked at me. "Eddie, when I saw you between the cars that day, you was just a little boy, and you saw what I did. I knew you was never gonna feel right until you collect." He rubbed his hands together. "I tole the bruja, 'I saw him. I saw the eye. Can I cut it out?' She tells me, 'If you use you own hand, it will multiply your suffering.' So I waited. I looked for you when you got big. I found you and I pulled you in. I wanted you with me, where I could watch you. I brought you into this work, praying, making offerings that somebody else would take care of you. A homeowner. A cop. Another títere. If somebody could just catch you where you don't belong and shoot you. Or maybe you kill somebody in a robbery and you go away forever. I wanted you to disappear from this world."

Pelón shook his head. He lifted his cane, turned the handle, and slowly pulled a long, shiny stiletto concealed within the rod. I leapt to my feet and tightened my grip on the knife and the Magnum.

Pelón let the stiletto reflect the moon. "I could have used this on you at any time. But I know it was pointless against you." He resheathed the knife and tossed his cane away from himself. "My brother didn't believe me. The armored truck? When I signaled that the police were coming so you all go inside? There was no police. I knew they had another guard inside the truck. I wanted you to be the first to go in and catch that bullet between the eyes. You was always the first inside. Remember? And you were supposed to go first that day too. But you never went. Instead"—Pelón held up his claw—"I lost pieces of myself as we went along. You was always destined to be the cacique."

Pelón pointed at his brother's corpse. "And now you see? You see what happens when you don't listen to the voice of God?"

"Why did you kill my father?"

Pelón shook his head. "My brother and me, we had this plot. We buy properties and torch them. You father, he was the fireman. He started the fires and we collect the insurance. He wanted a bigger piece. So my brother and I, we decide we hire somebody else."

"That's it?" I said. "That's why he died?"

Pelón said, "Is there an answer that'll make you satisfied?"

Neither of us looked at each other. Neither did we look at the corpse. We just stared into the dark earth.

Pelón said in Spanish, "Everything comes to an end."

I made eye contact with him. "Yes."

He looked at the gun in my hand. "At least leave me a final dignity, Eduardo. You can take the money."

"That isn't what I came for."

Pelón looked me in the eye again. "I know. But you and me is even now. Arrepiéntete. Repent."

I stood over Pelón. The gun was in my hand. He was on his knees now next to his brother, waiting, eyes pleading. I paused. Then I turned the handle toward him, and handed him the gun. I waited. Pelón did not shoot me.

I sheathed my knife, and began down the hill, in the opposite direction of the point where I entered the woods. Five minutes later I heard the shot crack and echo across the dark silence. I paused for a second of grief over Pelón, which surprised me. Then I hiked and I sweated, and it was all woods, trees, thorny bushes, and soft, moist leaves underfoot.

I came upon a group of deer as they watered themselves at a stream, and froze. They stood in place, in silence, and watched me. They stopped drinking and stared at my strange form. I stared at theirs in a standoff of mutual wonder. Suddenly, without warning, the deer exploded into a sprint. Agile movements that barely touched the earth. They vanished into the darkness.

I dropped to my knees at the edge of the water and saw my reflection. So much blood had flown in the car and next to that fallen tree that it was all over me, all over my face, my T-shirt. I stuck my head in the water and washed my face and drank. The water was cold and flavorless and I drank until I was full. I felt tired, but I continued. After a long time the forest began to change. The edge of it became purple. The sky became purple, then violet, then red, orange, yellow. I headed east, and after another long time I found a clearing, and then a road.

In the early-morning mist I came upon a home at the edge of a suburb. I watched from the bushes as the family left for a day at school and the office, and was relieved that the husband was a large man, about my size. I let myself into their home through a kitchen window that faced the backyard and put on a flannel shirt and a hat and sun-glasses that belonged to the man of the house. I watched the car in the driveway next door for twenty minutes.

Relying once again on the shit I learned on the streets of West Town, I walked out the front door, went straight

to the car as if I owned it, jimmied the door open using a
bent wire hanger from the house, hot-wired it, and drove
myself toward Chicago. I found the Loop FM and left it
there. They played a classic about rock and roll itself, by
Neil Young, and when he launched into a guitar solo, I
knew that Little Tony was with me on that road.

EPÍLOGO

I have worn lots of white for almost a year now. Chiva is my teacher. He helped me since I got here, like I knew that he would. Everyone needs family of some type.

Chiva gave me a new identity, a new name. He was always good at the paper crimes. He fell back into that as soon as he got down here—there's lots of business here for anybody who is good at forging documents. So Chiva hooked me up.

Criminal record? Gone.

Prison record? Nonexistent.

Work history? Steady. Just ask Social Security. Turns out I've been paying into it since I was sixteen. At least that's what their records show. I'm a new man, but not a newborn. And the IRS is very satisfied. No problems with my account. Even my credit is good. I'm still a Puerto Rican. I have an American passport. I even got a clean driving record, so my insurance rates are nice and low. It's the fresh start that everybody dreams of.

One thing was weird: looking at my own death certificate.

I figured it was necessary. A crafty detective might ID Tony's body, run his sheet, look up his old case files, find that I was his codefendant on the armored-car heist, discover that I had been released a month before the casino job, and figure me as a prime suspect for the guy in the gorilla suit. It was also possible, though not likely, that they would lift a print off the Magnum. If any of that ever happened, I needed the trail to me to lead to a finding of SUSPECT DECEASED for the case file.

Chiva showed me the forged death certificate for EDUARDO SANTIAGO ROSARIO and the medical examiner's report.

I touched myself in the ribs. "Why did it have to be that I was eaten by sharks?"

Chiva said, "No body to present, no body to dig up and test against DNA or dental records. You just certified dead. Nobody know where to find the tiburones that ate you. Besides," he said, "a dramatic guy like you? I couldn't just take you out with the flu."

I can't say here what my identity is. But I will reveal that it takes some getting used to, people calling me by a different name. It can be frustrating, although mostly it's all right.

Of course you can't erase memory. A person's more than just the record of who they are. That's why I'm in atonement now.

Chiva instructs me on how to hollow out the shell of the drum. There are very specific tools and techniques. It's firm, but somehow gentle, the way he does it. He shows no frustration with my rough hand, though I'm sure it offends him.

I pay attention and try to do it the way he tells me. I get lost in the act and mostly I think of nothing, or I think of the things I've learned since I got here, and it feels like I am studying something, I'm training, I'm growing, I'm learning, I'm becoming, my life has a purpose.

Sometimes I think of the past. How much I lost. How close I came. I think of Xochitl often. She caressed me in those final days, and she was right that we had been kind. I will always be grateful.

Xochitl was at the motel after the heist, like I asked. I ditched the car downtown and caught a train, changed trains, changed cars, changed directions even, then switched to a bus and walked part of the way with the baseball cap I stole from that house pulled low over my face. I kept the shades on in case my mug shots had been on the news. When I finally made it to the motel, I was so tired, I could barely knock on the door. Xochitl waited inside.

She pulled me in and shut the door behind me. I collapsed on the bed. Xochitl looked nervous and stood over me.

"Are you all right?"

I didn't have the energy to really answer. But no, I was not all right.

"I'm scared," she said.

"Don't be."

"Was that you?"

"What?"

"In the news?"

"What'd they say?"

"Some guys stole money from a casino."

"Anything else?"

"They got away."

"What makes you think it was me?"

She didn't answer.

I sat on the edge of the bed. "Don't believe everything you see on TV, Xochitl. Put it on."

We watched the midday WGN news. The reports were of a daring Halloween heist on a casino boat. They had video stills of the three of us: Tony, the clown, up on the blackjack table, Cabezón, the lion, with his shotgun, and me, the gorilla, giving orders. Nobody was hurt. Brian, the kid who maneuvered the dinghy, was interviewed on camera. He said at first he was afraid, but the guy in the gorilla suit was "real polite."

Police scoured the area. I knew it would be no time at all before they found the skid marks where we went off the road, found the wreckage and Tony's corpse, found the bodies in the woods. The bloodhounds would find my scent and it would lead them to the house where I stole the clothes and the stolen car report from next door. The car itself would then turn up downtown.

But I was far from downtown. All that hustling I'd done on the subway system would throw off any bloodhounds. I still had time.

"Shut it off."

Xochitl killed the TV.

"You got my money?"

"It's under the bed."

I got down on all fours and found it down there. My money belt. I opened it. It was filled with green. On top of it was the Purple Heart that Coltrane stole from me my first night back in Chicago. I zipped the money belt shut.

"Did you count it?"

"Ten thousand."

I knew that Coltrane and Johnson would have never agreed to release my full forty G's, even if they thought they would double-cross me later and get it back. Why risk losing the whole egg? I took what I could get my hands on.

"Beautiful." I tossed the money on the bed. "You got my tape player?"

Xochitl dug it out of her purse. She gave me my cell phone too. "Eddie, if you needed money, you should have come to me."

"What, so you could ask your husband for it? I didn't need money. I had my own stash that I needed to recover. That's all. Did you listen to the tape?"

"You told me not to."

"Good. Were you able to rent a car?"

"Yes."

"In your own name, Xochitl?"

"Of course. It's the white one right outside the door here. The keys are on the dresser, next to the room key. Am I gonna be implicated?"

"I already told you no. I'll drop the car at Miami-Dade and that'll be that." I added: "If I get caught, I'll just say that I forced you. Threatened to hurt your kids if you talked—that kind of thing. You say the same thing. OK? You bring my change of clothes?"

"In the bathroom."

I went in and shut the door behind me. I took the fastest shower and changed, but did not put on a shirt. When I came out, Xochitl was standing by the exit with her purse on her shoulder, looking nervous and sad. She winced when she saw the bruise on my bare chest.

"You need to get that x-rayed."

"I'll survive."

She touched the bruise lightly, but did not ask what happened. She said, "Why are you trusting me with all this?"

I thought about it for a second. "You have the most unforgettable smile."

Xochitl hadn't smiled once that day. And she didn't do so now. I stood in front of her by the door.

A kiss on the lips would not have been appropriate or fair to either of us. Xochitl put her fingertips just above my bruised skin. Her eyes watered. She leaned in and kissed me soft on the collarbone. I hugged her, and smelled her hair for the last time.

"Xochitl..."

"Please don't."

We were in each other's eyes now. Xochitl opened the door.

"Cuídate," she said.

I would have understood if she said, "Please don't ever call me again," but she didn't.

I sat on the bed. I desperately wanted to take a nap, but I had one more task to confront, and it made sense to take care of it as soon as possible, before I got in the car and rode away from the motel.

I dialed Coltrane's cell.

"Santiago!"

"What up, cowpoke?"

"Where the fuck are you? You lied to us."

I had told Coltrane and Johnson about the heist all right. But I had given them all the wrong information.

And I made sure that they did the money drop for Xochitl at the exact time when the crew left Pelón's, to make sure they didn't just follow us. At the time when we were in one state holding up one casino boat, these morons were more than a hundred miles away, in another state, thinking some other casino boat was about to get robbed. They waited at a fake rendezvous spot.

Coltrane said, "You think you're pretty clever, don't you?"

"So will you when you hear what else I got."

I put the tape recorder close to the receiver on my cell and pressed play. It was a recording of the conversation I had with Coltrane and Johnson by Buckingham Fountain. You could plainly hear each detective, who I repeatedly refer to by name, as they conspired with me to rob Tony, Pelón, and Cabezón after the casino heist. You hear them negotiate me down to ten thousand on the return of my stash, and also the part where they agreed to provide me with a bulletproof vest.

I shut off the tape. "Have you heard enough?"

Coltrane said, "What the fuck do you think you're gonna do with that?"

I said, "The quality's not the best, but you can clearly hear what's being said, right? You recognize the voices, don't you? I've made several copies."

"Go on."

"I have friends, Coltrane."

"Bully for you."

I said, "Anything happens to me? I get locked up? I disappear? That tape and a letter I've written explaining everything—explaining who all the players are—will be mailed to CPD Internal Affairs, the FBI, the Justice

Department, the state attorney general, and every major news outlet in this city. You follow?"

Coltrane did not say a word. I could hear him breathe.

I said, "Don't come after me, Coltrane. Don't tell anybody you know I was the fourth man, because you are now in this to your tits and you don't want that coming out. Make believe like I never hit your radar."

Coltrane said, "Boy, you're gonna shoot yourself in the foot one day."

"Maybe. But at least I'll be in control."

After that, I jumped in the rental and split. Xochitl left the CD she bought me in the player, cued to "Go Your Own Way." I slept a couple of times in rest areas, but never comfortably, since I kept expecting a contingent of state highway patrol officers to sneak up on me. They never came. I was in Miami by early afternoon.

I have followed the story since I got down here, on the Internet. Investigators found the car wreck, Tony's body, the brothers in the woods. According to the news, the money was fully recovered. It is unclear who double-crossed who, since there were two homicides, one suicide, and the fourth man, the one in the gorilla suit, disappeared but did not take the cash. I don't know if anyone is after me. I've never been named as a suspect. So far as I can tell from the news, the investigation seems to be at a dead end.

One news story did catch my attention: About six months after I left, two killers confessed to shooting that kid in the Humboldt Park bathroom. It was Nieve, aka "Sweetleaf," and Nena, the girls Tony and I had hooked up with on day one. They got picked up for smoking a joint on the Hot Corner. Once they were fingerprinted, their fingerprints matched the ones recovered from the murder scene in the bathroom in the park. Confronted with this, they caved in and confessed that they had lured the kid to the bathroom with the promise of a blow job. They shot him to get props in the gang. No one had put them up to it. The gun was never recovered.

The *Sun-Times* ran a picture of the killers on its Web site as they were led out of the station by the arresting officers, Coltrane and Johnson. The landlords were cleaning up their neighborhood after all.

Chiva tells me to pay attention. "You gonna make this thing pleasing to the Orishas, you gotta do it right." He shows me again how to tighten the skin of my handmade batá. The large one finally. It's full-bodied and shaped like an hourglass, which makes sense, since it is female.

"Mira. Así."

I do as Chiva tells me. Finally, the drum is ready. We both stand and admire it.

"It looks good," he says in Spanish. "Bellísima."

Me and Chiva and a couple of other investors work hard. Our little salsa label is off the ground. I got a woman I visit sometimes. Her kids are grown. I just bought myself an old motorcycle, and I have fun with it, although mostly I ride it slow.

But all of that is out of my mind right now. I look at my drum. It has no polish. It ain't ever made a sound. But it's my own creation. And I feel like, *This is it. This is why I came here.*

"Cúrate," says Chiva. "Play it."

I sit on a stump and lay the drum across my lap. The skin on both ends feels just right. I slap the smaller head and stroke bass tones out of the other end that speak like nascent thunder.

Chiva and I smile.

He winks at me. "Aché pa' ti, Boricua. Your ancestors are listening to you."

My drum sounds that good.

FIN

READING GROUP GUIDE

Questions for Discussion

1. *Gunmetal Black* may be described as many things, including urban literature, crime fiction, commercial thriller, pulp, noir, and Latino fiction. How would you describe it and why? What are the distinctions between these categories?

2. Is Eddie just a good guy caught in a bad situation? Is he a victim? A product of his environment? How did witnessing his father's murder change him? And why did he go into a life of crime?

3. How did setting and imagery affect the story?

4. Eddie was incarcerated for a decade immediately preceding the start of the novel. Do you have a sense of how he feels about that? What impact did incarceration have on him? He claims his debt to society is paid. Is it? Could Eddie be considered reformed?

5. One of the themes of the novel is that of missing or emotionally distant parents, especially fathers. What impact does this alienated affection and guidance have on the lives of the characters?

6. It is clear for most of the novel that Little Tony is on a downward spiral. Why does Eddie feel responsible for Tony? Was Eddie's loyalty misplaced?

7. What did you think of the use of music throughout the novel? What does Eddie's commitment to drumming and studying with Chiva tell you about him?

8. Eddie expresses antagonism toward Pelón throughout the story. What did you think of Pelón? How did his account of childhood poverty and the death of his little brother affect your opinion? How did you feel when Pelón smashed the disabled man's skull with an elephant tusk?

9. How do issues of race, gender, and culture manifest themselves in the lives of these characters? What about issues of class?

10. Eddie indicates a growing desire not just for sex, but for intimacy with a woman. Why has this need not been there before? What is different now? How does what Eddie learns about the love lives of Tony, Pelón, Blutarski, and Xochitl affect him?

11. What did you think of Xochitl? Why did she get involved with Eddie? At one point, Eddie says that Xochitl made the right choice in ending it. Why does he believe that? What was the value of their relationship? Could Eddie and Xochitl have had a future together?

12. What does money mean to these characters and why? Why did Eddie choose to work at the ink mill while he angled against Coltrane and Johnson to recover the forty thousand dollars? Should Eddie have accepted the loss and left for Miami after that first disastrous day out of prison? Why did he leave the casino's money with the bodies in the woods?

13. What did you think of the use of Spanish and slang throughout the novel? What does it add? How would the novel be different without these?

14. C, the Italian gangbanger, ordered Eddie and Tony to shoot the black kids in retaliation for a gang-related attack. When Eddie recalled that C viewed Puerto Ricans as derisively as he did blacks, he wondered why he and Tony ever sided with C about anything in life. Eddie claims to not know the answer. Do you?

15. Why *did* Eddie shoot those black kids? What choice did he have? How would you have handled the pressure that teenaged Eddie was under to take such violent action?

16. How is this novel's depiction of gangs unique? Did you see anything to relate to? What distinguishes gangs from fraternities, the military, or a tribe? What is the appeal for people who commit their lives to their gang? What alternatives might they be offered that would derail their involvement?

17. What is the role of spirituality, morality, or religion for these characters and throughout the novel? Each major character either explicitly or implicitly expresses

belief in a higher power, yet they all make choices that may be described as "immoral." Why is that?

18. How is *Gunmetal Black* similar to other works, books, and movies that you are familiar with? How does it relate to the Great Books? Is it in conversation with any of them? What makes *Gunmetal Black* a novel?

19. Pelón tells Eddie and Tony that if they hunger for the American Dream they better seize it. He says, "These people've been running things in this part of the world for five hundred years. You think they gonna stop *now*?" What does he mean? Do you agree? What are the arguments for and against Pelón's point of view?

20. How did you feel when Eddie avenged his father's and Tony's murder by crushing Cabezón's head with a rock? Was he justified? Wasn't he taking the law into his own hands? When, if ever, is that acceptable? Does it matter that Eddie's experience of law enforcement is that of corruption?

21. Eddie tells us that after he heard the shot marking Pelón's suicide he was surprised to experience grief. If Pelón was Eddie's nemesis, why did Eddie cry over his death? And why did he hand Pelón the gun?

22. Were you surprised that Xochitl was at the motel after the casino heist? Did you expect her to ride off with Eddie? Were you disappointed when she didn't? What would you have thought of her if she did?

23. The final scene finds Eddie in a state of peace and contrition. He is in Florida somewhere with a new

identity and a new mission, doing something he loves. How does the rest of his story go? Do you think Eddie will be able to live out his days in relative quiet? Or is Eddie, as Little Tony puts it, "a straight-up *magnet* for trouble"? What do you expect to see in the sequel to *Gunmetal Black*?

ACKNOWLEDGMENTS

Since *Gunmetal Black* is my first novel, its completion and publication are part of a larger story of how I became a novelist. Many people contributed to this development in many ways, great and small, and I cannot possibly recall every kindness. To everyone who supported or encouraged me in any way, thank you. What follows are more particular expressions of gratitude.

Praise be to God for giving me the words and vision.

To my mother again, the strongest person I know, for giving me life, and teaching me so much. And to my step-father, Marcelo "Yuyo" Aguiar, for taking such good care of her.

To my wife, Yajaira Yepez, Esq., for sharing your brains, beauty, passion, laughter, and love.

To my father, Hilario Serrano (1943–2002), a tough prince of salsa and the greatest storyteller I'll ever know. Thanks, Pop, for letting me in.

To my beloved brother Alexander Serrano (1973–2003), a brave man and a genius of love. I miss you, baby brother.

To my beloved brother Ruben Serrano, a wordsmith, musician, athlete, and coach. Thanks for listening with a poet's ear.

To my huge extended family, and para mi gente de Puerto Rico, Chicago, Philly/Bristol, and Nueva York.

To my badass uncle Eddie Pacheco. You were a real father figure when you didn't need to be.

To Raymond Reyes. Thanks for letting me use your encyclopedia.

To my fourth grade teacher, Mrs. Chang, who cried the first time she heard me read.

To my sixth grade teacher, Mr. Paul Tomasello, who taught responsibility, compassion, and self-control; and that every piece of writing must be rewritten and sanded like a piece of wood that you wish to make smooth.

To Peter Hilton, who ran the tutoring program and mentored teens at Onward Neighborhood House. Thanks for reading my one-page autobiography of the first thirteen years and coming to find me.

To Steve Lara, brother and lifelong friend. Thanks for digging the parts that I knew you would, but mostly for your huge heart.

To Annette Louise "Netty" Vargas, a true homegirl and the sister that I never had. Thanks for having my back, and for finishing the novel and leaving me a voice mail saying that it was good.

To the teachers and my fellow students at Wells High School in Chicago, especially the members of the Academic Olympics English Team that won first place three years in a row: Eli Martinez, Adriana Medina, Olga Rizo, and Christina Napoles.

To Tim Schellenberg, for listening to a true story

involving my dad and a baseball bat covered in blood, and saying that if I wrote it someone might actually *pay* to publish it. That was the exact first moment I considered becoming a writer.

To the Suarez sisters, Anita, Genoa, and Lucha, for all the movies, and the many gifts, especially that summer all those years ago, when you gave me a journal and said that I should write something.

To Jose Valle, friend, mentor, and photographer, for interrupting my speech on writing with, "Dude, *first* you write. *Then* you're a writer." Brilliant.

To Jane Jerrard for drafting a critique of my first effort, even though you didn't know me.

To my cousin Jeannie Vazquez for reading that first effort and passing it to a friend to read on a plane.

To my paisan Daniel Foerst, el salsero, for feeling this novel so much and letting me know with such enthusiasm.

To Carmen Santiago for finishing the last page and immediately saying that you couldn't wait to see the movie.

To Cleo and Duke, two mutts, for keeping me company.

To Fanny Mei Po Moy for many reasons.

To the faculty, staff, and my fellow students at Shimer College, where I studied the classics and produced the first draft of *Gunmetal Black* as my thesis.

To the faculty and staff at St. John's University School of Law, where I became a more disciplined writer.

To the instructors and students at the Frederick Douglass Creative Arts Center in New York City, where I worked on both *Gunmetal Black* and *Boogie Down*.

To Dr. Adam Lynn and the other members of our little tribe. Thanks for listening.

To my excellent agent, Jennifer Cayea of Avenue A Literary, LLC. Thanks for representing me and also for giving me such terrific feedback. Your suggestions deepen the work.

To Karen Thomas, my editor at Grand Central Publishing. Thanks for seeing the potential.

And last, but never least, to Mrs. Marsha Brody, guardian angel and teacher of high school English. Without knowing me, based only on what you heard in the teachers' lounge, you pulled a fast one and changed my schedule to enroll me in your creative writing class. It was the start of a beautiful journey. I never stop learning from you and I doubt that I could have become an attorney or a novelist without your influence. Thank you forever. I hope you are proud.

More gritty fiction from

Daniel Serrano

Please turn the page
for a preview of

BOOGIE DOWN

Available now
from Grand Central Publishing

CHAPTER 1

CEMETERY HILL

Cassandra was an NYPD detective, an undercover assigned to stop a monster.

The newspapers called him the Marathon Slasher. He stalked female joggers at night. He shredded their faces with a scalpel.

Cassandra's job was to lure the Slasher out of hiding. To act the part of a lonely jogger, unaware, reckless in her choice of shadowy cinder trails at dusk.

Cassandra was nervous. Undercover work was always dangerous.

Plus she had seen the photos in the case files. The scars. The grief in the victims' eyes.

Her department-issued semiautomatic was holstered inside her waistpack.

Two male undercovers shadowed her. Ghosts, they were called. Their job was to protect Cassandra yet stay out of sight. Each pretended to be a lone jogger, one ahead, the other behind Cassandra, about a twentieth of a mile, approximately one city block.

Compost in a nearby field mixed with the July heat to deliver a sweet, disgusting smell. That summer had been a scorcher.

Cassandra spoke up: "Jennings, what's your twenty?"

They communicated using radios rigged to look like MP3 players.

"Behind you, Detective, about an eighth of a klick."

"All clear?" she said.

"Yes."

"Pace?"

"Ten-minute miles."

Cassandra glanced at her watch. "Ten-zero exactly?"

That would put Jennings thirty seconds back.

"Ten point oh exactly, Detective. Nobody's gonna sneak up on you."

Tactical teams throughout the park monitored their transmissions and tracked them on satellite.

Each jogger had a GPS chip on his or her person. Cassandra's was tied to her sneaker. A command post managed the entire set from inside a fake Metropolitan Transportation Authority repair truck, parked on Broadway, under the number 1 train.

Cassandra radioed the lead ghost: "Jones? What's your twenty?"

She envisioned Jones checking the GPS watch he had coaxed from Technical Assistance. "A block ahead of you, Detective. Ten-minute miles."

Six miles an hour. Fast for her, this late into the run. Sweat salted her eyes.

Jones called. "Approaching the bridge, Detective. Ready for Cemetery Hill?"

Runners talked about the Hill. They feared it.

It was called Cemetery Hill because the city's first native-born mayor had been buried up there. It was known as a spirit-breaker for runners, but supposedly rewarded your effort with a special view of Manhattan's distant spires.

Previously Cassandra had always been too fatigued by this point to take the Hill and had stayed on the flats. This night she wanted to push herself.

"Stick it."

"Ten-four."

Cassandra imagined the lead runner crossing the bridge that connected to the back hills. Thirty seconds later she came to the span herself. She crossed it.

Trees on either side of the trail reached for one another with their branches like laced fingers. They formed a dark canopy over the trail that enveloped all who passed beneath.

Cassandra pumped her knees. Her earphones radiated silence beneath her ghosts' heavy breathing. She bopped her head and pretended to listen to music to appear like an easy target. In her mind, she got to the Spanish part of "Diamond Girl."

The first hill rose. It quickly became vertical. Like running in sand. With boots on.

Cassandra immediately regretted her decision to take the Hill.

She felt jumpy. It was dark. A raccoon scampered from a bush and she flinched. Cassandra's heart rate was off the chart. She labored to breathe.

She glanced back and saw only shadows. She glanced again and caught the flash of a man suddenly in, then suddenly out of sight on the curved path behind.

A *running* man.

Cassandra's heart skipped. *Where did you go?*

She slowed to let the running man round the bend. He didn't.

Where are you?

She whispered into her mic. "Jennings?"

"Yeah?"

"You see him?"

"Who?"

"In front of you. John Doe running man."

"Where?"

"Just ahead of you, maybe half a klick."

Jennings cleared his throat. "Negative."

"On the Hill."

"The Hill? I thought you said, 'Skip it'?"

"What?"

Jones cut in. He could see their locations on his special watch. "Detective, it looks like Jennings didn't take the cutoff, he stayed on the flats. I'm heading back—"

Cassandra stage-whispered, "Negative. Slow your pace and stand by. Tactical units stand down."

A lieutenant inside the fake repair truck radioed.

"Detective, you have to abort. It's too dangerous. Jones, turn around and rendezvous with her. Jennings—"

Cassandra cut in: "No, Lou, please don't. If it's him, he ain't made me. Don't blow my cover."

"Detective—"

"I'm fine, Lieutenant. I have my firearm."

It got harder to breathe.

The lieutenant hesitated. "Ten-four."

Cassandra didn't waste oxygen thanking him. "Jennings, are you hauling back?"

"Fast as I can."

"Floor it."

Cassandra glanced behind. Nothing.

I saw you. I know you're back there, running man.

Cassandra touched the cherished gold ring on the chain around her neck. She said a two-second prayer and quietly unzipped her waistpack. She felt the gun and removed a small can of pepper spray.

"Jennings?"

Her feet were like buckets of wet cement.

"Halfway up the Hill, Detective. Don't see nobody."

How is that possible? The curvature of the trail was not so great; one of them should be able to see someone between them.

Cassandra glanced back.

Nothing.

When she turned to face forward the Marathon Slasher leaped from behind a tree with his scalpel out.

"It's him!"

He swung.

Cassandra snapped her head back. The blade missed her throat by a whisper but sliced the earphone wires. The Slasher swung his free hand and tore her necklace off.

Cassandra aimed the spray but the Slasher knocked her hand and the aerosol discharged into her face.

"Aaahhh!"

The sting exploded up her nostrils. It lit her eyes on fire. The can dropped from her hand.

Cassandra's eyes welded shut. She threw a wild punch.

The Slasher slapped her with a hand like cast iron. He grabbed her ponytail and yanked her off the trail into some trees.

"No!" She kicked. "Stop!" She could not see.

Her sneaker with the tracking chip came off.

Opening her eyes, Cassandra plunged her hand into her waistpack.

The Slasher threw himself on top of her. They tumbled downhill, grabbing each other.

Suddenly he was above her, scalpel high.

Cassandra jammed the gun under his chin.

"Freeze!"

He froze.

She strained to keep her eyes open. "Toss the blade!"

He hesitated.

She flicked the safety and cocked the hammer. "I swear to God!"

The Slasher tossed the scalpel.

Cassandra pressed the muzzle to his carotid. "Off me! Kiss the dirt!"

The Slasher moved slowly.

Cassandra got to her knees and jammed the muzzle into the back of his head. She forced him facedown and scrambled for the cuffs in her waistpack. She restrained his hands behind his back, then spun away to empty her water bottle into her eyes.

"Oh, God!"

She gagged, hands on knees.

There was something in her bra. She felt it.

Her special ring!

The necklace was gone, but the ring had fallen into her cleavage. Cassandra held back a sob.

The Slasher spoke to her in Spanish. "I will peel your face away and the world shall see who you really are."

His accent was unfamiliar to her. He was not Puerto

Rican, Mexican, or Dominican. Cassandra's backups, Jones and Jennings, called from the running trail.

Her eyes swollen almost shut, she bent and grabbed the links between the cuffs. She put her foot on the Slasher's shoulder and yanked. His rotator cuff popped.

"¡Ayy!"

She spoke Spanish. "Threaten me again and I'll kill you."

Her ghosts ran up with flashlights and guns drawn. Jones had a finger through the laces of her running shoe.

Cassandra snatched it and pointed. "Weapon's in the bushes. Locate it for Crime Scene."

Jones searched for the scalpel. The Slasher squirmed and moaned. Blue and white lights flashed through the trees. Sirens approached.

Jennings bent toward Cassandra. "Great work, Detective. You collared the Marathon Slasher." He put his hand on her lower back. "Wanna go for a drink after the paperwork?"

Mucus dripped from Cassandra's nose. She looked into the man's face. He had been assigned to protect her.

She thought of something sarcastic to say, but heaved on his sneakers before she could get it out.

CHAPTER 2

MOTHER'S MILK

The following morning Cassandra was in the kitchen of her house on Virgil Place, in Castle Hill, in front of the stove in her robe and slippers.

She was sore. Her face stung as if she'd fallen asleep in the sun. Her throat was irritated. But she was alive, Praise God, in one piece, and making breakfast for her son.

Yellow butter sizzled in the frying pan. The smell of it filled Cassandra's kitchen. She poured pancake batter into perfect circles.

"Jason, honey, I need you to clear the table."

The boy was playing with toy cars, as he did every morning. He did not respond. He lined the cars side by side, counted them, recited their colors in order. Then he scrambled the cars and lined them up again exactly as they had been. He counted and recited their colors again.

Cassandra interrupted before he restarted the process. "Jason."

He stopped but did not look up.

"Please put your cars away so we can eat. Thank you."

Her son's eyes did not find hers. Cassandra stood in front of him, collected the cars, placed them in his hands.

"Go put them in your room. Wash your hands; breakfast is almost ready."

Jason slid slowly off the chair and went to his bedroom. She grabbed the spatula.

Children with autism require routine. Cassandra had learned that.

What she had never imagined was how much *she* would need these mornings with her son. Nothing could take away her guilt and constant worry about how much work kept her away from him. She was not there to attend to or protect him for most of the day. That bothered her.

But their quiet time, when they ate together, that gave Cassandra great satisfaction.

Seven in the morning and already the heat was making the back of Cassandra's neck sweat. Her mother returned from the corner store with bananas and an armful of newspapers.

"Wait until you see!"

Cassandra had made front-page news.

The *New York Post* and the *Daily News* had run virtually identical full-page color photos of the Marathon Slasher as he was wheeled from an ambulance into the emergency room, hands cuffed to the sides of his gurney like Hannibal Lecter.

In each picture Cassandra was escorting the prisoner in her running gear. The gold detective's shield dangled across her chest.

Both papers featured the same headline: CAPTURED!

One ran a caption: *NYPD Det. Cassandra Maldonado*

hauls alleged Marathon Slasher to hospital after daring Bronx foot chase.

Her mother read the news account. She stopped and looked up at Cassandra.

"That man tried to cut you?"

"Mom, reporters exaggerate. Want a pancake?"

"Too fattening."

"You always say no, then end up eating one of mine."

"Cassandra, you did not tell me this was gonna be dangerous."

"Want some scrambled eggs?"

"Cholesterol." Her mother went back to reading.

Cassandra told her mother that the commissioner's office had called about a press conference with the mayor.

"The mayor? Think you can get a desk job?"

"I told you, Mami, I wanna go to HI-PRO."

"What's that?"

"High-profile crimes. Celebrities. Cases that make big news."

"Out on the streets?"

"Sometimes. But not like before. No more buy-and-bust operations with drug dealers." Cassandra pointed the spatula at the newspapers. "I can't do undercover work anymore. The whole world knows I'm a cop."

"What about the hours?"

Cassandra knew her schedule had been a strain on her mother, who took up the slack in caring for Jason. It was only the three of them now. Cassandra's recent stint at Missing Persons had given her a predictable 8:00 a.m. to 4:00 p.m. schedule. No overtime, and she was home in the evenings to care for her son. Her mother feared a return to old ways.

"I don't think I'll work so much overtime when I get

my promotion. It comes with a raise. I can still keep coming home at a decent hour. You'll keep your evenings."

"I'm not complaining."

"I know, Mami. Egg white omelet?"

"Uy, no. Don't taste like anything." Her mother pointed at the Slasher on the front page. "How did *he* get hurt?"

Cassandra stacked pancakes on a plate.

"Slipped on a banana peel trying to escape."

Cassandra peeled a banana, sliced it, made a smiley face on the top pancake out of it. She poured her son a glass of milk.

"Jason!"

He bounded into the kitchen, sat at the table, and picked up his fork.

Cassandra's mother looked at Jason through the top part of her bifocals. "What, Grandma's like a piece of furniture around here?"

The boy climbed from his chair and went to her. She raspberried him on the neck and he giggled. She pointed at Cassandra on the front page.

"You see who that is?"

He looked at the paper.

"Who is that, Jason?"

"Mommy."

"Who?"

"Mommy."

"That's right. Your mommy's famous. She stopped a bad guy. Now we don't have to worry about him no more."

Jason looked Cassandra in the eye and smiled. She smiled back.

Her mother patted him on the butt. "All right, Papito, sit down and eat."

Jason sat and ate one banana slice at a time. First the eyes, then the nose, finally the smile. Always in that order.

Cassandra poured pancake batter. She included an extra one for her mother. She spied her child from the corner of her eye and felt the fullness of love.